DAVID M. BERGMAN

Until The End

A Novel

Until The End

For Eliza, my firstborn
I gift to you, my first novel

Copyright © 2021 by David M. Bergman
All rights reserved.

This book is a work of fiction. Names, characters, places, and incidents either are products of the author's imagination or are used fictitiously. Any resemblance to actual events or locales or persons, living or dead, is entirely coincidental.

ISBN 9798711576211
ISBN 9780989061612 (ebook)

Also available as an ebook from Amazon Kindle

Part One

"Do you like *love stories*?"

He asked her as he settled back in his seat. He had retrieved the paperback that had been jostled from her tray table as the Amtrak train lunged along a ragged track section. She was startled awake by the movement. He wished she hadn't.

For the last hour her face remained solely to himself. She was strikingly beautiful to admire. Young and peaceful in repose, her left temple and ear buttressed against a plush travel pillow, her position in a rather graceful angle, almost in the fetal position yet fully grown into the empty seat beside her. Eyebrows gently tweezed to symmetric perfection. Lips soft with a fine sheen of balm that he noticed her periodically reapply over the journey. He observed no trace of makeup to her cheeks. A kind complexion that had likely skirted through her teenage years with hardly a blemish. Her mane was a lush chestnut, flowing waves that temporarily ended in a sandy colored hairband, then continued beneath it as it ran down the side of her face into a seemingly polished groove of her neck. Her outstretched right arm and tilt of her adroit neck reminded him of Bernini's great marble work, *Apollo and Daphne*. He had sketched the masterpiece from every possible angle when he wandered upon it at the vast ornamental halls of the Uffizi in Florence. It was some years ago. Those *were* good times in Florence, he reminisced. No – he caught himself – be honest now –

passionate times. Passion was the singular word that summed it up. But how remarkably similar was this live statue now laying before him. *Daphne* – imagine that! – meeting her like this on a lumbering westbound train.

He had the time, while his Daphne was napping, to study the rest of her too. An athletic build, lean and toned at the shoulders and thighs. Her tangerine-colored capris pants ended near the top of her calf muscles which were well defined like the rest of her. Smooth and slender legs. Sockless, he admired her toned skin down to her ankles where her feet were tucked into her soft- soled velour flats. All the parts put together like nature had intended a female beauty to be. At least to his taste, he figured. Well proportioned everywhere, he realized. Perhaps in her mid-twenties, at most, he wondered. Perhaps only a half-dozen or so years younger than himself, if that. Just to admire her beauty was more than enough entertainment for him to pass the mesmerizing train time.

He glanced at the title again and then placed the paperback on her table. He recognized it immediately. It was the last love story he had read. A handful of years had passed since then. He didn't miss reading the genre. More memories came rushing to the forefront of his mind before he purposely let them ebb into the depths, where he usually preferred them. He couldn't help the episodes which sometimes came like waves crashing on the shore. Usually, it seemed like time had passed by rather swiftly since then, like the quick turn of a book page. He had moved on, thankfully, reminding himself once again.

"Good morning, by the way" he said gently to her with a brief yet kindhearted smile. It was the waning afternoon but he always liked to say the phrase 'good morning' to anyone caught napping and then startled awake – at *any* time of the day. Just a peeve of his that he kept over the years. It was a tacit acceptance of another person's need for rest and rejuvenation despite the time. No better time than the morning, to start off a new day with a clean slate. A good enough welcome for any soul awakening from sweet slumber.

The measure of time, he always felt, was so arbitrary. Man made. Better to understand the cycles of celestial events like the moon's waxing and waning, or a comet's passage, or a planet's orbit than to feel the constant urge to glance at a wristwatch or a cell phone screen to tell him what he already knew. Dawn's magnificent aura. The morning rays teeming over the horizon. Afternoon splashes that washed out nature's colors, albeit temporarily. And then evening repose, a cooling and calming and cleansing. A layering of thick emulsions of colors across the landscape. The softer palates. Ceruleans yielding to cardinal reds and orange poppies and yellow tangs as the sunsets receded, reluctantly, into the crepuscular hour. Crickets. Fireflies. The marks of passage into a starry night, and then slumber, and infinitum.

She received the book into her slender-fingered hands, checking that her bookmark remained where she had left it. It had held in place. She tilted the book towards him like the tip of a hat for a greeting – a gesture of thanks. And then she smiled for him and aligned herself in her seat. He noticed her nails were manicured with a light touch of lilac colored polish. A soft pastel color. Not brash like many women wear, which somehow annoyed him. Enough to accentuate the beauty of her fingers and hands in motion. Hands were like poems to him, animated with their own vocabulary for the reader to absorb and respond in kind.

She glanced at his eyes. They were soulful and nonjudgmental. She realized they hadn't spoken since a few cordial welcoming words of *'Hello'* were passed between them a few days prior as he boarded and sat down – her privacy invaded at that very moment for the duration of the train's journey.

His question remained lingering in his placid smile.

Probably OK to give him an answer, she judged.

"I do," she replied. She smiled again, this time more coyly, a bit embarrassed by her admission of a kind of inner secret to an utter stranger. But she did like love stories – very much so. They were comforting to her. Dreamy, of course, but also very nourishing. She wondered if he could see her blushing. She didn't even know his name, nor he hers. She felt vulnerable – almost slightly naked in the moment – and so she retreated the book towards her blouse for cover.

The train car jostled again, more abruptly this time, and she was lunged forward out of her seat. His right hand caught hers as she instinctively reached for support and grasped onto his left thigh. A waft of jasmine from her hair as he caught her awkward fall that landed her forward into his chest. Her hair brushed against his face momentarily but he didn't mind.

She was intensely beautiful, no doubt. All his furtive glances towards her confirmed his suspicions numerous times since boarding the cross country train from Penn Station. He had noticed her hazel green marbled eyes that periodically winced while she stared dreamily out the train window. Golden bursts, small shards emanated from the area close to each pupil. For one wakeful period he was able to sneak a much longer glimpse at her while pretending to read the newspaper. He noted a subtle coloboma in her left pupil. The slightest of imperfection. To find one is rare. Colobomas happen in less than one in a thousand people, he remembered. But her overall beauty, he acknowledged, was more like less than one in a million across the whole world. He had traveled enough by then to acknowledge that. He wondered if the coloboma affected her vision at all. No glasses. Perhaps she had contacts in but such a small defect, he knew, was unlikely to have caused any visual impairment.

Her lips parted gently while she sighed and they

periodically uncovered the fringes of well-aligned rows of glistening ivory teeth. She adjusted her position and flipped her hair behind her neck. Thick creamy waves with the slightest of curls, he noted, at the margins. *What was it about her hair that was almost appetizing in its sensualness?* Florence rushed forward again. *Yes, of course!* He shouted in a silent inner voice. *That's it! Gelato!* – Her hair was like the sensuous and rich gelato displayed through the glass panes of the local gelateria shops on nearly every corner. He had certainly consumed his share back then with Sami. He could have wandered the streets and alleyways of Florence forever in one lifetime and never be bored. The lighting. The settings. For an amateur photographer back then, it was a dream. He could have settled in Florence forever with Sami and been more than happy. He wondered if he'd ever return. But it would never match what he experienced. What they shared together in that place and time.

And now, her proximity to him only confirmed what he already knew from the moment he boarded the train and sat across from her. Nature's magic. A human being, a woman entering her fecund vital prime of life, as nearly perfect as any tropical sunset. He couldn't deny the fantasy of washing ashore with her in his arms on a deserted island.

Yet, on this train, boarding late while running to the platform just before embarking, it was the only comfortable seat remaining, across but diagonally from her. He ensconced himself adjacent to the window, drawn to the scenery as it unfolded, each with an empty seat beside them. And he gladly accepted the occasional glancing pleasurable view of her for as long as it might present itself. Daphne – *yes*, she was as near a reincarnation as he could imagine.

"Can you merely *like* something, or someone, you truly care about deeply? You know, from the source…" He lifted his right hand and pressed it against his chest. "Or is love simply pure love?" he asked her next.

He thought – it always seemed an odd affectation, to *like*, as if it was almost imperceptible, dispassionate, untrustworthy, and untruthful to oneself. He imagined 'like' is how most would experience a light sun shower drizzle by merely admiring the color of their umbrellas serving as catchers for unpleasantness. But that's where their simple joy began and ended. Why not soak in the droplets from heaven, he wondered. Let them be tasted like manna as if for the very first time in childhood awe. But no – the 'likers' merely would absorb the moment utterly devoid of zeal. Only a brief passing of interest or fancy – if that. To *love* was to engross oneself in the moment, a wonderment – to be an adult inside a child who is in full and complete awareness of bliss. Fantasticness. Humility. Completeness. How could there be *like* when one can choose *love*?!

He held his glance towards her paperback book as he recalled the plot of the romance. She hadn't yet responded to his question.

"It's a good love story. I enjoyed it a few years back. At the time it helped me to forgive and move on," he added.

That's all he said and then silence as he repositioned his eyes from hers to something outside the window that caught his attention.

She glanced outward as well – a kind of sea flowing toward the undulating horizon. A vastness of wheat and corn fields and grasses. She could see the breeze gusting through the tall grasses outside the window that she now desperately wished she could feel. The air was hardly refreshing these many hours cramped inside this tin vessel. A bit of suffering in exchange for what she impatiently awaited for on her arrival at this journey's end. It will end soon enough, she hoped. The train ride had taken its toll –

by now nearly two full days west of New York. But the musty sensation had settled in for yet another seemingly inexhaustible stretch of countryside. Lots of sameness it seemed to her. The window might as well have been painted with one scene alone.

"Where are you going?" He asked while not trying to lose himself inside the waving grasses and rolled hay bales.

"I was just going to ask you the same question," she replied with a turn of her head followed by a brief smile. But he remained focused on the scenery. From his peripheral vision he absorbed her smile and found it comforting. Warming. She was interested in conversation. A start.

The pain was indeed subsiding. Time heals, indeed.

"I asked you first," he insisted. She crimped her knees to her chest. Her capris fit perfectly, like a bicycle sun sleeve over his toned arms, he remembered.

"I'm heading to grad school. Seattle. They let me arrange a combined program – environmental sciences and landscape architecture. I like nature. No, I *love* nature." She smiled again, this time with a brief gaggle of nervous laughter and then glanced again outside their window. *What was he staring at so intently?* she wondered. A quiet peaceful pause balanced between them.

He unzipped the front of his thermolite vest and pulled out a small satin satchel from the inside zippered chest pocket. Then he loosened the draw cord and carefully tipped over the bag's content into his palm.

"Speaking of nature… I found this walking east along 42nd Street in Manhattan. I had departed from the research room at the public library next to Bryant Park and was walking towards Penn Station to board this train." He held up the object to check that everything remained intact.

"The sidewalk was rush-hour busy but this was laying in the gutter and its shape just caught my eye. Don't worry –

I've washed it well and then put a bit of polish cloth to it. I like collecting things to admire later."

He looked it over once more and then glanced at her eyes in a manner that asked, without stating, whether she wanted to have a closer look herself. His right arm carefully moved away from him and she extended hers to meet his. He passed it to her.

It was a seashell.

"It's an *Ark clam*. Like Noah's Ark. The flood. Drifting all that time until sunshine and beaches and seasons returned... She's a beauty, alright," he said excitedly. "Her kind are commonly found on the Atlantic coastline from North Carolina's outer banks to Florida. I wonder why she found a home in Manhattan. I'm sure she has a story to tell us." Sometimes, he knew, his shell fancies were a bit exaggerated for those who didn't quite see the world like he did.

She smiled again as her fingers gently stroked the beaded texture. She admired it without replying. A sudden memory flash from childhood rushed into her view. Seashells. Laughter. Running along a beach and escaping with Ansley from a fleet of blue-headed stinging jellyfish bobbing along the shoreline. They were running... screaming for their lives, it seemed. *Exhilaration.* Laughter upon reaching their sun-bleached blankets. Cool sand below piping hot sand and if you squished and squirmed your toes deep enough you were rewarded with even cooler ocean water seeping from below... *Happiness!* She smiled without saying a word.

"Here – try this." He pulled out a jeweler's mini magnifier loupe from his outside pocket. He twisted the hinge cover and handed the magnifier to her. "It's even better if you look real close at it."

She was genuinely curious, he realized. "Try to follow the flow of the ridges. You see how identical every bead is? That was made by a real organism. Not a machine.

Incredible, if you ask me. I find it more amazing now than when I was a little kid collecting buckets of these."

He was an intense type, she thought. But the diversion from the monotony was surely welcoming to her. She held the magnifier loupe and peered closely. A new world to her. One she never really thought much of. Microscopes and biology class weren't her thing, really, even though she liked science in general. Forests and streams and rivers were *her* thing.

The big picture, she thought. The macro fascinated her more than the micro, she figured. A fighter for Earth's preservation. Fresh air. Clean water. Ecologically sensible living. Grad school was to be her stepping stone to make her life count, leave something behind that made a difference on this troubled planet. Millions… billions needed her help. And she intended to reward them by absorbing herself in her studies – classroom and field studies – to learn what she needed to know to get from A to Z.

There was a hole perfectly positioned towards the top of the shell with a thin chocolate brown lanyard string attached. She looked at him.

"Did you bore this hole in the shell to make a necklace?"

"No, didn't need to. Nature did. The hole was made by a hungry moon snail."

He smiled at her for the first time. She giggled.

"A hungry moon snail? Yeah, right?!" she replied skeptically.

"No, seriously. Well, you need to see the whole picture. You're holding only half of the full clam. Like holding a glass half-full. This shell had a partner. Think of a pair of castanets – you know, the Spanish hand-held clapping instrument. Flamenco dancers, all the rest." He lifted his arms to mimic castanets in each hand as he snapped his fingers and hummed a catchy tune.

She laughed from the gesture and nodded. "I got it,

thanks" as she kept giggling. "Nice performance," she said in an exaggerated tone.

He continued. "So there were once two shells hinged together at the top, just above that hole." He reached for the shell in her hand while gently touching her fingers for the first time. They were warm and slender and soft. "When the moon snail is hungry it goes hunting for a clam like this one. It releases an acid that softens the shell layer and then, with its toothed tongue, known as a radula, it bores a hole into the softened shell, penetrates the clam, and gobbles up the clam's insides. Clam chowder for a hungry moon snail! Well, at least raw chowder. That's nature for you. The *grand* design. But if that hungry moon snail didn't exist then I wouldn't be able offer you this gift now, would I?"

He did say, 'glass half-full.' She wondered if she should correct him or was 'glass half-empty' really the way the phrase was supposed to be said? She wasn't sure of herself in the moment.

"It's beautifully simple yet very elegant," she replied as if she was a very serious professional shell critic. "I'm sorry it had to die for the sake of a hungry moon snail," she smirked. "Someday I'd like to meet this snail, not that I don't believe you. It does sound quite fascinating."

"May I?" He glanced at her neck and elevated the lanyard towards the top of her head. She didn't resist as he gently lassoed the cord into place around her neck.

The Ark clam rested perfectly between her loosened blouse buttons.

"Thank you, uh… your name… I don't even know your name?"

He paused, looked toward their window, and then into her eyes. Her coloboma was more pronounced now as he observed her pupils dilating.

"Name is Brad – Bradlee actually, with two e's at the end, but I haven't been called that since…" he thought about what would fit best for his story… "since the 3rd

grade."

"Thank you, Bradlee, double-e," she said with a chuckle. She paused.

"There are too many Brad's in this world, by the way. Too many shortened names in general. I like Bradlee. Your mother made a fine choice." Another pause as she touched the shell.

"I think you should keep it," she continued.

"No, it's yours... *Please*... A *gift* for you."

"No, Mr. Bradlee Seashell, I meant your *name*." She giggled again. "You should keep your full and proper name. But thank you again. It is a beautiful necklace. I like how it feels. Brings back some nice memories... *Thank you*."

She curled the lanyard between her fingers and then returned to the shell while glancing a few times between his eyes and the window scenery. The shell seemed very comforting. Stroking its smooth ridges she was reminded of a book she had read once, a Native American tale, about finding a special rock that was yours only, no one else's, one that would be forever comforting to hold.

"I also really like the curly swirly shaped ones," she said. "The ones that look like little twisters."

"You mean *Busycotypus canaliculatus*, or the *channeled whelk*. Yes, they are very pleasing to hold with smooth body whorls. They remind me of a twirling ballerina dancer. I hate to upset you but it's actually a predatory sea snail not unlike our little friend, the hungry moon snail. You know it's quite fascinating that almost all the channeled whelks are right-handed in their aperture – that's the snail's shell opening. I was lucky to find a few left-handed ones on P.E.I. last winter."

"*Prince Edward Island?*" she was surprised. "I used to *love* going there when I was a kid. But haven't been there in the wintertime. Summers only. Must have been some harsh winds in winter. Darn cold! But it looks like you survived none the worse. No frostbite on those salty shell fingertips, are there?"

His mind was focused on the task at hand but he filed away her comments for later. Perhaps, P.E.I. was something meaningful that they had in common, perhaps some stories to share if there was enough time on the train. He wondered which beaches or lighthouses she had frequented on the island.

He returned to the topic. "Hey, I think I have a juvenile version of a whelk in my bag. Too bad he washed up onshore. He would have grown five times the size had he lived to a ripe old age......... *Shell* I retrieve it?" He said with a straight face.

"Nice try, shellman," she replied. "Very punny."

She was witty, alright. He liked that and smiled back at her.

He reached up to the storage rack above his seat where his backpack was stowed, retrieved a larger string satchel and rummaged through it. As he arose she took a quick glance at his torso. Quite the muscular build. He must take care of himself, physically, she thought, like she does. Dark brown hair with wisps of some grizzly bear lighter brown streaks. Fit and agile. Strong thighs that stretched his jeans in a pleasing caressing manner. Full hands, sure of themselves. He wasn't uncomfortable in his movements. Free-flowing. At peace, yes – a peaceful yet handsome strong demeanor, that would be the best description, she thought.

He sat down and pulled out another shell for full display between them. "Here it is…" He held it in his palm - "a *lightning whelk*." He watched her eyes light up again.

"Now these guys are virtually all left-handers. They're called '*lightning*' because of their brown streaks running down their bodies like lightning bolts." He handed the specimen to her and let go. She swirled it back and forth between her index finger and thumb.

Another sudden flashback arrived from childhood – she was holding a summer soft ice cream cone coated with rainbow jimmies. Her hand brought the whelk towards her mouth. Flashbacks fired again – now it was as if her brain was tasting the rainforest soft vanilla drizzled on top with maple syrup and sugary sprinkles like it was yesterday.

She rubbed her forehead briefly to collect herself.

"So Bradlee, how do you know so much about shells? Besides, what do you call someone who is a shell expert anyway?"

"A malacologist, actually. Although the ones that study mollusk shells only – they're known as conchologists."

"Conchologists? That sounds like a headache expert chasing after concussions, if you ask me." She smiled coyly and rubbed her forehead to demonstrate. "But malacologist? Now *that's* a very cool name."

"It comes from the Greek, '*malakos*,' which means soft. Besides mollusks, malacologists study snails and slugs and octopus and squid – malakos because these are all invertebrates – none of those creatures have backbones, of course. You might say in a general sort of way – these are the squishy types of the invertebrate life forms."

"So you might say, Bradlee Seashell, that you have a *soft* heart for these creatures?" She giggled again.

Her laughter was the kind that asked for nothing in return. Just the pure enjoyment that he could tell she had deep inside. Snarky but also inoffensive. It seemed she enjoyed friendly teasing banter, a quickness at repartee. No sadness in her voice. A kindling of goodness that resided in a woman who remembered her childhood – his instincts suggested that she probably had a good and full childhood – and wasn't afraid to never escape from it. He liked that in her. He liked that trait, he knew, in anybody who possessed it since he also liked that in himself. He wished more people had it. Why grow up entirely if you can summon the essence of childhood deep within. Some essential innocence. Like admiring shapes of animals and people when staring at the clouds. Stardust sprinkled on only the wisest – at least it seemed to him – and he didn't care if anyone felt any less of him for this principle to a happy life. All the better to discover it in your youth than before it's too late.

"How does it go?" she asked. Her eyes glanced upward for a few seconds in thought.

"Sally" – she paused and then methodically continued with careful hyper-articulation – "sells seashells by the seashore. Yeah – *that's it!*"

"Bradlee Double-e Seashell, bet you can't say it for me five times fast!" she requested.

"*Sally?* Bradlee answered quizzically. I learned it was '*Sasha.*' Sasha makes it even harder to say fast. Go ahead and try it with Sasha, instead," he asked her teasingly.

The coincidence caught her off guard. "*Sasha?!*" She paused in a quick memory. "OK – I'll play."

"Sasha shells shesells by the sheshore," she blurted out.

She giggled wildly in disbelief and placed her hand to cover her mouth. He noticed the necklace glistening in the late afternoon sun rays that were dancing through the trees and wrestling to enter through the tinted window. The streaks of light tendered a slightly golden tint to the shell grooves. Her white silky soft blouse, unbuttoned three notches from the neckline, revealed a hint of cleavage. It was impossible for his eyes to avoid a quick look downward. Just a half-second was enough. Surely she wouldn't notice, he reasoned.

"Must go more slowly"... she lowered her voice to a whisper and now more methodically...

"Sasha sells shesells... Gosh – why can't I get it?!" Another giggle and she started again.

"Shasha sh, no… sells seashells by the seashore." Then she started a little faster…

"Sasha shells seashells by the sheshore." She flubbed it yet again.

"Sasha sells seashells by the sea" – "she paused for a quick second – "*seashore!*"

"*Got it!!!*" She screamed in delight followed by laughter.

A few passengers were roused from their seats, stirring and glancing over to them. It didn't bother her at all. She gave Bradlee a googly-eyed look, as if to say I don't care if they stare when I'm having fun, before settling back into her seat.

"So, Mr. – or is it – Dr. Bradlee? Are you really a malacologist? Ph.D. sort?"

He smiled at her and chuckled.

"You might say I'm an amateur one. Maybe a wannabe. I do enjoy the field. But no. I have no advanced degree. Mostly self-taught, you might say as well."

"Then what do you *really* do?"

He paused to glance out the window again and collect his thoughts. He ran the fingers of his right hand along his chin and then his index finger brushed a few strokes across his lips.

She admired his poise. His sense of self. He seemed quite comfortable in conversation, certainly not at all nervous unless he hid it well, sitting all these hours across from her in silence. She knew she could turn heads readily since pubertal changes erupted about ten years ago. She was too desirable a catch, at least according to her mother, who was quite the beauty in her own prime. Their teen photos, separated by thirty years, were nearly a carbon copy. And her father always said she would have her hands full with the boys, just as her own mother did before her parents met and tied the knot.

Yes – no concern with male admirers but she had her flings and a few close relationships that didn't survive the usual angsts and healings from high school and college, self discovery, and all the rest of becoming an adult woman in the modern world. The finding of herself, as she came to realize, the soul within that yearns for its working partner – her heart that had suffered enough and healed. She had a very good mind, she knew. But it was in the self-discovery that she loved nature too much to see it all go to waste in her lifetime – that was the heart telling her what her soul already and forever knew who she was. Passion was born. All she needed now was the proper education and mentoring, the right push here and criticism there, to gain an expertise and become what she wanted of herself. What she demanded of herself. All that was waiting to begin. And to make her parents and grandparents very proud. She was committed to her career and she knew the next big step would begin from her first steps off this train in Seattle.

Bradlee was ready to let go a bit more.

"I do what I love. I travel. I explore. I photograph what I think is worthy to the eye. At least I think I have a good eye. Maybe even enough patience to wait for the right moment." He lifted his hands and played as if he was holding a camera, readying for her to pose before him. She turned her head to the left and then smiled at him with her right cheek. He clicked.

"I write freelance articles for adventure and travel magazines, sometimes newspapers. Mostly online stuff now but I've had a few photos enlarged and hung in some galleries here and there. A few sales as well. My writings and photographs pay my bills comfortably enough. A big bonus comes if I can land a hefty price for an enlarged framed beauty – usually some wealthy client who might happen to wander into a gallery and take a liking to my work. But in my free time I also sketch and write poetry and work with wood." He stared out the window in thought.

"I study the things I enjoy learning. Not really the kind of stuff we learned about in school. Like seashells, for instance. Pretty straightforward life, I suppose."

"Lately, I've been trying my hand at carving driftwood. But I'm patient for the right piece to wash up on shore near my home. Sometimes a long walk along the beach searching for that right piece is the best therapy..." He held that thought until it dissipated, slowly.

"I dabble here and there, you might say. Just an amateur but I enjoy the variety."

"That's quite a list," she stepped in. "I'd like to see some of your photographs sometime. I like photography too. Not very good at it myself but I'm willing to learn more someday when I have the time. Gardening's more my thing – well, when I have the time for that too."

Bradlee noticed she had pulled out a canvas, some colorful threads, and a long needle from her pouch purse. The image on the canvas had begun to resemble a bird, he thought, from what he could tell – a pair of wings beginning to take shape in the pattern.

She was working a rectangular needlepoint from time to time since the train departed from New York. Stitching methodically was calming over these many years. She enjoyed the hobby very much. And creative, she thought, despite following the pattern that came with the packaging. Occasionally, as her technique improved over the past few years, she liked to challenge herself and deviate a bit. Follow her own instinct and alter the pattern enough to feel like it was her own when it was all completed. After framing, initially she kept all of them for herself. She had accumulated a whole wall of hummingbird needlepoints – various shapes and sizes that adorned her room nearly from floor to ceiling. They were very soothing to look at, especially upon awakening in the morning and seeing the sunlight strike the threads into sparkles. Other times she labored until her fingers were quite sore into the late fall season, trying to finish a bunch to offer as handcrafted gifts to family and close friends for the holidays.

Hummingbirds were her specialty. She knew the impetus – the source for her fixation. It started from her family winter break trip to Costa Rica when she was just eight years old. Going back to the moment always brought her happiness. The whole scene was genuinely *her* happy place to return to if ever there were moments of lingering stress or despair.

She took a break from stitching and shut her eyes to focus – it usually allowed the memory to flow into the present at her will... She was in the backseat of the car rental with her brother. Her father at the wheel and mother beside him. They were driving along a pothole strewn bumpy road, weaving to higher and cooler elevations through the mountains from the Arenal Volcano towards the Monteverde Cloud Forest. She was looking forward to visiting her first rainforest the next day. The evening was approaching and a cool opaque mist hovered over the road. It began to significantly impair their view causing nervous tensions to rise inside their vehicle. Her parents, worried by the slippery conditions, noticed a road sign next to a pleasant home coated with fresh flowers in window boxes. 'Casa Jacinta's Farmhouse' – that was the name, she recalled again now as she visualized the sign. So they parked and she, her younger brother, and her parents ended up staying the night in simple yet comfortable and clean rooms in the main farmhouse alongside the road.

The next morning, the proprietor's teenage daughter came knocking and asked if she and her brother were interested in milking a cow. Her 'Papi,' as the teenager called her father, was in the barn and was offering to show them how it's done. So, all excited now, she and her brother ran off with the older girl to the barn. The property extended for quite a ways from the road and they arrived at a simple barn where there was just one Holstein cow parked in the open hay pen next to a pretty looking golden horse that nibbled on her hair teasingly. Papi stood from his small bench and uttered something in Spanish to his daughter who then interpreted – "Papi says it's your turn now to milk the cow."

She sat down and grasped and squeezed at the cow's teats but not a single drop dripped into the bucket. Papi and his daughter had a nice laugh on account of her but then Papi gave her a slow motion demonstration of the milking process by grasping and kneading the udder, then pressing and pulling and squeezing on the cow's teats all in one rhythmic quick motion. She sat down again and after some more practice and adjustments, sure enough, the milk began to flow into the bucket in spurts. The cow rewarded her with quite a good singing 'Moo' and she flushed with pride. The animal was probably larger than any she had ever been close enough to touch before but it was gentle despite her prodding. But most memorably, she felt connected to nature in that instant, that feeling of awareness with the earth and its inhabitants, away from the comfortable suburban life she had always known. She recalled Papi saying – "For cereal... American cereal... Froot Loops" – in a broken English before he started laughing again with a big smile. She enjoyed the milking but it was difficult work for her small hands. Her brother lingered longer to have his own chance next but she knew, what he was really waiting for, was to help tend to the family's horse since he was seemingly born to be a horse lover – even to this day.

Papi's daughter grabbed her hand and then off they went dashing over to the chicken coup parked adjacent to the barn. They collected a basketful of fresh hen eggs and then skipped back to the farmhouse and deposited them on the kitchen counter. The chubby lady with the big rosy cheeks – the daughter's 'Mami,' was very kind - all smiles and hugs and nodding. No English at all, except 'hello' and 'welcome' and 'thank you.' Chores done for the breakfast that Mami was fixing for her guests, she turned and started exiting towards the open veranda.

And there they were – it was a magical moment! Hummingbirds with rainbows of radiant colors – the whole spectrum, glistening in the morning sun. Larger ones mixed with the tiniest and cutest ones. All sputtering about, darting forward and suddenly reversing backward, landing briefly at one feeder and then alighting to the next. Then they would dart off out of sight and, soon enough, return for more in a whirling wing-buzzing array. A feeding frenzy! Sipping at the feeders and tasting the variety of breakfast fruit nectars.

She gently grabbed a small squishy overripe orange slice laying on one of the feeder stands that was hung by a long cord from the roof edge of the veranda. And then she lifted her arm and stretched out her palm with the warm fragrant orange at the center. Then it really happened! – One of the smaller hummingbirds immediately flew to her palm and landed softly. It had an exquisite iridescent emerald green back that joined into a ruby red throat patch, with jet black wings that held still to its side. The hummingbird delicately tasted the orange nectar and then paused and turned its head in curiosity and stared into her eyes and briefly studied her smiling face. She remembered the wings tickling her palm but she held still long enough for this delicate dreamy creature to taste some more, to enjoy its breakfast meal. Eating right out of the palm of her hand! – The memory to this day still tickled her palm just thinking about it.

And then she heard laughter behind her as Mami, observing the scene unfolding from the kitchen, started whistling a tune. And then she broke into a song. It was in

Spanish and she didn't understand it, but still Mami's words sounded mellifluous, perhaps a little melancholic as well, and the little bird flew away. Later, she asked Mami's daughter, on departing from the farmhouse, what it was her mother sang and she informed her it was a Costa Rican children's folk song. Like a lullaby.

The girl sang it softly herself and then interpreted it for her. *"Gentle flies hummingbird in hand, health and love forever bestowed, in your home and land."* She said it was considered great fortune in her culture if a hummingbird lands in a child's outstretched hand. "It means the hummingbird trusts you more than others. The hummingbird already instinctively knows who to trust and because you cared for it in your palm, the most fragile of beings, then you will also choose to care for the whole world. And in our tradition," she continued, "your reward is that the hummingbird transferred a part of its very soul into you so that you will have a most blessed life."

It was a beautiful sentiment and she asked the girl to write it down and she brought it home with her on the flight. Years later she stitched the words of the song into her favorite needlepoint – the one that hung above her childhood bed. It had remained there for a long time. She was always comforted by that needlepoint until the end of high school.

She breathed softly to inhale the memory one more time deeply inside her. And then she opened her eyes. Bradlee's eyes were focused on hers before darting away towards the canvas that she had set on the seat beside her.

"It's a needlepoint," she began. "A hobby I've enjoyed for a long time." She smiled and he glanced upward to match hers with his own.

"It's very beautiful. I have always enjoyed a mishmash of colors, whether in a painting or a photograph. I find it astonishing how beautiful nature expresses herself through her enormous palette." She blinked a few times and then squinted with another smile as her lips parted. She decided to reveal more.

"You might say I have a hummingbird fetish. *All* of my needlepoints are of hummingbirds."

She paused to remember some of the facts that she always enjoyed sharing for those who were interested. She thought Bradlee appeared to be genuinely curious.

"Did you know that there are over three-hundred species of hummingbirds on Planet Earth but only twenty-three can be found in North America? The rest are scattered in Central and South America. And they aren't anywhere else in the world – just the Western Hemisphere. I've always felt honored to have been born in a part of the world where I can coexist with them. I guess you can say I feel a deep kinship with them... Maybe I was a hummingbird in a previous life?!"

Bradlee listened intently. She had a passion to share, no different from his shell collecting. And he admired her eyes when she spoke. Vibrant. Her coloboma ebbing and flowing, transforming her pupillary aperture with the changes in her temperament – from excitement to relaxation. It was fascinating to see it all in action, rather than in medical textbooks or on computer screens.

And then she smiled at him in a surly way and extended her arms to each side and began to hurriedly flap them, faster and faster. Her sudden action stirred Bradlee into laughter as well and then he began to make a buzzing noise and flapped his arms mimicking her movements until they both were exhausted by the pure fun of it all.

"I didn't know *any* of those facts. I would have thought we had far more species here in North America. Goes to show you how critical it is that our rainforests are preserved," Bradlee said.

"And Alaska and the whole of the northern forests as well," she interrupted him. "Hummingbirds are everywhere

– from Alaska to the tip of South America!"

He considered for a moment. "You know, maybe the hummingbird is one of the bellwethers – what I learned on one of my recent assignments – what scientists call *indicator species* for worrisome environmental damage. Measurable changes to the whole ecosystem as a result of their presence or absence that could possibly be reversed with the proper intervention. A resetting back to the natural balance and order if we had the political will to take the required steps. It's complicated to figure all of that out because it's like playing multidimensional chess or checkers. Kind of mind boggling to map all the possible interactions and decisions before settling on the most effective strategies. You might want to look into that in your upcoming studies."

Bradlee frowned before continuing. "Sorry to get political on you but, if you ask me, I don't think we will get very far with environmental improvements if we *only* mostly rely on individual, person by person, changes in behaviors. Guess most scientists think we could be quickly running out of time. I do agree that what each of us does helps but we need more massive change and it starts at the highest level of political and social and economic reforms. Anyway, just a suggestion… the indicator species idea, I mean."

Bradlee was tired but he knew he was also enjoying their conversation. She *was* listening. And it made sense to her. She couldn't deny the complexity of environmental sciences. Her upcoming studies would need more emphasis on public policy if she were to make any difference. She made a mental note to look into the proper course electives that would help her. Perhaps she would need to sacrifice landscape architecture for public policy. She sat back in her seat and wondered about all of this for awhile. She started back on her needlepoint again. That would settle her nervousness, she knew.

"So Bradlee journeyman, where are *you* headed on this rambling train?"

"I have a date in North Dakota that I'm heading to. In the Badlands," he replied.

His comment took her by surprise. *A date?* Figured as much. *Well, at least he's being honest with me*, she thought, with a hint of disappointment. *Could it be jealousy? Strange. Why would I feel jealous?* She tried to quickly dissolve the feeling away. She had only been chatting with him for a few minutes, after all. *But I don't even know his full name? He is handsome*, she realized. And adventurous. And seemed caring. *His work and travels must expose him to so many things out there beyond academia.* The real world that she knew was going to be challenging to change. He sounded mysterious to her, an Indiana Jones kind of life you only see in movies but without the cowboy hat.

She composed herself and looked straight at him now without a hint of emotion. A monotone voice came forth.

"I see. Is she *your* love story?"

He smiled and looked away from her stare and started chuckling. Then a whole stammering of staccato laughter spilled out before he inhaled deeply and then sighed relaxingly back into his seat.

"No, not that kind of date. She's a mare. Actually, she's lots of mares and probably a handful of stallions too." He chuckled briefly again. "There's a herd of wild mustangs that I've been asked to do a story about for a tourism board in North Dakota. I'm heading for Medora, the small town at the base of the Badlands. Teddy Roosevelt's old stomping grounds from his travels out west. I'm really looking forward to the assignment. Should be there for a week or so before I head onward."

"How far are we from Medora?" she asked.

Bradlee pulled out the Amtrak map. "I think we're approaching the Rugby station in about ten minutes, then we pass through Minot, Stanley, and then Williston in about three hours from now. I need to depart at Williston and then rent a car to head another few hours south to Medora. I'll be checking into my hotel close to midnight if all goes as planned." He paused and then had a quick flashback.

"Hey – did you know we're about at the geographic center of North America? At least that's what Rugby, North Dakota is largely known for – there's a stone signpost with that notation on it. It's just next to a tasty Mexican restaurant along Highway 2 in case you ever pass through these parts again."

"I gather you've been through here before?"

"Yeah – the Burrito Grande was darn tasty!" He paused to observe the window scenery once again and then turned towards her.

"I rode a bike across – " He paused. "Hey – you haven't told me *your name* yet."

"You haven't *asked* me yet," she replied curtly.

"Oh – OK, Ms. environmental sciences," he said while rolling his eyes.

"And landscape architect, to you" she replied with a smirk.

"Yes, of course. How shall I greet you in case, perchance, we so happen to get stuck sharing a train again?"

"Has it been that painful for you?" she laughed, this time flirtatiously.

"No. I'm enjoying our conversation. Wish we could have started it some twenty hours earlier out of New York. But I could be a bit shy, reserved at times."

"*Sasha!*" she blurted out. "That's *actually* my name. As in *Sasha sells sheshells*." It was her turn to have a good laugh.

"My full name is Lyra Sasha Flurey but I've preferred my middle name since the end of high school."

"*Sasha*, really?!" he asked in astonishment.

"Yup," she replied and giggled.

"Well how about *that* coincidence?!" he replied with amazement. "Well, both are pretty names for a pretty woman. Nice to meet you…….. *Lyra!*"

She crimped her nose at him and blushed and then looked towards the window.

Wheat fields glistening like golden spools of thread in the setting sun. Rolled hay bales like Tinker toy wheels tossed about. The monotony was becoming very soothing. The same feeling she had when she caressed her new shell necklace. She continued to enjoy the view as the train bobbed and rocked gently. Maybe there are good reasons people choose to live out here in this part of the country.

"So, you were mentioning something about a bike?" She opened a new line of conversation. She was enjoying getting to know this Bradlee man.

"Oh, yeah... I rode a bicycle across the country when I was younger. Passed through this region. Great journey with a few friends."

"Is that why you've been studying the scenery so intently out this window since we first started chatting?"

"You might say that. Good memories. Flashbacks happen a lot for me. Don't read me wrong. I don't have PTSD, nothing traumatic happened. Just layers of memories from my travels. I guess those layers get convoluted and jumbled, almost like playing Boggle – you know, the word game – where your eyes are racing around the letters, trying to construct meaning out of randomness. You look long enough and eventually you start finding the five and six letter words, even a rare seven, besides the simple three letter ones that are easy pluckers for most everyone. I like when those moments happen. At least that's when I think maybe I've outsmarted my opponent." He let out a few quick bursts of laughter and then continued.

"Some memories come quickly to me and dissipate just

as fast. But others – well, just more complex and nuanced. Like a fine wine, so they say – one of those you're supposed to inhale deeply and swirl and taste gently, letting it linger on the tongue and palate. You know what I mean? I can't usually tell much difference myself in wines but that's what the experts tell us. To each his own skill set." She nodded while she worked the needlepoint into the canvas.

"Well, the memories that linger longer – I tend to prefer those," he added. "They have more meaning. They sink deeper, they're etched more permanently each time they pop into a daydream. I never really know what may pop up next in my mind sometimes. Just who I am, I guess. It's made for some very interesting dreams."

"I *love* hearing other people's dreams. I find them fascinating to try to interpret," she replied. "Not sure if I dream any more or less than anyone else but when I have one of those really clear ones, incredibly detailed," she paused in thought – "what do they call it?..."

He interrupted her – "you mean *lucid* dreams?"

"Yeah, that's right," she remembered now.

"When I wake up from one of those I try to pop out of bed immediately and start scribbling down what I can remember. It may be for ten seconds, sometimes I can get to thirty, even a fitful minute before it all vanishes into mush. Sometimes I even pound my forehead a few times to see if I can knock out a few more details." She banged her forehead gently with her palm in mock demonstration. They laughed together at her gesture.

"Then I re-read my notes and it's like pure fantasy sometimes. Wild creatures, angels, gigantic ships, ultra-colorful flying objects. Other times, like I'm a cave woman or I'm living in an old village in Poland. Not sure why Poland but I can hear people speaking Polish, calling out 'Lyra, Lyra' and singing to me in Polish in my dream and it's as if I understand it all. Like I've lived there my whole life. Very odd. And then in other dreams it's like science fiction, you know – like I'm living way in the future. I'm a crew member on a spaceship heading to a new galaxy." She was quite animated, her hands gesticulating with the needlepoint. Bradlee was admiring her movements, as if she was conducting a symphony with her baton.

No hesitation to share, he thought. Maybe the long train ride begged her for company. Some human connection. Or just to hear her own voice after all these hours of monastic silence. It's one thing to go for a solitary walk along a beach or through the woods for a few hours. But, after twenty-two straight hours on a train it is understandable that anyone would crave some company and storytelling. That probably hadn't changed across the millennia, he surmised.

"I wish I had lucid dreams *every* night," he replied. "I agree. They can be fascinating to make sense of. But I like your approach. Maybe I'll try it sometime as well. The writing part. If I can drag myself out of bed…" He smiled at her.

The train slowed gradually and came to a stop. One of the Amtrak crew members came through announcing the arrival to Rugby Station. North Dakota had a handful of brief station stops. A few passengers disembarked. Most on the train seemed headed to Seattle, the final destination.

'Coasters,' he called them. Those who were exclusively traveling coast-to-coast. Most, he figured, probably never have enjoyed a single day discovering the interior of this beautiful country. *A shame*, he thought. *Such beauty in time slowed to the pace of a wandering wheat stalk in a Midwestern breeze.* 'A wandering wheat stalk in a Midwestern breeze' – he repeated the phrase in his mind again. He liked it – no, he loved it, and made a mental note to insert it into a future poem he had yet to compose. Maybe a lyric in a song…?

It was a brief stop in Rugby. Only a few minutes before the wheels starting churning again. Three more hours until he would arrive at Williston Station and head south to Medora. Wild horses. He closed his eyes and returned to a moment in time on his bike journey. It was seared as good as any memory he had ever had of an ecstatic event. One that made him feel so alive inside. Adrenaline rush. Pure unbridled happiness. The kind that probably made your face glow. A face that could be seen by others for miles. Perhaps the memory would remain for many more decades to come in his lifetime. A telling to his grandkids and great-grandkids someday.

Bradlee replayed the memory tape. He was in Kansas, the southeast part – Flint Hills, tallgrass prairie and plenty of hilly terrain for a bicycle wanderer to enjoy with his buddy, his wingman for the grand journey. It was a quiet road that undulated like a caterpillar through a massive valley. Mid-afternoon light. Skies drifting from hot June sunshine to overcast cloudy threats. A slight breeze. Nothing but rolling hills of farmland to his right. To his left, he and his buddy spotted a clump of wild horses up on the hillside on a bluff overlooking the road. Miles of grasses as far as the eye could see. And a fence all along beside the road. They passed a posted road placard beside the fencing – "Bureau of Land Management. Wild Horse Conservation Area. Keep Out." And as they cycled along the mustangs came trotting down the hill to join them. No saddles, no people, no cowboys in sight. Just hooves in motion and open land. First a handful, then a whole bushel of them started towards the road, and then too many followed to count. Bradlee screamed out to his buddy – *'Let's Ride!'* And the two of them jammed on the pedals faster, faster, and then Bradlee let out a loud and wild *'Giddy Up!'* followed by a holler of energy from deep in his throat.

The lead stallion, a full jet black beauty from mane to hooves, bulging torso muscles, took the bait and started into a full gallop beside them. The whole lot of mustangs followed. The cyclists had a long downhill stretch of road and so they burned rubber. Speedometers racing to thirty, thirty-five, forty, forty-five miles per hour. And the horses. Damn – here they came up beside them. Matching their mark stride for stride. A stampede that shook the ground beneath them like an earthquake. Did thirty seconds elapse or five minutes in time, he couldn't remember. Probably somewhere in between.

But then ahead was a high fence running perpendicular to them and cutting through the horse country. It had to end. The horses eased off as he and his friend raced onward... A moment in time. The telling in his mind never ceased to reward him with pleasure. Pure adrenaline. The chase. Vigor. Wildness. He figured he'd be telling the tale to his great grandkids someday on a front stoop rocker. Maybe they'll enjoy the story. Maybe not. Such are memories.

He knew, sadly, that for most life events, the meaning comes from having been there. The experience unique to oneself. For everyone else, truly, they are just another passing story. It's to the storyteller to paint the picture just right. But the listener needs a sense of place and time to fully absorb and digest it. But the *feeling* of that moment – no, that was for him to savor forever. That could never be fully shared. He knew it. But it didn't stop him from trying. It would probably serve as a conversation starter at times. Or a way to pass time. Maybe he needed to improve the telling and enliven it more. Vocabulary. The right words or body language. Add some more arm gallop gesticulations and stand up to do the telling. Show his audience through imagery how it is to hop on a bicycle and shift gears and head down a steep hill with wild mustangs chasing you by your side. Yeah – that would probably help, he figured.

"You're lost in thought, aren't you, Mr. Bradlee daydreamer?" He opened his eyes and saw her looking at him with her head slightly rotated. That infectious smile of hers.

"Let me guess – you're picking raspberries on a hot summer day? Cycling down to the bottom of the Grand Canyon? Kitesurfing in Aruba?" She giggled.

He nodded. "Something like that," he replied. "I was thinking about wild horses, that's all. "I'm looking forward to seeing them again —— " He paused.

"Again? Care to share?" she asked.

"Oh, it's a fine story. Perhaps when I'm feeling more energetic."

"Cabin fever, have you?"

"Yup – you might say that. Haven't been on this long a train journey – ever," he replied.

"Me neither. But it beats having to pedal all the way across the country, doesn't it?" she said.

He thought for a few seconds before responding to her.

"Hmm, depends on the memories you take with you, I suppose. Maybe even who you meet along the way."

She opened her book again to the bookmarked page. She was about half way through, he figured, from the looks of the page folds. The two lovers probably already had their first intimate kiss, he thought, thinking back to the book's storyline.

He wondered what it would be like to kiss her. His head wandered back towards the window.

Lyra. A beautiful name. Original. He had never met a Lyra before. Harp? He thought he remembered a little Greek mythology. That's what it means, right? A constellation – something from Greek or was it a Roman god? He didn't know for sure and didn't think it was critical to take out his cell phone to search for the meaning of her name just then. Perhaps later when she was napping again and he could compare her appearance to the Gods.

Lyra. Daphne. It figured as much that she had a mythic name. Well – Greek always sounded more exotic to him.

And then he started to fantasize about kissing her along a sparkly crystal beach somewhere in the Greek islands. He hadn't been yet but still, a white sandy beach was a white sandy beach. An azure blue Mediterranean Sea reflecting a cloudless sky. Whitewashed homes on the hillside and shells of all sizes and colors strewn about for the picking. He closed his eyes again and breathed slowly, taking in the scene in his mind. It was wonderful.

The kiss was long and soft and just happy. It was the kind of kiss that made him unaware of where he ended and she began. She was absolutely gorgeous in her one piece Canary yellow bathing suit slightly covered in a peacock feather-designed macramé shawl. The suit cut high across her thigh bones and revealed just enough of her defined muscular buttocks that he wanted to absorb all of her into his arms. Dough that needed gentle kneading in his strong grip and arms that sought embracing. The coconut oil scent from her sun lotion mixed with that aroma of jasmine lingering on her neck – her signature aroma from her shampoo? – or was it just her natural animal scent? – as her head pressed against his bare chest… He nodded off into a deeper sleep.

The train continued onward while he awoke but remained inside his lingering daydream. Lyra was playing music softly through her headphones and Bradlee was enjoying overhearing her selections. A Carole King ballad was returning him to his own quiet place hiking along a mountain ridge. The lyrical refrain came around again. Lyra was humming it quietly in her seat:

'Winter, spring, summer, or fall… All you have to do is call… And I'll be there, yes I will... You've got a friend…' He stirred to adjust to a more comfortable position as if being rocked in his mother's arms and continued to drift off.

Then a shriek of the brakes came followed by a sudden deceleration. He was startled awake as Lyra was grasping onto the tray table once again. The train abruptly came to a full stop.

They settled back into their seats and immediately looked out their window. It was still light enough outside to make out that the train wasn't parked at the next station. They were somewhere in between, in the countryside. They waited a minute or so.

A reassuring voice on the intercom:

"Good evening folks – this is your conductor, Harold Stokowski. Call me Harry, though. Sorry y'all about that quick maneuver. It appears we have a mechanical issue with one of the track switchin' units ahead. The braking system went into automatic stop mode like your anti-lock brakes on your cars. The system is controlled by computers so… not much I could do to override it… Don't think y'all want to end up in Albuquerque by tomorrow afternoon followin' a crawlin' cattle car over a thous'n miles so we're gunna just sit tight here and wait for the switch operators to fix the darn track. I should have word back from these folks in about twenty or so minutes once they're done with their inspection. Hope y'all been enjoying the ride." He paused a few seconds.

"And for your inconvenience, we'll be offering a free glass of wine or soft drink in the Bar Car for anyone interested in stretchin' those frog legs out a bit. It's on the house, folks. Just tell my darlin' Susie to put it on ol' Harry's bar tab." He started into a guffaw. "Good for the ol' circulation, if I may say so myself. I'll be back on this line in a jiff. Enjoy! Over."

"Friendly chap," Lyra said.

"I think he enjoys his job," Bradlee replied. "I mean – think about it," Bradlee continued. "How many boys did you know – sorry to be sexist, but I'm speaking realistically here – how many boys did you know growing up who used to say they wanted to be a train conductor? Toot, toot! Goes the whistle. All those engine noises, holding up their trains to show them off at show-and-tell and playing for hours with their toy train sets?"

"True," she replied. "My younger brother for one. Lots. Also honestly don't remember any girls I knew who went around the same way." She paused and smiled at him. "Apology accepted... but only this one exception." She winked at him. He continued.

"So here's what I think. Here's a grown man I'm thinking an older gentleman from the sound of his voice, maybe not quite an '*ol geezer*' as they say – who's been living the dream for, I don't know... forty, fifty years, maybe more. He sounds happy. You can hear it in his voice. Not jaded or wiped out. Fresh after all these years, I guess."

"Yeah, I agree" she replied.

"Well, I'd like to be like him when I'm on the far side of fifty or sixty years old."

"Me too," she whispered while setting her book down.

A silent pause ensued between them. Bradlee thought for a moment. What to ask her next?

He realized he was hungry.

"Your *favorite* food in the whole world... that's not a dessert...?" He blurted loudly.

Lyra thought for a few seconds and responded – "Hot pancakes. For *dinner*, not breakfast...! Oh, and topped with Grade A dark amber maple syrup! Vermont preferred but Maine will also do." She laughed loudly and then covered her face with her hand.

"Well, that's quite specific now?!" Bradlee smiled in reply. "You clearly haven't tried Canadian maple syrup... *a shame*." He tried to keep a serious face but failed.

"And yours?" Lyra asked.

"Hmm... homemade pasta topped with tomato sauce.

Pasta flour has to be hand-kneaded, hand-rolled and hand-cranked. Sauce has to be homemade too – *nothing* out of a jar. Lots of garlic, roasted tomatoes, some peppers and oregano. Oh, and *must* have paprika... not too spicy. Simmered over the stove for hours... and devoured... for *breakfast*!"

"Breakfast, really?! And talk about being specific?!" Lyra laughed again and Bradlee joined in.

"What do you say we go for a walk?" He asked her. "I'm kind of hungry and thirsty."

"I'm in." She put on her flats and he waited for her to exit their little world of four seats and a tray table, strewn about with a few light pullover sweaters, travel pillows and snack bar wrappers.

He walked behind her down the aisle and through the next few train cars. She was probably about five or six inches shorter than him. He observed how her back gently curved into her pelvis and how she kept a sureness to her posture. A lightness to her steps. Good balance. Effortless. Maybe she was a gymnast or had dance lessons growing up. A figure skater, perhaps? There was nothing in the view that he didn't enjoy.

The bar car was already teeming with passengers. Noisy but tolerable. They had to wait a bit before the barmaid approached them.

"Good evening folks, I'm *'darlin' Susie,'* as Harry likes to call me." She smiled at them slyly. "How can I help you?" Susie had to shout at them and over the energy in the crowd. She looked like she had been on this train for thirty years. An older woman, Susie knew her way around the bar car like a barn cat in the night.

"Ginger Ale please!" – They screamed out the identical order simultaneously and then looked at each other instantly. "*Ginger Ale*?! *Really?*" Bradlee said surprised. The coincidence instinctively brought on a good laugh together.

"I *always* order ginger ale when traveling – but *only* when traveling. Don't know why or when it started years ago but that's just a part of me now so much that I refuse to try something else," Bradlee went on. Lyra laughed again.

"Same for you?" he asked.

"Well – yes, actually" she replied. "And I thought I was the only strange one with this fetish?!"

Their drinks arrived in tall glasses filled with ice cubes and volcanic gingery bubbliness. They clinked their glasses together.

"Looks refreshing! Cheers to you and your future, Ms. Lyra, harpist to the galaxies, and future environmental scientist extraordinaire."

"And landscape architect, you forget," she reminded him with a wide smile showing off her beautifully aligned teeth for him.

"And to you as well, Mr. Bradlee Seashell by the Seashore. Wild horse chaser. Grand traveler."

Another round of laughter ensued. Susie started tossing small airplane-sized bags of salted peanuts and chocolate chip cookies to her patrons. The party continued as they enjoyed the company of others despite the cramped space to maneuver very much.

Before departing Bradlee proceeded to the bar top, opened his wallet, and placed a five dollar bill in the tip jar for Susie.

"That was nice of you. Thank you," Lyra said. "Do you like tipping?" she asked him.

"Yes, I think it's important to tip those who make the world a happier place. We could all use confirmation from others that who we are or what we do is important… And besides, giving is really just the same as receiving. Just a mirror image of life's dualities. You know… like the Yin and Yang symbol. The grand unifying connections through life and beyond. Well, that's my attitude… We all need to eat too and enjoy whatever it is money provides toward that end."

"I agree," she replied. "Nice life tip," she said, as she smiled at him again, turned, and then started back towards their train car.

The train started up again soon after they settled into their seats. The evening was waning outside the window. Heading just about due west in a train was hardly conducive to enjoying a sunset. One could only glance north or south out the windows on either side but there was still enough dispersed light to enjoy some crimson and orange streaks above the horizon dotted with wisps of pillowy clouds.

"You like sunsets, Lyra?" he asked her, noting how her name rolled off his tongue and palate for only the second time.

"Of course! Don't think you can *only* just *like* a sunset." She was teasing him about his '*like and love*' ideas that he expressed earlier. "I *love* them!"

She glanced out the window. "When I was in college back east I used to hike to the top of Mt Marcy most clear Friday evenings in the spring and fall to enjoy the view. I think I climbed that mountain at least thirty times during those years. I ended up being a volunteer guide for the local Girl Scout and Boy Scout troops by my senior year of college. Some of my sorority sisters even started teasing me by nicknaming me 'Marcy' that year. I didn't mind it – all in good play."

"I think Lyra suits you much better, if I may say," he cut in. "I'm still enjoying hearing the name… quite *beautiful*. Really like it. But if you prefer Sasha I can relent."

She blushed a bit.

"That's all right. The way you say it makes me think of my childhood again, for some reason."

"Well, hiking was honestly better than any frat party I'd ever been to. I especially liked the view from the peak over the miles of forest land. Pristine land. I hardly ever even filtered my water along the streams back then. Never got sick either. Those were magical walks. I admit that at some point during those hikes I convinced myself that my career would be focused on the environment. And so here I am today. On a diesel spewing locomotive heading three thousand miles cross country to save the world from itself. I'd *hate* to calculate what my carbon footprint is for *this* trip." She rolled her eyes and sighed. Then she smiled at him.

She seemed content to him. Settled in her mind. Genuine idealism. The world could use more Lyra Sasha F..." He realized he couldn't remember her last name... well, more of her type, that's for sure, he thought, with all the stress to the planet. He knew it well having studied the issues for some of his journal pieces. These were all hot topics in the media, no pun intended – global warming, environmental pollution, humanity's encroachment and destruction of wilderness, increasing numbers of threatened species, more massive hurricanes and prolonged droughts, political lack of will, rainforest burns – the whole of it all was quite depressing to him. He'd traveled to enough places already to see some of the changes going on with his own eyes and catalogued enough photos to fill a memorial museum to the history of a destroyed planet Earth, if it came to that.

He tried not to think about the big picture too much when he was traveling and writing and photographing. Might as well go home, he would have to say to himself, if all of this effort would be for nothing in another generation or two. But he had to will himself to not believe that would be the case. Maybe, in his own way, his articles and photos could make a difference if he reached enough people who could appreciate his work. Maybe the world will awaken, once and for all, and make the changes needed so that the air and oceans and trees and all living things had a better chance together. Harmony, at last. Nirvana.

His own idealism was still attached like an umbilical cord. Nourishing his soul with the completion of each and every article that saw the light of day in a magazine or newspaper. If only. *Or what was the alternative...?* Depressing. He put it out of mind – had to, he told himself countless times. *Be an optimist. Forge ahead. Keep at it. You are doing what you love to do. Not what someone else's dreams were for you. That time is over now. You're your own man with your own conscience. That's what's most important and can and will make a difference in this world.* That was his speech to himself and he knew the more he thought it he would fully accept it in time. If there was enough time left out there in the natural world to make a difference.

The conductor's voice returned to the intercom.

"Well folks, Harry here again. Hope y'all are perked up a bit more back there. Susie sends a bucket of peachy thanks to y'all who came on down to her place at the bar. And I was told I need to wish a lit'l ol' Happy Birthday to William Armstrong, triple I - all *five* years old today. William Armstrong the third, it is! Keep on training, son. No better way to see America than out the window of a train!" Harry said excitedly. The intercom then relayed a high pitched whistle toot sound for a few seconds.

"So folks – sure sounds like there was a nice little party y'all had goin' on. Good on y'all! I like a happy train. Always have, always will." He paused while Bradlee and Lyra smirked at each other. "This guy's a hoot," she said. Bradlee nodded.

Harry beeped back on. "OK folks – so I have some good news and some bad for y'all. About that track switchin' issue I said earlier. The problem is just west of Minot, just outside of town. The switch operators and line engineer folks are tellin' me that the problem is tougher than a hungry mamma bear to fix than they first realized. It's gonna take at least eight hours of overnight fixin' time on their part to get us goin' onward on the right track headin' west over to See...attle. That's the bad news – but not a longer delay expected than that. Somethin' about needin' to weld a new piece of track and fittin' it in place and running quality and safety tests using a dinkey parked in Minot. Pain in the ass, I'm sure, for those guys. I imagine not exactly what these linesmen wanted to probably be doin' on a Friday night in Minot. But heck, I'd wager the overnight pay won't be too chintzy for'um. Bright side to everythin', right?"

"Now we *could* attach another locomotive to our rear end and I can shimmy into it and take us backtracking to Chicago, then take an alternate route west but that would put us in to L.A. in about four more days and I can't imagine any of you kind folk would be up to sittin' on your hineys for that much longer and then havin' to figure out how y'all goin' to get to See...attle. I sure ain't." He chuckled, but his voice had that kind grandfatherly lilt that no one could possible blame him for the train's troubles.

A toot noise again came over the intercom followed by a short burst of laughter.

"Folks, that's a gift for my granddaughter, Bella," Harry continued on – "when I get back home to See...attle. She's sweet al 'right. All six years of her soul. Bella and her parents are flying out to See...attle in just a few days to visit ol' grampa and grammy. They live down in Georgia, where I'm from orig'ly if you haven't yet gathered from my drawl. Little Bella is just itchin' like cooters on a coon to help me drive this big ol' machine across country one day. Company says twelve years old and she's good for a stretch next to ol' Harry here but I don't think I'm goin' to keep on goin' in this ol' seat by the time she's ready. Retirement ain't too far off, I'm afraid folks. Oh well."

He took a long sigh breath into the microphone. Any remaining passengers that hadn't yet fully tuned in certainly were by now. Harry was rambling but also comforting. Like visiting your own grandpa.

"So folks, as I was sayin'. Bella – she already loves trains just like I did at her age. Runs in the bloodlines, I guess. My papa was also a conductor – imagine that! I figured this train whistle tootin' horn would be the *cat's meow* for her birthday gift." He tooted it again followed by another pause as the intercom faded to muffled dialogue.

"So, I've received an update about what we're all goin' to need to do just ahead. We're fixin' to pull into the station at Minot, North Dakota in just about five minutes from now. We'll all need to exit this train and stay overnight in Minot. Now, I know, no one was expecting this but I assure you that our Amtrak folks back in D.C. headquarters and on the ground in Minot are working on arrangements at the local hotels and motels that will accommodate *all* of us. So that's the good news – not so bad after all," he chuckled.

"Heck – some of y'all may just want to explore a bit of Minot on a nice walkabout if you want to stretch those rigor mortis legs of yours. The weather looks comfy enough from the forecast if you like a little North Dakota cool whip frosty winds."

"Now let me reassure y'all - I've been through these parts countless times. Minot's a good town. Good and honest people. They like visitors and Lord knows your tourist dollars will go a long way in keepin' food on their tables and winter clothes on their backs. And the cost of your hotel stay is on us. No need to shell out any of your hard workin' dollars. Y'all will also receive a little grease money in your pocket – that's fifty US dollars into each of your pockets to spend as you like on any extras – food and drink and such while in town. Whatever isn't spent is yours to keep but I sure hope you spend it here in Minot. I'd say the D.C. folks at headquarters are doin' their best to make

41

for some happy customers aboard this train. I've been working this outfit for the past thirty-five years. They do it right by you – at least I think so. Let's be optimistic and try to keep the whinin' to a Coonhound minimum. This will all be a little fun diversion, I would hope, for all you good folk. A surprise adventure. Sure, we'll be arriving a little late into See...attle than expected but some'ya may just be leaving your hearts in Minot." Harry laughed again, this time more gregariously than usual.

Some of the fellow passengers in Bradlee's and Lyra's train car starting guffawing. The conductor had their attention, all right! The intercom started again.

"OK folks – here's some more important stuff so listen up. We've got some small vans that will be meeting us at the station and will drop y'all off at various hotels around town. They're rolling out the red carpet for y'all. It might take a few trips to get everyone situated so we ask that elderly folk and families with youngins go first on the vans, please. Common sense folks. We'll all get tucked into soft clean sheets in short time. Maybe some cookies and milk too if y'all are nice to your hotel hosts." He stopped to laugh again. "The vans will make mornin' pick-up rounds at your hotels and motels in the mornin' starting at 07:00 and bring you back to the station. Some of you will be picked up by 08:00 sharp, the latest, in the last van rounds - so please be ready to go when they arrive. Hopefully y'all have a restful night sleep. This train should be departin' with Harry, yours truly, here at the helm at exactly 08:42 tomorrow mornin'. That's 08:42 on the Rudolph Reindeer's button nose – Please kindly make a note." There was a brief pause and then the sound through the intercom of liquid being gulped, followed by throat clearing.

"Sorry folks, all this talkin' made my cords run dry," Harry uttered before continuing further.

"With a fixed up track and some clear skies we just might be able to make up a little of that lost time headin' west across Big Sky country in Montana and up into Glacier. Maybe a good tailwind will help too," he chuckled at his own joke. "You won't want to miss that section, by the way. Big Sky and Glacier are a beaut! Never get tired of seeing those mountains. Maybe some elk too, if we're lucky. Take note again folks – you miss this train tomorrow mornin' and you're here to stay for awhile 'cause our next company train passin' through and headin' west won't be passin' here for another three days. And twelve hundred miles from here to See…attle is a *long* walk, al' right." He laughed again. "See – you later –attle!," he couldn't help himself from laughing now.

He sure was a hoot with a captive audience, Bradlee thought. *Love that Southern twang*. The conductor let out yet another burst of laughter before continuing.

"So, God bless and thanks for listenin', folks. See you at the station in just a few. I'm the one with the purple top hat on and rotund belly – can't miss me if you tried. Say hi to Harry, won't you? See you on the platform. '*Sleep tight by the firefly light*,' as pops used to say." And then the intercom went silent.

The passengers began to assemble their belongings. Bradlee looked over to Lyra.

"Well Lyra, it was very nice chatting with you the past few hours. I enjoyed it. Not sure if we'll run into each other again on the train tomorrow. I just have a short time on the train in the morning to get to the Williston stop. So I want to wish you good luck with your studies."

"Yes," she replied. "It was very nice to meet you as well, Bradlee Seashell." She paused before realizing – "hey, that rhymes swell…" She gave him a big smile and reached out her hand. Bradlee grasped it gently and took one last glance at this Daphne of a woman. He wondered if they would ever meet again. Their hands separated. Bradlee lowered Lyra's duffel bag from the storage compartment and they proceeded to pack their belongings.

Finished with her tasks, Lyra sat down as the train approached the station platform in a crawl. She was watching Bradlee reassemble his backpack. He had pulled out some more shell satchels to check on them and then spent a minute adjusting his extensive camera gear. A voice she hadn't heard inside herself for quite some time compelled her to speak.

"Bradlee ——" He turned towards her. "Don't take this the wrong way, but I thought maybe we could at least keep each other company overnight. You know – same hotel, perhaps? I'm just a little nervous about being on my own. Not sure why. It's just who I am. Always been that way. I get a little nervous in new places and it's dark out there now. Just get the heebie jeebies, you know. It just is... I'll treat you to breakfast in town though, before we board again, if you say yes?" She gave him a kind smile, one that couldn't be refused.

"Sure, happy to bunk with you Lyra." He smiled and raised his eyebrows.

"I didn't mean it like that," she responded but still smiled nevertheless.

"I know – just joshing you. We'll be all right. I'll help sort things out for us on the platform," he said.

He grabbed her duffel and hoisted it over his shoulder. "Holy cow! – you got a case of bricks in here?"

"Tree trunks, sorry. For my environmental sciences studies," she giggled.

The train came to a stop on the platform. Minot Station. As promised, various uniformed officials with walkie-talkies and clipboards in hand were there to greet the passengers filing off their respective train cars. Bradlee and Lyra disembarked. Bradlee struggled a bit balancing his backpack and camera bag over his left shoulder and Lyra's duffel over his right. They were met by a brisk temperature.

Sundown was nearly over. A cool breeze picked up. "Sweater weather, that's for sure" Lyra said. They deposited their belongings on the platform and pulled out their warmest fleece and parkas. A bit of a shiver ran through the platform's commotion. One of the train attendants handed an envelope to each of them. It was their overnight fifty-dollar cash stipend. Bradlee and Lyra opened the envelopes and stuffed the fifty-dollar bills into their wallets.

"Lyra, follow me. I have an idea."

They picked up their bags and headed through the crowd and into the station. It was certainly much warmer inside.

"Wait here a sec."

Bradlee exited the station onto the front street. A few taxis were alongside each other in the parking lot hoping for some business to arrive. Lyra watched Bradlee chat for a minute with one of the drivers who then deposited his backpack in the trunk and Bradlee joined the driver in the front of the taxi. The taxi spun around the station loop road and Bradlee jumped out. The driver was more methodical due to his age. A gray haired senior, well over six feet of a burly frame slightly bent at the chest, a light shuffle in his step. A long face, cheeks lined with small red capillaries, and a wide chiseled jaw.

"Lyra, this is James."

"Pleasure to meet you, Lyra. Pretty name, you've got." James gathered up Lyra's right hand as if it was a child's inside a gentle giant's.

"James says he has a good spot he thinks we'll like for tonight. I figured we can get settled quicker this way and I usually trust the locals anyway when picking an overnight spot wherever I'm traveling. Almost never fails. Don't worry about the cost – we'll settle up with Amtrak tomorrow. I'm sure it'll be fine.

"Well, alright then. Thanks for doing this, Bradlee. I like the plan. Nice to meet you as well, James. Thanks for being here for us."

"My pleasure, ma'am."

Lyra's duffel was swept up by James before Bradlee could flinch and it was deposited into the trunk. Lyra hopped into the backseat. Bradlee returned to the front with James who was dialing up a number on his cell phone. It rang a few times and then a click. Someone answered, thankfully, Lyra thought.

"Thomas, this is James. Good evening to you. I apologize for the late call. How are you and Nancy feeling?" He paused.

"Haven't spoken to you in – how long has it been? – At least a few weeks since the fall. Nancy stable since coming home?" Lyra couldn't hear the man's reply with any clarity. Just snippets of words that were awkward to string together into any meaningful flow.

"That's good. I know she's been through some rough patches. Both of you. I think about you both a lot. We go way back, don't we, Thomas? I'm praying for her."

Another pause.

"Good to hear. Say, you ever get around to fixing that roof leak above the Pandora Room?" More mumblings that Lyra couldn't make out.

"Well, if you need help with it just give me a call. I'll hook you up with my grandson's outfit. You remember Zach, don't you? Fully grown now. Big and strong like his papa. They don't grow Anderson's to be pint sized in North Dakota these many generations." He chuckled. "They do top notch work around town. Best in Minot from what folks tell me who read the internet stuff – 'Reviews,' I think they call 'em." More mumbling on the other end.

"Sounds good."

"Thomas, listen – I know it's late notice for you but I've got a couple of passengers who need a place for tonight. They just got off Amtrak's Empire Builder." A pause.

"Yeah, stranded overnight. Guess everyone in town's

heard about it by now. Train track needs some overnight fixin' just west of town. The boys are on it from what I saw – whole bunch of 'em were headed inside the station when I pulled up to wait about a half hour ago. Must have been that crazy late summer hailstorm last weekend. Who knows, maybe dented the track – I can believe that – those things were like giant snowballs." His voice was animated now and he laughed wholeheartedly. Then James looked at Bradlee while fashioning the outline of a rather large ball with his leathered hands for acknowledgment.

A pause as James listened closely.

"Got it. Very kind of you. I'll bring 'em right over. Thanks Thomas. I owe you one."

James started the car and turned towards Bradlee. "It's late. It'll take us only about ten or fifteen minutes to get across town to your place tonight. On the meter, usually, it's about a fifteen dollar fare with some daytime traffic, maybe more, but ten bucks tonight at this late hour is enough for this old man. Besides, the damn clicking noise from the meter drives me crazy. Ten's enough to bring home a nice pie from Ruby's for the Mrs. Does that sound all right to you?"

"Sounds perfect to me," Bradlee replied.

Bradlee turned to Lyra and smiled. James pressed a button on the meter and the LED lights and staccato clicking noises stopped.

"Sweet Caroline," he muttered happily. "Besides, I can show you a few clicks of downtown Minot, for what it's worth to you. Consider me your tour guide for the duration of the evening." He followed that with a good belly chuckle.

They started out of the station as James turned left onto 1st Avenue, crossed Broadway and then turned left onto Main Street.

Bradlee started. "Say James, what do you say we take a little detour to Ruby's first, before you drop us off. If I'm lucky she'll remember me and we can pick up some to-go dinner and pie for me and Lyra here as well?"

James turned to Bradlee, quite surprised.

"You know Ruby? How so?"

"Oh, I was a hungry biker a few years back. Came through here famished and left like a bear bedding down for hibernation." James laughed, as did Lyra who was recalling Harry's unique kind of personal dialogue.

"The guy went across the whole country from coast to coast on a bike!" Lyra crowed from the backseat.

"Is that so?!" James replied. "This town gets plenty of motor bikers coming through. Usually a lot rougher looking dudes than you look tonight."

"No, not that kind of cycling," Bradlee said. "I was on a bicycle. No engine. Just these thighs – '*Beatrice and Bessy.*' That's what I call them. They've never failed me."

Bradley pressed his hands into the flesh of each thigh and gave them a squeeze – "at least once I'm in top shape. They can climb any mountain after a hearty dinner and a good night's sleep." Bradlee was starting to like speaking in a folksy dialogue.

"Beatrice and Bessy!" Lyra chimed in – "You have names for your thighs?!" She cracked up laughing to that one. James started in as well.

James turned right onto Central Avenue. The ride was jovial as James relayed some history to them about Minot. By the time they parked in front of Ruby's they had heard the synopsis of James' life story. Fiftieth anniversary with his 'Sweet Caroline,' as he kept calling her, was around the corner in just a few months.

"October 18th – a grand day it was fifty years ago…" He relayed the wedding scene.

"We met way before that, though. We were just kids really. Schoolmates. We didn't really have much to do with each other in those child years. But we both grew up locally. We met up again in high school but only a passing few words here and there kept us in any sort of cordial contact. I'd say my sweet honey was a late bloomer as the docs would call it – physically and all, if you get my drift. Not a real looker back in high school when that was what most of us boys focused on. Probably still do – not sure if *that's* changed over all these years?"

"So high school graduation comes around and I go off to work in the mines and Caroline stayed on her family farm – her daddy worked the red winter wheat... combined them for miles. Big piece of farmland just outside of town. Silos you could see for miles – still standing today. Sometimes he would switch the crops out for hay or alfalfa but mostly it was wheat – a whole lot of it! Her daddy tried to hire me around that time as a farm hand but farming wasn't for me. Anyway, as my early twenties came around, I was looking to settle down and Caroline comes walking into this dance hall located just off Main Street over there one night that start of summer..." He motioned with his hand at a passage between a few buildings. "She was wearing this purple dress – her '*Lucky Lilac* dress,' my Sweet Caroline used to call it – and my blast furnace jaw just dropped to Antarctica!" James chuckled. "She was as *gorgeous* as I could ever imagine a girl to be. She was sure a woman by then and I hadn't seen her those past few years since end of high school, finishing up puberty and all. I about would 'a had a heart attack if I held my breath any longer!"

Lyra started to giggle uncontrollably in the backseat. She was tuned in to James' story.

"It's darn true, ma'am. Every word." James paused to collect his thoughts.

"So, I tried my darn best to have her like me that night even though I couldn't dance worth a dime and it turns out all along that she had her eyes on me since early high school but never talked – at least to me – about it. She really liked seeing me in my basketball shorts, she confessed later once we got to know each other better.

See... I was a varsity player, top scorer, played the center position on the one and only high school team in Minot back then. We had made it to the state finals my senior year. Lost by one point – darn opponents from over east in Fargo – much bigger school I might add – their shooting guard sank a field goal with nothing left on the clock. No instant replay back then, I might add. Caused quite a ruckus after the game ended but what the heck – that was a long time ago, as they say." He chuckled and was lost in thought for a moment. "Those were *fun times*." James paused for a breather.

"We got hitched just three months later and never looked back. I love her more now than I ever have, my Sweet Caroline. We couldn't keep our hands off each other during those three months of courting that our folks just had to let the wedding happen before there was trouble."

"It was a simple wedding. Families weren't with a lot of means back then. Straight hard-working middle class folks. Farmers, miners, builders, drivers... Enough to scrape by with a comfortable home, pay the bills, put a little savings away in the local savings and loan for special occasions and a bit towards retirement if you were lucky to live past sixty five or so. Most didn't back then. We all had fun at the wedding though. It was a real nice Indian summer day. Painted skies. An afternoon wedding outside the Lady Slipper under the gazebo. Thomas was there. You'll meet him soon enough... Good man, Thomas. When Nancy came along she made him an even better man – I'll say. She cleaned him up and helped him carry on with the family business running the inn together all these years. Good Christians... from the heart. They mean well to everyone they meet."

"Where was I?" James continued. "The wedding, right. Blessings and rice throwing followed by a nice party. Key Lime wedding cake – imagine that?! Right here in Minot, North Dakota. Caroline's mother had the limes flown in from Florida – special delivery. A whole case of them! Never tasted anything like it in my life! Still can taste that sweet and tart combination with the whipped cream and raspberries on top."

He licked his lips. Bradlee glanced back at Lyra and smiled at her and squinted his eyes.

"So the mines were a bit too dangerous back then and Sweet Caroline begged me to look for something else safer now that we had our first little one on the way soon after we married. I learned the railroad trades and worked the lines, helping with the track building and the maintenance, but that was harsh in winters up in these parts. Took its toll on my body. So I moved on to home and office construction as Minot went through a building boom. I was stronger than an ox back then and these hands could work a pipe fitting wrench in my right while I could drill at the same time with my left. Ambidextrous. A trait passed down for generations of Andersons since we came over from Norway in the late 1800's and settled here. Norsemen, we say – tough as nails to live through all these Dakota winters."

James kept on talking while Bradlee and Lyra enjoyed listening.

"Fifty years. Imagine that," he declared. "All good, may I add. OK, true – we had our little moments and squabbles but you forget those over the long run. You two kids remember that." James paused briefly to let his words sink in. At least he hoped they would.

"The mind forgets what it's supposed to, you know. It's the good times that really matter, that you want to hold onto and keep repeating 'cause there's nothing more important as you get to my kind of aging." He paused again. They were stopped at a red light and James reached for his handkerchief and blotted his eyes quickly.

"Sorry. I sometimes get emotional telling stories. My doc says it's a normal part of aging. Hope he's right." He took a slow breath and composed himself.

"You tired of hearing me wrangle on?" he asked them.

"No, not at all," Lyra responded. "James, please continue."

"Well, alright then. So Zach's working on securing a venue for the extended family and friends to all congregate for our fiftieth. Sweet Caroline wants a small ceremony where she and I can state our vows again. And I can't resist her wishes. She's worn me down after fifty years, I'll say." He started with a kind laugh.

"Here's another take-home for you two; well, really for you Bradlee – women sometimes need that kind of regular reassurance and telling that they are loved. A lot more, I think, than men. Maybe I'm wrong but I don't think so in most instances." James looked over to Bradlee and then into the rearview mirror to check on Lyra before continuing.

"But Zach and all the other grandkids wanted to throw a big party for us instead of a small ceremony. So, we all decided to give my Sweet Caroline a nice big surprise bash, ceremony and all included. They say half the town might just show up. Four grown kids and nine grandkids in all. One more on the way tossing about in her mama's combine. That's one of my daughters-in-law. Her fourth coming out just before our anniversary. I've been blessed."

James carried the look of happiness. No – more than that – *contentment* is the better word, Bradlee realized. He figured by now that James probably was one of those elders who knew just about everyone in town. Sometimes life is just all about who you meet, Bradlee thought. Serendipity. Pure and simple.

"Well, we're here." The glowing neon green cursive sign was hung vertically from the brick façade:

Ruby's on the River

James parked along the curb and they went inside. Busy

place, waiters and waitresses dashing about. A buzz of activity. More modern finishings than Bradlee remembered it. There was even a square dance floor installed since he was here.

"If you'll excuse me folks I need to head to the loo for a moment," James informed them.

Bradlee and Lyra approached the lectern and asked for a menu. The hostess greeted them. "Welcome to Ruby's. We'll be closing the kitchen in about ten minutes. You just made it! You folks here overnighting in town on account of the train? We've got a whole bunch we just seated. Crew is working overtime to feed them all but we appreciate the business." She was quite jovial.

Bradlee glanced at the wall clock – 8:50pm. "I think we're in for take-out tonight, thanks," he said. "If you give us a minute we can hopefully get you our orders quickly." He and Lyra took a seat on the entryway banquette and mulled over the selections. Bradlee heard James' voice and then recognized Ruby who was walking beside James, their arms clasped around their elbows. Ruby was as tall as Bradlee and wide at the waistline and gussied up in a floral dress. All kinds of costume jewelry hanging from her neck and ears and she had on multiple rings curled around her clubby fingers.

"Ruby, you look sensational!" Bradlee announced as he rose to greet her. "Just as I remember you!" But it was her radiant smile and warmth that he most remembered taking home with him that summer.

"Well, look at *you*, you *handsome* young man, all grown up now, in those jeans and hiking shoes – and a lot longer hair than I remember! So good to see you back here, Brad Abraham Lee!"

"Thanks Ruby – it's good to be back. It wasn't quite in the plans just now but such is my luck. It's great to see you again." Lyra was observing their encounter. She was an outsider at a reunion, certainly not even like one of the extended family – a bit awkward. But the excitement and energy in a social gathering, a bustling restaurant, was refreshing after two long days alone on the train.

"You still have those steel cut fries with that spicy mayo secret sauce? All I remember was our table gobbling up about three servings-full back when we came riding into town in near starvation. You know Ruby – the locals all recommended your place and I'm sure glad for that 'cause it was one of our most memorable and tasty meals of the whole journey. We arrived pretty late that evening into town and hadn't booked a place yet to crash overnight. You visited our table, and by half an hour later, telling our stories and hearing some of yours, you were like a second mother to me – making calls and all and getting us settled in just right in town for the night." Bradlee gave Ruby a big hug and she welcomed it with open arms and looked straight into his eyes. There was a bond between them, Lyra noticed – and a warmth that she wished she could have again someday if she could let it in.

"Now tell me – where are you doctoring these days?" Ruby inquired. "You must be done with your studies by now?"

Ruby checked his left hand for a ring and then glanced over to Lyra. "*Well! There's* a looker! Hope she's as sassy as she is pretty." Bradlee twisted his torso and glanced towards Lyra who had started to blush. He returned his eyes to Ruby's.

"Well, turns out I made a few difficult decisions and had some life changes after returning from my bike trip. But they were for the best, I think." He turned again towards Lyra to see if she was still observing them. She was.

"Oh, sorry, let me introduce you – this is Lyra. She's my —— " Bradlee paused to think of the right words to use – "my *train* date. We're heading west together."

Lyra looked at Bradlee and pouted at him coyly before standing. She reached for Bradlee's ear and whispered teasingly, "Doctor Seashell, huh? Abraham? I *knew* you were some kind of doctor" before extending her hand to Ruby. Ruby gobbled Lyra's arm up into her usual bear hug. Lyra didn't mind the affection. She realized she hadn't been hugged in…

The thought stuck in her mind. How long had it really been? Weeks, months? Gosh – it *had* already been years since her grandma had last hugged her like Ruby. But it *did* feel inviting and she enjoyed the rush of warmth inside her now after all that time.

"It's nice to meet you, Lyra. This boy of yours is quite the adventurer type. Not sure if you know what you're getting into but be ready for some wind in your sails. I'm *sure* he's the finest doctor in town back home." She laughed and gave Bradlee another hug. Bradlee figured Ruby didn't quite understand what he had tried to tell her about his life changes. The place was plenty noisy and busy. So he let it stand and figured nothing worse of it.

"So glad that train broke down," Ruby said. "Just look at this place tonight – must be half of that train load inside here just now. I just told the kitchen staff that we need to keep on going for at least another hour. I've been getting more calls for tables than I can remember since the power went out across town – when was that James? – '77? I think." James nodded.

"Yup, I remember that." James turned to Bradlee and Lyra.

"I was here too that night with Sweet Caroline and our four young ones back then. Three of 'em were still in diapers. Ruby's place here was on the only block that still had electricity and heat in town – we packed in hundreds with Red Cross emergency cots and blankets and plenty of hot coffee."

"Cooking pies too! Until 2 a.m. that night, didn't we James?" Ruby declared. They smiled at each other knowingly. Memories they shared – with looks and nods

55

that transcended time.

"Oh – I added a few specials since you were last here Brad," Ruby continued. "Had a chef pass through here from San Francisco one day a few years back. He liked the quiet country so much that he asked me for a job. Turns out he was an important chef for some fancy-schmancy restaurant in the Golden Gate city and got burned out chasing Michelin stars. This place and menu were, quite frankly, getting a little stale over the years anyway. I knew I just needed a little push to make some changes and he just showed up on my doorstep at just the right time. So we closed shop for a few months, renovated and modernized to attract the young college-age kids and yuppies – as I hear they like calling themselves these days – and opened up the view to the kitchen area so folks can watch the chefs do their thing, and added this dance floor." She pointed towards it.

"This place can be rocking on a Saturday night – mix of bluegrass, rock and roll, country western, you name it, although I can't do that rap music – just too much thumping noise to my ears; gives me a migraine just thinking about it. We have some local bands who come by, regulars now on their small concert circuit through the towns in the region. Just loving the energy in here now!"

Bradlee was happy for her. Ruby seemed fully alive. Present. What was the term, he thought...? 'A woman in full bloom' – Y*es, that's it* – with her floral dress to match, how appropriate – if only she could bottle her positive energy and sell it, she could make a *fortune*. He smiled to himself.

"But enough about Ruby's," she said. "I'm sure you're all hungry. If it were me I'd go for the Dakota Burger with everything on it. Neil here, the chef I mentioned – well, he had an idea to inject some kind of soft goat cheese into the heart of a half-pound prime Dakota burger that we order from Jerry's cattle ranch and slaughterhouse just north of town – Jerry's got quite the operation, all grass-fed, one of those organic farming set-ups like you read about in the papers – and this burger has taken this city by storm ever since. My best seller, by far!"

James chimed in. "Jerry's a former classmate and close friend of my grandson, Zach – they're both entrepreneurial fellows."

"And I've still got those fries that I'm sure you're still dreaming about since you pulled out of town on that fancy racing bicycle of yours. Add a nice glass of Chianti from Italy and you'll sleep real well tonight," Ruby added.

"Thanks, Ruby," Bradlee replied. The two embraced warmly again. Lyra was beginning to feel jealous that she couldn't receive another hug as well.

"Take care now," Ruby replied. "Oh, and want you to know, Brad, that I still have that pretty postcard you sent me from P.E.I. when you finished your trip. Still tacked to the corkboard just above my office desk in the back of the restaurant. And those fancy Jenny's chocolates you sent me – the ones shaped like a whole mix of seashells – they were just divine. Don't you think I forget when someone gives me chocolates, now?!" She gave a hearty laugh as she rubbed and patted her belly. "Could hardly share them! You are a sweet thing, Dr. Brad Lee." Ruby waved with a flurry and blew a few kisses at them as she turned and proceeded to visit some of the other guests, making the rounds from table to table.

"Vivacious, isn't she?" James said towards Lyra.

"*I'll say!*" she responded.

Lyra tugged on Bradlee's jacket and whispered again into his ear. "Your last name is Lee? I thought Ruby was just pausing with her speech between Brad and Lee," she asked him.

"Yeah, that's my full name," Bradlee replied. "Now you know why I prefer Brad." He paused, wondering if he should lead her on some more and then figured there'd be no harm from it. The double 'lee' – Bradlee Lee – probably would sound just too corny if he were truly on the playground getting harassed for it.

He leaned his head down towards Lyra's ear to whisper back at her. "Lee, lee lee, lee lee, lee, Bradlee's gotta pee pee – the guys would tease me singing that damn song in grade school. Sometimes even the girls chimed in too. It took its toll on me back then."

"Ah, got it. Still like Bradlee better," Lyra responded, "but you can call me Sasha if I must call you Brad - Dr. Brad that is."

"No thanks," he replied. "Besides, Lyra's already grown on me too much by now. It reminds me of a Greek goddess and a constellation and you…"

He stopped for a moment before speaking further – "you are very very beautiful, Lyra." Bradlee smiled at her as she blushed. "But – I'm not a doctor so you can save the prefix for someone else who's earned it" he said rather nonchalantly. "Maybe you'll earn it yourself, someday down the road."

James said hello to a few of the wait staff as they were dashing by and then turned to Bradlee and Lyra. "There's more to Ruby's story, of course. A Bostonian transplant right here in Minot. A civic gem by now. Ruby's been here for over forty years, most of those operating right out of this restaurant. *Everyone* loves Ruby," as James filled in a few more details.

Hunger pains were beckoning. "I'll take the special," Bradlee announced. "You too, James?"

"You betcha," James replied affirmatively. Lyra was still reviewing the menu.

"What'll it be, my train lady?" Bradlee teased her.

"Well, in another place and time I'd choose that burger hands down," Lyra replied. "But I've been a vegetarian for the past five years. No sense changing now just because I'm in cattle country. I'll take the Vege burger with those spicy mayo fries you've been dreaming about." She winked at Bradlee and smiled.

Gosh, she can be a tease, can't she? Bradlee thought. *Wish I knew more about her.*

"Oh, and a glass of that Chianti too," Lyra added with another smile.

They placed their take out orders with the hostess but were informed the Chianti wasn't going to happen. The hostess reminded them that there's rules about not having alcohol for take-out and they had to abide by them.

James turned to Bradlee and Lyra out of earshot of the hostess – "Don't you worry, I'll take care of it. Make yourselves comfortable while we wait for our orders. Be back in a jiffy." James wandered down the hallway towards the kitchen. He returned a few minutes later. He was holding a wood box by a rope cord. Some Italian words were scorched into the panels on each side. They smiled at him as James smirked and gave them a quick wink while he slinked past the hostess who was busy attending to other guests. Guess Ruby fixed him up real quick, Bradlee surmised.

Their orders arrived in take-out bags that made their stomachs growl from the aromas. Bradlee took care of the bill with a swipe of his credit card as James thanked him for covering his dinner order. In a separate bag were stacked four circular pie tins. They were just the right tin size for perhaps two to share a pie, or maybe just one person who was a glutton for Ruby's pies. James hadn't forgotten about the pies, although Bradlee and Lyra had. He had placed an order directly from the kitchen, since the staff all knew him well, when he went back to retrieve the Chianti from Ruby. Ruby had a waiter shuttle the pies to the hostess.

"Ruby said these are on the house," the waiter whispered to the hostess. "And no questions asked, as usual" as he smiled knowingly. The hostess was used to these little handouts. She knew Ruby's generosity came with the territory.

"One for each of us – thought you might enjoy some of Ruby's magic," James said as he opened the backseat car door for Lyra. They settled back into the taxi. "She's been baking these pies all these years and I swear there's something magical in them. Like a love potion that you read about in fairy tales – only you got to eat the whole pie to get at the potion baked inside these sweet and tart heavenly creations." He rummaged through the bag to see if the pies were labeled, which they were.

"There's a peach-raspberry, straight-up blueberry, a lime meringue, and a strawberry-rhubarb. The rhubarb is for Sweet Caroline, her favorite, so you'll have to come around these parts again if you want to try it." He smiled at Lyra.

"Thank you James," Lyra replied. "I'll have the peach. I'm sure it'll be the best pie I ever tasted. I'm a raspberry lover, actually. Used to eat them straight from the vines in the pick-your-own fields near my home along the Connecticut shoreline when I was a little girl – my parents would have to hose me down from the juices that dripped down my legs all the way to my toes!" She was animated retelling the story. "Dr. Bradlee here can have the blueberry. Don't doctors always say a healthy dose of berries are good for you?"

"Gee thanks for nothing, Lyra," he teased her. "I absolutely abhor blueberries, by the way. I shall suffer for your happiness." He smiled again, this time with a little gleam of dishonesty in his eyes, and a smirk of his raised right cheek, that Lyra gathered was his retribution.

James exited the parking space and headed south to loop around the Scandinavian Heritage Park. There was just enough northern twilight in the sky to make out a hazy view of the Gol Stave Church from the roadside, perched on the hillside. He paused the taxi along the quiet road to take in the scene.

"Too bad for the late hour just now 'cause the flowers here in the park are still blooming – just a fine looking place to have a picnic with your hunny one day." James glanced over to Bradlee.

"You might be interested to know, Bradlee, that one of our local docs here in Minot chaired the committee that built this replica of the old church in Norway. And yours truly here got his hands dirty helping with the building of it some twenty or so years ago. Fine and solid structure, if I may boast a bit."

James started driving again. "You two lovebirds…" – he lifted his right hand off the wheel and overlapped his middle and index fingers and waved them together while giving a quick smile – "you two will need to return someday to check out the carvings. Real fine detail work done by some woodcarving masters brought in from out of town. Oh, and that picnic I mentioned – no finer spot to pass a few hours in Minot – maybe get some afternoon shut-eye." He chuckled to himself. "Makes me very proud of my heritage. There's plenty of us old-blooded Scandinavians still around these parts."

James pointed out a few statues in the park and the small windmill adjacent to the side entrance. Then he turned north up Broadway, crossed the Souris River, and took a left turn onto 4th Avenue.

"Your cozy inn awaits you," James announced as he pulled up in front and parked.

But for the whole drive from Ruby's, despite her hunger pains brewing, the mystery of who Bradlee Abraham Lee really was had begun to intensify within Lyra.

Part Two

LYRA EXITED THE TAXI and walked over to the white fence that bordered the property along its entire perimeter. Adjacent to the entrance gate she examined the decorative sign. Its words were scrawled in pleasant flowing calligraphy and block patterns:

The Lady Slipper Inn
Established, 1923
{ Welcome All Sojourners Through This Land }

Dusk had arrived to Minot. The lawn extended for a long stretch from the fence to the inn. The sweet aroma from blooming roses wafted towards Lyra in the gentle evening breeze. The temperature had settled and warmed since she and Bradlee arrived at the station. She inhaled and sensed a comforting feeling within her. As if she had been here before, perhaps in a different lifetime.

A bright sliver of moon was rising over the roofline and the constellations were announcing their presence in the northern sky. She looked upwards and spotted Vega twinkling proudly inside her own constellation. There it was, indeed – Lyra in the sky. Her namesake. When she was old enough to be trusted with adult matters, her mother told her the story. Her daddy selected her name. 'If the baby was to be a blessed girl, her name must be Lyra,' he would tell her mother. It was because her daddy loved the harp more than any instrument. He was an emotional man, full of love for his family and friends. And to his sense of peace, the harp was the embodiment of the music of the gods. To listen to the harp – the Lyra – was to transcend time. To touch the infinite and embrace it. But her mother, Leah, also loved the name. She informed Lyra that 'Grandma Leora' – Leah's mother – was also nicknamed 'Lyra' by her parents from the time she was a baby, according to family folklore. And now, this present comforting feeling under the clear skies only intensified how much Lyra missed her family. She wiped her eyes on her jacket sleeve and peered at the inn once again.

James opened the trunk and pulled out Lyra's duffel bag and Bradlee's backpack. He proceeded to carry the luggage items as if they were simple twigs in his burly arms as he opened the white picket gate and lumbered steadily to the porch. Bradlee and Lyra followed behind along the walkway that was lined with flowers. A porch light turned on as they approached the main steps to the doorway. Then the screen door screeched open as a man stepped outside to greet them.

"Thomas, we made it. Sorry again for the very late hour," James spoke softly. "We ran by Ruby's to pick up some dinner for these starving out-of-towners." He set the bags down on the porch, walked over to Thomas, and extended his hand for a grasping handshake. That was followed by an embrace with a few stern pats on each other's backs.

"Good to see you, my old friend," Thomas said affectionately.

Thomas turned to his new guests to address them. "Thomas Johansen… Welcome to the Lady Slipper Inn." Bradlee and Lyra introduced themselves and shook Thomas' hand warmly. "Very kind of you to host us tonight under the circumstances," Lyra said.

"When a stranger sojourns with you in your land, you shall not do him wrong," Thomas replied with a gentle smile. "That's from Leviticus. Chapter 19, verses 33 and

34." He spoke in a relaxed manner, devoid of any anger or frustration for the late hour.

"Nancy and I are happy to be here for you. She's tucked in for the night but I'm sure you'll have the opportunity to meet her tomorrow morning. Our home is your home for tonight. We wish you could stay longer but we understand you need to catch that train again early in the morning. Well... at least we'll feed you a hearty North Dakota breakfast before you're off. Breakfast is served between seven and eight. Best if you're here early to be able to feast well and enjoy the meal before you need to go.

James turned to Bradlee and Lyra. "If you'd like, I'll swing by here in the morning at 8:00 sharp and deliver you back to the station. No stops this time." He smiled. "Will have you on that platform just ten clicks later. Plenty of time for you two to board and find you some good seats. Maybe cozy up with a good morning nap together to help digest a full breakfast. Still a long journey ahead of you... Hey, by the way, I never asked, come to think of it. You two headed to Seattle like most of the rest on that train?"

"Not me – I've got just another few hours to Williston. Will need to say my goodbyes to Lyra there," Bradlee responded first. "Heading by rental car to Medora. Some business there to tend to." He turned towards Lyra.

"I am. Off to grad school in Seattle." And then the thought of never seeing Bradlee again crossed her mind. She wondered if he felt the same way at all about her.

"This here is for Nancy." James handed Ruby's take-out bag to Thomas that contained the lime meringue pie. "Please give her my love. Look forward to visiting in the morning if she's able."

"Thanks James. Her favorite as we both know. I'm sure she'll enjoy it... Very thoughtful of you. I don't think she'll have too much trouble chewing and swallowing it now in small spoonfuls. She's been making great progress, thankfully," Thomas informed him.

James turned to Bradlee and Lyra. "Now you lovebirds enjoy your evening. See you in the morning." He winked at them again and started off down the path as they entered the inn.

"We'll take care of the bill in the morning," Thomas said in the foyer. "But please go ahead and complete the registration form, thank you. One form is sufficient for husband and wife." He handed it to Bradlee along with a feathery quill ink pen. Lyra excused herself to the restroom down the hallway.

Bradlee studied the pen for a moment. "Nancy's idea – this pen's a bit old fashioned but it adds a little charm for the guests on check-in." He smiled. "She loves everything birdsy... You'll see lots of decorative pieces throughout the inn that she's collected over the years. All bird related. Amateur ornithologist and top state birder in her prime. She has the eyes of a red-tailed hawk, I'd say, even without binoculars! Audubon lifetime member." He paused. "I love her dearly."

The craftsmanship was unique. Bradlee admired the pen's long and slender pheasant tail feather dotted with symmetric ebony markings running at short regular intervals the full length of the shaft to the quill. The quill was bound by a series of tightly wound Indian bridle cords to an intricately carved wooden stick. The stick pattern resembled Native American designs he had observed along his bicycle journey while passing through the Dakotas. The wood carving narrowed to an elegant gold plated nib.

"Beautiful pen! A one of a kind, I would think" Bradlee turned his head. "Did you make this yourself, Thomas?"

"No, that was a gift from a fellow, an extended guest many years ago – one of the wood carvers who stayed with us when the Scandinavian church was being constructed over on the south side of town."

Bradlee twirled the pen and then ran his fingers along the wood carving again and stopped where he noticed a band of very small letters etched into the wood where it met the bridle cords. They were Hebrew letters – very odd, he thought.

"Did the maker carve his initials here?" as he pointed at them.

"Yes, he was a very pious man. Jewish. A rabbi, but I remember him telling me that he wasn't the full-time kind of rabbi who had a congregation of worshippers. His passion was to make people happy with his wood carvings and furniture pieces – all one of a kind, mostly by hand. Always wore a black suit and pressed white button-down shirt with a black hat and skull cap underneath... Robust beard... Prayed often while he stayed with us. He always faced east, he explained to me when he prayed – towards Jerusalem. He was a fine young man, I might add. But that was over twenty years ago."

Bradlee studied the Hebrew letters carefully and then slowly and softly interpreted them aloud in English to Thomas... "Rav Eliezer Levitsky." The woodcarver's name, Bradlee presumed. It *must* be.

"Yes, that's him. I remember now," Thomas replied. "Rabbi Levitsky, he called himself." Bradlee peered down the hallway in thought.

"You know how to read Hebrew, young man?" Thomas asked.

"Oh, I learned a bit as a child, that's all," Bradlee replied.

"Doc Cohen recruited Rabbi Levitsky to Minot to work on the church carvings. Said he knew a friend back east who could carve wood like Michelangelo could carve a marble masterpiece. It's a grand building at the Scandinavian Park... and those carvings are *truly* masterpieces to see over all these years."

"Yes, James swung by to show us a bit of it on our way here," Bradlee replied.

"Nancy and I really enjoyed having this rabbi stay here

with us. She and I are spiritual types, if you haven't gathered yet. We believe in souls and heaven and being kind to your fellow traveler. Doesn't matter to us what religion you practice or what race you are as long as you have a good heart and soul. But this young man was quite learned in the Old Testament and so we would spend hours together with him around our dining table discussing the Bible into the late hours. Those were special times in our lives."

Lyra returned and joined them in the foyer. "I gather, from your last name, Johansen – that you're Scandinavian as well?" Lyra inquired.

"Yes, from the northern part of Norway. My father's roots are from a small village... Straumnes. It's located in Nordland County on the island of Austvagoya. Part of the Lofoten Islands tucked just inside the Arctic Circle. There's an old but quite accurate map of Norway decorating a wall in the parlor room if you'd like to have a look in the morning. You know, many visitors to Norway say the Lofotens are the most beautiful region," he said with a touch of pride. "If you two ever visit that area you'll need to experience the northern lights. One of those rapturous moments... Like G-d shining his countenance upon you."

Bradlee noted the spiritual allusion and didn't mind. It was comforting, wholesome in this setting. He twirled the pen once more in his hands.

"Times were hard after World War I and so the family cobbled their funds together and sent him off. He was just sixteen years old but strong, and braver than the rest, I would imagine, when he set sail for New York harbor and passed through Ellis Island in search of a better life here in the States. The usual work-hard immigrant tale. Worked his tail off in the fish market down on Fulton in lower Manhattan after he first arrived. Saved enough as an early-riser fishmonger at the docks over a few years there but then he started dreaming about heading west and buying some land to farm and settle down, have a family. And so he found his way to Minot and bought this plot of land right here where we're standing. There were already plenty of Scandinavians in Minot so he felt like he hadn't completely left home..." Thomas paused and then pointed to the framed oil portrait in the sitting room off the foyer.

"There's my old man. Painter did a nice job portraying his demeanor. He was a proud man. I'd say he felt he had lived a full life and did right by his family... He passed on some years ago but I'll always remember his affection for me and the memories he shared of his childhood in Norway. When he came here to the States he never did see his parents – my grandparents, again..." Thomas paused and closed his eyes prayerfully to compose himself.

"The Lady Slipper Inn didn't start out that way on this property. I grew up in a small family home that still stands off to the side of this main house. My parents used to take in traveling guests through these parts who stayed in a guest bedroom inside our home and were provided with my mother's hearty dinners and breakfasts, hot bath water, and a comfortable bed. Our inn caretaker lives over in that original home now. It's been plenty renovated over the years. We're actually standing where the family farm existed back then. When I inherited the land after my father passed, along with a decent bank account that he had saved, Nancy and I were only married for a short while and we decided to build this main house as a larger welcoming inn for travelers. We enjoyed the company and dreamed of traveling to far off places ourselves. I think we made the right choice after all these years. We've enjoyed chatting and getting to know so many guests. And plenty of them return every year for a long weekend just because they've enjoyed visiting the inn so much over the years..."

"I can smell your dinner," Thomas sniffed. "Ruby's kitchen – quite tasty. She's a sweetheart around here. Known her for years. Everybody loves Ruby... And her pies...! Wow...! Enjoy the magic."

Thomas proceeded to give Bradlee and Lyra a brief tour of the main level. "Our kitchen is just down the corridor and to the left. You can enjoy your meal in the dining room over here. I've left out a pot of coffee for you on the warming burner. It's decaf. Figured you wouldn't want a jolt of the high-energy stuff at this late hour. There's some herbal tea packets and hot water adjacent to the coffee pot if you prefer, so help yourselves."

"Very kind of you, Thomas," Lyra replied. "I'll have a quick look around at these decorative pieces and a nice sip of chamomile before bed. I happen to love birds, as well."

"The house is full with guests at the moment," Thomas continued. Quiet hour now but when the van pulled up an hour ago with some of your fellow train friends, this place was teeming with activity. Everyone's already tucked in upstairs. But I saved you the last room available. It's our Hummingbird Room. It's up the stairwell and then follow the corridor until the end. You can't miss it with the hallway nightlights on – there's a magnificent painted hummingbird on the emerald green door."

Lyra glanced at Bradlee in disbelief as her eyelids widened. *Hummingbird Room! – did Thomas really say that?!* She reached over to squeeze Bradlee's hand for a brief moment. Her smile was as wide as she could stretch her cheeks.

"You'll see that from the door to the bedspreads, and just about everything else in the room, Nancy decorated the color scheme to resemble a ruby-throated hummingbird... They are very beautiful creatures, I must admit, especially the males," Thomas remarked. "Sometimes we see them around these parts in the summer. But – I'm very sorry for the inconvenience. The room has two single beds. We usually can place them together and fix them into a king on request but with the short notice and the late hour... I just didn't have the chance to help arrange that for you."

Bradlee and Lyra glanced at each other and smiled. Bradlee felt an opening.

"That's OK, Thomas. The Mrs. and I are exhausted after a long train ride, anyway. We'll need plenty of rest after we gobble down our dinner and head upstairs. I'm sure we'll be tucked into bed in a very short while... Lyra and I sincerely thank you for your hospitality."

"Thank you, Thomas," Lyra replied while leaning into Bradlee and pinching the back of his left thigh – just enough to have Bradlee realize a little cringe of pain as payback for his fibbing.

"Lyra?" Thomas inquired in thought... "That's a beautiful name, ma'am. Haven't ever met a woman with that name before... In fact, I was admiring your namesake – your constellation – when tidying up the porch just before your arrival... How about that?! Now that's a coincidence if I've ever had one...! Maybe your stars are aligned tonight?!" Thomas let out a chuckle.

Bradlee took a seat at the entrance table to fill out the registration form. He paused where it asked for the usual details. Then he dipped the nib into the inkwell and scribbled:

Guest Name: Mr. and Mrs. Bradlee A. Lee
Address: Northside Rd, East Point, P.E.I.

He handed the form to Thomas who slipped on a pair of reading glasses. Thomas glanced at the information and looked up with a broad smile.

"You two are a long way from home! Nancy and I visited P.E.I. many years ago. It was our honeymoon – imagine that! Gosh! – I think we were probably about your ages at the time. Still remember cycling along those quiet roads with her and enjoying the salty air... We were just kids in 'Spring Love' back then... Brings back some fine memories."

"OK, off to sleep myself. Best I check on Nancy. We'll talk more in the morning, I hope. Have a blessed evening…" He started to turn away but caught himself. "Oh, and one last item… I almost forgot. There's a gift waiting for the Mrs. on one of the beds in your room. Our caretaker's specialty. It's been a Lady Slipper Inn tradition for many years. Hope you enjoy it." Thomas nodded and then walked down the corridor and disappeared past the kitchen.

Bradlee and Lyra were famished. They sat beside each other at the grand dining table that looked like it could fill a room with sixteen guests. Lyra went into the kitchen and collected two wine glasses for the Chianti. They dined together, voraciously enjoying Ruby's offerings. They talked about Lyra's upcoming courses and her research interests. And then Bradlee grabbed his camera bag and shared some recent photographs on his camera screen, discussing techniques he was mindful of while on assignment – angles and lighting, setting of the subject and balance in the composition.

Lyra agreed – the fries were among the best she had ever eaten and wondered if North Dakota had any award-winning fries contests like she used to enjoy back home in Connecticut when the main event for the year as a child – the fall town fairs – would arrive with hayrides and horseback corrals and cotton candy and piping hot fries in paper chutes. They shared the wine until the Chianti was nearly drained. The Chianti brought flashbacks to Bradlee. He was transported to Florence, once again – a café table set along the cobblestones of the Piazza della Signoria on a pleasant summer evening. Sami beside him as he waited for the most opportune moment to capture the softer evening light on the sculptures and the pastel painted decorative shops and restaurants that lined the piazza.

"Bradlee," Lyra nudged his arm. "Where are you *now*, Bradlee Seashell?" she teased him. He came to the present and smiled at Lyra. "Just a quick memory, that's all. I told you they happen from time to time. It was a good memory."

"Well, I'd like to hear more of your memories" Lyra replied.

The peach-raspberry and blueberry pies remained in their tins on the table. "Bradlee, I'm sure these pies would be delicious tonight, but can we save them for the morning train ride instead? I don't think I can consume another bite."

"Sure Lyra, I agree. Something to look forward to tomorrow."

Lyra excused herself to ready for bed as she climbed the stairs to the Hummingbird Room. Bradlee cleaned up the table and dishes and headed to the porch to enjoy one more taste of the North Dakota fresh air, just the same as he had inhaled peacefully on his cycling journey. *What is it about this place,* he wondered, *that feels right? It shouldn't,* he thought. It was not from where he came. Hardly anything resembled his childhood back home in Toronto or on P.E.I, the two places he shuttled between throughout his earthly years to date. *Is it the air? The farmland?* – Perhaps he was a farmer in a previous reincarnated life, he ruminated. If only we lived many lives – past and future – turning our souls – maybe meeting some of the same souls but through different lives and places and events – and yet we had to live in the present. And here was a place in North Dakota where it seemed people did genuinely live in the present. They cared. Life was slowed down just enough to make meaning out of simple and beautiful and important events. Living amidst nature. The cycle of the seasons. Reflection. Just plain caring for each other – *was it because they needed to or because they wanted to...* His thoughts rambled onward. He knew it was sometimes difficult to shut his mind down and here was Lyra on the train. *Reincarnation?* He grinned. Maybe it's all true.

Lyra entered the room, softly lit by the nightstand bulbs. Emerald green satiny curtains were covering the large window bays. These were complemented with matching doilies on the nightstands. A comfortable ruby-red velour wingback sitting chair was set beside the window. The bedspreads were of a fine weave that resembled intricately decorated Persian rugs with innumerable varieties of hummingbirds in flight. On top of the far bed lay a pair of beautiful woven slippers. She entered and placed her duffel and purse down and studied them. Exquisitely crafted, with an embroidered beaded colorful flower surrounded by hummingbirds in flight and sipping nectar. The bases were constructed of moccasin deerskin. She slipped them on her feet. They were ever soft and embraced her toes with warmth and comfort. *Slippers... The Lady Slipper Inn. A gift for you*, Thomas had said. *Masterpieces! I must thank Thomas and Nancy in the morning* – she made a note in her mind.

Bradlee gathered his backpack and camera bag in the foyer and continued upstairs. *So quiet*, he thought. Just so quiet and peaceful here. The door to the room was left open a crack and he knocked and waited a moment but there was no answer. He opened the door and then heard the shower running. Lyra's duffel was opened and clothes and personal items strewn about to the far side of the spacious room. He noticed the bedspreads and paused... they were as if plucked from the royal bedrooms of the Pitti Palace or Versailles. He turned to glance at the bathroom door. Light emanated from its entrance as he noticed that it was a few inches ajar.

Bradlee laid back against the headboard of the bed closest to the doorway. His angle allowed a sliver of a view to the bathroom mirror. He waited silently. Lyra exited from the shower and reached for her towel. A glimpse of her beauty in the mirror. Movement. The curvature of her abdomen swirling into the grooves of her back. Then bursts of hair being dried forcefully. A hint of a fold of breast tissue. She was exposed. He felt like a hunter, camouflaged, waiting for the right moment. He looked away in embarrassment. She was someone he hardly knew and yet he couldn't deny his desire. Such beauty. If she knew he was spying she would never forgive him.

He rolled to his side and away from his coveted view. He opened his camera bag, pretending to inspect and clean the lenses as Lyra exited the bathroom.

"Your turn – that was incredibly refreshing, my love, after nearly two days at sea," she announced sarcastically. "I hope I saved you a few drops of hot water, my dear." She was teasing him again about the married couple ruse. She smiled at him. She had applied a knee-length white satiny camisole in the bathroom and Bradlee could not escape from glancing as it shaped her beautiful lines. How he wished he could sketch her, Bradlee thought, in her nakedness… a seductive pose like Daphne for Apollo.

"Thank you sweetheart. As thoughtful as always," Bradlee responded, enjoying their continued repartee while his imagination ran wild.

He agreed with the delightfulness of a hot cleansing shower. The inn had provided a generous supply of fragrant soaps and shampoos. He lathered and basked in the hot water streams. He ran his hand across the scar on the right side of his chest. Touching it was his way of never forgetting and it had become a ritual nearly every night before bed. In time, it had allowed him to sleep better, a solace and a salve. Finishing, he slipped on a pair of boxers, shaved, and brushed his teeth and slid into his inviting bed.

Lyra was tucked under her covers and applying a few more stitches to her needlepoint. She was nearly finished with it except for a small section towards the bottom right corner. Her eyelids began to fade. She turned to Bradlee whose head was not more than three or four feet across from her. "Bradlee, I want to sincerely thank you for tonight. I feel like I am sharing a luxurious dormitory room with a close friend. It is just so *beautiful*. And inspiring. So thank you again... I'm exhausted... Sweet dreams, sleep well, Bradlee Seashell." Lyra laughed at the rhyme once again and closed her eyes. A few minutes passed as Bradlee's eyes surveyed the room one more time in thought.

"Thank you, Lyra. Sleep well, too. I hope your needlepoint springs to life, a Hummy dancing in the moonlight..." Silence. He heard only the breath from her lungs across from him. She had fallen asleep. *So beautiful*, he said to himself, *so beautiful*, as he glanced to study her face, now cuddled against the plush down pillow. "Sweet dreams, my dear..."

Bradlee nodded off soon afterwards. Memories flooded his dream space and were interlaced with his imagination. He was on a research vessel in the Galapagos interviewing marine biologists. Then his mind turned to Alaska and photographs of the Inuit village along the Aleutian coastline and their harvest of caribou and seals. An argument with his father. His mother trying to defend him yet torn between the two men she loved dearly. A wild horse stampede. He was running from them now down a grassy field in the mountains. Faster, adrenaline racing, his heart pounding to avoid being trampled. He screamed out in his dream. "Sami no! Don't go...! Hold on...! Stay with me! Stay With Me...! No...! And then he wept and cried out again. "No! Sami no! Don't Go...!!!"

Lyra was startled awake by his outcry and she quickly turned in fright. She glanced at the alarm clock – 04:08am. *He must have been dreaming, a nightmare.* Bradlee was breathing in fits alternating with silence and then a few jerking movements of his arms and legs, as if running, followed by more cries.

She lifted his covers and sat on his bedside, stroking his hair. He woke immediately and stared into blackness and then at her face. Sweat to his brow.

"Bradlee, shh, you were having a nightmare. It's OK now." She looked into his eyes. His tears now flowing. "It must have been a painful one... I'm sorry." She continued to calm him.

"You kept saying – 'Sammy, don't go'... Care to talk about it...?" she whispered. "Who's Sammy?"

Bradlee laid on his back and stared towards the blank ceiling and closed his eyes to erase the dream. He was fully awake now, in the present.

"I'm sorry for waking you, Lyra. Sometimes I have an occasional bad dream, that's all."

She pulled down his bedspread and slid next to him under the soft sheet. It had been some time since she had embraced another man in bed. She was on her side facing him and she held onto him, her right hand resting on his chest. She ran her fingers gently through his hair. He didn't resist. He reached with his left arm and stroked her shoulder and continued to her forearm. Her skin was soft. The aroma of jasmine immersed him. *Was it her hair or her perfume or just her own scent*? He wondered. She rotated her position above him and stretched her legs over his. She laid her head and cheek against his chest. The rhythm of his breathing settled as he gently embraced her with his arms and stroked her back. He was gentle and her instincts told her to trust him. She wanted his affection.

Lyra turned to face him. "Bradlee... will you kiss me......?" He stared into her eyes for a moment, once more admiring her beauty. Moonlight crept between the curtains and cast a glow on her cheeks. He placed his index and middle finger to her lips and gently studied their texture. She teased him, threatening to bite his fingers with open teeth. And then, he lunged forward and their lips entangled and enveloped. She tasted like sunshine and then like a refreshing skinny dipping stream. Maple syrup drizzled on vanilla ice cream followed by the soft texture of a moist brownie. Deliciously sweet. Then, a separation as their eyes locked followed by another plunge as her lips met his again and again. He moved to her forehead and her cheeks and then returned to her soft lips as his hands caressed the firmness of her breasts. He kissed her nose and chin and she reached back as he devoured her neck delicately and playfully. She giggled and released his grasp and then plunged forward again as she held his arms to his side and kissed him back even more.

Lyra was straddling his pelvis. Her head resting against his chest. She noted his scar and gently examined it with her fingers. She looked into Bradlee's eyes with curiosity and then leaned her lips forward, gently offering a series of kisses along the scar's length.

"And this here on your chest, she whispered… Why?" she asked softly but he didn't respond.

Her arms released his and she slowly explored his torso downward to the side of his abdomen and pelvis as they continued to explore each other's lips. She held on to his pelvic bone, massaging and caressing it before continuing further to his groin. She rested her hand over him. His bulge was tight and firm inside his boxers. He moaned and pressed against her as she stroked. Lyra smiled and searched his eyes as they held another long moist kiss.

"Looks like I've awakened a hungry moon snail," she whispered into his ear and laughed playfully.

Bradlee could not deny he wanted to be inside her at that very moment. To offer her pleasure and be pleasured in return. But it was happening too fast. Fear and vulnerability and frustration seeped into his mind. He wanted a relationship but one that offered commitment and security. Not a one night stand with a woman he hardly knew. His mobile career surely allowed for this kind of overnight romance but he didn't want a long distance relationship that would tear at his heart. And then thoughts of his nightmare came rushing through his mind. Sami's face appeared before him. His heart started pounding and he released Lyra and swept her to his side.

"Lyra, you are so beautiful. I want to have you so very much… but please understand. I need time. We need to be practical. We may never see each other again after tomorrow."

Lyra looked away with tears welling in her eyes. She remained silent as Bradlee continued talking but she wasn't listening, lost in her thoughts. A jumble of excitement and attraction came crashing down to a cool reality. She would be heading to Seattle tomorrow. There would be no more Bradlee Seashell to occupy any space in her life. She stood and walked to the bathroom to rinse her face. A ritual cleansing, she thought. She returned to her own bed and laid silently and focused on the darkness that now enveloped her as she tried to shut out Bradlee and hummingbirds and seashells and her past. Whether they spoke another word again no longer mattered to her. She closed her eyes, enveloped in more silent tears.

Her alarm buzzed at six-thirty. Lyra took a moment to gather herself as she stared at the light streaking through the emerald curtains alighting the room with a blaze of reflected colors. Lyra felt disoriented after a fretful sleep. She turned towards Bradlee but his bed was empty and his backpack gone. Yet, his camera bag was unzipped and laying beside his pillow. She rose and inspected it and found only a few contents – some additional lenses, flashes, a stabilizer, and some unopened flash drives. The main compartment was emptied of his camera.

She walked over to the window and parted the curtains. A magnificent array of flowers and bushes greeted her eyes. A landscaping marvel of creative beauty as she traced the garden view to identify the feast before her. She had studied enough horticulture in school to know many details of this extravagant terrain. And then she spotted Bradlee, in the garden at the front of the inn, dressed for the cool weather, and focusing his camera lens on the flower beds.

The sun's rays were streaming through the plantings leaving a misty haze with morning dew glistening on the petals and mowed grass. *The lighting... of course!* she realized. Softer, usually the better. A photographer always seeks the best lighting – first light and late afternoon leaning towards sunset, she remembered him telling her on the train. At least he was still here at the inn, she thought. A goodbye would not hurt with a cordial send-off.

She washed and dressed and packed. She found her needlepoint canvas beside her bed. She sat in the wing chair adjacent to the window. It allowed her an unimpeded view of the garden from her right side vantage as she worked to complete the canvas. Only the blank corner remained. The pattern could easily finish itself.

She glanced out the window to see Bradlee studying his garden subjects. He aligned and straightened a crop of lilies and then focused on a stand of pink and white and orange rhododendrons. Then he moved on to the Black-eyed Susans and yellow marigolds. Then an enormous grove of ornamental roses of innumerable varieties – from Princess Alexandra to Mother of Pearl, Tuscan Superb, and many more. A botanist of immense devotion surely must tend to this garden, she realized. He photographed them all, persistent and exacting in his quest from every angle. Then on to briefly scenting some Eternal Flame roses before he settled below a magnificent trellis partitioning one section of the garden from the other. The trellis was completely encased by Star Jasmine vines. Bradlee approached and placed his head into the mass of hanging vines as he absorbed their sensually sweet and intense fragrance. His eyes closed as he tilted his head high and she noted him smiling broadly. Minutes passed as Lyra watched him from the window. *"Who is this man who lingers amidst jasmine?"* she asked herself.

Lyra returned to her needlepoint and began to fill the empty corner with her own design. She selected some colorful spools of yarn and worked quickly, her imagination flowing freely.

It will be a gift from my heart... she felt, *even if I were to never see him again.* She selected a golden spool for the finale and crafted a swirling shell, a replica of the lightning whelk that Bradlee had handed to her to admire on the train. She completed it by sewing two red heart insignias bordering her initials – but which initials to place first? *Who am I now? Am I Sasha or am I Lyra...?* His passion last night flooded her mind with happiness. In calligraphy, she embroidered the "L" first; her renewed name, a return to childhood and loving memories. It felt right. She sewed with a flourish... L... S... F...

There it is, she admired the finished product. One of her most beautiful hummingbird canvases, indeed. She reached for her purse and retrieved a thin glass perfume bottle and sprayed a light mist to permeate the canvas surface. *He sure seems to like jasmine, doesn't he?* as she glanced again at Bradlee soaking in the trellis vines. *Then I shall give him his jasmine to remember me, if he chooses.* She wrapped the canvas inside a linen scarf with a hummingbird motif and composed a letter on the inn's stationery.

> *Bradlee – Thank you for last night and for your shell necklace.*
> *You will remain mysterious, as it should be, perhaps...*
> *A gift in return to you from my heart.*
> *Your Trochlidaeologist, Lyra.*

And then she added below it:
> *PS–if ever the need arises to unload some heavy baggage, call me...*

She wrote her phone number below, folded the letter into the envelope and wrapped it inside the scarf with the needlepoint. She located Ruby's uneaten pie tins, enclosed Bradlee's blueberry pie into a plastic bag that also contained the wrapped needlepoint and card and deposited the gift collection into a corner pocket of his camera bag underneath some of his extra lenses.

The breakfast table was a busy affair. Most of the guests assembled and collected their buffet items set out in the kitchen and found their seats in the dining room. The overflow bundled up in their sweaters and dined on the porch overlooking the garden. It was the last week in August but already the morning temperatures in Minot had descended to just above freezing. Lyra knew the flowers in the garden would not survive very much longer for the season.

She noticed Bradlee entering through the front steps onto the porch. He set his camera on one of the open small marble bistro tables. Lyra's plate was stuffed with fresh berries and melons and orange slices, a vegetable omelet, a few bite-size muffins and cheese slices. They met at the front porch screen door and Lyra could smell the jasmine vines on his clothes.

"Good morning," she greeted him. "You were an early riser today. Here. Take this plate from me. I'd like to go back for another helping anyway, before it's all gone. This place is hopping this morning…! Coffee, herbal tea, or juice perhaps?"

She looked refreshed and peaceful, Bradlee noticed, and she was wearing a grassy green stretchy soft cotton dress that hugged her torso and waist and accentuated the flecks of green in her hazel eyes. Lyra was incredibly beautiful in any color, he realized. He was concerned she would be more upset with him this morning after what happened during the night. Or, what didn't happen. Bradlee accepted the plate with a "Good Morning and Thank You" and kindly requested a glass of juice.

They dined together and admired the garden. Bradlee described some more of the techniques he used to adjust the light with the appropriate aperture settings and color filters to enhance the images. Some of these methods were done during the shoot and others were refined later, he explained, and that he would need to spend many hours on his computer to select and define the photographs that best captured what he chose to express. Often, only a handful from hundreds of photos made the grade for potential publication. But these flowers in the garden this morning – he had been photographing them merely for the fun of it. There was no article to write about the Lady Slipper Inn. "Sometimes, photographers take pictures just because they enjoy what they see," he went on…

Thomas was making the rounds with a friendly good morning to the inn guests. Nancy was beside him making slow progress with the aid of a walker. The couple approached Lyra's and Bradlee's table and Thomas introduced Nancy to them. Nancy's speech was disjointed and slurred and her right arm was hanging rather limp to her side in a brace. Thomas explained in a hushed tone.

"Nancy had a stroke just over four weeks ago. She was in the kitchen preparing breakfast on a morning just as beautiful as today. But then she suddenly collapsed to the floor. Oji found her right away and screamed out for me. I called Doc Cohen immediately who sent for an ambulance. She was stabilized in the intensive care unit over a number of days at the regional hospital here in town, then transferred down the corridor to the main hospital unit for another few weeks of care where she started learning how to eat and drink again. She was moved to a rehab center for the past few weeks until I picked her up. Nancy arrived back home just a few days before you came in late last night. Oji, our all-around caretaker helper at the inn – she's like family to us, another daughter by now after all these years here – well, she's been helping me look after Nancy on top of the usual daily work of running this place for guests."

Lyra reached out her right hand and Nancy met hers with a gentle handshake with her left.

"You're a very beau'ful woman," Nancy said with a slur. Lyra blushed.

"I'll second that Nancy," Thomas added with a gracious smile.

"Thank you," Lyra responded. "I feel refreshed thanks to both of you and I feel very fortunate to have slept in the Hummingbird Room. You might say my interest in hummingbirds goes back to when I was a little girl... The Lady Slipper Inn is truly a beautiful and special place."

"Nancy's been making steady progress with this walker," Thomas continued. "And her speech is picking up as well these past few days. And I can tell she's still as clever and witty as ever!" Nancy smiled awkwardly due to partial paralysis of the right side of her face but her eyes gleamed as Thomas gave her a cheeky kiss.

"The therapists said Nancy's gait, her arm, and speech will take quite some time, if ever, to fully recover. But we're optimistic and trust in the Lord. I'm just so thankful for all the docs and staff at the hospital and rehab center who saved her life. We are blessed with good people here in Minot."

Oji opened the porch door carrying a pitcher of coffee in one hand and orange juice in the other. She made the rounds topping off glasses for the seated guests and was waved over by Thomas to their table.

"This is our sweet Oji," Thomas introduced her with a gentle hug as she blushed. She looked a bit older than Lyra, Bradlee surmised, with slight creases to her forehead and the beginnings of crow's feet adjacent to her eyelids. Lyra admired her conspicuous Native American features with high cheekbones and almond shaped eyes with gorgeous braided jet black hair that extended to the small of her back.

Thomas noticed Lyra studying Oji. "Oji's a Lakota Native American. Her ancestors inhabited these parts of North Dakota long before us folks got here. Her family lives not too far from here on a reservation. Oji joined us as a young teenager. She stays with us here most of the time in the old house that I mentioned to you last night where I grew up – it's the one over there on the edge of the property…" Thomas pointed towards it. "But her husband and little boy do come and stay here as well throughout the year and Oji returns to the reservation to see her family on a regular basis. We always enjoy having her family visit us here for holidays from time to time and other special occasions." Lyra met Oji's eyes and then Lyra seemed to feel some deeper connection with her. It was a comforting feeling.

"Oji is short for '*Ojinjintka,*'" Thomas continued. Her name means '*Rose*' in the Lakota language." Lyra turned her head and once again admired the variety of ornamental roses blooming in the garden. She turned back.

"Oji, are you the gardener responsible for all of this beauty? And all of those fantastic roses?!" Oji blushed again and nodded.

"Yes ma'am, cultivating roses has been a great hobby of mine ever since I was a little girl. I guess my name was appropriately chosen for me," she said with a broad smile.

"They are stunning, Oji, just as incredibly beautiful as you are," Lyra replied. "Someday I'd like to meet your family. I've never been on a reservation before," Lyra said.

"I would be happy to take you there when you have some free time," Oji responded with genuine affection.

"Oji also makes the decorative slippers here," said Thomas. "All sewn by hand, I should add. Lakota inspired, you might say, with some modern additions. Each one is a unique and original work of art but they are durable and *can* be worn and enjoyed for many years… Our inn's special take-home present for our guests.

"Lyra, I trust you found your set of Lady Slippers on one of the bedspreads last night?"

"Yes, Thomas. They are *incredibly* beautiful. Nothing I have ever seen before… Thank you, Oji – you are a woman of many talents, that's for sure."

"Would you like to see how I make a pair?" Oji asked. Lyra glanced at her watch. Twenty minutes until eight o'clock. James will be arriving soon to return them to the train station.

Oji walked Lyra quickly through the garden and invited her into her home. There was a studio arranged in the living room with all kinds of decorative materials piled about.

"To make a proper moccasin, one must have a strong and balanced foundation," Oji started. She sat at a table and demonstrated how she cut the dried deerskin hide into different sizes and then, with a small machine in front of her – she stretched and shaped the deerskin until it was soft and tender and more pliable. Next came the stitching to fashion the shape of a moccasin shoe. For this step, Oji pulled out a long single strand of brown leather lanyard.

"In the old days this lanyard was made from sinew, the intestines of buffalo or deer, but no longer." She attached the strand to a stiff awl-like needle - not much different than her needlepoint, Lyra thought.

"We begin here, at the beginning of course," Oji laughed innocently as she pierced a hole with the needle at the very base of the shoe. "And then, step by step, I weave the lanyard through each puncture, hole to hole. If it isn't precisely done then the shoe will be awkward and imbalanced, out of symmetry, and will not last… If I am careful with my work, and if I craft with a genuine loving mind and heart, then a pair of moccasins will become a worthy gift."

Oji glanced at the various craft supplies in the room.

"These are... how shall I say... window-dressing. The glass beads and bows and colorful cloths and further sewing patterns that make each pair unique for the ladies. Modern touches. But it is the foundation of the moccasin," she pointed to the yet unfinished one in her hand, "that has the most meaning to me in our tradition."

Oji focused again and returned to sewing the moccasin. She was humming a traditional song, Lyra gathered, while she worked. After a few minutes, Lyra asked.

"Where do you stop sewing the lanyard?"

"In one continuous motion I continue around the entire moccasin... until the end."

Oji finished the final sewing loop and held up the foundation of the moccasin for Lyra to inspect. "In my village we have a traditional saying handed down from our foremothers for many generations," Oji continued.

"A pair of moccasins are like two lovers. Sewn from the heart, the moccasins will last a lifetime. Just as two who share love that is right, and pure, will love until the end..."

Oji looked at Lyra who had tears beginning to well in her eyes. "Only we cannot take moccasins with us after we die... But love... Love is eternal. Until the end... and beyond." Oji pressed her hand to her heart.

Lyra's tears began to flow down her cheeks. For her family. For her wish that Bradlee could understand her growing feelings for him.

"You have a troubled heart," Oji squeezed Lyra's hand. "But a troubled heart means that you are one who understands the power of love. It is impossible to love without also feeling pain, just as a flower cannot bloom without rain."

Lyra looked at Oji and smiled despite her tears.

"Thank you for understanding, Oji."

"Lyra, you are in North Dakota. Dakota means *"friend"*

in my native tongue. I can sense which people harbor good souls within them. It is another birth gift from my ancestors. I've been told some of them were shamans, in their time. You and I are united by friendship now, and I hope, forever."

They hugged and exited Oji's home to return through the garden. Lyra lingered a moment when she came to the jasmine trellis and bathed herself in its flowers.

"Might as well enjoy the real thing!" she said to Oji, who joined her happily twirling through the vines. Oji turned to embrace Lyra one more time.

"The handsome man at your table... he has a good soul too. Also hurting inside, like you" Oji said as her index finger gently poked her chest. Then she departed to the kitchen as Lyra viewed the garden for a few last moments.

As Lyra began heading toward the porch, she spotted Bradlee standing with his arm outstretched. She stopped and observed him closely. And then she noticed that there were a series of hummingbird feeders dangling from the far side of the wrap-around portico. Bradlee was holding an orange slice from his plate that he placed in his palm. A ruby-throated hummingbird darted towards Bradlee at that instant and then rested in Bradlee's palm and nuzzled the orange slice. After a few moments to enjoy its breakfast feast, the hummingbird then glanced at Bradlee, darted off, and flew directly at and over Lyra's head as she quickly ducked. Bradlee had turned and watched Lyra's actions and his laughter was like a child's at play. Lyra's mind flashbacked to Costa Rica when she was a child. A hummingbird in her palm. Mami's story and phrase rushed into her memory. *Such coincidences must have a reason – they must!* she had to rationalize. The same scene, only a different place, and time, and person.

James parked the taxi at the curb and entered through the gate. It was shaping up to be a beautiful sun-filled morning and so he paused to admire the glistening flowers in the garden before greeting Lyra. Then he climbed the porch steps and proceeded to embrace Thomas and Nancy with a few gentle bear hugs and warm smiles. They exchanged kind words and some laughter as Thomas and Nancy thanked James for the delicious lime meringue pie from Ruby's.

"Time to hit the road, folks" he turned towards Bradlee and Lyra. "Your choo-choo is fired up and ready to chug!" he yelled out as he did a little dance trying to resemble a rumbling train. He retrieved Lyra's duffel bag and Bradlee's backpack that were both parked beside the path and then proceeded towards the taxi. Bradlee chased after him.

"James, hold up," Bradlee said. "I've decided to stay in Minot for the day instead of heading to Williston. I've changed my car rental reservation. I'll be arriving in Medora tonight anyway, as planned. The distance is pretty much the same from here to Medora by car."

"Oh? And your sweetheart over there?" James glanced towards Lyra.

"Lyra? She's got bigger plans. Great plans, actually, waiting at the end of the tracks. I'm sure she'll be fine on her own." Bradlee took out the fifty-dollar bill from his pocket that the train attendant had given to each of them.

"James, please pass this to Lyra in the taxi. Tell her it's a pass-through gift from me. Ask her to give it to the first street musician she meets in Seattle who plays her a sweet tune. Tell her it will bring her good luck if she does."

"Will do." James deposited the bill in his pocket.

Lyra was standing on the patio, listening to bits of their exchange. That was it. She would go her way and Bradlee his, in just another minute. James gave a hearty shake of his hand to Bradlee and wished him well and hoped to see him again someday. He picked up Lyra's duffel again.

"See you in a jiff, Lyra. Don't linger now 'cause that train isn't going to wait for long." He turned and walked back towards the taxi.

Lyra descended from the porch onto the walkway and approached Bradlee.

"Lyra, I wanted to check out the wood carvings at the church that we passed last night. I might know someone who helped make those carvings. Also thought there might be an interesting story there with an angle that hasn't been covered yet. Maybe it'll also take me to Norway someday soon, if I'm lucky. From the looks of that map I studied in the parlor room this morning, there's plenty of places to explore in Norway. Haven't been yet." Bradlee knew he was rambling. "I don't know. Maybe a publication would be interested in sponsoring..." She looked away.

"About last night, Lyra... I'm sorry again. Maybe someday we'll meet again... There's lots of trains out th — ___"

"Well, blahbity blah blah!" Lyra blurted out in a sarcastic tone as she quickly glanced at him and looked away before regaining her poise.

"It's OK, Bradlee, I understand... See you at the seashore someday..." She tried to smile.

"Goodbye Lyra," Bradlee said softly.

They gave each other a gentle embrace. Enough time, Lyra thought, for Bradlee to inhale her jasmine aroma one last time.

"Bradlee Seashell... sometimes you remind me of a child I once knew..." Then she turned her lips to his ear and whispered... "*Gentle flies hummingbird in hand, health and love forever bestowed, in your home and land.*" Bradlee peered at Lyra curiously as they separated their entangled arms. Lyra found one last smile to offer him followed by a quick and gentle kiss on his cheek and then she turned away.

Part Three

James departed with Lyra to the train station just a few blocks away as Bradlee said his goodbyes to Thomas and Nancy and set on foot with his pack strapped to his back and his camera bag across his shoulder. After spending an early morning hour outside in the garden it felt good to be free to roam outside again in the fresh air. The sun warmed his face and the temperature was just right for a brisk morning walk into town to stretch his legs after a long train passage.

The temperate weather reminded him of the arrival of autumn on Prince Edward Island when the tourists emptied and the island grew quieter – only then could the ocean waves thoroughly cleanse the beach sands of sunscreen and lost toys as the grassy marshes and dunes rested peacefully and were hardened by the fall winds and rains for the coming winter. The fall season was his favorite time on P.E.I. and, despite spending most of the year in school growing up in Toronto in his family home, he grew particularly fond of enjoying outings each fall as a young adult – often visiting the family's vacation home on P.E.I. by himself. The solitude allowed him to enjoy quiet time – time to think and observe nature, to interact with the natural rhythms of each day. He also enjoyed his hobbies during these academic respites – poetry writing in small journal books, sketching and painting on his walks along the beach and through the marsh grasses, observing the variety of migratory birds, and bicycling along the quiet and peaceful lanes and bays and small towns. Occasionally, he would take a sunfish out to the ocean and sail along the coast, tacking into the wind, the salt sprays refreshing him. But it was his wood carving hobby that was most consuming of his time and creative energy.

His father's brother, 'Uncle Eddie' as Bradlee used to call him as a toddler – and the name stuck thereafter – noticed Bradlee's eye for the right kind of fallen wood to select from the forest or a piece of knotted driftwood along the beach. Uncle Eddie was very patient with Bradlee as he tutored him in the art of woodcarving during summer stays with the family. Hours would pass together in the work shed, scraping and shaping, etching and polishing. Bradlee was a novice but Uncle Eddie was a master craftsman and his career allowed him to travel far and wide. Sometimes, he brought back special gifts for the family from his journeys. Always unique curiosities that kept Bradlee's attention.

As Bradlee strolled into Minot, memories came forward and he wished he had remained in touch with his uncle after the events a handful of years ago. *Why didn't he?* he asked himself. Uncle Eddie had nothing to do with what happened. Bradlee felt a wave of shame and he tried to displace it by chatting cordially with strangers outside on their lawns on this beautiful weekend morning.

The family vacation home on P.E.I. was a wonderful escape from the bustling urban life of Toronto where his father, Nathaniel, was a busy physician, chief of trauma surgery at the university hospital, and professor at the medical school. He recalled how his parents would also devote time and finances to sustain the Toronto community through donations for building endowments for their spiritual center and many charities. If there was a need, his parents would find it and provide.

Bradlee thought of some pleasurable moments with his father as a child during those summers on P.E.I. – they would start the day in quiet prayer together on the goat farm, sometimes sail along the bay, or build small wooden model ships together. And on other days there were chores to take care of – fence mending and lawn cutting, house painting and many more. When woodcarving wasn't calling him, Bradlee most looked forward to helping with the goats on the family's ten acre lot. The front lot was a long sprawling flat stretch to the roadside and contained a fenced-in pasture while the backyard was wild with gently sloped marshes that ebbed into the ocean beyond. The few dozen goats in the herd were largely tended year-round by an older couple that lived in the guest suite above the generous garage. But Bradlee had many opportunities to milk the goats in the morning and bathe and brush their coats in the evening. He loved how they would nibble at his clothes and his hair when he was a young child sending him into wild fits of giggles. Those were good times, he knew, and he secured those memories deep in his mind for safe-keeping.

The goat milk was sold to a local cheese factory that packaged and labeled the brand under the name for his family summer home; the home and business each adorned the signpost at the entrance to the farm:

~~~ *The Marshpillow Home* ~~~
Marshpillow Organic Goat Cheese, Inc.

The business was the small family enterprise run out of the farm by his parents. It grew over many years as did the substantial profits from the sale of the prized cheese on the island. Some of these funds were invested into a trust account for Bradlee's use in adulthood.

By the time Bradlee had finished high school the older couple tending the goats had retired and the family was spending less time there anyway – so the goats were donated to other area farms as the business could no longer be sustained. In college now, Bradlee converted the guest room above the garage into his own apartment for use anytime he wished to return throughout the year. More recently, other than his periodic travels to support his struggling photojournalism career, Bradlee spent most of his time back on P.E.I. and he didn't mind. He lived simply above the garage, almost never entering the main house, and he provided what he needed for himself. But he did need to periodically tap into some of his funds set aside from the goat cheese business ever since he returned from his bicycle trip cross-country and made some important decisions.

His mother, Jenny, would periodically call but she rarely visited him while he was at the Marshpillow over the past number of years. She used to manage a small personalized chocolate shop for many years that was open only during the peak summer season on P.E.I. His mother was a creative type who also loved the ocean, and so she had a local factory create custom molds to her design specifications for her melted chocolate concoctions – milk and dark chocolate, and her specialty, her best-seller – the one the tourists waited in lines that extended down the street for gift boxes – her *'goat's milk chocolate seashells.'* They were the same ones that Bradlee had shipped to Ruby when he returned from his cycling trip.

Alone at the Marshpillow for various periods of adolescence and young adulthood allowed Bradlee time to think or heal or attend to his creative impulses and projects. He knew he needed these sabbaticals from his academic studies to reinvigorate his spirit. His father was often traveling for work, giving guest lectures at hospitals and medical conferences. His career, by nearly all measures, a grand success judging by his time commitments as a sought-after consulting surgeon, research grant writer, composer of many textbook chapters on advances in surgical techniques, and his teaching responsibilities at the medical school and university hospital. Bradlee paused in thought – it had been over five years already since he and his father had last spoken. By now, the fallout with his father had settled enough in his mind that he didn't dwell on it. It was done and he couldn't imagine any scenario to repair the wounds other than to continue to let the scars form and harden. He was young and had his whole adult life ahead of him. He needed to make his own way. There would be no long shadow cast from his father ever again. And as for his dear mother, she was conflicted between her love for two men – her husband and her son. Diplomatic in her intentions to maintain cordiality, the rift had taken its toll on her psyche and so she had largely withdrawn from Bradlee to maintain her own sanity. He spoke to his mother on occasion, usually for ritual holidays or his birthday, but Bradlee felt that his relationship with her remained increasingly fragile.

On many early mornings, Bradlee would hop on his bicycle, pedal around the bend in the road from the farm and then turn left onto Lighthouse Road. It was a straight jaunt to the East Point Lighthouse. He felt like it was the end of the world as he would face into a grand sunrise or challenge the wind or rain or snow flurries in his face and peer out over the ocean. On pristine clear days he could even make out the rocky outcropping of Cape Breton Highlands. The land was like a jagged impenetrable fortress in daring defense of the ocean's incessant assaults against the shore. The northeastern tip of Nova Scotia. He had conquered a cycling trip around the Cape in the summer before his cross country journey. It was his prerequisite and it held many fond memories shared with Ezra, his best friend from early childhood. In circumnavigating the Cape he felt anything was possible. He would continue across North America, he dreamed then, then perhaps onward through Europe and over the Alps and the Balkans, and then across the vastness of Asia from Turkey to the Caspian Sea, across Kazakhstan to the Altai Mountains, push forward through Mongolia and dip into China until he would run out of land at the Yellow Sea. He dreamed of circling the globe on two wheels and knew that he could. He knew that his body was fit and strong and blessed with the kind of tough-mindedness that could see any journey through. A confidence in adventure for adventure's sake. Yes, the dream of adventure and conquest was an old story; he had read plenty of Caruso, Shackleton and Parry, Meriwether Lewis, Langdon Warner, and the gifted Piccard family, among many other sagas of adventure and sacrifice. But this was his story, his life, and he was smart enough to know that at his gut level, the journey was what truly mattered; it was the journey that contained the stories that arose from the pumping of the heart, the daily newness of people and places, the thrill of overcoming any obstacle – these were all far greater than the excitement of the finish.

    He looked at the Cape as his transitioning, his becoming into manhood. Independence. Ability to survive within the elements. The travel magazines all raved about the Cape as a Top-10 location in the world for cycling adventures, and it was in his backyard to enjoy! Steep climbs and hair-raising descents as the Cabot Trail winds and hugs the massive rocky coastline from Cheticamp, then turns inland to a higher plateau where moose roam freely. Then descending again to Ingonish Beach before climbing Cape Smokey to a majestic apex overlook – where ocean meets a wall of granite and switchback hairpin serpentine turns await – a cyclist's dream that also requires skill and fearlessness. But he did it all and the memories rushed like waves across his mind when he chose to welcome them.

    He wondered if Lyra cycled at all. Perhaps spin classes at the gym with those toned legs of hers. *Lyra*... why was she popping into his mind so frequently this morning? He thought about last night. *Why did I turn away from her? Why can't I enjoy what I used to enjoy? Will I ever again?* She was perceptive, curious, smart, witty, sensitive, and just incredibly beautiful to him. She wasn't pushy to know his past when he couldn't have the courage to tell her everything. *Why? Why can't I stop thinking of Lyra now?* These feelings had not brewed inside of him since Sami. *Has enough time passed to heal? Maybe*, he wondered.

JAMES EXITED THE DRIVER'S SEAT and pulled Lyra's duffel from the taxi trunk. They had an abbreviated but cordial conversation on the way to the station. James handed Lyra the fifty-dollar bill from Bradlee and let her know about his suggestion. James was surprised to hear that Lyra and Bradlee had not eaten Ruby's pies last night for dessert. *Darn shame*, he felt. *Maybe they wouldn't be going their separate ways this morning if they had?* Lyra wasn't in much of a chatty mood. *That*, he could sure tell. In the ride over to the station he periodically glanced at her through the rear view mirror. She would reach for a tissue from her purse, blotting occasional tears that spotted her cheeks as she stared out the window, mostly in silence.

He gave her a gentle hug and held her for an extra moment wrapped in his long arms that enveloped her like an octopus. He thought she needed that.

"Thanks James," Lyra said. "You've been very kind."

"My pleasure Lyra. I enjoyed meeting you both last night. Sure hope you lovebirds fix up these patches between you. I don't know the whole story, that's for sure, but I'd say you two won't be able to keep your distance for very long. I'm a grown man who's already lived his love story. Still am with my Sweet Caroline... until the end, you know. Until the end."

Until the end? Did James just say that too?! She turned her eyes quickly and stared at him.

"I hope so, James. I know this may sound crazy but I...... I think I'm in love with him." Lyra turned away as she felt a rush of tears welling. James studied her face for a moment and brushed a tuft of hair from her cheek. He wrapped her up in his arms once again with a long gentle squeeze.

"Not crazy, Lyra. Just the way love is. And that feeling won't ever end when it's shared right... This Bradlee fellow – he'll come around again. Have some faith in the stars."

She started to tear again. "Take care, James."

She lifted her duffel and headed to the station platform. The place was bustling with activity as passengers were embarking and food and drink carts were stacked waiting for their items to be delivered to the bar car. Harry, the conductor, was welcoming passengers on board into one of the front cars. He had on his purple top hat and a black shiny waistcoat. Lyra's mood changed when she saw him. Harry was the epitome of a jolly old man, she thought. All smiles and kindness. He was just about exactly as she had imagined he would look like now seeing him for the first time on the platform. *Was he the wizard from the Wizard of Oz? Gosh, the resemblance was uncanny*, she chuckled to herself as she approached the train.

"Well, good mornin' my sweet lady," Harry opened. "And a fine mornin' it is here in Minot to board a train bound for... and where is it you're goin', ma'am...? He waited for Lyra's response.

"I'm going......." she held the thought for a few seconds and the delay caused Harry's eyebrows to lift in surprise, "until the end," Lyra responded and chuckled.

Harry looked closely at her and noticed a faint residue of tears in her swollen eyelids. "My dear, *'until the end'* is the finest place to be goin', now isn't it? Whether on a train or in life. May I wish you a most pleasant journey... and what's this pretty lady's name, may I ask?"

"Sash —— " she caught herself. "It's Lyra Flurey, sir. Pleasure to meet you, Harry. And thank you for giving me many smiles." He winked at Lyra.

Lyra boarded and found a comfortable seat by the window once again. *Definitely a wizard*, Lyra thought, she just knew it. Her mood was quickly uplifting. A quick fantasy came and went as she stared out the window to the platform bustle. *Would Bradlee come running as the train started to pull away?* Her emotions swayed like a dingy in a storm. *Only in the movies*, she realized sadly.

The train departed on time, just as Harry had promised last night. She noticed the train's pace quickening as it headed westward across the countryside. After Williston, the train soon crossed into eastern Montana. It would be another long day of travel but she was looking forward now to some new scenery, departing farmland for the glacier peaks. The sun was streaking through the window. She lowered the shade and napped for awhile until hunger pains awoke her.

Lyra strolled to the bar car and took a seat at one of the swivel chairs. Susie was working. She poured Lyra a cup of coffee as Lyra ordered from the menu. They chatted briefly, mostly small talk about Lyra's upcoming plans, her master's degree, and Susie's life working as a barmaid on a cross country Amtrak train... Lyra let in that she had met a man on the train yesterday.

"Yeah, I remember him," Susie said. "He was here with you when you ordered your drinks yesterday evening. Straight ginger-ale-on-the-rocks kind of guy. Handsome, I might add. I kind of could tell he liked you. Kept his eyes on *you* the whole time." Susie gave Lyra one of those knowing looks and a smirk. Lyra blushed and then briefly looked away in thought.

"Well, he's off somewhere exploring now... It's OK. You mentioned the word *time*, Susie. I've realized already that timing is so often critical in life... Just not the right time for a relationship, I guess," Lyra responded but not quite thoroughly believing her words.

"Look Lyra. You found a nice guy. And he found you. Perfect coincidence. Talk about timing! What about coincidences, you know?! I believe more in *them* than I do what time of day it is. Heck, most of the time working on this tin can I can't even tell what time it is! But I've had plenty of coincidences. Old passengers turning up after years not seeing them – we just happen to meet on the same train going the same direction while I'm working just the right shift in this bar car. Or, just missing a storm blowing through or getting stuck on the tracks somewhere due to a mechanical and then other things come about from these events, some of them extraordinary. And Harry and I have wondered plenty ourselves about coincidences. Anyway, coincidences are real and I believe in them."

"Take these fortune cookies right here," Susie pointed to the collection piled high in a large cardboard box marked with a row of Chinese characters. The box was sitting off to the side on the bar ledge. "Harry picked up a new shipment of these in Minot since we had time to restock overnight. Something fun that I like tossing to customers during Happy Hour."

"Now a fortune cookie is an interesting thing. For some people, they open the cookie and read their fortune and it's about as bland and innutritious as spam on white bread. But every once in awhile, there's a customer who I just know that fortune cookie hit the right spot. How do I know? Because if you look closely at that person's face and study their body language you can tell. They won't leave that message on the table when they finish up here in the bar car. No, they hold it or pocket it or keep on re-reading it and then stare out the window in some kind of daydream…" Susie stared out the window with a straight face in mimicry and Lyra laughed. "Not sure if they're having a good memory or a fantasy." Lyra laughed again as Susie kept a serious face.

"Suit yourself if you don't believe me. But I think, in

that moment, that either the fortune cookie found the right person or the person found the right fortune. Don't really matter. But the coincidence happened. And it was real…"

Susie turned and walked over to the overflowing box. She dug her hand in and pulled out one of the clear plastic wrapped fortune cookies.

"Here, I'd like to give you one now. Hold out your palm for me." Lyra reached out and Susie gently grasped her hand for a moment before depositing the fortune into her palm. She stared into Lyra's doleful eyes. "Maybe it'll bring some good luck your way?"

"Thanks Susie, and thanks for the words of train wisdom."

Lyra returned to her seat. She pulled out the book she hadn't finished yet. The love story she had been nursing since the train departed from New York. Only a few chapters *until the end*, she realized. Then she stopped in sudden recognition and said softly to herself – "Until the end… There's that phrase again." She smiled but wasn't sure why. It was humorous, the coincidences that all occurred in less than twenty-four hours. *Maybe Susie was right.* The scenes flashed before her. *We boarded the same train heading west. Bradlee's opening words to her about her paperback, ginger ale, the Hummingbird Room, Oji's comments, a hummingbird landing on Bradlee's palm…* But sitting here now, book opened to the bookmarked page, she paused and stared out the window. *What does it all mean? Did any of that really happen to me? Maybe it was just all a lucid dream?*

She returned to the book and finished reading the final chapters. The lovers had overcome what they needed to. Problems resolved. The ending was truly the beginning as the lovers were set to live happily ever after. She wondered if they could remain that way forever… until the end. She smiled. It was a pleasant story. She enjoyed reading these kinds of stories. It consoled a deeper sadness that resided within her. Gave her hope that life truly does have meaning – that it must go on despite misfortune. At least these kinds of stories almost always have a good ending. *Fiction, she thought – why can't reality be at all the same, ever?!*

Misfortune... the word reminded her of the fortune cookie tucked in her breast pocket. She pulled it out and unwrapped it from its plastic sheath, then cracked open the cookie and enjoyed a piece of the sweet sugary treat. A flashback to summer, again. Eating a sugar cone laden with mint-chocolate chip ice cream along a boardwalk with Ansley. Bikinis and flip-flops on. They were so young, too young to care about boys yet, with sunburned cheeks and noses and shoulders and sun-bleached flowing hair. Seagulls squawking as she tossed small pieces of sugar cone to them and admired how they could catch them in mid-air. "Sky acrobats!" Lyra shouted out. Happiness and laughter with Ansley. And with her little brother, Jared, and her parents. Everyone enjoying their own cones beside them on a boardwalk bench. They were sharing licks and having great fun at that moment.......... The image faded.

Lyra spread the fortune cookie message and read it to herself:

Nothing is Impossible to a Willing Heart.

She read it again and then stared out the window, wondering.

BRADLEE TURNED DOWN BROADWAY and entered the Scandinavian Heritage Park at the Danish windmill adjacent to the flag poles. It was a gorgeous day. Just as James had said, the flowers along the path and through the gardens were in full bloom. He passed a few statues commemorating some native sons – skiers of some renown from North Dakota's past. Then past a bronze statue of Hans Christian Andersen. Old Hans was holding a book in his right hand, his page marked by his long index finger; his left arm was outstretched and he was admiring a duckling in his palm – *'The Ugly Duckling' – it must be the image from his classic tale*, Bradlee recalled, as he stared peacefully and kindly at this little creation in Hans' hand and thought – *just like my friendly hummingbird this morning!* Bradlee flashbacked to breakfast on the inn porch. Then, Lyra ducking as the hummingbird darted straight for her. Ducks, hummingbirds, outstretched palms – coincidences... strange he thought. He paused to think about old Hans. Bradlee loved when his mother would read Hans' stories to him as a young child cuddled in bed together. Some years later he recalled learning that Hans was also a novelist and poet and even wrote adventurous travel articles. Bradlee wished he could have met Hans had he lived in the past, sure in his thoughts that they had much in common to share.

He continued down the path and past an enormous Swedish horse replica ribboned with painted flowers for its saddle and harness. It was pointing the way along the path as Bradlee continued and then climbed the steps to the church plaza. There was a sign erected at the entrance: "Sunday Service to Commemorate Our 25th Anniversary." He would miss it. The date was scheduled for tomorrow. But today, Saturday, the church plaza was empty of other visitors. From the outside, Bradlee could tell that the church was crafted entirely of wood. He approached the front portal and placed his hand on the wood carvings, studying their curled intricacies – a web of interlaced carvings from the base to the very top. He felt the grains of wood beneath his fingertips and he smiled.

It must be him. I know the work of his hands.

Bradlee entered through the portal and stopped along the

nave to take in the breadth of the humble and simple beauty before him. He felt the massive stave posts and looked skyward to the craftsmanship that extended to the wood support beams. The church was empty except for two older men chatting to the side of the altar, studying a bench that was placed just below a carved diorama of Da Vinci's painting, *'The Last Supper.'* One man was quite expressive with his hands as the two chatted. Bradlee noted he was wearing a beige colored suit and a peach colored shirt with mother of pearl cufflinks. The cufflinks were inscribed with the Staff of Aesculapius, an ancient Greek symbol of a serpent entwined around a wooden staff. Bradlee knew the symbol was usually adorned by a physician as it represented the staff of the mythical Greek god of healing and medicine. The other gentleman had his torso and face angled away from where Bradlee stood. He had a long flowing speckled gray and black beard and was dressed conservatively in a black suit and white shirt. On his head was a simple black skullcap. The man with the beard was listening intently, eyes focused, as he pulled and shaped his beard with his right hand. His hands appeared larger than expected for his average stature and Bradlee noted that his fingers were long and muscular and his finger pads callused. The evidence of a hand craftsman, Bradlee surmised.

Bradlee approached the two men. He overheard them discussing some details of the bench carving and enjoying the moment together. They turned towards Bradlee. At once, Bradlee knew.

"Uncle Eddie!" Bradlee said. "It's you! It's good to see you… But how is this possible?!"

The bearded man gave a wide smile.

"Baruch Avraham, why this is quite a surprise?! Here in Minot, North Dakota of all places! God works in mysterious ways…" Bradlee's uncle referred to him by his Hebrew name. Bradlee stood in shock – here in front of him, just at this moment, stood his uncle, the woodcarver. Bradlee approached and he gave his uncle a warm embrace.

"Tell me, Uncle Eddie – is this all of your work?!" Bradlee rotated around and looked up to the ceiling in admiration and smiled.

"Uncle Eddie?" the other man inquired. Bradlee's uncle chuckled with a warm smile as he reached to hug Bradlee's shoulders once again.

"Funny story, Ben... I'll tell you the short version. When Baruch here was still in diapers he had trouble pronouncing his L's. They sounded like D's. So, when I came to visit Baruch and his family from time to time on the Jewish holidays or at their summer home, Bradlee had trouble saying my name. Actually my shorthand name – '*Eli*,' as you refer to me as well on occasion, Ben, instead of my full name – Eliezer. When Bradlee would say my name it sounded like 'Edi' and so, for his family, it evolved into simply '*Uncle Eddie.*' It stuck and I was branded with it as a family nickname."

"Well, Rabbi Eliezer Levitsky, in all these years knowing each other, you never told me *that* one before!" the other man said and then the two friends enjoyed a round of laughter.

"Please, let me introduce you," the rabbi said. "Baruch, this is Doctor Benjamin Cohen beside me. He is a physician here in Minot. Ben, this is my favorite— Well... also my *only* dear nephew... my brother's only child."

The rabbi turned to his nephew. "Ben and I have known each other since we were five years old in kindergarten together."

"Pleasure to meet you, Dr. Cohen. "The name's Bradlee..." Bradlee paused before continuing. "Bradlee Levitsky." He shook Ben's hand. Bradlee noted the doctor's grip was firm and confident.

"Bradlee – your common name, I see," Ben started in. "Your uncle and I were best pals as kids. Stayed that way all these years despite the distance." Ben eyed the rabbi with affection.

"After my medical school training and residency back east in family medicine I moved out west and accepted a position with the IHS here in North Dakota – that's the Indian Health Service. I know it sounds odd but I was fascinated as a child by anything Indian... Native American, as we say today more respectfully. As I was growing up I always wanted to work as a doctor on an Indian Reservation – and so I did."

Rabbi Levitsky explained further. "During his IHS service, Ben had fallen in love with the Dakotas and so he was recruited to stay here in Minot where he has been a pillar of the medical community for many years. He's the founder of the small Jewish community here as well. Baruch – there are Jews just about *everywhere*, as I'm sure you know by now. Yes, we all have differing religious affiliations and beliefs and practices. But still – *a Jew is a Jew*. Even a child with one sixteenth Jewish blood can be considered." The Rabbi looked at Bradlee and winked with a smile.

"You know how much I like lox, Rabbi?! Ben said with a raise of his bushy eyebrows. "Well, when I moved to Minot from the reservation I couldn't believe I would find lox here in North Dakota. But there it was in the grocery stores sitting right next to the cream cheese. Turns out that my Norwegian friends discovered they liked lox probably long before us." Ben gave a hearty belly laugh. "Now I'd call up Eli here from time to time to ask for a shipment of bagels from Toronto since – darned if I could find a good bagel in town..." More laughter. "But over time, my Scandinavian neighbors and patients just about adopted me as one of their own over Sunday meals together with bagels and lox." The three men shared a knowing round of laughter. Morning prayers followed by bagels and lox and a shmear of cream cheese. Customs. Traditions.

"Your uncle is a wonderful man and an exceptional craftsman," Ben announced proudly. "When I was asked to head the committee to erect this church in honor of the many Scandinavians who settled here – many of them patients in my practice for the past thirty years here – I could not refuse the honor and the obligation... This site is both religious and communal. Yes, this is a church – a replica of a real old one in Norway, and it is well used by the community for services. I've been to plenty of fine weddings inside here over the years. Many of those couples were patients of mine. Many still are. A few I even introduced to each other at my office across the hallway's exam rooms," Ben laughed. "But this building also hosts wonderful music concerts and poetry readings and such that Hannah – that's my wife – and I have enjoyed together these many years."

Bradlee's uncle turned and warmly embraced him again. "It's been a long time, Baruch" he said.

"I know, Uncle Eddie, and I'm very sorry about that. I shouldn't have lost our connection over the past number of years." Bradlee felt his eyes well with tears. He did all he could to hold back his emotions.

"It's OK, Baruch, time moves on. You and I understand each other..." the rabbi responded softly and tussled Bradlee's hair in childish jest.

There were plenty of intriguing questions that needed answering. Bradlee explained how he accidentally ended up in Minot overnight. That he was passing through and heading to Medora later in the day. And the pen inscribed at the Lady Slipper Inn. How he had recognized his uncle's name and wondered if he was the one who actually worked on the church carvings when the building was being constructed – and so he decided to have a look for himself in town. But never did Bradlee imagine he would meet his uncle today at this place.

"And why are *you* here today, Uncle Eddie?" Bradlee inquired.

"Ben has been helping with preparations for the site's twenty-fifth anniversary celebrations tomorrow. Actually, he is being honored for all of his efforts raising funds for the community. The community can sense that Ben isn't too far away from retirement. He's an adopted son in these parts, as Ben mentioned earlier. This center has been quite the mitzvah project!" the rabbi chuckled. "And Ben extended a kind invitation to me as head of the rededication committee. Unfortunately, it has been more than a few years since he and I have seen each other so I decided to fly out here a few days ago and stay over for the Sabbath weekend... The grounds look magnificent, I might add. Ben and his committee have done a wonderful job with the preparations... Oh... and Baruch, in case you were wondering since I am a rabbi... Yes, I know, this is a church, but it is also a center for Scandinavian culture and heritage and Ben has told me how wonderful these people are here in Minot and throughout this region. God didn't make them Jewish, but he should have!" the rabbi laughed again. "Their values are our values, just the same. '*Do unto others as you have others do unto you.*' Yes? The Golden Rule. It is the foundation of humanity's peaceful coexistence, God willing."

"Look, over there Baruch." The rabbi pointed to the words carved into the horizontal wood beams above them along the nave. Bradlee turned and looked with astonishment. On one side was written the Golden Rule passage from the Old Testament. Leviticus 19:18. It was in Hebrew in a beautiful calligraphy pattern. On the other side was etched the translation into English in matching calligraphy.

"You see, Baruch, we are one people in any sanctuary where God resides. Placing these passages here was my idea and Ben encouraged the committee to accept it as a token of appreciation to the Jewish community that helped support this endeavor. And never... *never* has anyone who stepped foot in this building departed without a greater sense of kinship. Of spirituality."

Bradlee's eyes were tearing. It had been a long time since he had set foot in any kind of house of worship. The thought of doing so remained too painful for him these many years. But listening to his uncle, hearing his message – it was healing. Uncle Eddie was right. And Bradlee realized that his uncle had grown with the years himself – into an even wiser and patient man.

"Baruch, you know I am a religious Jew but also a liberal one. I have one foot firmly planted in the times we live in. And I know a religious life is not for everyone. But I have learned in my travels to truly appreciate the wonders of different peoples and cultures and their traditions. We are all in God's hands, Baruch. Every one of us. Yes, it is true, I chose not to work on the wood carvings that adorn the altar or the wooden crosses in the interior of this church. That is not my place as a Jew beholden to his faith. But when Ben invited me here twenty five years ago to help make something wonderful for the people here, I couldn't refuse my best friend. I worked on the entrances and the portals – the ones with the intricately woven lattices. There were a few other wonderful craftsmen who helped me and they worked on all the rest that you see inside here. We had wonderful moments collaborating as artists who happened to also be of different faiths. But we shared the same values. And our *hands*... the same gifts from our single Creator." The rabbi turned to admire the work throughout the church. "But the portals and these etched passages – they were done with *these* tired hands," he added proudly to his nephew.

The rabbi paused and closed his eyes. "Let us turn towards Jerusalem, as is our tradition." He turned to face east. Ben and Bradlee followed his lead. The rabbi held a long moment of silence before speaking.

"I pray with all my loving heart, all my soul, all my might: Someday, God willing, all of God's children will be able to pray under one roof together in peace… and let us say… Amen." Ben and Bradlee replied with a heartfelt "Amen."

The three men chatted further and shared more stories with Bradlee from the years that had past. Bradlee enjoyed their conversation but realized it was time he continued onward.

"Gentlemen, I sure wish I could stay overnight for the ceremony tomorrow but I need to be in Medora for business in the morning. But I do want to take a closer look at this craftsmanship, maybe shoot some photos…"

Bradlee turned to address his uncle directly. "I've been working on my photojournalism career for the past number of years, Uncle Eddie. Don't think you knew that. It's been a struggle to make a living but it is enjoyable. I haven't gotten back much to wood carving since school ended. I took up photography instead but I do miss our time together. Those were great memories I have of you and me carving wood in the storage shed on P.E.I. until late at night. I want to thank you for your teaching and your love back then. Those are memories I'll never forget from my childhood." Bradlee quickly pulled out his professional digital camera from his bag and displayed it to his uncle and Ben as evidence of his current work.

The rabbi turned to Ben. "The Levitsky family has been making a long line of doctors and rabbis since even prior to departing from the Polish-Russian border and settling in America and Canada. Baruch here was quite the medical student a handful of years ago. *Top in his class*, if I may add. But some personal problems arose and…"

Ben butted in. "I understand. These things happen. I had my doubts as well during my medical studies. Medical school can be stressful. I don't think it's my place to know all the details. But I can tell you this, Bradlee. I trust my old friend here. He may be your uncle but he's been my best friend just about my entire life. That kind of bond means more than you can understand at your young age. But you are still very young, Bradlee. And if your uncle tells me you've changed your mind one day and want to finish up your medical studies, then I will promise you, Bradlee, that I'll do what I can to make it happen."

"Thank you, Dr. Cohen... Very kind of you," Bradlee replied.

"Baruch," his uncle added. "Keep in touch, will you? I've missed hearing from you as well. You are like a son to me, always have been."

The rabbi took Bradlee aside a handful of steps away from Ben. "Baruch, your father asks about you from time to time. He had hoped that you might contact me at some point. May I tell him that I have seen you and you are well?"

"That will be fine. I'm not sure if we'll ever be able to patch things up. Don't see how," Bradlee responded and looked away. "I'll keep in touch now, Uncle Eddie. I promise you. I love you like a father."

"Your father still loves you, Baruch. You two must find a way," his uncle replied with the look only an uncle can give to a nephew he dearly loved.

A long hug ensued followed by affectionate pats on the back. Rabbi Levitsky and Ben departed from the sanctuary and strolled through the gardens. Bradlee could sense their bond of friendship as he observed them from a distance. He lingered with his camera in hand and took some close-ups of the wood carvings, and particularly, his uncle's works. Then he departed the center and walked towards the car rental agency.

THE TRAIN PASSED THROUGH SHELBY and arrived at East Glacier in the mid-afternoon. The long hardscrabble farmland was giving way to a rise in the continent's elevation. The tracks had reached the transition zone – from the great North American prairie to the soaring Rockies. The transition was quick and stunning from the train window. Lyra grew increasingly excited to see the snow capped mountains off in the distance. The train hugged a ridge, a nail biting drop-off, as it chugged along and through the heart of Glacier National Park. Lyra ran to the portal between the adjacent cars. She opened the door and inhaled. *Cool fresh air!* The smell of Douglas fir cones and cedar and spruce permeated the train car. She basked in it and then returned to her seat. The other passengers thanked her for the welcome refresher. She had made a few new friends along the way. Enough to stave off the loneliness and solitude. But barely enough to minimize her racing thoughts of Bradlee and their time together at the inn. That intense moment in time now receding quickly as the grinding of the wheels shrieked across the mountain pass. By the early morning tomorrow, the train would be pulling in to Seattle.

As the train departed from Whitefish station, Lyra extended herself across the seats and comforted with her travel pillow and light blanket. The evening passed into darkness. From her duffel bag she retrieved her course manual and orientation packet for graduate school and began focusing on what laid ahead. It would be a long nine months of intense study to earn her master's degree. Master's *degrees*, plural, she corrected herself – '*doing the double-dip,*' as she would say to her sorority sisters - *Environmental Sciences and Landscape Architecture* – it would be. A package deal, she convinced herself. She added the landscape degree because she couldn't help not to. She loved imagining the idea of designing garden spaces from nothing. A blank slab of earth that needed some loving. Seeing Oji's beautiful garden at the inn only enhanced her interest now in honing her skills. Lyra knew most names of plants and could easily identify them through her own self study during her college years. Her duffel was stuffed with plant identification manuals and thick hardcover architectural design books by various masters. Heavy books. *'Bricks'*... she laughed. Bradlee called them bricks. She smiled out the window, briefly recalling his surly look at her when he lifted her bag off the train in Minot. But the landscape degree would lend credibility if she wanted to be hired for those kinds of jobs. A fallback, perhaps. She liked the fact that she had the time now to learn and to experiment and explore her interests in greater detail. And if not? If her life took her elsewhere with her environmental studies, then she figured landscape architecture could always remain a hobby. Besides, the additional master's degree was only a minimal additional cost for her tuition.

But the environmental sciences program... She had specifically targeted the graduate program in Seattle to study with one of the university's esteemed faculty members, Dr. Carol Bonheim. In her research as a tenured professor, Dr. Bonheim specialized in air and water quality indicators across various ecosystems. The impact of humans on the environment and vice versa. Despite the professor's global travels to share her cutting edge research, her lectures, and appointments to government oversight committees, Lyra's persistence enabled her to strike up correspondence with Dr. Bonheim via email – enough to allow Lyra's acceptance into the program and a guarantee that she could work in Dr. Bonheim's lab. Perhaps even a chance to join her in field research should the opportunity and funding arise. Lyra's father was a high school science teacher in her home town. She had fond memories, awkward as they were, from her time as a student in his 9th grade Biology class. Some teasing from the other students as well, being 'daddy's little girl.' But that's in the past and she thought back to those times at home in the evenings when her father would share far greater insights into biology and the natural world around the dinner table than the other students could have ever received. Her father realized he had a budding scientist on his hands and gave Lyra the gift of time together. Lyra's mother was an artist – spending hours painting and experimenting in her own ways with various media. An award winning artist in local circles. Her works hung in galleries and were strewn throughout their family home. Lyra loved her mother's work. Colorful, usually abstract, but all meaningful in one interpretation or another. Her mother was a kind soul. She baked and prepared the family dinners most nights and arranged Lyra's and her brother Jared's lunches each morning before school, often with an added hand-crafted napkin stuck inside the lunchbox – one of mom's decorative colorful pen doodles that Lyra would always admire – and the words in her mom's cursive style: *I Love You Lyra... Mom* – drawn with an added heart shape. Lyra wished she had her mom's artistic flair for drawing and painting but in time she realized she had inherited more of her dad's scientific and analytical bent.

Lyra pulled out a small framed watercolor from her purse. It was one of her mom's paintings of Lyra and Jared when they were quite young, sitting beside each other on a set of playground swings. The frame always traveled with Lyra wherever home would take her – from her college dorm room to weeklong vacations at Ansley's home, and now to Seattle. She wished she and Jared kept in touch more often over the past few years other than sporadic moments. But he had settled a long way from Connecticut. She understood his reasons. Like Lyra, Jared eventually followed his own dream. And his dream was to be around horses, to be a cowboy, she figured – and so after high school he skipped college and applied for a job, and a lifestyle, he knew nothing about and ended up on a ranch in Kansas. The last few years of high school were a very difficult time for her little brother and the changes in location and lifestyle were sorely needed. She was happy for him and Lyra knew he was generally happier now as well.

The train motored onward into the night. The cabin side lights automatically dimmed at ten o'clock. Lyra adjusted her head against her travel pillow and shut her overhead reading light. Time for some needed rest on the home stretch into Seattle. She closed her eyes and could only think of one thing that might help her to sleep. After all, repeating the words were as soothing as any mantra – like counting sheep. "Sasha shells seashells at the sheshore." She giggled and tried again, over and over, until perfected just like yesterday, as sleep finally arrived. The name Sasha almost sounded foreign to her now. A person from her past, perhaps. It was receding quickly from her mind.

THE CABIN LIGHTS FLICKERED ON at six-thirty the next morning. Lyra had indeed slept well. She was more exhausted than she had realized. She freshened up in the bathroom at the end of the train car and packed up her overnight items when the intercom started to crackle.

"*Goooooood... Mornin'!*" Lyra recognized the voice immediately and smiled. It was Harry rousing the troops. "I hope y'all slept like baby gators in a swamp 'cause we're just a few minutes from givin' this ol' locomotive a welcome rest in *See*-attle. *Yee Ha*!!!" Harry exclaimed wildly. "This ol' mare has chugged a long way, folks. And like y'ur own special hunny, I've learned to treat'er right all these years! She'll go in for some cleanin' and polishin' and gear greasin' and, not before too long, she'll be rearin' her hind legs to head on east again!" Harry was on his game again and the passengers were loving it. Already, laughter was making its way down the train car as passengers stretched their arms skyward.

"And in case y'all were wonderin', I've already had my two cups of mornin' joe. Suggest you consider the same... Susie will be making the rounds down the aisle handin' out some of that fresh brewed dark liquor in case y'all are int'rested." Harry broke out in laughter. "Start prep 'in folks. Pack those bags and don't forget any belongin's. We've got a museum of lost treasures at home – don't want to add any more junk to it. Bye, y'all... Oh – and I'll be welcoming y'all on the platform once again. Now be nice and give ol' Harry a hug g'bye?!" He signed off. Lyra knew she would miss Harry's comforting Southern twang.

The train pulled into Seattle's Kings Street Station. Lyra hailed a taxi. The driver proceeded along Interstate-5 and then turned to cross the Montlake Bridge, past the Husky football stadium, and into the tree-bordered section of Montlake Boulevard as the road cut through the University of Washington's sprawling campus buildings and athletic fields. There was the outdoor track on the right side. Memories of Lyra's cross country and track-and-field days back in high school flooded her mind. She was a state champion in cross country and top-10 finisher in the mile as an elite Varsity runner. Good memories. All the while, working hard and pulling top grades in her classes. She took pride in her work effort and she knew her parents were very proud of her accomplishments. That was some time ago but going for runs and hiking into the mountains remained steady consistent pleasures since she had moved on to college. "Idea factories," as she called these times taking a good long run or hiking a mountain. Running and hiking were the ways she enjoyed clearing her mind of distractions and allowing a relaxed creativity to swell to the surface.

The taxi veered onto NE 45th Street, then turned right onto 41st Street followed by a quick right onto 36th Avenue and pulled up at a well-manicured home at the corner. It overlooked the entrance to the 'Botanic Gardens and Center for Urban Horticulture' just across the street. It was an experimental research center that belonged to the University. Lyra exited and took in the scenery. She felt fortunate. The house was prettier than the photographs that came in the envelope with the keys. It was a lovely setting and would allow her many hours to enjoy meandering though the backyard plantings in support of her gardening passion. She quickly thought of Oji and wondered if she had ever been to Seattle. She made a note to try to reach her someday and invite her for a visit. The house was built for a family and she would have it all to herself. A bit daunting but quite an upgrade from her simple shared apartment in college. She was very fortunate. The home belonged to one of Dr. Bonheim's colleagues, a professor of geology at the university, who would be departing for a research sabbatical in Patagonia, South America. While responsibly tending to the upkeep of the home for the academic year, Lyra would pay no rent other than her utility bills.

Lyra spent the rest of the morning getting situated. She borrowed a bicycle, which contained a rear-loaded basket, from the shed and stocked up at the local market. On return, the lovely sunny afternoon could not resist a good run. She changed into her sports bra and shorts, laced up her new pair of running shoes, and then studied a map of the area on her cell phone to create a jogging route. As Lyra was removing the house keys from her large purse she noted Ruby's pie, still wrapped and smelling of raspberries and peaches inside. She picked up the pie and smiled as images came forward of Minot and meeting Ruby at her restaurant. James' comforting words. Bradlee hugging Ruby. *Why did Ruby and Bradlee share a deeper sort of bond?* She wondered now. Lyra set the raspberry-peach pie onto the kitchen counter. It would be a very welcome snack after a good lookabout run. She exited and locked the front door, hid the house keys inside the flower pot, inhaled and exhaled deeply a handful of times, and bound down the street towards the Union Bay wetlands loop trail.

BRADLEE DEPARTED FROM MINOT taking the more scenic route, retracing his bicycle route from some years ago. He passed Lake Sakakawea as he crossed over the Missouri River at Four Bears Village and then turned left to head south along Route 22. Rolling farmlands and cows dotting the landscape towards the horizon. Hay bales intermixed with incessantly bobbing oil-drilling rigs that resembled grazing prehistoric dinosaurs. When he was on his bicycle he had most enjoyed these quiet long sections of open land, the gentle rise and dips as the earth undulated beneath his wheels. He was like a caterpillar making slow and steady progress across the Great Plains, stopping here and there to listen to the stillness, interrupted only by a periodic wind rushing against his tanned cheeks. Wristwatch time was meaningless, replaced by what he felt was even more immeasurably important and inspiring – sunrises and sunsets. The repetition of the natural order repairing his soul and allowing love and goodness to seep back into the dormant crevices that always remained inside him. He knew he was a child with a kind and sensitive heart but the early adult years had brought sadness and discord and bitterness. That bicycle trip was the beginning of his healing. He knew it. And now retracing these roads brought with it some of the painful memories and layered scars.

He looked at his outstretched hand and fingers. Five fingers. *Five years from the last time I'd been on this road gradually heading home. Searching for answers.* He turned his hand horizontally and measured the number of fingers that fit between the horizon and the waning sun. Four fingers of sunlight remained. *About another hour left before sundown.* He chuckled to himself. How simple a technique it was to use a hand to tell time. His ancestors probably did just the same for thousands of years. Primitive and yet sufficient despite the modern world's complexities. Was he happier now for his decisions after returning home from that trip? Perhaps. Wins and losses. Concessions made. He had wrung himself through the mental bargaining and depression and anger phases. In a way he felt forged by his independence now. His ability to remain disconnected, detached from allegiances and relationships if they didn't suit his needs. To travel and explore. Shoot random photographs while detached from truly interacting with his subjects – while also trying to drum up some business as a result. A financial exchange that often was devoid of meaningful personal exchange. Some would think he was just bumming around without an exacting career. But he felt reasonably satisfied with the current plan. He worried if the money in his personal account would run dry sooner than later and he'd need to seek a different job, something steadier than freelance photojournalism. But that was too far into the future to worry about. He had a nice opportunity waiting for him just up the road in Medora.

    He passed the sign for the turnoff to Medicine Hole. The name stuck with him ever since he had passed through here previously and it was indeed through these very parts along his bicycle trip that he stewed on his decision to leave medical school and then made up his mind to follow through with it. To '*drop out*' as his parents repeatedly said to him later, condescendingly. But his pain wasn't theirs at that time. And he felt like he was descending through a hole of his own making in life. A hole he needed to fall through to save himself. No one could possibly understand, but himself. And so he grasped at whatever footing he could find until he could breathe freely and overcome his searing pain. But now, five years later, Bradlee also knew he had replaced one pain for another. The breach with his family, and particularly with his father, had remained a dormant yet smoldering sore in an otherwise pleasant past number of years venturing forward. He was hardened now, though. Perhaps more inured to tolerate pains of the heart. Or was it his past aching heart that prevented him from loving again? The images of Sami and Lyra flashed through his mind as Bradlee stepped on the gas and left Medicine Hole behind as quickly as he could. He turned west onto Route 200, south on Route 85, and then west onto Interstate-94 before exiting. The sun was setting over the petrified sandy hills as he continued along the final stretch on Pacific Avenue and arrived to Medora.

He checked into his room at the inn on Broadway and walked over to the Badlands Saloon for dinner and a craft beer. He ordered a heaping plate of spaghetti and meatballs with garlic bread and a side salad. Tasty and filling. The place sure had some character to it as if right out of a western movie. Cowboy hats hung from the ceiling and gunslinger pistols were bolted as door handles. A few clients even had their horses hitched right in front to the old posts. He made a note to return here for some photographs for his story. The saloon was quiet with only a few customers tonight. His kind of place. Bradlee lingered at the bar sipping his beer and chatting a bit with the bartender, a young man named Kirk who was probably close to his own age, Bradlee surmised. Bradlee watched the scene as it unfolded. Kirk's girlfriend came wandering in as Bradlee was enjoying the quiet, his thoughts turning to his business meeting in the morning. The girlfriend approached the bar and she motioned for Kirk to take a walk down the hallway into the storage shelf area. Bradlee glanced over. It didn't take long before the pair were just about tangled up into a pretzel stick, lipstick smothering kisses and groans. *Passion*, Bradlee thought. He missed that kind of affection. Why did he pass on that opportunity last night? *You're a fool, Brad Lee*, he chided himself. *Go drown your sorrows in another beer. See if that will fix it.* Bradlee looked away from the couple.

Above the cabinets behind the bar were shelves laden with vintage toy trains set along their tracks. His demure mood transposed slightly to a more upbeat intoxication as he thought about what Harry would say to him just now. Maybe he'd be cheering him up from his self pity. Lyra's smile came into view. *She was beautiful alright! And quick on the draw with a wittiness that he really enjoyed. Nothing wishy-washy about her dreams!* Bradlee thought. Brains and beauty and desire to make the world a better place. *You are a damn fool Brad Lee*, he said to himself. *A real fool. And you don't even have her phone number. Heck, you don't even know what university she's heading for in Seattle even if you wanted to reach her. What do you know about her?* Bradlee concentrated on her name... Lyra Sasha... *damn, what was her last name? She told me it and now I can't even remember it. It was a soft spoken name, no staccato or harsh syllables to it, and it flowed gently off her tongue and lips. But what was it?* He walked back to the inn in disgust with his failed memory, plopped onto the bed and turned on the TV for a few mind-numbing minutes of late-hour talk shows. He didn't even bother to undress before falling asleep on the lumpy mattress.

The alarm shook Bradlee nervously out of sleep at seven o'clock the next morning. He washed and shaved and then changed into a new pair of black-dyed jeans with a stonewashed buttoned denim shirt that he had purchased for the meeting. Appearances do matter, he realized. He glanced at the mirror. The black and blue color combination was staring at him and he smirked. *Bruise-colored clothes to match a bruised ego... Nice choice, partner.* His head felt like it was being squeezed by a vise as the alcohol hadn't fully processed yet. He had a sand-colored cowboy hat with him that he had picked up along his bicycle journey at a western outfitter store in Valentine, Nebraska. It was a fine piece of work with a couple of bird feathers inserted into the diamond-patterned leather band. He fit it onto his head, tilted the brim downward, and peered into the mirror – *'now you're lookin' like a fine cowboy, aren't you?!'* He chuckled and then set his remaining clothes in his room drawer since he knew he'd be staying for at least a few more days in Medora. Bradlee grabbed his camera bag and ate breakfast in the foyer. Then he strolled down Broadway and turned right onto Main Street. He noted the bicycle shop at the corner as he continued to his meeting place at the Badlands Cowboy Heritage Center.

He approached the front desk and tipped the brim of his hat towards the receptionist. "Good morning, ma'am. The name is Brad Lee, freelance photojournalist. I have a meeting arranged here with Thomas Cotton and Frank Ramus."

"Yes, young man, they are expecting you," the receptionist replied. "Down the hallway and to the left you'll find our large gallery and reception room." She pointed Bradlee in the right direction. "Sure hope you can change their minds…"

While she was speaking Bradlee was glancing at the walls covered with memorabilia before his brain registered the last comment. He glanced back curiously towards the receptionist. *'Change their minds'* – that was an odd comment. She gave Bradlee a concerned look by raising her eyebrows. Bradlee continued down the hallway.

There were three men waiting for him in the gallery room. Thomas and Frank stood for introductions and proper handshakes while an older gentleman remained sitting alone.

"Pleasure to meet you Mr. Lee. I'm Tom Cotton. This here is Frank Ramus."

"Pleasure is mine, gentlemen. And Brad will be just fine instead, sir."

Thomas continued. "Brad—— Frank and I have been looking forward to this project. This here is Jim Clayburn, one of our board members as well." Thomas motioned to the older seated gentleman at the other end of the table who was wearing a cowboy hat and a bolo necktie fastened by a silver medallion. Dangling from the medallion was a turquoise stone carved into the shape of a buffalo horn. Bradlee could make out a hint of Native American features in his face and eyes. Bradlee noted that time had worn deepened vertical lines running in the grooves of the man's cheeks matching the layers of etched horizontal lines on his forehead. He seemed to have a permanent thickened leathery tan to his face and arms with the same kind of callused hands that reminded Bradlee of his Uncle Eddie.

"Jim is from the Fort Berthold Reservation nearby here. He's attending this meeting as the senior representative from the Three Affiliated Tribes government and as an honorary board member of the Heritage Center. The reservation spans both sides of the Missouri River and is comprised of the Mandan, Hidatsa, and Arikara Nation." Bradlee reached out his hand. "Good to meet you, sir." Jim hesitated before extending his hand to Bradlee without saying a word.

"I hope you had a satisfying train journey, Brad. Haven't done the cross-country rail trip myself. Sure hope you had some friendly chatter and enjoyed the scenery despite probably departing with a sore back. That was one long-ass haul from New York City…" Thomas snickered.

"Yes, I did, as a matter of fact," Bradlee said with an abbreviated smile. Instantly, Bradlee's mind flashed to an image of Lyra laying on top of him in their room at the Lady Slipper Inn. He shook it away as quickly as it arrived.

"Please, let's be seated," Thomas responded as they settled into comfortable leather-backed chairs around the conference table.

"Brad, when we talked over the phone last month about having you come out west and do this story and photo shoot of the wild horses in the park, Frank and I were excited to make this happen. As we discussed, the Heritage Center here in Medora wanted to do some advertising to attract more visitors here, drum up some needed revenue to maintain the building and our museum artifacts and such and we thought a photo shoot would be just perfect for this gallery space and street windows accompanied by your written story about the history of the wild horses in the Badlands. We have quite a few tourists who come through town. But most of them only visit briefly, get themselves some candy or an ice cream cone with lunch, and head to the national park next door. Our site here has been seeing fewer visitors over the past number of years with the economy slumping as it has and we're worried we might not be able to make ends meet with our projected budget."

Frank jumped in. "Brad— Tom and I need to be straight with you. Since we last spoke the Heritage Center board has had to make cutbacks in spending. We're bleeding in the red and we missed out on our usual much needed summer fundraiser on account of a tornado that came through here just recently and nearly tore off the roof of the building. That repair alone is going to cost us many thousands. So, here it is straight up – we still want you to do the wild horse story but we can't pay you what we agreed to. We're awfully sorry about that but the board just decided on this late last night in an urgent meeting knowing you'd be arriving here today." Frank paused, understanding the disappointment in bearing bad news.

"Now the board has agreed to repay you for your travel expenses here if you decide not to take the project – that's only fair…" Bradlee began to squirm in his chair before straightening his torso and squinting his eyes at Frank with disappointment.

"Gentlemen, I was hired to give you twenty five of my most artistic and interesting photos of the wild horses in the Badlands of Teddy Roosevelt National Park here in North Dakota. We agreed that those images would be relinquished to the Heritage Center for your sole ownership, not mine, to do with them as you wish for print or online marketing. And that I would oversee the printing and framing of those large images to adorn this gallery space or wherever else you wish to hang them. You mentioned to me that you had plans for a gala evening celebration in the gallery to kick-off a fundraising campaign and that I would be invited, all expenses paid, to return for that occasion. That gala alone would be quite important to me to help further my career as a photojournalist through the contacts I might make. And I was to write an accompanying story about the history of the wild horses in the park and further history about this region." Bradlee was clearly irritated. "That's a *lot* of work... You know, most of that work is done when I return home to my studio and pore over hundreds – perhaps thousands – of images and plenty of notes from library research and phone calls and self study. So, my time and effort has a price. We agreed to ten thousand dollars for these efforts and I signed a contract stating just that."

"Yes, we know Brad," Frank said. "Tom and I are not pleased about having to discuss this with you on such short notice. But... the board gave us no alternatives. Look, we are a nonprofit organization and we've been struggling lately with collecting sufficient donations from wealthier folks and a reduction in paying visitors to the center. The board is asking you to try to understand our financial position and be willing to do the job for a lot less. Maybe someday we can bonus you but there wouldn't be any written guarantee that we can offer you that."

"What are we talking about?" Bradlee responded frustratingly.

Frank glanced at Tom who nodded back at him before Frank continued. "Two thousand dollars. That's the best we can offer you on behalf of the board… Listen Brad, the board was going to nix the entire contract at the risk of having you sue them but you and I both know that a lawsuit would cost you, and the board, a whole lot more in legal fees than your salary for the job. It just doesn't add up and we sincerely apologize." Frank paused and set his cowboy hat on the table. Bradlee turned his head away and glared out the window while gently shaking his head.

"Look Brad, I know this is not what you were expecting," Tom added. "But we've seen your work. We hired you because we think you can do the job and do it real well. You are young, you have your whole career ahead of you. I still think you'll get some of those connections you were seeking from doing this story and photo shoot for us that a few thousand dollars less income now won't make a hill of soybeans difference down the road."

Bradlee stared ahead glancing briefly at Jim directly across from him at the end of the table. Then he averted his eyes upward to the far wall where a large framed photograph occupied most of the wall space – the photo image captured a cowboy mounted on horseback lassoing a calf inside a rodeo arena. He admired the photographer's lighting and choice of focus on the moment the rope landed over the steer's head. The steer's eyes were bulging. *Was it primal fear or was it due to the rope's tautness? A chokehold?* He couldn't tell. Bradlee wondered if the stress on the animal was even considered as an issue in this rodeo sport.

A few thousand dollars less? Try eighty-percent less, he sneered to himself. *Might as well do the whole damn project for free!* He tried to calm his frustrations by peering out the window. The Badlands sandy hills could be seen in the distance. He remembered back to his bicycle ride through them. The climbs and descents. The buffalo encounters and the wild horses who were seemingly unafraid of him back then as he stopped to observe them foraging adjacent to the road. They were magnificent in the midst of the wild terrain.

Bradlee turned toward Tom. "And Mr. Clayburn here – what is his role in these affairs?"

"Jim here has been a guide in the national park for nearly forty years. He knows every nook and cranny in the Badlands better than anyone I've ever met. He's an honorary founding member of the Heritage Center and has a lifetime appointment to the board for his knowledge and services to the people in this region and the tourists who spend their dollars passing through these parts. Frank and I, as fellow board members, asked Jim to attend this meeting so that you two could meet. We'd like for you to do your work with Jim's help. Jim knows where the wild horses usually reside in the park. You two can saddle up on horseback and spend a few days together if you're willing to accept the project for a lot less pay."

Bradlee glanced over at Jim. He was aware that Jim hadn't yet taken his eyes off of him since Bradlee first sat down. As if he was studying Bradlee's every move and facial expressions. Bradlee was feeling uncomfortable. "Excuse me gents, I need to take a walk outside for a moment to think about it," Bradlee responded sternly and rose to head back to the foyer.

Bradlee hustled past the receptionist and out the front door into the quiet street. *Damn it*, he said to himself. *You get a nice break and then the money just doesn't add up. I'm going to be spending hundreds of hours on this project and for what?! – might as well do it for free,* he thought again. *But I can't afford to do it for free! I need income to live on and support future projects. At least that's my plan. To keep at this career.* But he had self-respect. He should go in there and tell them to go to hell. And then head straight home to P.E.I. and figure out what comes next.

Bradlee turned to head back inside the building. Jim was standing outside the entrance against a hitching post. He was staring at Bradlee with his arms crossed.

"You're upset," Jim started. His voice was deep and grainy.

"You ever stop *staring*, Jim?!" Bradlee raised his voice in anger. Jim just kept staring straight into Bradlee's eyes without changing his stiff-lipped expression. "Of course I'm upset! Who wouldn't be?! This is my *damn* career!" Bradlee scoffed and then kicked the toe of his hiking boot into the curb.

"A man's got to decide what's best for him," Jim replied. "But before you walk back inside here and cancel this project and head back home, wherever home is... I want you to know that it'll be alright, either way. This center will figure out another way. It will likely survive just as it had done plenty of times since its founding years ago. And the horses – they'll still be out there waiting for you too, either way you choose to handle this. They will be replaced by the next generation soon enough and then the next and so on. My people have understood this from the beginning of time. They will understand it until the end..."

Jim paused to let his words sink in a bit. "Mr. Lee, where I come from a man works to change the world one small measure after another. Make it better. More just. More equitable. More compassionate. What are *your* roots, Mr. Lee?"

Jim waited for a reply. Bradlee stared off towards the Badlands hills again. The lighting was nearly perfect this morning as the sun accentuated the desert sand colors.

"I'm from Toronto and I live on Price Edward Island most of the year when I'm not traveling for work. But quite frankly, I haven't had very many opportunities in the past few years with the economy as it's been. Seems like my line of work is drying up with print journals closing shop.

Sure, there's online travel magazines and websites but they're not paying much these days for photojournalists – and National Geographic magazine isn't quite knocking on my door just yet." Bradlee laughed sarcastically and paused in thought while looking away again. "I've sold a few nice prints in galleries over the past year but still not enough to make a living at this…"

"You've chosen a tough business to make ends meet as a young man. About the same as a lot of farmers out here in the harsh Dakotas. Planting soybeans and sugar beets and wheat and then sitting back and praying for rain during the short growing season. Sometimes it comes just right, other times too much, and then plenty of other years, not enough. Unless it's just right a large part of the fields die from drowning or thirst. Add to that the issues we all face with global warming trends and these farmers have their hands full. Still primitive that we rely on Mother Nature as much as we need to after thousands of years. True, the fancy irrigation systems help, mark my word, but the crop yields still sometimes don't add up for lots of farmers near these Badlands, including on our tribal lands. And on top of Mother Nature's wrath, we've had plenty of oil spills over the years from the pipeline running nearby our lands to contaminate our drinking and irrigation water…" Jim realized he was straying off topic so he paused.

"You pray at all, Brad?" Jim's question struck Bradlee by surprise. Images of Bradlee's childhood and times spent with his father in synagogue services, or during summers at the Marshpillow home, confronted him. "I used to when I was younger. Doesn't appeal to me much as I've grown. I'm Jewish, Jim, but don't practice much of the religion and rituals. You might say I still hold onto a certain sense of spirituality. Nature is where I find solace and connection and I've been OK with that for the past many years."

"I was studying you, Brad, inside the gallery room. Something different about you that I can sense from your eyes. A good soul. I can smell one from a distance. I like to think I understand people well after all these years working with all kinds who show up here… So Brad, tell me, what does your faith teach you about how to live a worthy life?" Jim inquired. "Does it not instruct you to be useful? To help improve the world? To leave something behind as your legacy to your family and this Earth that is meaningful…?" Jim let the questions linger for a moment. "I've met plenty of Jewish folks in my time while they've passed through here on family vacations. A nice and slow horseback ride gives me plenty of time to get to know folks and strike up some wholesome conversations outdoors. Something about this land that evokes a certain humbleness and openness to chat freely… You know, I haven't traveled much myself away from my tribal lands over my lifetime, Brad, but the world has come to me here and I've learned a great deal about many peoples and faiths and ways of life."

"It's called '*Tikun Olam*,'" Bradlee interjected. "'*Repair and improve the world*' – it's a foundation of Judaism."

"Tikun Olam? Hmm… The phrase almost sounds like something in my Native American tongue. *Tikun Olam*. I like it… Brad, you've been given a special gift with those perceptive eyes of yours. And what about your hands? Are they not also a gift from our Creator? Your ability to work your camera. Quickly adjust the lens settings and zooms and whatever else you do with that fancy gadget. A cameraman's hands are like a surgeon's hands. I've looked at some of your images online last night while attending the board meeting. They *are* good. Vibrant. Soulful. One even brought tears to my eyes. You remember? – The one you posted on your website of the toxic waste spill into Hudson Bay. It was an image of a wasteland of decaying fish along the shoreline. In that photo you focused on their dying eyes. Mournful. Those fish had souls, I believe, just like you and me, Brad. I cried for their souls and asked for forgiveness for man's faults. And I knew you were the man for this photo shoot of the wild horses. My gut tells me that you understand and respect nature just like my people."

Bradlee's anger was dissipating listening to Jim's comforting words.

"Come here, young man, let's take a walk." Jim motioned to him. He put his arm around Bradlee's shoulder as they strolled towards the grassy field at Chimney Park just down the road. Bradlee noticed Jim's gait had a subtle limp as he slightly favored his left leg.

"You see this chimney here," Jim said to Bradlee. "This is the last standing structure of what was once a large slaughterhouse and meat packing plant that operated on this site over a hundred years ago. My ancestors were chased from this land to make way for the buildings that once stood here. We did not slaughter animals for mass consumption. As you know from your history lessons, we lived off the land and migrated to follow the buffalo and the elk and the deer for our survival. The animals were a blessing to us and we understood that kinship to nature. Maybe less so today but I am an elder of my tribe. The stories remain within me from my parents and grandparents who lived here when the park was not what it is today as a tourism destination. Some of my ancestors even met and knew Teddy Roosevelt when he used to come stay out here way before he was the President. I was told stories in my youth that a few of my ancestors even served as his guides on horseback through the Badlands. Same kind of work as I've been doing nearly my whole adult life. And those mustangs in the park boundaries? They are the descendants of the last survivors of a round-up that occurred many years ago. Their ancestors escaped detection but these mustangs still have no official and permanent government protections as elsewhere on western forest service lands. I consider these feral horses my spirit brothers and sisters. And so do my people on the nearby reservation who once traversed these lands." Jim pointed to the park entrance station and the winding road past the gate.

"It is a beautiful and wild place, Brad. Join me and you will not regret it." Bradlee stared at the old slaughterhouse chimney. A monument to death. He once wanted to save lives as a future doctor. To follow in his father's footsteps. He knew the family line of doctors extended for at least six generations that he was told about from his youth. Some of those doctors were also learned rabbis like Uncle Eddie. Bradlee had heard the stories as well, although he never got the chance to meet him – of his grandfather who immigrated to Toronto from Poland after the Second World War. In Poland, he was an esteemed physician and rabbi but he died from sorrow before Bradlee was even born. His wife had perished in Auschwitz but he was able to save his two sons – Bradlee's father and Eliezer – and they came to Toronto to make a new life.

Bradlee looked again at the chimney. It triggered a discordant feeling about the suffering of many of his ancestors in the Holocaust. Faces and minds he would never know. He felt a wave of guilt now rising from his gut. He had indeed enjoyed his medical studies. But things happened. The name Levitsky had grown distasteful as a reminder of his past. And especially of his father. Bradlee decided to shorten it and so he used the name 'Lee' instead for any non-legal affairs since he hadn't gotten the full courage to officially file the name change through the courthouse. A more anonymous name – Lee. Quicker and easier to say. And he had decided his eyes and hands would be put to work in other ways, perhaps more like his Uncle Eddie's artistry than his father's surgical prowess.

"Jim, I was here five years ago," Bradlee spoke. "On a tourism adventure of my own. Wish I could have met you back then. Maybe things would have turned out differently for me since then. Always wanted to return here and visit the wild horses... I was very excited about this project, Jim. It meant something very personal to me."

"I understand. The Badlands isn't to everyone's liking but to some – there is a certain spiritual connection that is real... Brad, listen... I'd like to show you the park like you could never have seen before."

"Thanks Jim. I understand where you're coming from. But, I'd prefer to meet you tomorrow morning instead. Today, I'd like to explore a bit of the park on my own."

Jim smiled at Bradlee for the first time. He could sense that the young man's demeanor had changed for the better.

"And you can tell Tom and Frank that I will do the job better than they could ever imagine. To hell with the big paycheck! I'll figure it out later," Bradlee declared with a shrug and frown.

They walked back to town and made plans to meet at the park stables the next morning. On the way to the inn Bradlee stopped into the local bicycle shop on Main Street. He spoke with the owner who agreed to lend him a bicycle for the day. A racing bike similar to the one he used to go cross-country. His *'white stallion,'* as he called his time-traveling machine that was waiting for him back home on P.E.I for another adventure someday ahead. Its smooth white frame and aerobars cut through the winds as he gripped the bright orange handlebar tape. Silver reflectors and flashing red lights adorned the front and rear wheel forks to ward off any passing cars or trucks.

In town, he picked up a sandwich and some energy bars. Then he returned to the inn, changed into his cycling bibs and jersey, filled a few water bottles and placed them in the rental bike's holders. He slipped his camera bag into a light backpack along with his lunch and snack items and started pedaling towards the national park entrance.

Bradlee paid the entrance fee at the gate along River Road and continued past the park welcome center and into the park. He remembered this spot like it was yesterday. A roller-coaster of twists and turns, ascents and descents that would challenge any cyclist's stamina. Today was a sunny day just as it was then. The road immediately climbed and wound to an apex. A wall of sandstone mesas and pyramid-like pillars accompanied him along the entranceway as he cycled onward and crossed over the Interstate-94 bridge and into the solitude of the park. The road wound and climbed again to a plateau. The effort was intense for his legs and he wished he hadn't been more recently lax in his training regimen before this trip commenced.

Riding through the plateau, he paused to enjoy a moment surrounded by a village of chirping prairie dogs darting playfully in and out of their burrows. Their village had expanded since he had last gone through here. He was pleased his friends were prospering, as cute and photogenic as they were. The land opened to broad vistas as Bradlee was able to relax his legs and his breathing from the climb. At the fork he turned left onto the Scenic Loop Drive and continued winding through walls of desert sandstones of shimmering sunset hues in the mid-afternoon light. Every shade of brown palette could be found sprinkled with scrub brush and cypress. The leaves of some of the cottonwoods were already transforming into brilliant golds. Blooming wildflowers – asters and rabbitbrush and large clumps of sunflowers – dotted the roadside and were interspersed between rock formations. Scurrying about in the scrub were cottontail rabbits and chipmunks. He startled a pronghorn antelope and then came upon a small herd of bison laying in a grassy field set off from the roadway. The solitude was only interrupted by the songs of the warblers and sparrows and cedar waxwings foraging for berries and insects in the brush.

The plateau did not last long. A series of searing climbs and brief descents followed. He had entered what he remembered describing as the 'roller coaster' section. His thighs – good ol' 'Beatrice and Bessy' – were firing away in fits and pains now as he realized they were not quite as inexhaustible as five years ago. But his quads responded well enough with sufficient prodding and massaging. He paused at a promontory to enjoy the vista that extended for many miles from each side of the road. It was a clear day. Sweat poured from his brow.

And there they were – off in the distance, in the descending and undulating landscape below the promontory. Foraging. Braying. Swatting flies with their handsome tails. Naked. Freely roaming. Browns and blacks and whites and golds with thick ungroomed manes. The wild horses of the Badlands.

Bradlee dismounted from his bicycle and took a seat on the bench at the overlook. It was a perfect resting point. He opened his backpack and retrieved his lunch. *Perhaps take some photos as well*, he thought, *despite a bit of color bleaching from the early afternoon sun*. He could adjust for that later in the editing. In his peripheral vision he spotted something darting near a collection of purple wildflowers. He focused and, from the flight pattern and wing speed, realized it must surely be a hummingbird. It rested briefly on the stem and then sipped the nectar. And then it settled onto the adjacent flower and then another.

Bradlee quickly opened his camera bag and rummaged through the lens compartment for the right afternoon filter and noted an odd plastic bag that he didn't recognize. He pulled it from the compartment and opened it. It was Ruby's blueberry pie! He hadn't remembered storing it in his camera bag. And there was more stowed in the bottom of the bag. He turned to look back for the hummingbird but it had flown away out of his sight now. He wished it would return again to join him for lunch.

He returned to the mystery bag and next pulled out a beautiful linen scarf with a hummingbird pattern. The aroma struck him at once. *Jasmine!* He unwrapped the scarf to discover Lyra's magnificent needlepoint. He chuckled as he admired the shell she had woven into the corner beside her initials. He opened Lyra's note card and read it. Then he read it again and inhaled the aroma from the needlepoint itself. The jasmine instantly brought his mind back to the Lady Slipper Inn. The gardens. The Hummingbird Room. Lyra exiting the shower. Glimpses of her beauty in the soft light through a crack in the door. His nightmare. Lyra's early morning comfort and their first kiss. Hummingbirds – Lyra's passion for the delicate creatures.

She had signed the card with the salutation, 'Your Trochlidaeologist.' *What is a Trochilidaeologist?* he wondered. He pulled out his cell phone and searched for the term... He found a match with Trochilidae: *Hummingbirds are birds native to the Americas and constituting the biological family, Trochilidae.... often brilliantly colored...* Bradlee laughed emphatically. Loud enough for the wild horses to pause and glance upward towards him with ear-perked curiosity. *Lyra, you clever one! Very clever indeed!*

He read more and followed a curious link to another entry page... *Trochilus Polytmus, also known as the red-billed streamertail hummingbird or 'doctor bird,' is the national symbol of Jamaica where it has been immortalized in Jamaican folklore and song. It lives nowhere else than on the island nation of Jamaica. The doctor bird received its name because of its black crest and double-pronged tail that resemble a top hat and tail coat as doctors used to wear in the years past... The native Arawaks on Jamaica believed that this hummingbird had magical powers. They referred to it as the 'God Bird' since it was believed to be born from the reincarnation of a dead soul.*

Bradlee closed his phone and observed his hummingbird friend once again as it returned for another helping of nectar. He was lost in a shower of memories. He turned back to Lyra's note. Then he shouted the numbers, one by one, to the hummingbird and the wild horses, with utter joy. Lyra had left her phone number at the bottom of her note card!

He grabbed the plastic fork that was packed inside the bag and devoured a heaping bite of Ruby's sunbaked blueberry pie. As delicious as he remembered her pie from years ago! He knew Ruby's advice was right back when he passed through Minot and happened to visit her restaurant – *'Brad, honey, you follow what resides inside your heart and your life will forever be meaningful'* – as she looked him in the eye then and stubbed his chest with her index finger. He knew Ruby's words sounded as corny as a fortune cookie saying but still, the thought lingered with him for the remainder of that bicycle journey. He had no significant regrets now for his decisions. But time still brought lingering pains. He looked towards the Badlands hills and tracked his new hummingbird friend until it disappeared into the horizon. Maybe it was time to let go of the rest of these remaining pains, he thought.

Bradlee admired the needlepoint one more time, gently brushing his fingertips across the delicate stitching, shaping the outline of Lyra's hummingbird. He recalled her working on it in spurts during the long train ride. He inhaled her perfume, embedded into the fabric. He decided to follow his instincts. Lunch and photos of the wild horses could stand to wait a few more minutes. He breathed a series of steady breaths to calm his racing heart. He had the promontory to himself. Solitude in the midst of such beauty before him. He spotted the hummingbird again as it returned for another taste of wildflower nectar. He studied the wild horses for another moment. Then, Bradlee quietly chanted Lyra's phone number until it was set to memory and dialed.

LYRA WAS ENJOYING HER AFTERNOON RUN along the waterfront trail through the nature park. The wetlands and ponds were host to a variety of birds that provided sanctuary adjacent to Union Bay. Lake Washington was to the east and she made note of the floating bridge that crossed the lake. Another area to explore on a future run, perhaps. Lyra exited south from the Union Bay waterfront trail, ran past the university rowing center, and then continued onto Walla Walla Road. The rowing teams were in full training modes on this Labor Day weekend as she overheard the steady calls of the coxswains barking out the pace for the muscular rowers in the bay. The school year was set to begin the next day. At the Montlake Bridge she turned left to cross over the waterway, picked up the Arboretum Waterfront Trail to Marsh Island, and then continued to Foster Point. It was to be her turnaround point after a lung-cleansing initial three miles. She pressed the stop button on her sport watch upon reaching the grassy knoll at the point. Twenty-four minutes had passed. Not too bad. Quite slower than her usual six to seven minute per mile pace but she was exploring her options today. Getting to know her new territory and campus surroundings on a pleasant early afternoon. She rested for a few minutes while sitting atop the bench overlooking the south side of Union Bay. It was a pretty site along the waterfront. The waves were ebbing against the rock edifice and she welcomed the cool breeze from the lake. After a brief rest she would be heading back to her new home tracing the same route. She removed a small water bottle from her fanny pack as her phone rang.

Lyra didn't recognize the phone number. She hesitated a few more rings but then pressed the answer button. It was a man's voice on the other end. He had a nervous laugh and was calling out her name. "Lyra… Lyra, is that you? It's me… Brad. I mean Bradlee." He laughed nervously. "I hope I'm not interrupting anything important, am I?"

Lyra decided that a bit of opportunistic playfulness was only fitting. She lowered her voice to a whisper. "Well Bradlee Seashell, this is a nice surprise! I just so happen to be in a very important meeting with the Lake Washington Mollusk Preservation Committee at this very moment. We are deciding the future of the lake's rare mollusks and I am trying to convince these people that I happen to know a brilliant malacologist who would be just right for a consulting job. Are you interested?" She paused. "I will place you on speaker phone right now if you are." Lyra kept a deadpan seriousness to her voice. Bradlee went silent.

"You still there, Bradlee Seashell?"

"Lyra," Bradlee started, "I don't know what to say. That's quite an offer."

Lyra burst into laughter. She threw herself onto her back on the grassy lawn and continued to laugh hysterically into the phone. She tried to compose herself. "Bradlee Seashell, you are *impossibly* naïve… or just full of yourself. Which one is it?" More laughter. Now Bradlee starting laughing together with her.

"OK, you got me, didn't you? I guess I deserved that," Bradlee answered. Lyra settled with a few more chuckles.

"Where are you now? I hear water gurgling in the background," Bradlee asked.

"I'm at a place called Foster Point. Quite pretty. It overlooks a bay near my new home. I'm taking a short breather after a nice run here to a half-way point… Bradlee, you must have found my note in your camera bag."

"I did, Lyra. And I wanted to call to thank you for your beautiful gift. The needlepoint is exquisite as is the scarf. You are very talented. And I see you personalized it with the shell and your initials and your jasmine perfume which is… well, a little intoxicating – in a good way I mean." Bradlee laughed now. "And thank you for your card. You know that jasmine aroma – well I haven't seemed to be able to wash it off no matter how hard I've tried these past few days." Bradlee was nervous, he knew it. That was an awkward way of putting it, he realized.

"Your welcome, Bradlee. You know, I wasn't really expecting to hear from you again but I'm glad you're calling me now. As I wrote, if you ever want someone to talk to I'm just a phone call away."

"Thank you, Lyra. I appreciate that. Listen, I wanted to share something with you. I discovered your gift and the blueberry pie while sitting here at a beautiful overlook. I'm in the Badlands right now near Medora. I rented a bicycle today and decided to search on my own for the wild horses. I'll be on guided horseback tomorrow. My work has begun here and this spot is just too beautiful to fully describe where I'm sitting." Bradlee paused and stared at the horses. "Lyra, the wild horses are grazing close by. They are absolutely fantastic just as I had remembered them and the more I look at them the more I can't seem to stop thinking about you."

Lyra blushed on the other end. "Well, if you could only see me now all hot and sweaty at the moment..." Lyra giggled into the phone.

"Doesn't matter, Lyra. I can imagine you as I wish and to me you are the bee's knees. Or, shall I say, a malacologist's dream bombshell."

"Bradlee Seashell, you are silly and intense all at the same time. But I like that about you."

"Lyra, I want to apologize for my behavior the other night. I didn't mean to..."

"Bradlee, enough of that. I said my peace back at the inn and I left you a thank you gift because I wanted you to know that I hold no hard feelings. I forgive you if that's the answer you are seeking. All right? Are we *straight* about that?"

Bradlee was taken aback by Lyra's abruptness but it was refreshing. Nothing needed to linger between them. "All right then, Lyra. Thank you... Lyra, I really would like to keep in touch with you. You have no idea how happy I am that you left your phone number in your note card."

"I'd like that very much, Bradlee. And now I have yours as well on my phone id. I'll add you to my contacts – maybe even insert you as one of my 'Favorites.'" Lyra laughed again and Bradlee thoroughly enjoyed hearing it despite her teasing.

"Great! Well, I'll let you go back to shvitzing – I mean, sweating. Have a good rest of your run. The wild horses say hi to you, by the way." He knew it was a corny statement but deep down Bradlee believed, in some way, that it was true. Nature provides when it needs to provide, he knew from enough life experiences from his travels. Coincidences happen for a good reason – his mind had come around to accepting that concept over the past number of years. And these wild horses brought him and Lyra together from the moment he boarded the train and took his seat across from her.

"Then please give them a good neigh from me." Lyra made a horse neighing sound into the phone. *What was she thinking?* She was nervous, really nervous, talking to Bradlee. Goosebumps on her skin.

"Cute," Bradlee responded. "Lyra, thanks for taking my call. Let's talk again soon."

"I'd like that Bradlee. Take care now. Bye." Lyra disconnected even though she didn't want to. Bradlee held the phone for a moment and stared at the screen. He saved Lyra's number into his call list and then realized he still didn't have her last name. Lyra would have to do. 'Lyra Sasha' – that's all he entered. And then he pressed, 'Add to Favorites.' On the other end, Lyra typed in 'Bradlee Lee.' She hesitated, deleted Lee, and inserted 'Seashell.' *Why not?* She had started calling him that for the most part. And then, she too pressed 'Add to Favorites.' She scrolled to the 'Notes' section towards the bottom of the 'Contacts' screen and thought for a moment before typing... 'Be patient. Has a wounded heart.' She smiled and glanced back at the waves before setting off on the trail again, energized, as she advanced her pace home to her usual speedy self.

Bradlee finished his lunch as he waited for the sun to arc further west until the right moment arrived. He had honed his photography skills through hours of self-teaching, adjustments, and improvements to his instruments. And by now, he was confident in his judgment of when to capture the most favorable light on his subjects. The wild horses remained in a shady area in the rambling scrub bushes below the overlook. He set his fold-out portable tripod on the ground. Then he inserted the diffuse light filter over the aperture of his DSLR camera, removed the lens cap, and added the matte box for some further shade cover. He spent a few minutes adjusting the zoom and focus rings as he peered through the viewfinder. He smiled knowingly. It was an internal joy that came forth from the emotions that stirred any artist to create – a wedding of a worthy subject to an artistic eye. He began to press the shutter release. The horses were the star performers. They were offering him his own magic show with the curtains wide open to nature's wild magnificence. All he needed to do was to stare and simply press the button countless times as a silent witness.

THE PHONE RANG.

"Dr. Bonheim's office. Bonnie speaking."

"Hello Bonnie, this is Lyra Flurey. Good morning." Lyra was collecting a few souvenirs at the university store before her first class was to begin.

"It's a pleasure to speak with you again, Ms. Flurey" Bonnie replied.

"It's been a few months since we last spoke," Lyra replied. "And thank you for helping to make all the arrangements for me for the professor's home. I love it!

Just moved in yesterday, in fact."

"Wonderful, glad I could help. I look forward to meeting you uh... *Lyra?*" Bonnie glanced at the student id badge that was clipped to a manila folder on her desk. It contained a welcome packet with various further last-minute curriculum details and maps of the university and local area around the campus. "Ms. Flurey, I thought your first name was *Sasha*? Wait..." Bonnie rummaged through her file cabinet and retrieved Ms. Flurey's application folder. "I'm sorry, my mistake, your application does say – *Lyra Sasha Flurey* – after all."

"Oh, you've got it right, Bonnie. I was using my middle name for some time but lately I've been leaning towards preferring Lyra so... let's go with that from now on for university correspondence, if it's OK with you too.

"No problem, Lyra. I'll make a note of your preference and adjust your university ID to state '*LYRA*' in bold print. I'll have it ready for you this afternoon."

"Thanks Bonnie."

"Very pretty name as well - *Lyra*. Your parents must have had a difficult choice deciding between them." Lyra laughed at Bonnie's comment.

"Bonnie, I look forward to meeting you. I'm just calling to confirm my four o'clock meeting today with Dr. Bonheim." She was more than excited to finally meet her advisor and learn about potential research opportunities for her year-end master's thesis.

"Yes, we have you listed for that time. Dr. Bonheim is flying in from Houston later this morning and I don't expect any delays at the moment. We will see you then."

"Thanks again, Bonnie. See you soon." Lyra hung up and finished purchasing a logo key chain and a stuffed animal. It was a husky, the university mascot. It would mind her bedroom pillow while she was away for long stretches studying at the university. A bit of a lucky charm, perhaps. She decided to name the stuffed animal, '*Foster*' -

in honor of Foster Point where she had run yesterday. But the real reason for the name, in case anyone asked who she really trusted with her secrets, was to remind her of the time and place that she and Bradlee had reconnected. And how happy she felt at that moment.

She was enjoying her first few classes that morning. The combined Environmental Sciences and Landscape Architecture departments had designed a dual degree program that filled her daily schedule from 9 a.m. to 5:00 p.m. except for Fridays when she was able to arrange to be done by noon. Each department had made some concessions to allow Lyra to complete her dual master's degrees in two packed semesters and Lyra was determined to finish the program in that time period. Dr. Bonheim waived some of Lyra's classroom course requirements in exchange for an intensive winter month between the two semesters when it was expected that Lyra would join Dr. Bonheim in field research – good enough to earn the remaining credits towards her degree. And the landscape program already awarded Lyra about a third of her required credits from her previous undergraduate advanced studies where she graduated summa cum laude. Lyra knew that she just needed to spend nearly all of her waking hours studying. And probably more than a few all-nighters as well poring over texts and research articles and writing her master's thesis itself.

Lyra arrived promptly for her meeting with Dr. Bonheim. She enjoyed a few minutes chatting with Bonnie in the reception area before being invited into Dr. Bonheim's office. Dr. Bonheim was still finishing with a phone call behind her desk as Lyra glanced around the spacious room. Dr. Bonheim waved her to come inside from the entrance door. Award plaques, certificates of appreciation, and honorary diplomas from a variety of major universities in the United States and internationally adorned the entirety of one wall and spilled into another of which was mostly comprised of photographs of Dr. Bonheim posed with various world leaders and dignitaries, many which Lyra recognized from television news and newspapers. The remaining wall contained some large framed aerial photographs of various locations in the world – Lyra recognized the Great Barrier Reef, the Hawaiian Islands, sand dunes in Saudi Arabia, the Amazon rainforest, and many others. Lyra walked over to the photos for closer inspection as Dr. Bonheim finished her call and joined Lyra.

"You have any hobbies, Sasha? Dr. Bonheim inquired immediately after ending her call. "It's an honor and pleasure to meet you, Dr. Bonheim. "It's Lyra, by the way. I prefer my first name now. I know when we last spoke I went by Sasha, but I've had a change of heart.

"I see" Dr. Bonheim replied as she tapped her desk. "Lyra, the lyre of Orpheus. Good old Orpheus. Quite the harpist. Now *he* had as fine a talent as any Greek god there ever was – or is, perhaps. Orpheus could charm the animals and make the trees dance with that lyre of his, so they say."

Lyra didn't know what to say. She was amazed by Dr. Bonheim's encyclopedic knowledge of mythology. "Hobbies, Lyra – the question I asked..."

"Oh, sorry Dr. Bonheim. I was admiring these aerial photos. Yes, I do have a few hobbies when I can find the time. I like to jog regularly to keep myself fit, if you call that a hobby. But I've always been mesmerized by hummingbirds ever since I was a young child. I do needlepoints of hummingbirds and have various hummingbird-related collectibles. I find that they keep me grounded – my spirit that is, despite the hummingbird's magnificent beauty in flight."

"Very interesting. Fine birds, I must agree" Dr. Bonheim responded. "We have our share around these parts in the Seattle area. There may be some different ones than you're used to observing in the northeast. Connecticut – Guilford area I see, to be precise. Just east of New Haven."

"Yes, that's right. The Connecticut shoreline. It's quite a nice wooded area adjacent to the Long Island Sound. I enjoyed growing up there. My father is from the Seattle area, born and raised in these parts, and my mother attended this university as an undergraduate when they met on campus. But they moved to Connecticut, where my mother was raised, before I was born," Lyra said.

"Yes, know it pretty well. I had spent some time at Yale University more than a few years back as a visiting professor. Quite a nice area. Prefer life out west here where I'm originally from but I have some friends back east from those times. Keep meaning to visit again but just too busy with work and lectures and travels for my research."

"You like those photos?" Dr. Bonheim inquired.

"Yes, I do actually. It is always fantastic to see the Earth from above, especially if removed far enough where humans are no longer visible in the frames. Makes you really appreciate the beauty of the planet that much more. The colors. The natural flows of the landscapes…"

"Those are my photos, Lyra. My hobby…" Dr. Bonheim let in. "One of the great benefits I've always appreciated about my career here at the university is the gift to travel and lecture and work on various projects that hopefully have made, and still are making, a difference around the world. These photographs were taken by me from various winged aircraft or helicopters over the years as the Institute's director. Still love looking at them periodically. Plenty more in my home stored in various shoe boxes. I've had a difficult time switching over to one of those fancy digital cameras. Afraid I might be too old now to learn all the new gadgetry… The images show the evolution over time. Humanity's impact can't be denied from aerial photos. The evidence presents itself too starkly. But – air and water quality. You know, Lyra, these are my specialties in environmental sciences. The very basics. Can't have a healthy Mother Earth without those two staples working well. Now there's a lot that goes into that equation, and I know you're here to learn about all of that over the next few semesters. You and I will be partnering together quite a bit. I've read your application and am impressed by your motivation and undergraduate performance. It'll be quite a step up from where you've been to our graduate school program. Your undergraduate professors - one of them I actually know quite well by the way - wrote some very nice things about you. And I know you've overcome some personal challenges in your life. So, I welcome you here Lyra to the mecca of environmental sciences. A brief oasis for you to draw water from and clear the air of past, perhaps misguided learnings. We will shape you into a scientist bar none." Dr. Bonheim pointed towards a photo of the Saudi Arabian sand dunes and chuckled. "That was quite a toasty day in the field!"

"Thank you, Dr. Bonheim. I'm very excited to be here," Lyra replied a bit sheepishly.

"Your course work is all planned for the two semesters. It will be a burdensome schedule but I imagine you will be one of our finest students if you focus on the tasks at hand and minimize distractions from entering your life." Dr. Bonheim paused and glanced at Lyra's hands. "No ring on any finger? I presume you are on your own accord at the moment?"

Lyra nodded yes and smiled. "Well then, you are a young woman and there is a campus full of other young folks who would be delighted to meet you, I'm sure. That's all part of the experience in due time. Just try to stay focused, Lyra. I was your age once myself."

Dr. Bonheim offered Lyra a seat across from her desk as she placed her reading glasses on and then glanced upward. Lyra folded her hands in her lap. "About this winter semester of field research that we briefly discussed a few months ago..." Dr. Bonheim continued.

Lyra was impressed at how Dr. Bonheim, as busy as she was, recalled the details of their conversation. "Yes, I know this is a great opportunity to work with you, Dr. Bonheim. I was hoping in that research there might be something original that I could use for my master's thesis."

"Of course. That is the plan. Not nearly to the extent of a Ph.D. my dear, but I will try to point you in the right direction. Our options......"

Dr. Bonheim gathered some manila folders together from the piles on each side of her desk. "I have here three considerations from the Institute's consulting services for the month of January, just after the holiday vacation period... Seems the Colorado River levels have been dropping for quite some time. There's concern downstream with potential contamination of water tables that need some further investigation in Utah and Arizona... And here's another... it's in south Louisiana. The Mississippi Delta has been silting for many years and shipping channels are concerned about safe passage into the Gulf of Mexico but my concern is whether the waterway can remain viable as a shipping channel and whether the wetlands ecosystem is being severely threatened. Of course, if we simply just let it keep on silting maybe the air quality will also improve as a result of less pollution from diesel burning cargo ships." Dr. Bonheim gave a few laughs. "But those are political and economic challenges. Environmental sciences gets messy sometimes... Oh... and the last option here... North Dakota pipeline concerns. Seems the oil companies are interested in building a wider and longer pipeline through that area to connect Canadian oil fields to American refineries further south. The company that intends to build this new pipeline is seeking government approval to pass through a section of Native American reservation lands. Those previous pipelines through that region leaked like a rusty drum and made a heck of a mess of some pristine waterways some years ago. Hate to see that mess happen again. This project will be tougher to analyze since it's got a thick layer of powerful business and political interests at stake, on top of Native American tribal rights. And it'll be darn cold in North Dakota in January, but it's another worthy project. And that's just in North America. But I've been traveling a lot internationally this past year. Personally, I'd prefer to remain in the States this winter so let's skip over any international options."

"Any of these appeal to you, Lyra?" Lyra's ears perked up when she heard the words, *North Dakota*.

"I think I prefer the pipeline project, Dr. Bonheim. I'd like to imagine working long-term on policy decisions. The experience studying the issues, and attending meetings alongside you with various politicians and powerbrokers, will be invaluable for my career. Besides, on a personal note, I took the train cross-country this past week and it passed right through the heart of North Dakota. Kind of enjoyed the landscape and the people a bit while passing through the region. It might be nice to return... just a hunch."

Dr. Bonheim gave Lyra a stern stare. Then she wrapped her arms around her chest and proceeded with a mock gesture of bitter-cold shivers. They broke out in laughter together at the thought of freezing temperatures. "You are a tough bird, aren't you, Lyra?! All right then – we'll plan for North Dakota in January. The Institute's director has her pick of the projects she chooses to participate in. Have never been to North Dakota myself... Cheers to a new venue for research."

Dr. Bonheim held up an imaginary glass and Lyra followed her lead. They clinked their palms together and gulped generous sips from the mystery glasses. Lyra was very pleased with Dr. Bonheim's jocular personality. She just knew at that moment that she had made a fine choice traveling about as far west as she could find for her studies. It was worth the journey.

THE NEXT MORNING, Bradlee awoke at dawn and quickly gathered his camera gear together. He finished off Ruby's blueberry pie tin while putting on the softest jeans he had with him and meandered out of the inn ready to start the day. Work boots on and cowboy hat in place. He didn't bother to check the mirror this morning. Just too sore to look at himself from embarrassment. He met Jim at the stables adjacent to the national park.

"You ride much?" Jim asked.

"Not really, I have a bit of experience here and there but it's been a few years since I've been on the back of a horse. Maybe it's best I take out a nice old steed to cushion this saddle sore bum. My bike trip yesterday just about knocked me out last night. My thighs are still screaming at me!"

Bradlee was all smiles and laughter this morning. Jim wondered what had changed his demeanor so quickly from yesterday's blues. He handed the reins to Bradlee.

"This here is Ms. Culpepper. She's our finest mare. A beauty in her prime. Named for a little girl who used to work at the stables here. She helped birth this mare. Turns out the little girl grew up to become a horse veterinarian..."

Jim paused and smiled. "That little girl's my granddaughter" he announced proudly and then laughed. "Brad, just feel that silky chocolate milk coat, a little weathered with time but still as smooth as little Ms. Culpepper's baby's bottom some time ago. She also happens to be our oldest mare at the stables. She won't mess much with you. And if you're nice to her she'll tickle your ears."

Jim laughed again as he placed his left foot in the stirrup and leaped to straddle his tall black stallion. To Bradlee, Jim was like a spry teenager despite the years that didn't deny his age from his drawn face and graying hair. The saddle was a beautiful work of art – custom etched leather with Native American motifs. Surely a one-of-a-kind, perhaps like Jim himself, Bradlee surmised.

"I've been admiring your saddle, Jim. It's a beauty!"

"Gift from my daughter-in-law on the day she married my son. She's from a different tribe. It was her family's… really her tribe's way of creating a sense of unity between our people. Used to be a custom back in the old days for the young couple to present handcrafted gifts to the parents of the bride and groom. A group of the finest artisans from each tribe would organize the gift making and the ceremonial giving. Very beautiful ceremonies back then when I was only a child. So, my daughter-in-law wanted to revive the customs, some of the old ways of our people. She's been mostly successful with the younger generation. They've been rediscovering the power of these traditions again. The kinship. Very proud of her for that. She has a very loving heart. My son, Jeremiah, is blessed and so am I. And here it is! This plush leather saddle is as silky soft and smooth as it will ever get after all these years holding my bottom." Jim chuckled as he slapped his behind. "And she gave me two grandchildren. One of them is the horse vet I mentioned to you. The other is my grandson. I'm grooming the little guy to help me manage our ranch properties on the reservation."

They steadied along the horse trail that wound into the park. The road disappeared quickly from view. Within minutes Bradlee realized this was a whole new experience than riding a bicycle along the park road. He was inside the national park yesterday but not fully immersed within it. What the eyes can't see from the roadways, even traveling on a slow-going bicycle compared to an automobile. Dial that down to sauntering on horseback through sand-footed terrain and the photographer within him didn't know where to look first – it was all majestic and picture worthy. Pure wildness.

Jim started where he left off yesterday. "Brad, the tour tape begins now..." He laughed. "Welcome to Teddy Roosevelt National Park." Jim clicked at an imaginary button on an imaginary device and smiled behind him towards Bradlee who was still trying to find the right position in his saddle. Bradlee winced a brief smile despite his discomfort as Jim continued.

"The Badlands here in North Dakota are cousins of the ones in South Dakota. Similar terrain but different histories. The land here was visited by Native Americans long before Rough Rider Teddy Roosevelt came through here in the 1880's and set up shop at a cabin just south of here where he hunted bison and took in the sites on horseback. He was a lonely man back when he first started visiting here. But before I tell you more of his story, Brad, let me explain these parts to you. We're standing on millions of years of geology doing its erosion work across the land. This place was once teeming with rivers. As the rivers ran through these sands the minerals leeched over time – that's the colorful sediments you see sprinkled everywhere in the rocks – and so these mesas and pyramid-like structures piled up high over time, however you want to measure it. It's really all just petrified sand dunes of one kind or another."

"The Lakota came through here years ago and called this area 'Maco Sica' which was translated as 'Land Bad' – ergo, the Badlands. Potable water was darn tough to find in these harsh dry hills where temperatures can bake you and freeze you, all in just twenty-four hours. But despite all that, take a look around. There's plenty of life here." Jim pointed out the various plantings and flowers as Bradlee had noted yesterday but the scenery was even more abundantly beautiful here in the heart of the park. "We've got plenty of small burrowing critters who eat the grasses and live off the flowers, I'd imagine. Guess they find enough water from the plants and the occasional rains that wash through here and periodically replenish that river down in the valley below."

The horses carried them onward along the primitive dirt and sand path. "Back to TR – President Theodore Roosevelt. As I was saying earlier… so young Teddy Jr. had inherited a nice fortune from his father when he was just nineteen on account of his father dying a bit unexpectedly from stomach cancer. His father had made out well in a plate-glass importing business in New York and left TR a multi-millionaire in today's dollars. TR was a young well-educated Harvard man who met his future first wife, Alice Hathaway Lee, while he was attending Harvard. They married on his twenty-second birthday and he continued his studies at Columbia Law School in New York City, his hometown. He had probably outgrown his difficult childhood asthma by then through vigorous exercise along with rowing and boxing at Harvard. Around the time he got hitched to Alice he made his first trip to these parts of the Dakotas in 1883, when he was just twenty-two, to hunt bison."

"Hey, by the way Brad, isn't your last name also Lee? Interesting coincidence." Jim waited for Bradlee to chime in but his voice was muffled from their horse tracks. Jim continued with the story.

"Two years later, Alice gave birth to their first and only child together, a healthy girl – also named Alice. But then tragedy struck. On the very same day, just two days after his daughter was born – first TR's mother dies from a fit of typhoid fever in the early morning. His mother's death is followed soon after on that afternoon by his wife, who succumbs to kidney failure. And here's the stick – the day both his mother and wife died? Valentine's Day, 1884. Imagine that!" Talk about having some hard luck and one heck of a sad love story for a young man to deal with at such a young age!"

Jim pulled up on the reins and his stallion stopped at attention. Bradlee followed Jim's lead with Ms. Culpepper. They had arrived at a plateau overlooking a broad swath of the park below them and off to the distance. It was more beautiful, Bradlee thought, than his overlook yesterday where the wild horses were grazing. Jim and Bradlee took a moment to slake their thirst from some cool water in their canteens.

    "Her family and friends all called Alice, TR's wife, '*Sunshine*' because of her very cheery demeanor. It was a nice nickname. And so, in TR's diary entry on the day she died, along with his mother, he put a giant X across the sheet and wrote the words – *The light has gone out of my life.*"

    "After that day he never really wanted to talk about his former wife. He tried to move on and that's when he returned out west here for more extended stays in these Badlands. They say he needed a good deal of healing of his heart and mind from his tragic sudden losses. I'd agree to that. And so he bought himself a ranch just north of the Badlands here and got on horseback and rode through these parts, often solo, to experience nature's healing powers. Right here. I think it's likely he stood where we're standing and took in this view… I might forgive him for getting into the bison shooting and selling business since, as you and I both know, he eventually largely became a nature conservationist and was the first President to set aside land to be undeveloped for all time – 230 million acres of it, in fact, during his time as President. He established the first National Parks – not this one, I might add, this patch came later – and he signed the Antiquities Act that has taken care of setting aside countless other lands as monuments to Mother Nature's creations. Not too shabby. Naming this land, Teddy Roosevelt National Park, in his honor, makes a lot of sense now that you've heard his story."

    Bradlee spotted the herd of wild horses off in the

distance. Their ears were signaling to each other as they made their way from a high butte and descended towards the valley floor. There was a long ribbon of a stream and Bradlee could see where they were headed to drink in a safe clearing. Jim turned towards Bradlee while pointing towards the horses but he noticed Bradlee was already intently focused on them.

They sat in silence and admired the wild horses for a few minutes before Jim continued on with a softer voice now so as not to garner their attention. "Young TR did write a personal tribute about Alice, his Sunshine, that was saved for us to appreciate today. I memorized it some years ago Brad, and would like to share it with you now." Bradlee nodded approvingly towards Jim. Jim cleared his throat with another sip of cool water from his canteen and stowed it away in his saddle. He lifted his cowboy hat off and held it to his saddle. Bradlee followed his lead and did the same as Jim began to recite:

"'*She was beautiful in face and form, and lovelier still in spirit; as a flower she grew, and as a fair beautiful young flower she died. Her life had been always in the sunshine; there had never come to her a single sorrow; and none ever knew her who did not love and revere her for the bright, sunny temper and her saintly unselfishness. Fair, pure, and joyous as a maiden; loving, tender, and happy. As a young wife; when she had just become a mother, when her life seemed to be just begun, and when the years seemed so bright before her—then, by a strange and terrible fate, death came to her. And when my heart's dearest died, the light went from my life forever.*'"

Jim returned to silence for a long moment. Bradlee's head was bowed and he was hiding his face beneath his cowboy hat as tears welled in his eyes.

"You OK, son? Jim asked. "I'm sorry. Must have hit a raw nerve... It's about your own girl, isn't it Brad? Some kind of pain. I sense it in your heart..." Jim paused to let Bradlee have a few moments to collect himself. Bradlee pulled out Lyra's linen hummingbird scarf from his pocket. He dried his eyes and cleaned his face from the settled dust.

"Brad, there's no pain deeper than losing someone you love. In the early days, the grieving is bad, real bad. But I've learned over time that if you look up on a cloudy day, you see formations sometimes. My ancestors appear to me. My own mother and father, my grandparents, my tribal elders. I could swear sometimes they are looking at me with a keen eye and all I can hope for is that they are pleased with who I am, my decisions in life, whether I'm leading life with my heart the way it's supposed to be." Jim paused as he glanced at the clouds.

"You want to talk about anything inside of you, Brad?" Bradlee wiped his eyes again and took some deep breaths.

"I'm OK, Jim. Thanks for asking. The tribute did hit a nerve, that's all." Bradlee sipped from his canteen.

"Thanks Jim. You're a good man. Wise. I appreciate that wisdom. I hadn't known much about TR's history. He was also a good man from what I can gather. I think I understand why he came out here after what he went through so young."

"Yeah, TR had a rough patch for awhile. But you know what, Brad. He went back east and reconnected with a childhood friend. He remarried and the pair had a gaggle of kids and you know the rest of the story as he eventually became our 26th President. Youngest there ever was up until that point in our nation's history... The power of nature, Brad. Power of healing."

Jim glanced at the view. The wild horses had their heads bowed to the stream.

"The point is Brad – life goes on and we all need some healing in our lifetimes. The wise ones discover the power of healing before it's too late. Because the heart knows how to repair and grow stronger. That's just how it's designed.

We just have to be willing to give our heart a chance to work its magic.

"Tell me something, Brad. You got a girl in your life? Cause I could swear you can't fool me with your emotions on as high a gear as they are."

"I'm beginning to see the light return to my life, Jim. And it feels really good inside. I recently met someone. She's a special woman already but I hardly know her well."

"Well, all right then. I knew it!" Jim laughed heartily. "OK, lover boy. Enough of this emotional stuff. I've said my peace. Let's giddy-up and head down to those wild horses while they're still mighty thirsty. You'll get yourself some nice photographs today."

Jim relaxed the reins and gave a gentle kick with his spurs. His stallion knew just what to do as the pair took off down the trail into a gallop leaving Bradlee choking in a dust cloud. Ms. Culpepper meandered along for a brief while, then started into a gentler trot as if she knew Brad wasn't quite the tough cowboy he wished he was.

Part Four

The Green Point Campground was enveloped in darkness by the time Bradlee parked his car. Halloween night was only a few nights ahead and Bradlee never cared much for the holiday. He enjoyed collecting the sweets, all right, but the spookiness always unnerved him when he was younger. But this pervasive darkness at the campground was indeed spooky and it reminded him of the approaching ghoulish holiday, especially since he was the only car parked at the campground entrance. He set his tent onto a flat grassy area and attached the rainfly over the top, leaving it partially recessed to observe the night sky. He inflated his camping pad, set himself into his down sleeping bag and rested his head on a small travel pillow. He zipped closed the tent flap. His back was to the ground and face to the heavens. The sky began its show, thankfully, a few moments later. First the stars began to glitter and then he noted shooters streaming across the heavens. The moon made a grand appearance as the clouds parted. He sat up and noted the moonlight glistening across the ocean. Then he laid down again and searched for the Lyra constellation. It should be somewhere out there, he knew. *Search for Vega, one of the brightest stars, and you can find Lyra*, he recalled from his recent research. It resembled the Dippers – Big and Small – *but where exactly to look in the night sky for her? For the nocturnal glowing harp?* Bradlee lost himself in the expansive stars. The view was eternal. Humbling. Silent wonderment. He held still for as long as he could and welcomed the loss of self and time.

BRADLEE NEEDED TO GET AWAY from Prince Edward Island after spending nearly sixteen-hour days, seven days a week, over the rest of September and October sifting through nearly three thousand digital images on his computer screen at the Marshpillow home. The glare was taking its toll and he was becoming irritated from incessantly studying optimal horse alignments, sandstone backgrounds, and pressing countless keyboard strokes with his photo editing software that he began to wonder if he was just cheating nature of her greater beauty in her natural unedited state. *Why mess with a photograph if the photo captured nature as it was.* At *that* very moment, *that* time of day, *that* sky, *that* weather pattern. As it should be appreciated. He had reasonably narrowed the field of final photo candidates for the Heritage Center gallery in Medora but he still had the writing piece to do. The accompanying essay that needed to be mostly about the history of the wild horses in the park. Jim's further elaboration about the park's history would prove invaluable to the final product. He grew fond of Jim's perceptiveness. Soulfulness. As if he understood Bradlee better than anyone except, perhaps, his Uncle Eddie always had.

There needed to be a relevant theme for the project. Something to bind the photos and words together that was universal. Perhaps he'd frame it all as a love story from him to the wild horses. No, that was too specific. Better – allow the wild horses to be quintessential ambassadors, examples of nature's eternal love story. The concept for the project was coming together in his mind and he needed a few days to step away and let creativity breathe again. He couldn't deny an artist's fatigue. And the income he was to receive from completing the project for the folks back in Medora was hardly enough motivation to wrap up his work quickly. Besides, he had nothing else secured to take its place. Travel magazines just weren't calling him back and the Halifax and Toronto art galleries hadn't had a new sale of any of his framed photographs in many months.

Bradlee also had about enough that he could take of horses. He thought back to how sore his buttocks felt, dismounting that evening after riding with Jim through the national park all day long. He figured it took him about a week alone to recover from that horseback campaign on top of the punishing bicycle ride the day prior – barely enough time to at least be able to sit in even the most cushioned chair without flinching every few minutes.

Bradlee sensed burnout rapidly approaching. He needed a short break and he had never visited Newfoundland before. Late October camping along the Newfoundland coast would be darn chilly and windy, possibly freezing temperatures overnight – that much he knew. And so he gathered his trail backpack and stuffed it full with his heaviest and warmest gear. He pulled down the unopened two-person tent box from the storage shelf in the garage and stripped off the cardboard packaging. He had never gotten around to opening the new tent since he hadn't had the desire to return to camping in many years. It was laying next to his old weathered tent, torn to shreds and riddled with insect holes after all these years set aside. But his nostalgia for the good times spent in that old tent was too strong to part with it.

He stared out the garage window towards the ocean. The sun was rising as the fog was lifting over the marshland. He wished he had his camera beside him at that moment to capture yet another miraculous morning in his own backyard. He slipped the bundled tent sleeve into his backpack, added a few water bottles into the side-zippered compartments, some dehydrated food packets, a multitool, mint tea packets, and a Jetboil stove with a couple of propane fuel canisters. Enough for a few days and nights to enjoy a place where few others had ventured in their lifetimes.

It was a relatively brief and pleasant drive to the P.E.I.

ferry terminal at Wood Islands. He stopped to visit the historic lighthouse there – one of his favorites, before boarding the ferry to Caribou on the Nova Scotia side of the Northumberland Strait. The ferry was quiet this time of year after the summer's busy tourist season had ended. From Caribou he took the more scenic Highway 4 through French River and then on to Antigonish where he picked up the Sunrise Trail and crossed the Canso Causeway bridge into Cape Breton Island. From there, he drove the southern route around Bras d'Or Lake through St. Peters, Hay Cove, Big Pond and East Bay. He camped overnight in East Bay and awoke the next morning to finish the brief jaunt to North Sydney where he boarded the six-hour choppy ferry crossing to Channel-Port aux Basques at the southwest tip of Newfoundland. It was five o'clock in the afternoon by the time the ferry docked. From there, it was another four hours of driving, dodging moose in his headlights along the Trans Canada Highway to the Deer Lake turnoff to Highway 430, the '*Viking Trail,*' as he meandered past the East Arm of Bonne Bay and finally reached Gros Morne.

The next day he thoroughly enjoyed hiking the bog trail and then taking a small cruise along Western Brook Pond, a massive glacial fjord. The rest of the day he relaxed and read from a few books amidst the solitude of the campground.

Later that night, as he turned in to his tent, Bradlee added a sugar cane packet to the steamy water in his Jetboil and stirred. Then he bobbed a mint tea bag and let it seep before taking a few sips. Nothing better than a hot cup of mint tea – it was his own preferred camping drink for cold nights inside a simple tent's shelter and his sips brought forth many fond memories of prior hiking and camping expeditions. He closed his eyes… the waves. They were gurgling, striking rhythmically, musically, against the rocky shoreline. Shuffling ashore and then retreating. Endless cycles. He focused on an image of Lyra's face that he recalled from the train. He had handed her the lightning whelk shell. Her head was tilted teasingly towards her left shoulder and her hair dangled like silken threads. She glanced at him from this photogenic view, her right eye studying him like a playful inquisitive dolphin in the ocean. Perceptive. Curious. Innocence. A coy smile. As if she was ready to pucker her lips and blow him a kiss. His Daphne. But Daphne had transformed – reincarnated into Lyra. The harpist. He imagined her playing the harp on a sunny breezy day on a seashell covered beach. A love song to the ocean. To the dolphins, perhaps, who whistled to her in return. He was sitting on a boulder enjoying her concert. She cocked her head gently once again at a provocative angle and smiled her lips over to him. Lyra knew Bradlee was admiring her and she was enjoying the attention he lavished her with his eyes.

Bradlee unzipped the chest pocket of his jacket and teased out Lyra's linen hummingbird scarf, brought it to his face and inhaled. The jasmine aroma was fading but remained like embers after a roaring fire. It had been three weeks since he had spoken with her. Lyra was immersed in her studies and he understood she had limited time to offer him. He figured she needed to settle into a natural rhythm and Bradlee knew that late-night conversations weren't going to help her focus on her intensive studies. It was difficult to resist the urges to call her. This was one of those moments. He really wanted to hear her voice.

He dialed. It rang seven times before Lyra's voicemail message began. He listened to her recording but then hung up. He checked his watch and calculated the evening time in Seattle. It would be five o'clock in a few more minutes. He waited and then called back at the top of the hour. This time Lyra picked up on the first ring.

"Bradlee Seashell, you are persistent aren't you?!" she giggled a bit.

"Lyra, it's good to hear your voice. I just wanted to say

hi, that's all. It's been a little while. I know you're very busy."

"I'm sorry Bradlee, I've been meaning to call you but… I know, no excuses when it comes to friendship… How's the project coming along? I imagine you're busier than I've been lately."

"Yeah, it's coming along. I needed a little break to decompress. Been horsing around too much!"

"Not funny, Bradlee… OK, a little funny." Lyra laughed. "It'd good to chat again. I'm just walking out of my landscape architecture drafting class. I love it! Garden design drawings. Urban building landscapes. Personal home gardens – wherever the imagination wants to flow. My environmental science professor is a real hoot – Dr. Bonheim, the one I mentioned to you the last time we chatted. She's my thesis advisor and the one I'll be doing research with in January. Oh… I didn't tell you yet. Some *really* neat news. I'll be back in *North Dakota* in January. Dr. Bonheim and I are working on a research project related to the safety of a proposed oil pipeline. Anyway, she's just real down to earth, serious about her work but has a great sense of humor. We've hit it off real well. I feel very fortunate. Oh, and I didn't tell you about her hobby – she's also a photographer, like you. Well, not quite for a career of course. She loves to take aerial photos when she needs to survey the landscape from above for her research or consulting work. She's got some framed photos in her office – I think you'd enjoy them…"

Bradlee just listened and sipped on his mint tea. Lyra's voice was a stark but now welcome contrast to the ebbing of the waves. Just hearing Lyra's voice was enough to make him feel content. Her words were all just bonuses. Every one.

"You OK, Bradlee? You're not saying a peep," Lyra continued.

"Oh, sorry Lyra – just enjoying hearing what's going on

by you. Yes, I'm just fine. I'm in a tent in Newfoundland at the moment. Enjoying the stars."

"You're kidding?! It's damn freezing cold, isn't it?!" Bradlee laughed. The tea was emitting steam as he held his cupped hands around it.

"I'm toasty in my down sleeping bag. As happy as a hummingbird sipping sweet nectar. Or maybe as happy as a bed bug?"

"That's kind of gross, Bradlee. Hope you don't have any of those kinds of visitors." They laughed together.

"Is that the ocean I hear in the background? And why exactly are you in Newfoundland?"

"Like I was saying, I just needed a little break, that's all. Newfoundland is fantastic! I left my camera on purpose at my home on P.E.I. but now wish I hadn't. Gros Morne Park is across the way from my campground by the ocean and I had a blast hiking there earlier today and enjoying a cruise along Western Brook Pond. Well, not quite a small puddle but that's what the Newfies call it here – the Pond is actually a huge fjord, probably similar to the ones in Norway. Pristine. Steep granite walls with waterfalls gushing into the water below. Water is freezing cold when I touched it on the boat ride. I imagine it will freeze up soon enough as winter sets in here. But I plan to hike the coastal trail nearby tomorrow. I heard it's absolutely spectacular from some of the locals in Rocky Harbour, the small town nearby here. Then I'd like to head over to visit the lighthouse at Lobster Cove and some of the craft artists at Woody Point... have I told you I really like visiting lighthouses? There's one very close to my home on P.E.I. Maybe someday I can show it to you, Lyra..."

"I'd like that, Bradlee... Gosh, I wish we were closer to each other."

"Yeah, me too."

A few seconds passed with some quiet breaths exchanged between them.

"Lyra, I just want you to know that I think about you often. OK – *a lot*. That's all. I know you're busy so I won't keep you. You have a good night."

"Thank you Bradlee. You're not too far from my mind too, you know. And Foster knows it too."

"*Foster*—— who's that?"

"Oh, just a good friend I met. He's harmless." Lyra laughed.

"Oh, OK then, I guess… well, good night Lyra. Sweet dreams."

"Bradlee, maybe for you – it's ten o'clock where you are, I think. Only five o'clock here. I'm a long way from dreaming. Plenty of sunshine this time of year before I light the midnight candle. I've still got miles of burn time before I hit the hay. Get it – hay." Lyra neighed into the phone just as she had done at Foster Point.

"It's improving," Bradlee chuckled in response. "Try not to get a horse voice." More laughter between them.

"I've got a massive paper due tomorrow for one of my classes. Ugh! Pile of work keeps getting higher…! Oh, got my first paper back earlier today, by the way. *A minus*. I'll take it. Gives me some room for improvement – will be a long year ahead…" Lyra laughed with a hint of exasperation.

"Bradlee, sleep well... Have a good dream for me this time, will you?"

Bradlee knew that Lyra was referring to his nightmare at the Lady Slipper Inn.

"I will, Lyra. I sure will… Cheers."

"Cheers back to you," Lyra responded and gave a long sigh breath as she hung up. Newfoundland must be darn cold, she thought. But then she realized she had plans to be in North Dakota in January. The thought conjured an image in her mind of floating on top of an iceberg surrounded by a pod of laughing dolphins in the middle of a vast ocean. Very strange image, she thought, and smiled trying to imagine what Newfoundland really looked like. Then a quick fantasy rushed through her mind as she passed a photo shop on her walk home from the university. She was cozying up to Bradlee inside a tent on top of the iceberg. They unzipped their sleeping bags. They were kissing again. This time without any hesitations. And then the iceberg was melting from the warmth of their bodies and they were both very happy in each other's arms.

Silence again. Bradlee finished the mint tea and turned to his side. He had enjoyed a beautiful day in Newfoundland. Just what he needed followed by a very welcome nightcap chatting with Lyra. Sleep came quickly.

BY THE SEVENTH STRAIGHT DAY WITHOUT SUNSHINE Lyra felt like she could palpate the invisible fog between her hands. If she held her hands apart, barely uncupped, the fog would roll inside between them and serve as resistance, like a repelling magnet. Seattle was absorbed in spongy dank air that refused to dry. Dampness pervaded any piece of clothing she wore to her classes and the fog hovered all morning and into nearly every afternoon. There might be a brief clearing at ground level but it was fleeting as the moisture cycle invariably repeated itself beginning with each overnight's incessant cloud journeys, marching inland from the ocean. There was no escaping from it.

Despite the gray end of October, Lyra continued to maintain her running schedule. Most days she would drop her backpack at her dining room table and head straight to her bedroom after she returned home in the early evening. A tossing off of dampness as she quickly changed into her running clothes, laced her dry pair of shoes and headed out the door. By the end of the rainy-foggy month she had learned to rotate two pair of running shoes to always have one set that was dry – at least for the start of a run. The other would be airing near a heater for use the next day. Today was no different. Just a bit spookier with Halloween decorations throughout the local neighborhoods. The skeletons and skulls added a heavier macabre gloom to the early evening. She was beginning to understand why many could not tolerate the long gray and wet winters. Depression was already being worn on the faces of some of her classmates. And there would be no break in her studies until Thanksgiving. A long three-week stretch of monotony ahead. She needed to run to preserve her optimism. Release the endorphins. Keep fit for a sunny day, whenever that kindness would ever return.

She was pacing herself ever since arriving to Seattle. She had set a personal goal to compete in a half-marathon by spring. Not just compete – she was going to try to win her amateur age group. The goal provided sufficient motivation to remain in top shape and she had noted how her energy and concentration levels were sharply honed in conjunction with the muscular tone in her arms and legs. This evening was a 'mark run' – the term she used to test her current max pace. To mark her progress towards dropping even more time for the half-marathon distance. She knew she wasn't far off from where she needed to be by mid-March.

This afternoon's plan was to follow the usual route through the fog of Union Bay and then continue south past the athletic fields, cross the bridge to Foster Point, and then add a loop south through the arboretum before tracing her route back home – 13.1 miles, precisely. She reset her stopwatch and pressed start as she darted from her front steps. After less than a minute she pushed the pace and accelerated towards the foggy Union Bay trails, past the Central Pond, then Carp Pond, and turned south on Canal Road. As she neared the rowing center she turned to take a brief loop around the Shellhouse Annex and noted about a dozen male rowers readying their boats, stretching their leg muscles and torsos on the deck, and utilizing the stationary flywheels to warm-up. As she rounded the curve one of the rowers was standing in the wooded path. He was considerably taller than Lyra with bulging shoulders emanating from beneath his tight crew shirt. Lyra couldn't deny that he had ruggedly handsome features. Golden brown hair and clean-shaven. She instantly recognized his face as she slowed since he was purposely blocking her path with his arms outstretched as if ready to teasingly catch her in stride. Lyra made the connection quickly – she recalled seeing him shopping in the aisles of the same local market she would frequent near her home over the past month. She recognized the matching boat anchor tattoos on each vein-engorged bicep. Sweat moistened his shirt at the mid-gut which was flat and toned. Lyra had no choice other than to press the pause button on her sport watch and then pull to a quick stop.

"Hey! I think I know you from somewhere," he said. Lyra needed a few more breaths before speaking. "You're quite the runner." He watched her chest rise and fall as she calmed her breathing.

"You look like you're in decent shape yourself," Lyra replied. "You work out a lot?"

"Mostly rowing but, yeah, I hit the weight room pretty hard back at the athletic center."

"You shop at the market on 45th Street, don't you?" Lyra asked.

"Sure do – yeah, that's it! I knew it! You just look different without your day clothes on." He studied her sculpted anatomy as Lyra placed her hands to her hips.

"Say – my fraternity brothers, we're having a little get together tonight for a Halloween Party at the house. Couples date thing. Seniors only. We're kicking everyone else out tonight. I'm still searching for a date and I'm feeling real lucky running into you like this."

"I think I ran into *you*! That's probably a *lot* more

accurate" Lyra replied but her tone was not irritating. She was rusty in the flirting game, face to face. She smiled at him.

"My boat is getting ready to set out on the bay for an hour of muscle motoring. Big regatta next week against Oregon and USC. Pac-12 Conference top-tier placement is on the line. Would you like to meet up after, maybe eight o'clock tonight? The pizza place over on 25th Ave – the one next to the flower shop – is real tasty and low budget enough. You prefer pepperoni or meatballs for toppings? We can split a pie."

"Actually, I'm a vegetarian. Sorry."

"OK then, that's still cool... sort of. I'll order some veges on one half and meats on the other."

"I didn't say yes, yet."

"Oh, OK – then what'll it be?" He folded his muscular arms around his torso and offered Lyra a sultry glance.

Lyra realized she'd be plenty hungry by eight after finishing this run. Halloween parties can be fun.

"All right then. I'll take you up on your offer... Might be good to at least know who I'm having dinner with."

"Yeah, sorry. Name is Matt. And you?"

"Lyra."

"Lyra...? Huh... *weird* name! See you at eight then."

He started walking back towards the rowing house and didn't glance back. Strange. Nearly any guy she met in the past glanced back at least once after walking away from her. Lyra held still observing him for another moment. He went over to some of the rowers preparing the boat oars and started to slap them irritatingly on their heads. They cringed from the blows. Then he turned towards the smallest of the group and lit into him with a foul mouth about something that Lyra could not discern. Probably freshmen getting hazed, Lyra figured. They looked so young to her.

Lyra pressed start again on her watch and sped south

along the trail, returning feverishly to her desired pace. She rounded Foster Point and looked out to the bay as she briefly thought of Bradlee. *Why doesn't he call more often?* It had been another busy few days since their last brief conversation. *He's in Newfoundland! About as far from where I am as Bradlee could be.* She admitted a hint of jealousy for his adventurous lifestyle. She worried if he was really OK and made a note to call him this coming weekend. And then she felt uneasy. A spreading loneliness. She had made a few friends in her classes but nothing that quite clicked yet. She was just too busy studying to enjoy a relaxing evening on the town and she wasn't the bar-hopping kind of grad student. Matt was probably a senior at the university. Maybe a year or two younger than her, at most. Some attention from a guy for a change of pace – might be nice... A simple night to meet new friends could be just what she needed to break up the monotony of her days and this languorous weather. Lyra turned her back to Foster Point and accelerated to the bridge crossing. She turned south to complete the arboretum loop before racing home. She stopped her watch timer. *Eighty nine minutes on the nose!* She was pleased – 6:48 minutes per mile pace. *That would do for now.* She knew she had plenty of power remaining in her legs for the future. And she had just earned some pizza.

Lyra showered, dried and curled her hair at the margins, and opened her closet door. *What to wear?* She didn't have a Halloween costume and she really didn't feel like wearing one anyway. She pulled out some hangers and rummaged through her dresser. She tried on various mixes and settled on a mid-thigh cream skirt and satiny black pullover blouse. She painted some rouge on her cheeks and added a few eyeliner whiskers below her nose. That would be enough of a costume, she figured, for a grad student.

Matt was already inside at the bar when Lyra arrived to

the pizza place. He had a pint of lager draft beer half-downed in his right hand. He was in jeans and a white cotton T-shirt. She stepped past the hostess and tapped on Matt's back. He turned.

"Hey Laura! Great to see you!" He eyed her outfit. "Nice whiskers. Mouse?"

"More guinea pig – I prefer them… It's *Lyra*, by the way – not Laura."

"Got you."

There was a single yellow rose laying on the table next to him. Lyra glanced at it. Matt picked it up and handed it to her. "Oh, sorry – I got you this from the flower shop next door. Hope you like it. They were out of red but I liked yellow, anyway." He handed the rose to Lyra who sniffed and stood holding it while glancing at the crowd.

"These here are some of my frat buddies." Matt introduced Lyra and they chatted over the ever rising noise at the stand-up bar tables. The pizzas arrived and Lyra was famished. She devoured three vegetarian slices with a half-pint of a pale ale local draft beer. Matt ate the rest of the pie and some more pepperoni slices from the platters served to his fraternity brothers. He encouraged Lyra to have another beer but she was already bloated.

After dinner was consumed, Matt chimed in. "OK, everyone, ante up. Let's take this party to the house!" He reached his palm out towards Lyra and she opened her purse, located her wallet and contributed a ten dollar bill. The group proceeded back to the frat house a few blocks away. Matt and his buddies periodically looked back to add Lyra into the friendly chit-chat but the comradery challenged her natural shyness.

Not everyone had a date. The large main room at the fraternity house was decked out with dry ice machines steaming vapor from the floor. There were decorative skulls and skeletons strung from the window frames and other Halloween paraphernalia in the hallway and bathroom. The place reeked of fermented beer and Lyra felt her flats sticking to the floor like chewing gum. A beer keg was set onto the foldable bar flap with a pink punch bowl beside it. Lyra excused herself to use the restroom. When she returned Matt had two plastic cups filled with ice and punch. He handed her one and they clinked them together. Matt guzzled and then shook his head from the ice cold brain freeze ache that ensued while Lyra took a few sips of the concentrated vodka punch. They chatted for a few more minutes before Lyra found a seat as Matt made the rounds catching up with some of his fraternity brothers. He'd periodically glance back at Lyra to check that she was still there. Lyra felt awkward. The party wasn't what she was expecting. She felt old now. A misfit among young boys now that her mind had switched channels to grad school and career ambitions. She wished Bradlee would walk through the door and whisk her away. She rose and started for the front door.

"Wait, wait, wait – not so fast." Matt chased after her and grasped Lyra's shoulder from behind. "You just got here. Come on – give me a chance now. I'm sorry. I got distracted by some of my buddies. We were talking shop about the regatta next weekend. Happy to have you come by and watch it if you have the time. Cheer us on, you know. Husky pride. We've got a great chance to win this thing outright!" he yelled behind him towards his teammates as they started to bark and howl in response. Matt removed his hand from Lyra's shoulder and Lyra turned towards him.

"Hey, I'd like to show you the frat house. Care for a tour?"

"Sure, but I think I'll be heading out afterwards. I've got some more studying ahead of me tonight."

"Sure thing. Whatever it is you're into here for your degree."

After four years of attending various fraternity parties in

college, Lyra wasn't at all interested in seeing the inside of yet another – but maybe things looked different on the west coast, she wondered.

He brought Lyra down the hallway and then up a flight of stairs. The place smelled musty to Lyra. A few dirty shirts and snack wrappers adorned the upstairs hallway.

"My place is down here to the right. Want to show you this cool lava lamp – retro 60's thing my cousin sent me last winter. I can stare at it all night." Matt held her hand as he opened the lock to his bedroom door and shut the door behind them. It was cramped inside with a futon along one side wall and shelving, a refrigerator, and desk on the other. There was a wardrobe in the corner stuffed with sports equipment. Typical tight dormitory space, Lyra thought. Nothing at all different from frat houses out east.

"Now look here." Matt reached for the lava lamp and handed it to her to hold. It was emitting globs of volcanic red goo from the base, creating the usual formations she had seen plenty of times before. Matt took a few steps and stood behind Lyra. He whispered into her ear. "I know how to make really good lava love, Lyra. The best you've ever had." He gripped her left hand forcefully. His right hand reached under Lyra's skirt and squeezed her buttocks.

"What are you doing?" Lyra attempted to break her left hand free from his grip but Matt refused. He started to kiss on her neck and then held his hands forcefully around Lyra's waist and then groped at her breasts. Lyra winced in pain as she tried to fend him off.

"Stop it, Matt!" Lyra's voice grew louder but he continued to grope. He picked up Lyra with a sudden push downward against her torso. Lyra was flung into his arms and he dropped her onto his futon. Then he tried to hold her legs in place. He pulled and lifted her shirt, tearing a seam at the shoulder, and then mounted his body on top of her pelvis, his legs scissoring Lyra's into a wrestler's hold.

"Get off me, Matt! Get off!" she screamed.

He ripped her underwear off from beneath her skirt and she felt a stinging pain from the elastic snapping against her vulva. He pulled down his jeans while holding her legs as she slapped at him to defend herself.

"Get off! Somebody help me!!!! Please! Help!!!"

Lyra screamed as loud as she could before he cupped his left hand over her mouth. She was muffled briefly but then she bit his hand and he withdrew it and stared momentarily at his bleeding palm and wiped the blood on her shirt. Then he stared at her menacingly and slapped her across the face with his bloodied hand.

"Don't you say another word or I'll really beat you!" as he lifted his right fist above her. Lyra turned her head to the side and cringed. She was crying now.

"Somebody help me!!!" she screamed again.

The next blow came with a right hook. His fist struck her left eye and the bridge of her nose and she felt a searing pain to the side of her head and upper eyelid. She screamed again and whimpered.

"Don't move or I'll hit you even harder!" he yelled at her.

"Somebody help me!!! I'm being raped!!!"

He pulled her legs apart and was ready to enter her.

The door to the room flung open at that moment.

"What's going on in here?!" A man yelled while staring at Matt.

"Matt, get off her now!" Lyra glanced at the man. He was a giant, at least a foot taller than Matt and he must have weighed three-hundred pounds with massive muscles to his upper torso, arms and thighs.

"Matt, what the *fuck* are you doing man?"

He pulled Matt by the collar and flung him into the dresser and then punched him hard in the gut. Matt fell to the ground.

"She wanted it, Carl! She asked me to do it with her. The bitch loves jocks."

Lyra was lying in the fetal position, whimpering. A metallic taste was flowing across her tongue. She touched her lip and noticed the blood.

The man turned to Lyra. "He was raping me," Lyra whimpered.

"You need to get out of here right now! I'm sorry this happened. I'll take care of this asshole. And I promise you I'm going to see that this dude never even thinks about trying this again – on any woman! My sister was raped in college. I nearly killed that guy. He's going to pay – real hard now. You have my word on that."

The man had rage in his face as he turned towards Matt and lifted him off the ground by merely using one hand around his neck. Lyra quickly stood and lowered her skirt. She grabbed the lava lamp and smashed it on the floor and watched the red liquid ooze out like a river towards where Matt was clutched in Carl's grip. She found her purse and ran out of the room and down the hallway, her hands trembling. Tears flowing. Heavy sobs and gasps for air. She located the stairway and guided her legs down the stairs while holding onto the banister and then escaped past the party room and out the front door. She made it one block. It was dark outside and quiet. The storefronts had already shut for the night. She sat down on the sidewalk in front of a lit store window in a haze of fear and pain. She was shivering. Blood still filling her mouth from the cut to her upper lip. She touched above her left eye and winced from the swelling pain.

A stranger stopped and stooped over on both knees.

"Are you OK, my child?" she asked Lyra in a soft tone. Lyra was frozen. Words just wouldn't come.

"You look terrible. Let me help you."

The woman lifted Lyra to her feet and wrapped her light winter coat around Lyra. She brought Lyra to her car that was parked nearby along the street and opened the door.

"Here, sit here in the backseat. I think you may need to

go to the hospital." The woman paused as Lyra stood defiantly at the car door without answering.

"Please talk to me... Do you speak English?"

"Please—— just take me *home*. Can you take me home now?" Lyra found her voice between frightened sobs. "I'll be alright. I don't think I'll need an emergency room. *Please* take me home," Lyra pleaded.

The woman squeezed Lyra's hand gently. She was able to extract Lyra's address from her before Lyra settled into the backseat and laid on her side. She continued to sob in spasms of pain and fear. The ride went by quickly without another word exchanged between them.

"We're here now." The woman parked her car in front of Lyra's home and exited. "Take my hand. Come on."

Lyra was continuing to whimper in between waves of tears. As Lyra arose the woman gave Lyra a steady hug.

"You're safe now. You're safe... The key?" They walked the path to the front door. Lyra pointed to the flower pot and the woman opened the front door, turned on the lights, and escorted Lyra to the living room couch. She went to the bathroom and brought two hand towels to the kitchen. She wet the first with cold water and wrapped the second with ice cubes from the freezer. She returned to the living room and cleaned Lyra's face gently with the cool washcloth, removing the blood from her cheeks and lip. The internal lip wound had already clotted but she was very gentle, being careful not to cause Lyra any more pain. She placed the ice cloth to Lyra's left eye. Lyra winced but she grasped it and held it in place.

"I'm a nurse. I just finished my evening shift at the children's hospital and was walking home when I found you on the sidewalk. I'm sorry this happened to you, Ms. ..."

"It's Lyra. Thank you for taking care of me."

Lyra began to sob once again. The woman held Lyra to her chest, wrapping her arms around her gently, and then she rocked Lyra like a newborn. The trauma was raw and unforgiving. Lyra held onto her and continued fits of sobbing until there were no more tears that could possibly flow. She began to quiet as the woman sang her a soft lullaby tune in Spanish. Somehow it seemed familiar to Lyra and it was very soothing. The hour passed in silence.

"I will need to head home now to my husband and my twins. They'll be worried about me. Will you be OK, Lyra? Are you all alone in this big house?" The woman looked around the room and down the hallway.

"Yes. But I think I'll be alright for now. Thank you. You are an angel… What's your name?"

"It's Angel." The woman laughed softly.

"Seriously?" Lyra was able to offer a hint of a smile.

"Yes. Angel Rodriguez, sweetie. That's who I try to be." She gave Lyra a big smile and another hug. "Please take care of yourself. You should see a doctor tomorrow morning to check on your injuries. The police should know about this tomorrow as well unless you were ——" She paused and looked away with a few tears of her own.

"Were you raped, Lyra? Because then you will need the emergency room and the police involved as soon as possible."

Lyra's eyes welled with tears again.

"No, he hit me hard. He tried to. But someone else stopped him…"

Lyra began to sob again and couldn't speak further. The memory was too raw and intense.

"Shh… settle down now." Angel held Lyra's hand gently and wiped her eyes with the cloth. "You need to shower and get some rest. I'm going to leave now. Lock up, please, behind me." Angel walked over to the kitchen and found a piece of paper and pen and scribbled.

"Here, this is my phone number. Please call me tomorrow. You need your privacy but I'm here to help you, Lyra, if you need or want to talk some more… if you need a friend. I don't live far away."

"Thank you, Angel."

She rose to depart. Lyra stood and escorted Angel to the front door. They hugged again and Lyra felt a kinship towards her that she couldn't quite place.

She noticed a small and delicate gold pendant hanging from Angel's necklace as Lyra handed Angel her winter coat. It was in the shape of a hummingbird. Angel departed down the path to her car. Lyra locked the front door securely and slumped to the ground, her back to the door. She began to cry inconsolably again as she held her hand to her swollen left eye.

She had fallen asleep for some time. Lyra pulled herself up and walked to her bedroom. She tore off her clothes and entered the shower and scrubbed her body with her soap bar. She grabbed the luffa sponge. She felt disgustingly dirty. As if toxic mud had seeped into her pores and she needed to decontaminate from a life-threatening contagion. She scrubbed everywhere she could reach. Added more soap and repeated it again from head to toe. Her skin burned from the luffa's roughness but she didn't care. She was clean. She dried and found a pair of pajamas and dressed. She sat on her bed and was too afraid to lay down. She got up and walked to the kitchen and made a cup of mint tea. Maybe it would help calm her. She glanced at the bloody towels that Angel left soaking in a soapy Tupperware in the kitchen sink. She returned to her bathroom. She touched her left eyelid and upper lip and then looked in the bathroom mirror. There was already a massive bruise forming over the entire left eyebrow and eyelid and her lip was swollen and meaty. Skin was scraped off the left side of her nose. She looked awful.

Lyra picked up her phone. It was just after midnight. She located Ansley's contact information, dialed and waited. It went to voicemail. She texted instead:

Please call me ASAP URGENT!

Lyra stared at her phone waiting for a response. It arrived.

One sec need to find a quiet spot

Lyra's phone rang a minute later.

"Lyra, so good to hear from you, my bestest friend! You settling into life in Seattle? Big change! West Coast life is awesome, isn't it?!"

Ansley didn't quite understand Lyra's urgency.

"Ansley, can you come here. I need someone to be with me. I've had a rough night. I got really beat up by a guy at a Halloween party."

Ansley was in San Francisco. She had moved to the Bay area with her boyfriend after high school graduation. They attended Berkeley together and then, she and Charles were each accepted to grad school programs at the university. Ansley continued into the law school while Charles was enrolled in the Ph.D. program in physics. But she and Lyra remained very close despite the distance during their college years and both looked forward to making the time for more frequent visits to each other now that they were just a short flight away.

Lyra could hear live jazz music playing in the background.

"Oh no! I think so. Lyra, that's *terrible*...! You know I love you girl. Let me check on flights. Give me a few minutes and I will call you back. Stay by your phone. OK, Lyra?"

"Yes, I will."

Ansley heard Lyra sobbing before she hung up. She quickly searched on her phone for flights to Seattle and located one that would be leaving in just over an hour.

She texted Lyra a copy of the flight itinerary and then wrote:

Lyra I'm coming soon. You be brave for me OK? Just as you have always been!
Lyra texted back:
I will be. THANKS Ansley - I love you too!

Ansley waved to her girlfriends in the club. It was girls' night out and she was enjoying herself. She motioned and pointed towards her phone screen while signaling that she had an urgent call. She ran into the street, hailed a taxi and directed the driver to speed to the airport. She made the flight just in time and landed in Seattle. It was 3 a.m. She texted Lyra as she ran to the sleepy taxi line.

Arrived. Lyra - Text me back now that you're OK.
Will be there soon.
Taxi on its way now.

Lyra heard the ping next to her teary damp pillow case. She was in a sleepy fog but typed:
I'm OK. Thanks. BE SAFE.

THE STONE POLISHER WAS BECOMING an enjoyable toy for Bradlee despite the steady grinding noise. It was plugged into the wall socket for the past three days inside his woodworking studio beside the garage and tumbling stones ever since he returned from Newfoundland. His creative juices were flowing on the return trip back from Gros Morne to the Marshpillow. He knew the brief trip had cured his mental fatigue and irritability from his long hours at work on the photography exhibit. An idea was developing from inside the depths of his heart. It was a feeling he had not been open to for many years. As if a key was turning and out flew the dark and scary goblins, now replaced by light, puffy clouds and rainbows. All he could think about was to create something special, a gift for Lyra for her birthday or for the winter holidays, whichever came first. He didn't even know when her birthday was. He just couldn't stop thinking about her. Maybe it was irrational given the distance but he couldn't deny how he felt. Something that just clicked every time he spoke with her, which wasn't often enough. He should call Lyra more often but didn't know what was best these past few months with the distance between them.

On the journey home from Newfoundland he resolved to ask Lyra if she would be willing to at least try to set a schedule to chat with him a few times each week. Maybe it could work out between them if they both wanted it to. If they could be patient. He knew that words over the phone created images, as if she was beside him, walking, holding hands along a shore or along a mountain path, or perhaps chasing him – or would it be him chasing her – along a wind-swept bicycle ride. Laughter. Good times in his imagination.

He had arisen early the next morning after his last night tent-camping at Green Point when he had last spoken with Lyra. He packed his gear into his car, strapped a small day pack onto his shoulders, and set out onto the adjacent coastal trail. The trail passed through a section of thick pine forest that covered a bluff overlooking the shoreline. Then it descended onto a section of beach strewn with driftwood pieces, volcanic rocks, and seashells. A rainbow of colors that gleamed as they were wetted by the ocean waves.

He collected a handful of stones into his hands and studied them. Some were sparkled and roughened while others were like the softness of formed clay pounded by the hands of a young child. Each stone had its beauty. Its uniqueness. Never were two the same just as the array of seashells beside them. He strolled and climbed and jostled through the slippery rocks – giant boulder fields intermixed with juveniles, as if the giants had birthed countless offspring and skipped them to the shore. Gifts to Poseidon, ruler of the seas, if the emperor was inclined to enjoy a day at the beach. As the tide ebbed the stones and seashells dried and the colors drained to a bare resemblance of their former water-embalmed majesty. He collected an assortment of the volcanic rock specimens and deposited them into his backpack until his shoulders could bare no more.

He moved on to seashells – white slippers, dog whelks, cockles, turrets, Atlantic surf clams, oyster drills, and even a few broken channeled whelks. He was finished collecting and inspecting and cleaning and he turned to depart from the blustery beach to continue along the trail. And there it was, lying humbly beside a shining emerald seaweed strand. He retrieved the delicate shell into his palm and studied it for any sign of a living inhabitant as he rinsed it in the shore waves. It was empty. He beamed with awareness. It was a Harp Lora. '*Oenopota harpularius*,' he recited to himself. It was a magnificently intact specimen. The color of Italian marble. The kind the great masters requested for their sculptures. Bernini's masterpiece – Apollo and Daphne – the sculpture he admired and sketched countless times at the Uffizi in Florence, rushed into his mind now. Lyra – the harp. The harp shell was resting as if it was the head of a goddess. The streaming strands of flowing seaweed emanating behind it. Daphne. Lyra. *Is it a sign from the heavens?* Bradlee rested on a boulder and peered at the ocean. Lyra was thousands of miles away along another shore but she was becoming nestled inside his heart and enveloping its beating chambers. He gently squeezed the harp shell in his palm. Tears came now. He was healing from the pain that he had sequestered inside these many years. It was rushing from him now like the waves in retreat. *Let it go*, he whispered to himself. *Let it go*. And so he sat on a large boulder for a long time along the shore, tears and solitude and thought until he released Sami to the ocean and the clouds and the heavens above. He let the pain of Sami go and then he realized that what remained behind, deeply within him, was pure and genuine. Pure love and kindness. An eternal light. And he knew this light would reside permanently within his very being. To light his way.

When he was finally ready to move on, he arose from the boulder. The trail continued south through wildflower fields and marshland and around a few lily ponds before exiting at the terminus onto the roadway. He thumbed a short ride back to his car at the Green Point campground, deposited his small pack, laden with stones and seashells, into the trunk and drove south. He wanted to visit someone who Uncle Eddie mentioned when Bradlee saw his uncle at the church in Minot.

'*Perhaps you may want to take a vacation to Newfoundland when you need one, and visit Leo, a good friend of mine, a fellow woodcarver. I think you two would have a lot in common to share,*' his uncle said to him then.

Bradlee turned off the highway and continued to the parking lot at Lobster Cove Head. He explored the lighthouse at the point and walked down to the water's edge. More massive boulders interspersed with shards of jagged striated rock formations, some laden with dried brown seaweed strands that seemed to serve as a perfect complement to the blue water. *Nature's glory.* The waves gently lapping at the rocks. A calmness he felt within that hadn't really been present in a long time. Infinite balance of softness with hardness, colors with plain grays. *Harmony.* That was the best word he could think of to explain what his eyes could see. Today, he was an observer. He didn't always need a camera in his hands to document these scenes. This morning his eyes and his mind were conspiring to convince his heart what he already had been coming to realize these past many weeks... *I'm falling in love with Lyra.*

He returned to his car and rolled the windows down. The coolness bit at his cheeks but he was enjoying all the elements of nature. The sun and the stones and the marshes and the pines, the waters and the winds. The winds guided him around the East Arm of Bonne Bay before turning west and arriving to Woody Point. There was a small strip of artisan galleries, shops, and restaurants. Some closed for the approaching winter, others with their doors open as a welcome invitation to the gentle ocean breezes. Bradlee parked and picked up some lunch along Water Street for his afternoon hike to the apex of 'Lookout Hills Trail.' One of the galleries had its front door open. An appealing wooden crafted sign was mounted beside the door. The words were intricately chiseled and then stained a golden hue:

~שא—— *Ash Woods Gallery* ——שא~

There was a younger man, perhaps similar to Bradlee's age, turning a raw block of wood attached to a large lathe. The high-pitched whorl from the belt was familiar to Bradlee from turning wood on his own lathe in his woodcarving studio at the Marshpillow. The man had his back turned to Bradlee as the lathe was arranged in front of a wide bank of windows overlooking Bonne Bay. Bradlee stared and admired the view. The air was permeated by the smell of wood varnishes and stains despite the open doors and windows. There were various clumpings of raw wood in one section. Some intricately carved wood pieces were hanging, drying from the ceiling in another corner. A young girl was sitting off to the right in what looked to Bradlee like an old-fashioned homemade school classroom chair and desk. She was dipping her paintbrush into a watercolor set and delicately painting brush strokes onto a canvas.

"Hi there!" Bradlee called out. He rang a small bell that

was dangling on the inside of the door and noticed that there was a beautiful wood carved mezuzah fastened to the doorpost. The man flicked a switch and the lathe came to a stop. He turned towards Bradlee, his right hand holding a sturdy carbide turning tool. He was wearing a well-worn apron and thick silicone orange gloves. He had long brown hair that descended along his back and was gathered by a hair band. His temples were ever slightly graying. He started towards Bradlee.

"Good day. Welcome to my shop. You can have a look about if you'd like. The name is Leo Ash. Good to meet you."

"Thanks. Bradlee Lee." Leo removed his right glove and they shook hands. "I do a little wood turning and carving myself back home. You have some beautiful pieces here." Bradlee stared at a large finished piece hanging on the wall. It was an oval shaped mirror with an intricately carved wood pattern surrounding its edges.

"That one is all hand carved. Alder wood. No machine touched those grains" Leo offered. "A few hundred hours of work on that one. Hate to part with her but if you're interested I can give you a bit of a better price than what's marked. We're into slow season now with the coming winter." He gleamed with pride as Bradlee stroked the mirror frame.

"Your technique resembles the work of my uncle in Toronto. He mentioned you to me a few months ago when I last saw him. That was back in North Dakota. Long story for another time, maybe… My uncle told me that there was a young man named Leo Ash who had attended a workshop some years ago that he had offered over in St. John's for beginning woodcarvers and you were the finest student of them all. You had that passion and drive to learn and that you had genuine God-given talent. He said you two had hit it off real well as teacher and student and became close friends over the years. My uncle suggested I visit you here in Newfoundland. Said he thought you and I might have a lot in common to share... Anyway, I was in the area on a short vacation these past few days and so here I am. Sorry for not calling before dropping in."

"*Rabbi Eliezer Levitsky!!!*" Leo shouted with a gleam in his eyes. "Well, what do you know?! Small world meeting you here in Woody Point! He's your uncle?!... And North Dakota, of all places! Would sure like to here more about that place. Never been myself. Boy, your uncle sure gets around, doesn't he?! He's an amazing artist. I learned everything I could from him. Still am, but mostly by video chat over the past few years. We share ideas and he is always offering me tips and recommendations... Honestly, I feel like a disciple of your uncle." Leo laughed heartily. "Your uncle is one of the finest people I've ever met. He's been my mentor for a lot of years. This shop was just a dream of mine when I was a teenager. It wouldn't exist now without your uncle's guidance and confidence that he instilled in me. It's a pleasure to have you here, Bradlee."

They chatted for a short while longer filling in some details of their lives. Leo showed Bradlee some of the other finished works in the shop. Then he demonstrated a handful of shop tools that Bradlee was not familiar with. Making a new friend felt good, Bradlee thought. And his uncle was right, he realized. He and Leo did share a lot in common, starting with their respect and love for Uncle Eddie.

"Daddy, who is this man in our shop?" The little girl stopped painting briefly at her school desk and glanced towards Leo and Bradlee.

"Oh, you two haven't met yet? This here is my daughter, Ruthy. She's all but seven years old but she helps me run the place now." He smiled at his daughter who gave him a toothy nose-scrunching grin. She returned to her painting.

"Bradlee, not too many visitors have passed through Woody Point in the past month. Most of the other shops have already closed for the season. I'm working on some large decorative pieces now for a few fancy hotels in Halifax. Pays my mortgage until the tourists return in the spring. Well, I'd love to chat more but I need to continue working at the lathe for a little while longer. Please look around more, if you'd like. Happy to meet up with you in a few hours if your plans allow for more time here."

"I'd like that," Bradlee said. He browsed further as Leo returned to the lathe. An asymmetrically shaped wood piece caught Bradlee's attention on the bottom of one of the display shelves. He held it up. It was made from maple wood and he noted that the grain was richly stained with a color that Bradlee thought resembled dark amber maple syrup. Bradlee's mind flashed to the train ride. Lyra's comment about her favorite dinner – *pancakes with maple syrup, Grade A dark amber.*' There were two darker oval-shaped knotty burls embedded in the turned wood as if the bowl had its own set of eyes. His finger pads felt their softened polished texture. The burls resembled a bird's eyes, he thought. He checked the sticker price at the base and winced. Two hundred and twenty dollars. His finances were tightening over the past number of months. He knew he had been spending far more than he was receiving from his work and his personal account was dwindling. But he just knew that Lyra would really like the pattern and design and feel of this bowl. And the dark amber maple syrup stain. He held it in his hands as he continued to stroll around the shop and then walked over to where Ruthy was painting and observed her for a minute.

"That's quite a nice selection of colors, Ruthy. What are you painting?"

"Thanks mister. It's the Tablelands," Ruthy replied. "The pancake flat mountains near here." Bradlee chuckled at the coincidence of her description as he held the maple bowl carefully in his hands.

"Where did you learn how to paint so beautifully?"

"My mommy. She showed me how to paint with

watercolors. She said my hands were like hers. A blessing to make people happy."

"Does your mom work at the shop too?" Bradlee asked her.

"No. She's up in the clouds now. And Rachel said that when she gets home soon she's going to take me on a hike to the Tablelands again. She doesn't mind it if I want to visit my mom. Rachel says that we're very blessed to live in such a beautiful place where my mom will always be too."

Bradlee tried to absorb what Ruthy meant. His gut understood. "I see. Well, your mother must have loved you a great deal. And I would certainly agree with Rachel. Newfoundland is a very beautiful place to live."

"What's your name, mister?" Ruthy asked him. She had returned to working her watercolor canvas with delicate strokes. She had just begun to fill in the sky with wisps of cumulus clouds. Bradlee admired her talent at such a young age. Then he noticed that Ruthy was wearing a necklace. A small silver Jewish star was attached and dangling from her neck.

Bradlee paused and thought about his name. *Who am I? A child deserves an honest reply.*

"Can you keep a secret?" he asked her in a whisper while putting on a serious face.

"Fingers crossed." She held up her hands to show him. "Sure can," she whispered back.

"My name is really *Baruch*. It means 'Blessing.' But I also go by *Bradlee*."

"That's neat. Nice to meet you, Baruch... ata Adonai..." She started giggling as she continued to recite more of the beginning phrase of a Jewish blessing.

"You too, Ruthy" and he laughed with her as he patted her gently on the top of her head before turning and browsing a few more minutes. Then, he stood at the register. Ruthy rose from her chair and brought over some gift paper. She wrapped the maple bowl for Bradlee before returning to her watercolor.

Leo stopped the lathe once again and walked over to the register. He checked the price of the maple bowl, winked at Bradlee with a friendly smile, and proceeded to mark down the price by fifty-percent. The bell on the doorway chimed as the credit card transaction completed.

"Bradlee, please stay for dinner if you can" Leo announced more loudly as he glanced towards the door.

"And who am I adding a plate for dinner tonight?" Bradlee turned around. A young woman was standing in the doorway and smiling with her hands on her hips.

"Rachel!" Ruthy stopped painting and ran over to the woman as fast as she could and wrapped her arms around her waist. Rachel lifted her up and kissed her cheeks repeatedly. "Hi, sweet angel. Good to be home again." Leo joined them and kissed Rachel gently on the lips while staring into her eyes. They touched forehead to forehead for a few intense seconds.

"Welcome home my love, I've really missed you," Bradlee heard Leo whisper into Rachel's ear.

"*We* really missed you," Ruthy corrected her daddy. They turned towards Bradlee and he noticed that Rachel was wearing a wooden-banded engagement ring with a small diamond set at the top.

"Bradlee, this is my fiancée, Rachel. We are to be married this spring." Leo nuzzled her neck as she handed Ruthy into Leo's arms.

"Can we go now, Rachel?" Ruthy pleaded.

"I just got home, Ruthy."

"Please…!"

"Let's see. It's two o'clock. The Tablelands is a long day hike. We're going to need to leave early in the morning tomorrow, my love, if we want to visit with the clouds. But how about if we hike to the top of Lookout Mountain this afternoon instead? We haven't been up there in awhile."

"But that's a lot of steps!" Ruthy pouted.

Bradlee chimed in. "I was planning to hike the same Lookout Hills Trail myself just now to the very top. My guidebook says it's a spectacular spot. I can carry Ruthy if she needs a boost from time to time. No worries."

"Cool with me," Leo added. "I've got a few more hours of work to do at the lathe on this piece." Leo turned towards Rachel. She had an awkward face.

"Bradlee here is Rabbi Eliezer Levitsky's nephew. The man I told you about who is my woodcarving mentor."

Rachel's eyes lit. "Well, why didn't you say so?! Nice of you to visit us here, Bradlee. It's a bit off the beaten path. Leo has told me some wonderful things about your uncle's woodcarving."

"Oh, almost forgot" Leo walked over to the doorpost. "The mezuzah here…… that was a gift from your uncle when I opened my shop."

"Did Leo tell you that your uncle introduced us to each other?" Rachel asked.

Bradlee raised his eyebrows in surprise.

"Well, he wasn't physically present when we met" Leo replied. "Bradlee, your uncle knows Rachel's family quite well. In fact, he prepared Rachel for her Bat-Mitzvah some years ago. They are from Toronto as well – they belong to the same temple as where your uncle serves as a part-time rabbi. So when your uncle heard that Rachel's family was planning a vacation trip to Newfoundland about six months ago, he called me up and, with Rachel's permission, I contacted her. Your uncle thought Rachel and I might be a good fit for each other and, well, honestly I was ready to meet someone to have a relationship again after…" Leo paused and his eyes turned away and studied the lathe before he composed himself. Rachel squeezed his hand.

"Rachel and her family stopped by the shop and, well, I looked at her and she looked at me, and well… we just knew there was something that just clicked. I don't know.

Something that would last between us until the end."

Leo smiled at Rachel and then continued. "How does anyone know why? It just is. So, by the end of her vacation week here at Gros Morne with her family, we just knew we shared a special bond. And so here we are, six months later..." Leo cuddled Rachel and kissed the top of her head.

"It's called *being in love*, Leo. Gosh, you are a terrible word mincer! And you don't have to tell everyone our *whole* story, do you?!" Rachel giggled and then kissed Leo on the lips.

"OK, to the top of Lookout Hills trail it is!" Rachel announced. "Troops, be ready in five minutes!"

Rachel kissed Leo again, this time a lot longer, ran out the door, jumped in her car, and sped down the street a short way to their small home. She brought her suitcase inside and set the groceries in the refrigerator and cabinets. Ruthy rolled up her watercolor at the shop and placed it inside a small cardboard tube. She stuffed the tube and her small paint set and brushes into her backpack, added a water bottle, and laced up her sneakers. Then she opened her desktop and carefully withdrew a small framed photograph that was laying inside and placed it into a zippered pocket of her pack. Bradlee went to his car, packed his lunch and other items into his day pack, and returned to the shop. Rachel rejoined Bradlee and Ruthy and the three hikers proceeded briefly down the road and turned at the entrance to the trailhead.

They met some resistance initially. The trail passed through sodden grassy fields with percolating rivulets that trickled from a swollen stream as it wound its way carving a path through the mountain. The footpath continued along the side of the stream. The gurgling and whooshing sounds from the stream, meandering through reeds and around boulders, were like a musical concert for Bradlee. He raised his hands as if he were a conductor and play-acted to Ruthy until she giggled feverishly. The trail opened and passed through fields clumped with tall amber grasses enjoying the afternoon breeze. Wildflowers were enticing bees. They passed remains of wild blueberry plants and Bradlee wished his visit could have been in summer when the blueberries were ripe and ready for mass consumption. Rachel spotted a moose in the distance and they all held still, silently observing its massive antlers. Hawks circled periodically above them.

They arrived to the stairway. All Bradlee could see were wooden steps that seemed to climb to the sky ahead of them. He turned towards Ruthy who already had her arms raised with a puckered face.

"OK Ruthy, I gave you my word," Bradlee said with a smile. He lifted Ruthy and placed her legs onto his shoulders as she straddled his neck.

"Giddy up horsee!" she blurted loudly.

"Oh really?" Bradlee replied as he neighed and then bent backwards to frighten Ruthy. She giggled instead while covering Bradlee's eyes with her hands. She wanted to play peek-a-boo with him and he obliged her.

"Now Ruthy, be nice," Rachel chimed in. "There's more than a few hundred steps to the top. When I say so I expect you to walk at least a few of those on your own." She glared at Ruthy who scrunched her nose. Bradlee hadn't held a child in quite a long time. Years, actually. He had avoided family get-togethers and holidays for the past number of years. He imagined many of his little cousins would have probably forgotten about him by now.

They were close to the apex as the stairs wound, tracing the edge of the mountain. Bradlee's shoulders were burning as he shifted Ruthy's weight from side to side.

"OK angel, time for your porter to place the princess down," Rachel called out. Bradlee set Ruthy on the steps and massaged his shoulders and slurped at his water bottle.

"Even a horsee has to drink sometimes," he said while neighing at Ruthy.

"Last one to the top is a rotten tomato sauce!" Ruthy shouted. She nudged Bradlee and then started to race up the steps.

"Hey, no fair!" Bradlee cried out.

"*Sauce?*" Bradlee turned towards Rachel.

"Have no idea where she got that from?" Rachel said, and then they chased after Ruthy.

They were laughing in stitches by the time they reached the apex of Lookout Mountain. Ruthy was already unpacking her small backpack and starting into her energy bar. She opened the cardboard tube and pulled out her watercolor, paint set and brushes and added a few drops of water to the till. She sat in one of the large Muskoka chairs on the platform and peered at the view and then up to the sky. Bradlee and Rachel arrived triumphantly a few minutes later.

Bradlee stepped onto the platform.

"Wow!" There was no better word to describe the magnitude of beauty that greeted him. It was the most beautiful view he had ever seen.

There was Bonne Bay in all its glory stretching out to the ocean beyond. To the east was the grandeur of Gros Morne Mountain. He turned to admire the snow dusted Tablelands to the south. He took it all in as he slowly turned in a full circle and raised his arms outward. If there was truly a Creator, Bradlee thought, then he was standing before one of her finest works she could have ever fashioned in all the universe. *Only a woman could have birthed such magnificent beauty!*

And then his mind turned immediately to what his heart already knew: *Lyra, I wish you were here with me to witness this awe. Someday*, he thought.

"Bradlee, if you don't mind looking after Ruthy for just a bit, I'm going to head a little ways further. Just a few minutes and I'll be back. I enjoy seeing the view from that ridge top over there." She pointed as Bradlee acknowledged it. He opened his daypack and started into his sandwich. He couldn't take his eyes off the view for very long.

Ruthy was studying the sky and carefully dipping her brush into the paint wells. Bradlee observed her as she added varying tones of gray and pink highlights to the undersides of her clouds.

"She's inside these clouds." Ruthy elevated her left arm and pointed her fingers towards the clouds hovering over Bonne Bay. "Mommy told me that's where she'll always be and all I need to do is to look up when I go outside and I'll find her smiling back at me." She continued to mix colors with drops of water until she found the right match to her liking.

"Do you see her, Baruch? She's right over there——" Ruthy pointed skyward.

Bradlee swallowed his sandwich bite. He looked towards where Ruthy was pointing and stared silently. Then he felt tears streaming down his cheeks. They made their way to the angles of his mouth and the salty flavor lingered there. He tried to regain his ability to speak.

"I see her, Ruthy. I really do" he whispered to Ruthy and then he ran his fingers gently through her hair. "Your mother is very beautiful. And she does love you very much."

"Not everyone can see her in the clouds. Only special ones. That must mean that you are special, Baruch. Mommy also told me that only the special ones are strong enough to love someone else after we can't see them anymore here where we live. That's why I love Rachel too. I know she's not my real mommy who gave birth to me. But I do love her. And I know my daddy really loves her too."

Bradlee didn't know what to say. Ruthy was wise beyond her little years. A child her age shouldn't need to know so much about life and death. He turned away as more tears flowed until he was able to control the spigot once again. He sniffled a bit and Ruthy turned her head towards him.

"You are sad. Is someone you love in the clouds too? Can you see?" Ruthy asked him.

"Yes, I do. Just over there." Bradlee pointed to a different cloud formation.

"You're right, Ruthy. When you love someone it never has to end... Loving never ends."

Ruthy reached into her pack. She unzipped a compartment and pulled out the picture frame that she had packed at the shop. She brought it with her on every hike to a mountain top. She peered at it for a few seconds, then back at the clouds, and smiled. Then she kissed the photo. She handed it to Bradlee.

"It's me with my mommy and daddy. I was four then. Mommy was very happy. I can see it in her smile. She got very sick and died. Daddy said it was cancer. I don't know what that is. Doesn't really matter. I didn't like seeing her when she was very sick anyway. This picture is the way I remember her. And every time I look up and see the clouds I see her there smiling at me just like she told me."

Bradlee studied the color photograph. Her mother was very beautiful and he could see how similar Ruthy's face and eyes were to her mother's. "Ruthy, I look at your mother and I see you too in this photo. Yes, your mommy is in the clouds. But also every time you look in the mirror your mother is there, right in front of your eyes."

Bradlee gently held Ruthy's hand and traced her finger along her mother's eyes and down the sides of her face in the photo. Then he brought Ruthy's hand to her own face and guided her fingers just the same. Ruthy understood and stared into her mommy's eyes and just kept on smiling with joy. She set the picture frame back into the zippered compartment and proceeded to determinedly finish her watercolor. Ruthy signed it with her initials at the bottom right, let it dry for a few minutes in the cool air, and then rolled the finished artwork and placed it back in the tube. She handed the tube to Bradlee.

"Baruch, a present for you. Because you are very special too. Thank you for being my friend. And a new friend for my daddy. He doesn't have very many. Oh, and for being a great horsee!" She giggled.

Bradlee accepted the tube from Ruthy. Then she leapt from her chair and wrapped her arms around Bradlee. He held on to her and stroked her head gently and peered at the clouds once again. She had tears in her eyes now. He held her closely for awhile.

"Sometimes, I really miss her," Ruthy sobbed.

"Yes, I know that feeling deep down inside. It's called loving, Ruthy. You go right on and keep painting those clouds." He smiled at her and then he held her close as his own tears began to flow. He thought of his moment sitting on the boulder at the beach as Ruthy quieted in his arms.

"Ruthy, let the pain go from that spot inside and let love fill it all up instead. Fill up your heart with love." He placed his hand against his heart and she did the same. "Yes, that's right. Mine's filling up too," he whispered with tears in his own eyes. She wiped her eyes with her sleeve and smiled at him and they knew they understood each other better than anyone could.

Rachel arrived as Bradlee and Ruthy were settled again in their chairs and enjoying the view together. "Did you finish your watercolor, sweetheart?"

"Sure did." Rachel wondered where it was laying to dry. "I decided to give it to Baruch as a present."

"Baruch? Who's Baruch?" Rachel asked quizzically.

"Uh oh," Ruthy snickered now with her hands to her cheeks. "Oopsy daisy." She glanced at Bradlee, as Rachel did as well but in confusion.

"Rachel, my name is really Baruch. Baruch Avraham Levitsky."

"I see. Then who is Bradlee?"

"Maybe we can talk on the way back down the trail to the shop. I could use a good catharsis about right now… Can I explain my story to you? That is, if you have a willing ear."

The late afternoon light was accentuating the colors and subtle hues that Bradlee most appreciated. They began their descent along the steps and into the tall grasses, now backlit and glowing in shades of ochre and umber and cinnabar. He stopped and removed his camera from his pack. He snapped photos as quickly as he could in this most perfect lighting of the day. He asked Rachel to pose with Ruthy and they enjoyed their photo shoot together with the grasses and the stream as beautiful backdrops.

Ruthy then ran ahead of them. Bradlee saw the opportunity. He told Rachel his story. All of it. And she listened well.

"Does Lyra know that you love her?" Rachel stopped and asked him.

"No, I haven't told her yet."

"Well, Baruch… Bradlee, whatever you wish to be called now… I can't fix the troubles that linger with your dad. But has the thought crossed your mind that Lyra just might be thinking and feeling the same as you?" Bradlee diverted his eyes from Rachel's and looked towards the ground.

"I can tell you that it was difficult for Leo to open up to me about how he felt. What he was afraid of. That he felt guilty. That it was too soon for him to move on. That it hurts deep down inside when you lose someone you loved so much and that you don't know if you could ever stand the risk of having it ever happen again. Leo's pain was probably similar to yours, Bradlee. Probably still is. But I looked Leo straight in the eye just a few weeks ago after we had been dating and calling and writing and texting each other since this past spring and I decided to make a trip back here to Woody Point – this out of the way quiet little place on the world map – and I marched right into his shop and asked him if he loved me. *Yes or No.* That I wanted to hear those words from him or I was leaving for good and never coming back."

"I would guess you got the answer you were seeking?" Bradlee responded sheepishly.

Rachel smiled. "Sure did or I wouldn't be here loving Leo and continuing to love this sweet little girl he helped create. And I love Ruthy now more than a mother bear could ever love feeding honey to her cubs. Hopefully, Leo and I will start another family together very soon... The point is Bradlee... that's *our* love story. Leo's and mine. You need to go out there and make your own love story. Just about everyone does. So, if I were you, I'd start working on a plan before Lyra moves on... You know Bradlee, a man can't spend all his time with his head in the clouds."

Bradlee spotted Ruthy on the trail and grinned.

Rachel quieted. She hoped her advice was not falling on deaf ears.

"'*A fish that's a worthy catch doesn't wait for the fisherman who forgets to load his hook with a juicy fly. Why, she just moves on and finds herself a new stream...*'"

Rachel recited the phrase with a low pitched manly voice. She repeated it again, this time with an even deeper voice.

"That's my dad's voice. He's passionate about his fly-fishing." Rachel let out a long belly laugh. "That was his advice before I jumped in my car in Toronto and sped away to give Leo his ultimatum face to face... you know, I think my dad was right now or I wouldn't be standing here with you. And now I'm as happy as any clam could ever be!"

Bradlee glanced at Rachel. Her face was glowing. It was as if her heart emitted a vapor that enveloped her being in a white cloud of love and kindness. She was the personification of a loving spirit in a woman's form.

Bradlee glanced down the trail again to check on Ruthy. She was skipping stones into the stream and splashing puddles. *Exactly what a seven year old child should be doing*, Bradlee thought, as he peered at the clouds above them one more time.

"Thank you, Rachel. You're right." And Bradlee let the last of his pain release from his heart like a stone skipping into a vast ocean. There were no more stones left to skip now. He felt lighter, unburdened, a sense of freedom and confidence he had not felt in many years. Rachel smiled at him and clasped Bradlee's arm around hers as they continued to hike along the trail adjacent to the stream as Ruthy skipped ahead.

ANSLEY STOOD AT LYRA'S DOORWAY ringing her bell numerous times. No answer. She didn't want to disturb the neighbors. It was almost four o'clock in the morning. She knocked with her fist against the door and tried to shout Lyra's name without being too boisterous. Still no answer. She slipped off her dress shoes and walked around the garden hedges to the side of the house and found a window covered by drapes. It looked like it should be a bedroom. Ansley knocked again – this time with the secret code, the knock sequence that she and Lyra did when they were kids. Their family homes were right next to each other on a leafy quiet street in Connecticut. And only they knew their special knock, alerting them outside their bedroom windows when one wanted to come over and spend time with the other after school. When they were teenagers those knocks often happened later at night and so they would secretly open the window and let each other in and tell their troubles and secrets. When they got their first period. Fights that needed resolving with parents, siblings, and friends. Thoughts about colleges and careers. And eventually, their many chats about boys, and which ones liked which of them, and how to properly kiss one – they would practice on plastic frogs - and all the rest of growing up. They were tighter than the triple knots that held their stitches together when they both fell and split their chins learning to ride their two-wheeled bikes on the same day of kindergarten. Their scars still matched in the same exact place, same number of stitches for each.

A light turned on and Lyra spread the drapes a sliver and peered out into the dark dampness. "Ansley, is that you?"

"Well of course it is Lyra, who else would know our knock? It's four o'clock in the morning and I'm freezing out here. You going to open this window or meet me at the front door?" Lyra knocked back the same sequence against the glass pane and then opened the window. She helped Ansley climb through to her bedroom. Ansley stood and stared at Lyra's mangled face before wrapping her in her arms.

"I'm so sorry, Lyra." Lyra thought she had nothing left to donate from her tear glands but the salt water rivulets again made their way down her bruised and battered cheeks. Her face and lip and left eyelid had massively swollen in the past six hours despite the repeated ice applications.

Ansley grew angrier by the second. "Whoever did this to you is going to pay. Or his damn parents will for raising such a vicious human being. I've got plenty of attorney contacts who can help you, Lyra. But we need to get you better first. Physically and mentally. I'm here for you, OK. I'm going to stay with you and keep you safe." Ansley started to sniffle as she held Lyra again. "Best friends, always!"

"I'm scared, Ansley. I don't know if I should go to the police in the morning or just try to heal and forget about all of this. I have so much work that I need to do for my studies. I don't have time to deal with the police and interviews and court appearances. I just can't."

"Let's figure that out another time, OK? Come on, I'm exhausted too. I had a few rounds at the bar with some law school girlfriends. Ladies night out earlier when you called me. I'll need some rest too to be strong for you." Lyra pulled out a set of pajama pants and a T-shirt and Ansley quickly washed-up and settled into Lyra's queen bed with her. She turned to Lyra who had her back turned.

"Come here Lyra, let me hold you. We'll talk more in the morning." Lyra cuddled into Ansley's shoulder and Ansley turned out the light.

The university medical clinic was busy on the morning after Halloween. The doctor assigned to Lyra at check-in was running late over the morning. But Lyra didn't mind. She had nowhere to go looking this bruised. The initial numbing rush of adrenaline after the attack had dissipated, replaced now only by gnawing consistent waves of pains all over her body. Lyra and Ansley chatted in the office waiting room about various details of their lives since they had last spoken before starting graduate school. They promised to get together over the winter holidays in Connecticut. Ansley invited Lyra to stay with her for a few days at her parents' home.

Lyra was brought to the exam room and handed a urine specimen cup by the nurse. She provided a sample in the bathroom and returned. At Lyra's request, Ansley joined her in the room for support but also to be sure the doctor was thorough with Lyra's examination. The medical report would be crucial for Lyra's legal case. Lyra removed her clothes and donned a medical gown. As she was undressing, Ansley glanced in horror at Lyra's bruised body. The nurse measured Lyra's vital signs. Her blood pressure was mildly elevated but the nurse explained that, without a history of high blood pressure, it was more likely due to stress from her trauma. Dr. Stoddard entered the room and greeted Lyra sympathetically and listened intently to Lyra's synopsis of last night's events.

She started her exam of Lyra's facial trauma. Her internal upper lip laceration and swelling would repair over time and would not require any sutures. Her cheeks were bruised but her jaw bite and teeth were properly set. Lyra's left eye was swollen shut so a visual acuity test was not possible but she gently opened her left eyelids and inspected each eye. Lyra's pupils dilated and constricted normally and her eye movements appeared to track normally through all visual fields. Dr. Stoddard noted the small coloboma in Lyra's left eye which Lyra acknowledged she always had since birth. Her right eye, slightly bruised, demonstrated superior vision, testing at 20/15 on the Snellen vision chart that hung from the back of the exam room door. "A hawk's eye," Dr. Stoddard remarked with a kind smile. There was a bite impression mark to Lyra's posterior right neck. Lyra was experiencing some pain with full breaths and her left rib cage was tender. Bruises ran down the length of the sides of her torso to her pelvic bone. Her breasts were sore and had bruised hand imprints to their undersides. A chest x-ray revealed no rib fractures and her lungs were clear. Dr. Stoddard donned medical gloves and continued gently with a pelvic exam. She asked Lyra if she was recently sexually active and Lyra replied no while glancing at Ansley with tears in her eyes. Her vulvar tissues were tender and slightly bruised but there was no evidence of lacerations, bleeding, or penetrating injury to her vulva or anal opening. Dr. Stoddard carefully inserted a few laboratory cotton swabs inside Lyra and then covered Lyra with her exam robe. The remainder of Lyra's physical exam was otherwise normal.

Dr. Stoddard elevated the exam table and sat on her rotating exam stool.

"Lyra, your injuries are substantial" she began. "Unfortunately, I've seen too many cases of physical abuse and date rape in my young career. I wish it weren't so... You're probably still in a bit of shock from the events that happened to you last night but I am going to recommend that you visit the police station nearby here and have them start an assault investigation. They have detectives who work on these cases, Lyra, and they are usually successful at finding the perpetrator and bringing him to justice." Lyra looked to the ground and began to sob again.

"I'm sorry, Lyra. I really wish this didn't happen to you." Dr. Stoddard held Lyra's hands in hers. "Listen, I'm going to give you a name of a social worker who works here at my clinic. She can speak with you and provide a referral to a psychologist... When you're ready... it may really help to talk to someone who is skilled at helping you heal from this. Sometimes people will suffer from PTSD... that's post-traumatic stress disorder... after these terrible altercations. You are young and, I'm sure, a very kind and loving person. Counseling can help you heal and be able to trust again in a personal relationship. In time." Dr. Stoddard paused hoping for some acknowledgement from Lyra that she understood her advice. Lyra nodded.

"Good. Now I can be reached here at the clinic throughout the week." She reached into her white coat and pulled out her business card. "I'm also writing my personal cell phone number on the back in case you need to reach me after hours." She looked at Lyra sympathetically and gave her a brief hug.

"I'll be back in a few minutes while you finish dressing." Dr. Stoddard exited to her personal office to complete the documentation of Lyra's visit into the computerized medical record. She returned to the exam room.

"Lyra, these are my exam notes and the social worker referral I mentioned to you. Please find the time to visit the police station. I've sealed a copy of my exam note in one envelope – you can provide that copy to the police officer at the precinct. The other copy is for your records, and your attorney's, who will assist you with prosecuting the man who did this to you. Now please go home and rest." Dr. Stoddard looked over to Ansley who nodded in agreement. "Lyra, I'd like to see you back here for a follow-up visit with me next week."

Lyra thanked Dr. Stoddard and exited with Ansley. They stopped in the hallway bathroom and applied some cover-up powder to Lyra's face and eyelids followed by a large pair of sunglasses. They departed the clinic and strolled along a quiet street. They collected some Chinese take-out for lunch and returned to Lyra's home.

"You and Charles doing well?" Lyra started.

"We have our moments, you know," Ansley replied. "It's been seven years that we're together already. Can you believe it?" Ansley seemed content chatting about him. The couple were quite inseparable. "He's happy with his physics Ph.D. program – settling into his graduate studies just like you and me. But we're together and he supports me mentally through this law school stuff and I give him what he needs as well." Ansley smiled as she suggestively lifted an egg roll to her mouth and licked it. Lyra gently shoved Ansley's shoulder. "Guys – sometimes they just need us to make love to them for that reassurance and to just take away their stress. All the pillow talking is fine but I get it after these many years together with Charles. They're just wired for the physical part more than us. Besides, he's a really good lover so no complaints here."

Lyra started to tear again. Ansley stopped.

"I should have known better. I should have followed my instincts and not gone up those steps. He didn't even remember my *name*." Lyra was crying furiously again into her palms.

"Lyra, now you look at me!" Ansley reached out to Lyra and gently lifted her chin until their eyes met. "What happened was N*ot – Your – Fault!* That punk meant to hurt you, probably from the moment he saw you. And I would guess that he probably has hurt others before you... I'm sorry. I didn't mean to remind you of last night." She hugged Lyra again.

Once settled again, Lyra nibbled at her lunch. Two wrapped fortune cookies remained on the table. Ansley turned and stared closely at Lyra's eyes while brushing aside her wisps of hair.

"Can we try to separate our minds from last night for a moment?" Ansley asked. Lyra nodded. "Good. I want to know if you've met anyone nice since you moved here at the end of the summer. Come on, spill the beans..."

Lyra told Ansley about her rigorous class schedule and after-hours endlessly studying environmental policy, air and soil sciences, the minutiae of alternative energy sources, writing papers, sketching imaginative landscape drawings, and preparing for her winter research project with Dr. Bonheim in North Dakota. There wasn't a single weekend that she didn't spend studying at home except for last night's terrible mistake. But there was a man she had met on the train coming to Seattle. He was sweet and tender and ruggedly handsome yet seemed to have a heavy heart. Lyra didn't know why but she had hoped that in time he might talk about whatever it was in his past that was unsettled. She just knew there was something that was a burden. And yet she thought about him most every day. To be truthful, she relayed, she thought about him multiple times every day. Just little flashbacks of his smile or the way he looked at her when he thought she wasn't noticing, and she kept the necklace that he gave her and wore it most every day except for when she went running. And these flashbacks happened very frequently. She didn't mind them at all. And she didn't know if he felt the same about her. He was so far away in Prince Edward Island or off traveling here or there. They just spoke again briefly recently and, of all places, he was in a tent in Newfoundland. Lyra just didn't know what to think but every time they spoke there was an energy there. A tingly spark as strong as when they chatted on the train and shared a room at an inn in North Dakota. Lyra explained it all to Ansley and what happened in the Hummingbird Room – actually, what didn't happen despite her desire to be loved by him.

Ansley held silent through Lyra's ramblings and sniffles.

"Well, gosh darn it Lyra, *you're in love*, aren't you?!" Ansley smiled at Lyra and sat back in her chair.

Lyra turned and stared out the kitchen window. It was turning into a beautiful day. Sunshine streaming into the room and lighting her face with warmth.

"I think so, Ansley. I really do."

"And does this guy have *any* idea how you feel about him?"

"We laugh together on the phone or when he texts me. He makes me laugh because he can be so serious and we tease each other and he has all these hobbies and interests and he was going to be a doctor but something happened and he's a really good photographer – that's his current job, and…"

"Lyra, you are rambling on and on… Look me in the eye…" Ansley could be headstrong. Lyra knew she appreciated that directness over the many years that they have been best friends.

"Do you or do you not love this man… what's his name…?"

"His name is Bradlee. Bradlee Lee. But I like calling him Bradlee Seashell."

"I see. You can explain that one later to me," Ansley said with a very curious raise of her eyebrows.

"I do love him, Ansley. If love is the feeling that you belong together. That you always belonged together and always will."

"Well, that's about as beautiful a description as I've ever heard for a loving pair," Ansley replied. Her facial expression eased into warmth. "Well, I can't pick up the phone and call him for you, Lyra, but I'd suggest you two have a heart to heart talk sometime soon. It may hurt you to find out that he's not interested or he's moved on. But love does hurt sometimes. A lot. It's all a matter of taking that chance. Am I right?"

Lyra listened as she absorbed Ansley's message. "Ansley, thank you for coming to help me. Can you stay another night to help me through this a bit more? I know you need to get back to your classes and to Charles."

"Deal! Hey, let's open these fortune cookies. Love 'em!"

Ansley wrestled hers open first and read it:

Friendship is richer than any treasure.

"Aw, that's very cute," Ansley remarked.
"Well, that fits you *perfectly*, Ansley!" Lyra exclaimed.
"OK, you're next."

Lyra unwrapped hers, read it to herself and then glanced into the light. She placed her hand across her face in shock.

Nothing is Impossible to a Willing Heart.

It was the exact same message as inside the fortune cookie that Susie gave her on the train.

She read it aloud to Ansley who then opened up with laughter.

"You see – your fortune has been told! Am I right or am I right?" and Ansley laughed again as Lyra really smiled for the first time in nearly twenty-four hours.

Lyra rested in her bedroom after lunch while Ansley made a few phone calls to a faculty member at her law school in Berkeley to discuss Lyra's physical abuse and attempted date rape and to ask for some legal advice. Her professor explained the procedures to follow in detail. After Lyra awoke from her nap, Ansley reviewed the legal options with Lyra. Despite multiple attempts to convince Lyra, Lyra refused to open a police investigation or seek an attorney. She just wanted peace and quiet and she needed space to return to her studies. Her degrees and her career were just too important to her to be swept up in the emotional roller-coaster of a seemingly never-ending legal case. What Lyra mostly began to think about was the man who likely saved her soul, maybe her life as well – Carl… that was his name… she remembered now. Carl saved her inside that room. She needed to thank him one day if she could find him. That there was goodness in this world from the depths of horror.

Ansley agreed with Lyra on the last point. She was pleased that Lyra was focusing on something positive from her terrible ordeal. She worried about Lyra, being alone in Seattle without a strong support group but she also knew that Lyra was tough. She was resilient. Ansley knew, as well, that the legal system was never a quick and easy process and the outcome hardly ever predetermined. And Lyra really had no significant financial resources available to fight the system. Ansley felt defeated but she understood Lyra's position. She begged Lyra to at least meet with a counselor when she was ready and Lyra promised she would look into it. They hugged and decided to not bring up the legal topic again.

They crossed the street and strolled through the university arboretum. It was closed to the public by the evening hour but Lyra had a key to the gate issued to her by the landscape architecture administrative office. Access after-hours provided Lyra with a relaxed undisturbed location to allow her thoughts and creativity to flow surrounded by the beauty of the experimental gardens and plantings. It was a garden always in flux. Always transforming. Lyra thought to herself:

Maybe it is time to tell Bradlee how I really feel about him. Ansley is right. But I need to heal first. I'd prefer to see Bradlee face to face when I tell him.

Lyra escorted Ansley around her private space as they moved on to discussing anything other than school and relationships.

Ansley stayed overnight comforting Lyra once again through her nightmare awakenings. She held her tight when Lyra awoke in fitful rages during the night. And just as Lyra's mother used to do when Lyra had bad dreams as a child, Ansley stroked her hair and hummed softly until Lyra returned to sleep each time.

Ansley awoke early the next morning and departed for the airport to return to San Francisco. Before she entered the taxi parked outside Lyra's home, Ansley turned back and shouted to Lyra while blowing a kiss goodbye. "Lyra, nothing is impossible to a willing heart. Nothing! Love you girl!"

Ansley held out her fist to the taxi door and gave it their secret knock code. Lyra smiled back at her as she repeated the code against her doorpost. And then Ansley was gone.

Part Five

THE HOUSE WAS IN DISARRAY by the fourth day of Lyra's self-imposed quarantine from the world she once gladly inhabited. She had spent nearly all of that time in her bed, alternating between self-loathing and anger with bouts of depression and despair, especially when she arose to use the bathroom and glanced in the mirror at her battered face and chest bruises. She was barely eating nor did she have an appetite. Foster remained steady on the adjacent pillow on her bed but even he received little regard from Lyra. She was in no mood for giving hugs, even to a stuffed animal. She didn't answer the phone or return any texts – it didn't matter, only a few messages were left regardless. She realized she wasn't exactly a socialite. Bonnie called the day prior to check on her whereabouts since she was informed by Dr. Bonheim that Lyra had been missing her classes and had skipped a scheduled meeting with her professor without bothering to cancel. Lyra didn't respond to Bonnie's message either. Bradlee called as well, but Lyra let it ring into her voicemail. She was not in any mood to talk to anyone – even Bradlee. The thought of trusting any man again troubled her as anger raged within. She wallowed in the darkness of her bedroom or living room with the drapes closed at all times. Darkness to envelop her anger at the world. At men. At how fragile she was. *Why didn't she fight back more? Why did she feel so lonely? Why did she have trouble making new friends?* She wanted to leave Seattle. But where could she go. Her brother was somewhere in Kansas on a horse ranch. Maybe she should go visit him, spend some time in the country. Help him with his work on the ranch, take care of some horses. But no. Their relationship wasn't on the best of terms either, having grown more distant in the past few years. Her brother had his own problems he had been working through. Maybe some other time, she rationalized.

She stared at her texts and landscape designs strewn about her bedroom and the kitchen table. Everything seemed meaningless now. Just all purposeless. Pointless. Just a stupid bunch of useless facts and ideas. She searched for alcohol, something to alter her mind and wash away her despair – anything she could find since she didn't usually purchase it herself. She rummaged through the kitchen cabinets, then over to the dining room buffet but couldn't find any in the damn house she now loathed for its overbearing size and constant upkeep. She returned to her shower and slunk to the floor. The hot water plunging onto her scalp and burning the bruised scabbed skin around her left eye, nose and lip. She stayed there for an hour while her tears mixed with the steady endless stream until the water ran cold. She stared at the drain wondering whether anyone would care if she too simply washed away into the bowels of this dark city. *Would they even retrieve my body from the depths of the ocean? No, a burial at sea would be just fine. I could be a final meal. Fish food. At least I would have some last use to the world.* As the cold water brought shivers, she arose from the shower, dried and donned a robe. She glanced at Bradlee's Ark shell necklace. It was hanging on the bathroom mirror frame. She felt like she too was lost on a vast ocean vessel waiting for something, anything, to rescue her from the tidal wave that would tear the ship into splinters. A tidal wave of fear. Her heart feeling pierced by shards of broken wood and her chest heavy from fallen beams as her ship was collapsing under the force of the tidal wave. She held the Ark shell curiously in her palm as if it was an exotic object from a foreign land.

She had a flashback to the train.

'*She has a story to tell us... It's even better if you look real close at it... Nature created this hole... A hungry moon snail... you need to see the whole picture... like holding a glass half-full...'*

A glass half-full, Lyra picked on the words. *Was Bradlee always so damn optimistic about life? No. I'm sure he's got his own issues to deal with. After all, I haven't exactly seen him knocking my door down to visit me with roses in his outstretched arms!*

Lyra set the Ark shell necklace around Foster's furry neck and dressed for the first time since Ansley departed. She checked on her backyard garden. It was a landscape in need of some tending with all the rains and thunderstorms. Herb pots coated with weeds. Tree branches and leaves in disarray just as she felt she was inside her own life. A squirrel scurried up a pine tree. It was followed by another, round and around the tree they wound, then back down again and across the lawn to the next tree. The cycle repeated until one squirrel held still as the other mounted. Raw backyard sex. Squirrels procreating right in front of her. Nature ensuring the next generation of furry creatures while also spreading acorn seeds in the process to grow the next stand of giant oaks. The sexual act seemed revolting to her now and she cringed wondering if the female felt any pain. *Why did she accept her mate?* Was it merely biological programming or did this pair have something more bonding, more loving, that they shared. After all, there were squirrels across the other side of the fence in the adjacent backyard. *What did these two have to offer each other that the neighbors didn't? Who knows?* The mounting ended quickly and the male scurried off in search of his lunch. But the pair did linger in their vicinity. Their nests in the same tree above her. She cleaned the garden space of debris and pruned the herb pots. She plucked off a few sprigs of mint leaves and returned to the kitchen.

Lyra realized she needed to talk with someone. The quiet space was like a breeding ground for fears and obsessions. She wondered when, or if, she could leave her home again anytime soon. She filled a tea kettle with water, added the mint sprigs, and set it to a simmering boil. She turned off the stove and let it seep before adding a spoonful of orange blossom honey. She inhaled the vapors. They were soothing. Quieting. An aroma that evoked nature's rebirth. She poured the elixir into her favorite pottery mug. The mug was a gift from Ansley's parents and was fired with decorative hummingbird motifs. Lyra was a young teenager at the time, entering high school, and she had kept the mug at Ansley's home in her best friend's pantry to enjoy on their frequent sleepovers. Lyra's passion for hummingbirds, at the time, was ever expanding ever since her encounter in Costa Rica. The mug had survived through high school and she brought it to college with her and now to Seattle. Lyra sipped the mint tea while staring out the kitchen window.

 The squirrels began another round of chasing. A piece of paper laying on the floor beside the table distracted her attention away from the backyard and so she retrieved it. It was Angel's name and phone number. *My Angel. My rescuer. She was so sweet to care for me.* Lyra collected her cell phone from her bedroom and dialed Angel's number. A man's voice answered and Lyra hesitated. Chills came with a rush of fear. The doctor warned her about PTSD. She hung up the phone and drank a few more sips of the mint tea. The calm returned. She called again. This time, a young girl's voice giggled into the phone before a woman's voice sent her away. Lyra recognized that it was Angel.

 "Hola, como estas?" the woman's voice answered.

 "Angel, is that you?" Lyra said.

 "Lyra, I recognize your voice. I was hoping you would call… Are you OK?"

 "Yes, Angel. Thank you."

 "My pleasure." Silence as Lyra didn't quite know what

to say next.

"Lyra, you wish to talk? Perhaps it is time."

"Angel, I'm just very lonely. I'm scared to even go outside."

"Yes, I understand. But you must try. Can you call a taxi? I am making dinner for my family when you called. I'd like you to join us. It's my specialty dish tonight. My husband's favorite."

The bruises. Lyra's face remained swollen but less so than the days prior.

"That's very kind of you Angel but…"

"Lyra, please. Summon a bit of courage and call a taxi. Where I come from we never talk with an empty stomach. If the stomach is not full then the heart cannot be fulfilled."

Lyra smiled. "Angel, you are very sweet. OK, I will come over. Thank you. I need to get ready first and put on some makeup but I will be there soon. I look forward to meeting your family."

Angel gave Lyra her address and they said goodbye.

Lyra finished her mint tea. She cleaned up the kitchen and family room and organized her books and papers. Then she returned to the garden and clipped some flowers for a bouquet for Angel. She found a few chocolate bars in the pantry and wrapped those as well for Angel's children.

She put on a long flowery dress and dabbed her facial bruises with cover makeup. Her face was presentable enough. The healing had begun to be noticeable. She called the taxi, grabbed the gifts and waited by the window sill.

Her phone rang. It was Bradlee. He had been trying to reach her for three days straight.

Lyra answered this time.

"Bradlee, you are persistent, aren't you. Can't you give a girl some space?"

"Lyra, I'm sorry. I was getting very worried. I just had a bad feeling, that's all. Don't know why. Are you OK?"

Lyra paused as she peered through an opening in the drapes. The truth hurt worse than the bruises now.

"Yes, Bradlee. I'm OK now. I, uh... I had a bad fall while running the other day and got pretty banged up. Just lots of bruises and all. No stitches. I'm getting better now... and how are you?"

"I'm sorry you hurt yourself. Do you need to see a doctor?"

"Bradlee—— I said I'll be alright." She was irritated now. "Yes, if it makes you feel better, I saw a doctor the next day and she said I'll heal in time. Nothing permanent." Lyra wasn't sure about that but it sounded like the right thing to say. She felt distant from Bradlee. The spark wasn't there. More like dullness. Devoid of the happiness she used to feel when she would see his name on her caller id.

"Glad to hear that. Well, I just wanted to say hello again. I missed chatting with you. I'm back home in P.E.I. and finishing up the wild horse project. I've told the Heritage Center in Medora that I can deliver the photographs and the write-up very soon and they invited me back for Thanksgiving break as was the original plan. Well, actually, the man I told you about who gave me the horseback tour of the Badlands – he invited me to stay at his ranch on his tribe's reservation land for the holiday. I'll be flying out to Minot the day before Thanksgiving. I'll need to rent an SUV at the airport. Never know how winter conditions will be out there. Then I'll head to his ranch. Really looking forward to meeting his family and seeing the reservation."

The taxi pulled up in front of Lyra's home and honked.

"Bradlee, I have to go now. I'm going out to dinner and meeting a new friend. Can I call you later? Thanks for checking up on me."

"Oh... OK then. Talk to you later, Lyra... I'll be up late tonight working so you can reach me later if you'd like."

"Let's see how the evening goes. I might need a rain check. Bye, Bradlee."

"Bye, Lyra." She hung up.

Lyra grabbed the bouquet and chocolates, exited, and locked the front door. She remembered that she forgot to wear Bradlee's Ark shell necklace. It was in her bedroom hanging around Foster's neck. *Oh well, doesn't really matter. It's just a silly seashell.* The taxi sped off to Angel's home.

BRADLEE WAS SEATED AT HIS WORK TABLE. He had purchased it a few years earlier from a used furniture store on P.E.I. It was actually a drafting table, the kind used by architects and artisans who preferred to lay their work like a large jigsaw puzzle, a collage of interconnected items. Detailed sketches perhaps. Building plans. The thought of a treasure map came to his mind. Treasure. *Was Lyra my treasure?* He missed yet another opportunity to tell her how he really felt about her.

Yet, he sensed something was off with the conversation. A disconnect. When they had always spoken previously it was like two magnets attracted to each other's poles. Drawing ever closer that it was as if they needed to try to exert some sort of negative energy, that neither welcomed, just to pull themselves apart. It just never happened before. But tonight was different. The Lyra he had come to know was affectionate, teasing but in a gentle way, an exceptional listener and responder. No platitudes like one would expect generated from a machine-learning computer with a sycophantic program. Something was different tonight. She was going out to dinner with a friend. *A date? Maybe she didn't want to hurt my feelings? Maybe this sort-of long distance relationship they were having wasn't fair to her. Just a useless waste of emotional energy. I am more than three thousand miles away. She's incredibly beautiful and has the most radiant sunshiny personality. Surely the men on campus could see that with their own wandering eyes or with a simple conversation face to face.*

Bradlee glanced at the final selections of his photographs. He had enlarged the images to poster size prints, and a few even larger that would serve as the cornerstone of his photography show at the Heritage Center gallery. He was pleased with them. All of them. He had captured the wild horses as he had hoped. With their full personalities. Their eyes could not disguise that these animals had souls. There was anger and rage and curiosity and need and sadness and love in those eyes and in their stances. They protected each other in the herd. And then there always seemed to be the solo sojourner, distanced from the herd. Off in the brush or by the bank of the river. A loner. Bradlee captured a brilliant image of one of these loners and so he studied the stallion's face as the print stared back at him.

Are you and I that similar? Destined for a quiet existence apart from the herd? No mate to keep one company? Are you and I to die alone when it comes to our end?

He wondered if the approaching winter would make any difference or did this horse remain alone. Was it by choice or was he excommunicated from the herd for a sin that would not allow for forgiveness followed by a welcome return.

It was approaching midnight. The thoughts troubled him and so he shut his table light and crawled into bed. The window was open a crack to let in the cool ocean breeze. He rested on top of the covers and peered at the moonlit clouds for a long moment and reflected. "*Goodnight moon*" he said. The old children's book came to mind and he chuckled. It was one of his favorites and he used to plead to his mother to read it to him repeatedly. Those were good times here at the Marshpillow. When the main home was bustling with activity and family and visitors. And then he thought of little Ruthy and stared again at the slowly moving clouds. But this time there were no tears that came.

"Goodnight Sami. I miss you very much right now. I will always love you."

ANGEL WELCOMED LYRA INTO HER HOME. It was along a street with interconnected rowhouses in an older more modest section of the city where trees lined the roadway beside the curb. The taxi had passed a small children's park around the corner. Lyra gave Angel a hug and presented her with the flower bouquet. The young twins giggled wildly as Lyra offered them the chocolate treats while they pointed towards Lyra's face and spoke in Spanish. Angel turned to introduce her children, Isabel and Gabriel, with pride followed by a stern stare and they stopped giggling at once and held still with serious faces before smiles returned. Lyra could see how beautiful they were. Radiant cheeks and grins and wide-eyed stares and jet black hair with milk-chocolaty smooth skin. Angel introduced her husband, Guillermo, who approached while slipping a clean shirt over his head and welcomed Lyra. Then he teasingly chased the kids away. But they lurked anyway behind doorways, giggling all the same, as Lyra strolled down the hallway while playing peek-a-boo with them. The aroma was intoxicating from the kitchen. Lyra finally felt hunger pains after days of meager portions that she could only muster to swallow for survival.

    The family joined together at the dinner table as the twins assisted and placed the finishing touches of silverware and condiments. The tablecloth fabric was a picturesque design of a volcano spewing red and orange lava into the light blue sky. Fruity branches hung along the margins of the cloth design and at the base was a sunset ocean strewn with turtles and whales. Lyra thought it was quite beautiful. Angel insisted that Lyra take a seat instead of helping in the kitchen and so she convinced Lyra to sit and relax at the table. Lyra tried to chat with the twins using whatever Spanish she could recall from her high school studies. She glanced over to Guillermo's hands. They looked well-worn with his finger pads thickened and nails roughened. He was a delicate man with a lithe sinewy frame and his teeth looked like they hadn't visited a dentist in some years. But she chatted disjointedly in Spanish intermixed with English due to their mutual limited proficiencies. Occasionally, the twins chimed in and spoke on his behalf as interpreters. He didn't mind it at all. Lyra noted that Guillermo also didn't ever focus on her facial bruises and her still slightly swollen lip. She was certain Angel must have told him of the reason for her condition but he didn't glare or study her face and she was glad for that.

Angel arrived from the kitchen laden with a serving tray. She laid it at the end of the table. "We will each make our own casado since I am not sure what foods you like, Lyra. Casado is a very traditional dish in our culture," Angel announced as the twins snickered.

Angel placed a large bowl of white rice onto the lazy Susan at the center of the table. This was followed by heaping bowls of black beans and fried sweet plantains. Another dish had chicken pieces hovering in a savory sauce and yet another had a few fish fillets. "This is dorado, a popular fish found along our coastline back at our old home. It is sweet and delicious if cooked properly. I prefer it with some butter and olive oil fried quickly in the pan."

Angel winked at Guillermo who returned the gesture with a blown kiss that made Angel blush. "Angel is an amazing cook," Guillermo said as he patted Lyra's forearm gently. Lyra noted that his gesture did not alarm her or send a rush of chills and fits of dark imagination.

"And this is Ensalada de Chayote," as Angel brought the

final dish to the table. "Isabel was a big helper in the kitchen for this one, mixing and tossing the ingredients." Angel smiled at her daughter affectionately. "It is made with our variety of pears that I can only find here in Seattle at a specialty market. I dice the firm pears and then we toss them with chopped red onions, roasted red peppers, olive oil, wine vinegar, cilantro leaves, freshly ground pepper, and a pinch of salt."

Angel reached for Guillermo's plate and dished generous helpings of each item onto his dinner plate and set it down in front of him. He reached over with his head and inhaled the aromas deeply with a comforting smile. Angel took her seat beside him. Guillermo rubbed his hands together, closed his eyes, and then held his hands vertically in front of his bowed face in silence. Angel and the children repeated the gesture followed by Lyra. Guillermo recited a brief prayer in Spanish and the family responded with '*Amen.*' This was immediately followed by the clinking of silverware as the children reached for their plates and bowls and Angel served them in turns.

"May I serve you your dish? Angel asked of Lyra.

"Please. I'm famished."

"You like to taste everything, Lyra?"

"Yes, everything. It all looks so delicious!" Lyra smiled brightly and Angel was very pleased.

Lyra's plate was loaded up and she proceeded to taste and devour it all with pleasant conversation.

After dinner, Guillermo looked exhausted and excused himself as he climbed the stairs. Isabel and Gabriel played in the small living room space as Angel and Lyra cleared the table and then moved to the backyard patio and relaxed into a few rocking chairs. It was a comfortable evening to enjoy some fresh air. The rains had stopped for the past few days and the birds had returned to their evening chirping.

"Thank you for a delicious dinner, Angel. That was very

kind of you to ask me over."

"It is my pleasure. I'm glad you could come and join us."

"Everything was fantastically delicious. I didn't realize how hungry I was! And I don't think I've had such a delicious meal in years!" Lyra rubbed her full belly delightfully and smiled.

"You mentioned casado, that it is a traditional dish. Which country is it from? Well, I guess I should say, where are you and Guillermo from originally?"

"Casado is our traditional dish of Costa Rica. My mother taught me all the recipes we enjoyed tonight. You must visit there one day. It is a beautiful country!"

Lyra's mind returned to being an eight year old. "But I've been already!" She smiled and giggled. "True, I was a small child then. A vacation trip with my parents and brother. We had a wonderful time. And I would like to return someday."

"That is wonderful!"

"Tell me how you came to Seattle," Lyra asked.

"Guillermo and I married when we were nineteen soon after high school finished for both of us. My father invited him to work on our family farm tending to our few cows and horses and our vegetable gardens. My father was aging quickly. Farming had taken its toll on his tired body and he could no longer handle the workload alone. My mother ran the family inn – or as they say here, the bed and breakfast. The guests slept upstairs overlooking the gardens but my parents – and Guillermo and I after we were married – slept downstairs and managed the inn and farm for a few more years. But my mother really was the manager of the inn and farm business. She brought the customers with her beautiful flowers always sprinkled throughout the inn and tended to all the little special homey room details – all the laundry, and of course, her delicious breakfasts, and sometimes dinners as well for hungry late-arrivals. But then she suddenly passed away from a heart attack. She was overweight and did not exercise much but my Mami knew things from our cultural traditions that few others did in our region. She was a very spiritual woman. My father struggled with depression and loneliness after she passed. His more limited English did not help. Really, he was purely a farmer at heart. Animals are what he has always loved. But the tourist business wasn't so good in Costa Rica then when the economy here in the US and in Europe entered more difficult times. Guillermo and I needed a better future for ourselves and we wanted to start our own family." Angel glanced at her three-year old twins as they played quietly together.

"Guillermo and I decided it would be best to try to come to America. I applied for nursing school and Guillermo is a very good truck mechanic. Diesel engines. We were granted immigration by the State Department and were settled here in Seattle by the government. I finished my nursing studies a few years ago and have been working at the children's hospital nearby ever since. I also studied English over many night classes. We are happy here. Our twins are also happy and enjoying their school and friends. Guillermo and I work hard. Long hours. But the money has been good. Enough to help my father back home with the upkeep on the family farmhouse and he is visited often by other relatives who agreed to help with his care. I do miss him very much, my Papi, but such is the sacrifice for the next generations."

Gabriel came rushing to join them on the patio followed by Isabel. They were begging for dessert and Angel tried to shoo them away but they persisted and she allowed each of them a few squares of milk chocolate from Lyra's gifts. Isabel returned inside while Gabriel lingered at his mother's lap as Angel stroked his hair. He stood and walked over to the birdfeeder. It was empty. He used the nearby scoop to collect the seed mixture in the corner of the patio under the eave. Then he climbed a small stepstool and filled the feeder to the brim. He returned and opened the water hose valve, filled a small pitcher of fresh water, and poured the cool water into the ceramic basin – a bird bath hanging beside the feeder. Gabriel stood back and waited. A few sparrows arrived and landed for a dinner meal at the feeder. Then a blue jay came to feast and he was soon chased away by a hungry magpie. He waited further. An iridescent green dragonfly darted towards the bird bath and landed on its edge and sipped from the cool water. It alighted and hovered in place and then skillfully, slowly maneuvered backwards. Gabriel reached out his right hand. The dragonfly landed in his palm and paused in perfect stillness. Gabriel gently moved his left hand closer to the dragonfly and slid his fingers in a caressing motion across its back and wings. He carefully pulled his left hand away and then held perfectly still and stared closely into the dragonfly's eyes. The dragonfly appeared to be doing the same in perfect stillness. Then Gabriel broke the silence and started to giggle and his hand vibrated. The dragonfly returned to flight. Gabriel giggled even more in delight and then ran back to his mother's arms.

Lyra was staring at the scene unfold as did Angel. "My son thinks he's a dragonfly whisperer. He has an old soul," Angel remarked as she kissed the crown of his head.

Angel began to softly sing a Spanish tune. Lyra's head turned towards her in surprise. She recognized the song immediately. She listened and then, after a few more seconds, Lyra began to hum along. Angel paused. Their eyes met and something familiar simultaneously clicked. They hummed together until the song's end and continued staring at each other, wondering how this could be.

"Angel, is your family's home very close to the Monteverde Cloud Forest?" Lyra asked.

"Yes, it is."

Does it have a small barn in the field behind the house

where cows are milked and a horse stable beside them?"

"Yes."

"And lining the entire porch off the kitchen where your Mami cooked, is there a long row of hummingbird feeders that attract incredibly beautiful birds."

"Yes, indeed there were... but we set them away after Mami passed on."

"Angel, I think we've met before." Lyra smiled knowingly. And then she reached out her right hand towards the bird feeder and recited the English words of the song.

"Gentle flies hummingbird in hand, health and love forever bestowed, in your home and land."

Angel's eyes began to tear. "My Mami's song. But how do you know this?"

"Angel, you were beside me on the patio when a hummingbird landed in my palm. We were guests at your farmhouse and you showed me and my brother the farm... Your Mami smiled and gave me her blessing. The hummingbird's soul that resides within me."

Angel closed her eyes and tried to return her mind to many years ago. To the scene on the patio at her home in Costa Rica. There was a small American girl, perhaps at least a handful of years younger than herself. "Did we collect hen eggs together in a large basket after you tried to milk the cow?" Lyra nodded and giggled.

"Yes, Angel, that was me! That little girl was me! And you must have been a teenager. I could tell by your dress. You were becoming a woman." Lyra pointed towards her own chest and smiled. "It was a magical morning and you were so kind, Angel. And your parents so generous and loving to me and my family."

Angel rose from her rocking chair and Lyra followed. She reached for Lyra and they embraced and held each other for a long time.

"Lyra? But that wasn't your name then, was it? I would have remembered such an unusual and beautiful name."

"No, I used to go back and forth between my first and middle names when I was a child. Just something fun that had no real reason to it. But when we met, I had preferred Sasha then. But it is Lyra now and I do love it. It was my mother's preferred name for me. I was named after my mother's mother but I had decided to rebel as a child and wanted my own unique name in the family... But Lyra has always been my first name and Lyra it is today again. It's been only recently how much I realize I've missed my grandma's name."

"Lyra, it is amazing! God works in mysterious ways. You know, I do believe that there are many things that happen to us for very good reasons. Important reasons. Who we meet on our journeys, what we hear and see. Yes, one can say these separate events in our lives are just coincidences because that's what they do seem to be. But I don't think so. A coincidence is placed there for us to make the right connection. It is like a lesson in school that needs to be learned. Each coincidence builds on the one that comes before. One upon another. Some call it our destiny when we discover these coincidences. Others say it is the will of God, a Creator, something that looks after us and the whole world, but I think that free will is the idea that one can choose, or not choose, to recognize these coincidences. They are like little fortune cookie messages that connect our lives together from the very beginning until the end. God's little secret messages being sent to us. Perhaps to guide us in the right direction through our lives. We just need to be aware that coincidences are just that – these meaningful messages. I think the prophets understood these messages and that's what enabled them to foretell or warn or motivate their people to change their ways – to be kinder, more forgiving, more at peace with each other. How else can we explain that you and I could meet like this separated by so many years apart... different worlds? Right here. Right now... That I passed you on that very street just a few days ago and you were there and in need of me to help you... Lyra, coincidences don't just happen for no reason. Do you feel that way too?"

Lyra kept holding on to Angel. There were no words to make sense of it all. Just emotion.

Gabriel returned again to the patio.

"Now you held the hummingbird in your hand when you were a little child. My son here... the dragonfly. Tonight is not the first time a dragonfly has landed in his palm. Not the first coincidence." Angel smiled.

"Like the hummingbird, my Mami taught me that in my culture there is a different belief about a dragonfly landing in one's hand. Angel closed her eyes and inhaled deeply...

"As sure as a dragonfly sees, so shall you see the fortunes and miseries of others."

My son is very observant. And he has a good heart. My daughter does too, thankfully, but her fortune has not yet been revealed. We will see what life brings for them. But, in some way, my son will be involved as a wise person assisting the fortunes and miseries of others. Such is his destiny.

"Then what is the symbolism of the dragonfly landing in your son's palm?" Lyra wanted to understand much more.

"Yes, I mentioned my son has an old soul, Lyra. Dragonflies are one of the oldest living species on this Earth. They are imbued with the wisdom of the ages and yet each one's adult lifespan is very short. A dragonfly has learned that the time we all have on Earth is very brief indeed. If we are fortunate, we realize the connection between the coincidences that come into our lives and seize the opportunities for personal reflection and growth. To live in the present. To live with awareness and with a loving heart. To be open to change just as a dragonfly transforms from its larval stage to adulthood. But because our time is fleeting, timing is critical in our lives. If a promising opportunity arises then we must seize it because it may not come around again. And a *green* dragonfly, as the one that visited Gabriel just now – green symbolizes the growing nature within our hearts. Our emotions and relationships. If you see a green dragonfly, it symbolizes that it is time for a new relationship to blossom while also nurturing the connection to those that were meaningful in the past or remain meaningful today. But these relationships must come from the depths of an honest heart, an open heart that does not conceal. It requires one to trust another soul. To merge two hearts together like a clam shell does its other half. From two equal halves becomes a greater, ever expanding whole immersed in love. And what is love but the eternal energy of the universe."

Angel paused in further contemplation. Then a gleam in her eyes as she raised her eyebrows and widened her globes. "Such is the wisdom of the dragonfly imbued in the one he touches kindly without biting." Angel laughed. She bit her jaws together in a mock biting motion and Lyra joined her in laugher.

It was time to return home. Lyra hugged Angel's children and promised she would return to play again someday. Angel kissed each of Lyra's cheeks. Then she brought her lips to Lyra's left eyebrow and gently kissed her swollen bruised skin.

"Thank you, Angel. And please thank Guillermo as well. He seems like a very fine man. Very kind and gentle."

"He is Lyra. Very much. Not all men are monsters."

Lyra looked away and held her lip. She batted away any thought of expending more tears. Angel sensed that Lyra was beginning to heal from her trauma. It was a good sign of her strength and resiliency.

"You have your mother's spirit don't you, Angel?"

"I suppose that I do. Mami remains inside here." Angel held her palm to her heart...

"Can I drive you home, Lyra, or shall I call a taxi for you?" Angel asked.

"No thanks. I think I will walk home tonight. I have this delicious dinner to digest. It is a beautiful evening and the stars are out. I think I'll be alright... But thank you, Angel. Maybe I'll meet a dragonfly along the way. Now that would be a coincidence!"

Lyra smiled sarcastically but in a gentle and meaningful way.

"Angel, you are a very special woman and friend. Someday I'd like to repay you."

"In my culture there is no repaying of love. Only the giving." Angel held out her palm as if searching for a hummingbird or a dragonfly and then laughed once again. She blew Lyra a kiss and Lyra exited.

The sky was clear after the most recent storms had moved inland and over the Cascades. Lyra strolled down the street and looked skyward. An archipelago of stars shining from the vast blackness of space. *Constellations!* She recognized a few but wished she knew more of their names and positions in the northern sky. But an amateur astronomer she was not. Maybe Bradlee knew of their locations and could name them all. He did know that 'Lyra' was one among them in the sky, she recalled. Angel's interpretation of the green dragonfly turned inside Lyra's mind as she steadfastly walked home undisturbed by a few other street sojourners who stared at her bruised face along the way. Angel's words reverberated within Lyra's mind...

'It is time for a new relationship to blossom. But it must come from the depths of an honest heart. Trust. Two hearts, joined together like two halves of a clam shell. Love is the eternal energy of the universe...'

Lyra was feeling her vitality emerge. She approached an elderly darker skinned gentleman who was playing his saxophone along the sidewalk. A street musician. Lyra hadn't come across any yet in Seattle near where she lived. His melody was lingering in the air between the buildings and quiet shops. It was soft with gentle harmonies as the music echoed down the street corridor. He smiled at Lyra and paused his playing. Lyra noticed that her battered face didn't seem to bother him at all. He spoke.

"A healing lover's tune for you perhaps, my sweet dear?"

He started playing again and Lyra stood silent and listened. It was a beautiful soulful melody. There was a Native American colorfully patterned blanket laying in front of him with an array of handmade necklaces made of colorful beads and small varieties of seashells. Lyra picked up one of the necklaces that caught her eye. She had never seen the kind of shells before as she studied the necklace in her palm.

"Ah, Mama san, you have chosen wisely," the musician said. "It is my most beautiful necklace of them all... My *Lyra shell* necklace." Lyra glanced quickly at his face. His eyes widened and he had a beaming smile. He tilted his head backwards and laughed into the night sky.

'*Coincidences don't just happen for no reason,*' Lyra thought again of Angel's words. She searched for a price tag but couldn't find one.

"Sir, how much for this necklace?"

The musician turned his head away towards the street and then glanced with his right eye at Lyra with a teasing yet comforting smile.

"For you, my most beautiful lady, this necklace is free. I feel inside as if this necklace has been on loan to me all this time and it has finally found its rightful owner. Please... my gift to you under these beautiful stars." He reached out his palms and Lyra handed the necklace to him. Then he placed it over her head and gently straightened it around her neck. "Most beautiful. Please... wear it well, Mama san."

Lyra ran the shells through her fingers. She thanked him and offered a kind smile.

She noted an old-fashioned wool felt derby hat lying beside the musician's chair. Lyra suddenly remembered Bradlee's fifty-dollar bill. It was still tucked inside her small wallet in her purse. She searched for it and then pulled out the folded bill and deposited it into the man's hat.

"This is from a friend of mine. And from me too. And for the next Lyra that happens to come along. Thank you for your beautiful music tonight." She gave him a generous smile. He brought his palms together and bowed gently towards Lyra.

"Thank you my lady, from the depths of my heart. And a blessed evening to you."

Lyra continued onward. Angel's words... *'From the depths of an honest heart, an open heart... must trust another soul... what is love but the eternal energy of the universe.'*

Her mind raced with memories. The fifty-dollar bill at the train station. Hummingbird moccasins. The Lady Slipper Inn. Oji. Roses. Bradlee's Ark necklace. She felt her neck and realized the Ark necklace wasn't there. *Where did I leave it at home or was it lost?*

Her walk became a slow jog. Her breathing accelerated and the pains in her chest and ribs were now more tolerable. She would overcome this. All of this rage. She was better than being destroyed by a madman. She held her purse tightly in one hand like a baton holder in a relay race. And then she began to run. Faster. Faster. She glanced at her watch and set a torrid pace for home. Lyra opened the door and quickly tore off her clothes and jumped into the shower. She was drenched with sweat. She used her hands to squeegee her sweat off of her arms and legs. Let it go. It was the kind of sweat that oozed out of her glands as if it was a Gila monster's venom that was harboring her anger and bitterness and hate and frustration at the world.

"Let it all go! Get rid of it...! Get Matt off of me!" Lyra screamed in the shower and scrubbed at her hair and skin vigorously once again. She cried and then screamed, over and over, until there was no more pain to set free.

THE NEXT MORNING LYRA AROSE EARLY and dressed for class. Foster was on the floor beside her bed. He must have fallen overnight. She returned him to his rightful pillow beside her. Bradlee's Ark necklace was dangling around Foster's neck. *There it is!* She lifted and placed it around her own neck and gently touched the ridges of the shell. It was as if it was a beacon of healing energy. She decided there would be no more makeup to her face. The bruises would be her badge of courage. That she would win the war even if she had lost one fight with humanity's darker elements.

Lyra marched into Dr. Bonheim's office and asked for forgiveness for skipping the scheduled meeting with her professor.

"It won't happen again. My word is my word or I do not deserve to be here at this university."

Dr. Bonheim sat Lyra down inside her office and closed the door. Lyra told her everything that occurred over the past week. He voice was subdued but without tears. She maintained her composure. Dr. Bonheim listened intently. She asked if Lyra was receiving proper psychological care and Lyra answered that it had already begun and that she was pleased with her progress. She would not let an evil madman deter her from her goals. Dr. Bonheim admired her courage. She decided to confide with Lyra. Dr. Bonheim told Lyra about a similar incident that happened to her when she was young and thought she was in love with a man who hurt her one night during her Ph.D. studies. A predatory professor who lured her into his home after a long day working side by side at the university lab together. Dr. Bonheim pulled her shirt collar up and slightly towards her left shoulder. She showed Lyra a scar that remained to this day. It ran along the length of her lower neck and towards her upper back. Dr. Bonheim was branded by the man's pocket knife because his student, the young Carol Bonheim, didn't quite appreciate that their relationship would need to be more physical, more sexual, should she wish to advance towards earning her doctorate. Dr. Bonheim stood from her desk and walked over to Lyra and gave her a long supportive hug.

"You will remain yourself, what is your good nature, and come out of this episode even stronger," she told Lyra.

Lyra thanked Dr. Bonheim for her support and revealed her feelings about Bradlee. That she sensed that she could trust him and wanted to become closer but that she was also much more nervous than before. Dr. Bonheim advised Lyra to be patient and allow for time to heal her wounds. That nearly all men have good souls and that Lyra happened upon the wrong one at the wrong time just as she had many years earlier.

"You must remember that it is not Lyra who must forgive herself for that night but the man who tortured you because he will live with the shame and guilt for what he has done to you, if he has any soul."

Dr. Bonheim returned to her desk chair. She knew it was time to change the subject. "Enough said."

Lyra nodded.

Both of them knew that a return to normalcy was essential. A return to being a hard working student. And Lyra was desperate for that return.

Dr. Bonheim revealed the reason for her desired meeting with Lyra earlier in the week.

Permitting for the North Dakota pipeline was being fast-tracked by the federal government. The National Environmental Policy Act, which had served for decades as a bedrock of legislation to promote effective and exhaustive review of any sizeable infrastructure project, was being weakened by the pro-business, pro-oil industry administration in Washington. The implications could have widespread and substantial environmental impact for the country. But now, through regulatory reinterpretation, the Environmental Protection Agency had recently decided to limit public review of such projects in order to reduce the so-called red tape that often held up projects for years to allow for extensive scientific impact analyses and public review.

"These exhaustive reviews have proved critical and justifiable in nearly all cases, thankfully," Dr. Bonheim added.

Well-paying jobs were at stake and the North Dakota pipeline project was being proposed as an essential national security initiative to stabilize the national strategic oil reserves long-term. The pipeline's fast-track was now being authorized by the President of the United States despite the intention of certain Congressional oversight committees who were seeking to take the administration to court over which body has final say over such regulations.

Dr. Bonheim explained that the folks shaping the pipeline outcome were powerful brokers in the halls of Washington and the energy industry. The Bureau of Indian Affairs within the Department of the Interior was also critically involved and they were negotiating a waiver for the pipeline to pass through a section of reservation land in exchange for substantial monetary payouts to the reservation council's operating budget. A legal quid pro quo between the federal government, the local tribes on the reservation land, and the oil industry.

However, there were some glitches. The local Native American tribal council in the North Dakota pipeline region was at odds amongst themselves in support or opposition to the proposed project. On the one hand, you had the younger generation of tribal leaders who advocated that the monetary influx would be substantial enough to raise the standard of living of every tribal member for many years ahead. After all, the deal was to allow for three revenue sources: the federal government was to pay a block grant of funds to the reservation if the council approved the pipeline to pass through tribal lands; there were to be contractual job guarantees for Native American workers from the reservation for the pipeline's construction; and an annuity was to be paid for the next twenty-five years to the tribal council from the oil industry that extracted and controlled the pipeline's flow.

But on the other hand, most of the elders on the tribal council were very hesitant or opposed to the project's scope out of concern for the health and safety of the tribal lands. They had lived through previous pipeline spills in their lifetimes. Spills that occurred adjacent to the tribal boundaries yet leaked into their underground waters on the reservation rendering their irrigation wells and streams toxic for numerous years. There was longstanding animosity since the federal government and oil industry did little to clean up those past toxic spells that leached onto the reservation in the past. The lands could not be farmed, livestock suffered and most needed premature slaughtering or euthanizing, and tribal poverty ensued. And now the tribal council was being asked to allow a substantial section of a new pipeline to pass *directly* through the reservation's land.

Dr. Bonheim explained to Lyra that, besides her professorial duties, she was the director of the Environmental Policy Institute adjacent to the university campus. A think-tank that also operated as a consulting service to government and industry drawing from the expertise of faculty across many sectors in the university departments and other hired professionals. The Institute agreed to a substantial contract offered by the EPA to prepare a risk assessment analysis of the North Dakota pipeline's potential impact to the environment on the reservation's lands. An impact study of what could go wrong and whether the pipeline's benefits outweighed those risks. The report was to be made available as well to the House and Senate oversight committees and to the Department of Energy and the Bureau of Indian Affairs. The Institute had a fast-track deadline to complete their analysis by the end of January as per the administration's demands. Time was of the essence. And so the Institute had already begun the process of selecting the experts and building the project team. This would include geologists, water and soil experts - particularly in watersheds and aquifers - civil engineers, pipeline construction consultants, and staff administrators. Trailer offices and accommodations were already available on the reservation to house the Institute's team of consultants adjacent to the small airstrip on the western edge of the reservation. The location already provided ease of access to the proposed pipeline site in the vicinity. Dr. Bonheim explained that Lyra was to wear multiple hats as an assistant on the project. She would conduct detailed background research as requested by the professional staff and serve to aggregate the analyzed data and expert recommendations into a draft document that Dr. Bonheim and others from the Institute would review and adjust before the final report was submitted to Congress and the various federal agencies involved. The report that Lyra drafted would serve as her de facto Master's thesis for her degree.

    Lyra was increasingly excited by the project. She knew the work would provide invaluable experience for her and possibly serve as leverage towards a future job after she earned her master's degrees.

"Lyra, you wanted to learn about real world geopolitics" Dr. Bonheim added. "Well, this is the real deal, young lady. I've been doing these very kinds of investigations for many years since I was about your age. Time to get your feet wet. But Lyra, understand this point well – when nature is at stake, sometimes we must look for the lesser of two evils. The pipeline very likely will be built regardless of your and my mutual interest, and the Institute's, in promoting alternative fuels for the future. But we will need to determine what direction that pipeline will take to minimize risk to the environment. That is our job this winter. And, while I mentioned to you previously that we would be spending most of January there, our work must begin earlier over the upcoming Thanksgiving holiday. You and I will need to head to North Dakota in just a few weeks as a small advance team to scout the project. Get to know the lay of the land. We will be there for three or four days over the holiday weekend. This way when we return in January we will have a head start on our work..." Dr. Bonheim paused as she let her briefing about the project sink in. Lyra nodded approvingly.

"So how do you feel about enjoying a Thanksgiving turkey on a Native American reservation?" Dr. Bonheim smiled.

"I'm a vegetarian" Lyra replied with her palms raised. "But count me in on everything else. I'm excited to get started on the research."

"Good. One of my colleagues at the Institute will be meeting with you shortly to update you on our preparations to date and brief you further about the politics on the ground. You and I will meet once more at my office before we head to North Dakota in just a few weeks. And Lyra, make sure you have a heavy winter coat, wool hat, and thick ski gloves. There are plenty of outfitters in this town who will readily supply your needs. The Institute will provide you with a small stipend to assist with these purchases. You do remember my shivers when you chose this project a few months ago?"

Dr. Bonheim gave a surly smile as she wrapped her arms once again around her torso in a mock shiver. Lyra laughed again and thanked Dr. Bonheim for the stipend. Lyra had no intention to freeze to death. After all, she's wasn't a cold blooded reptile. They made plans for their next meeting before they would embark for North Dakota for the Thanksgiving weekend.

For the remainder of the day, Lyra immersed herself in her lectures and readings and landscape drawings. Her misshapen face received plenty of stares from fellow classmates but she focused her eyes towards her work, ignored the glances, and maintained her composure. She returned home and changed into her running gear. The stress of her first day back into her studies deserved a reward. She added her small fanny pack around her waist and deposited a mace aerosol spray into the zippered compartment. It was Ansley's insistence and Lyra agreed that it might bring added peace of mind. Lyra decided to follow her usual path towards the Washington Park Arboretum despite the steady flow of fellow runners and walkers she knew she would pass along the trail network. More stares but she had grown inured by now.

She jogged around Union Bay as her muscles, stiffened from inactivity and trauma, began to loosen from her demanding strides. She turned past the athletic fields and approached the rowing shellhouse. Her stride increased with her rush of nervousness. *Would Matt be there with the fellow rowers?* She fought off the deeper emotional signals imploring her to turn around and run home. This was *her* route and she wasn't going to alter it. She could hear the rowing crew sniping with each other as they readied their boats along the shoreline. There was a young man sitting quietly on a bench and he was overlooking the activities at the boat ramp. His back was facing Lyra as she completed the turn along the trail and he was loosely wearing a warm-up jacket around his shoulders. She stopped suddenly when she recognized the word "MATT" plastered in purple lettering along the jacket's upper back flap. Lyra's adrenaline flowed with anger and rage. She cracked off a thick stump from a fallen tree branch and quietly approached him from behind. There was a rustle from some leaves beneath her feet and he slowly turned his torso while remaining seated and looked right at her. Lyra brought her weapon to her side and stared. He slipped off his wool hat. He had a foot long row of perhaps over a hundred small stitches running along the length of his left brow, down his temple, and then along his left cheek to beneath his lower jawline. His eyes were both massively swollen and bruised and he was wearing a white patch over his left eye socket. His nose had dried blood congealed at the entrance to his nares and there were additional stitches that repaired a flap of tissue that had been torn from the area of his left nostril. A thick white bandage flared across his nasal bridge and was attached underneath his eyelids. Lyra noted that four of his middle upper front teeth and two middle lower teeth were missing and his lips were grotesquely swollen and crusted with dried blood and multiple sutures. A large swollen contusion jutted from his upper right scalp. His right hand, wrist, and forearm were casted up to his elbow and his left wrist and thumb were splinted above a series of swollen and bruised fingers. Another cast descended from just below his left knee to his ankle. A pair of crutches were resting on the bench beside him. Matt looked at Lyra briefly and then his eyes averted to the ground. Lyra approached cautiously, circled to the front of the bench, and then stood in front of him.

"Matt, you hurt me." Lyra held her composure despite

shaking inside herself in fear. "Maybe you've hurt others just like me before. But if you ever go near me again I will finish what Carl started. I will kill you." She stared at Matt and he glanced back at her with utter sadness and then averted his gaze again to the ground at her feet.

He spoke with difficulty and his articulation was severely challenged.

"I'm so sorry, Lyra. I was drinking heavily that night. And no, I promise you I did not hurt another woman before." A few tears ran down his cheeks. "I guess I deserved this beating. Carl almost killed me. My left eye has been banged up so much that the eye doc said I'll be blind in that eye the rest of my life... When Carl was finished with me in my room he told me that *'living with the pain for what I had done to you, would be worse. Just like a woman who must always live with the pain of being abused or raped.'*

"Lyra, I can't ask you to forgive me. That wouldn't be fair. But I am very sorry that it happened. I have no excuse for my behavior. I've been sitting here the past few days and wondering what went wrong with me these past few years in college. I know I need to get help. Make some changes with who I am. How I treat other people. Maybe this was what I needed. A good beating to knock some sense into me..."

He looked up and held his gaze on Lyra. "And I *will* stay away from you. I promise you that I will." He reached out his splinted left arm and opened his palm towards Lyra. Lyra wanted to bash Matt's hand with the heavy stick. Instead, she dropped it beside the crutches. He lowered his arm to his side and then turned away to look out on the bay as the team began to row away from the dock.

Lyra turned and walked back to the trail. Then she started to run again. *An eye for an eye*, she thought to herself. She couldn't stop her tears from flowing but she fought them off quickly and let the salty taste linger in her mouth before spitting out her saliva. Then she sipped from her water bottle. *It is done. Justice served,* she thought. Maybe Matt was speaking truthfully. It didn't matter. She would prevail and Matt would never forget what he had done to her. She rounded Foster Point and continued to the Arboretum and raced home just the same as the week prior. She'd need to regain her strength and stamina as her bruises healed. But she was determined to return to her usual running form.

Lyra fixed a healthy salad for dinner and paired it with thin slices of fried eggplant with olive oil, parmesan cheese and red sauce. She sprinkled some oregano flakes from her spice rack and then reached for the paprika. *Bradlee! He did say he liked paprika with his pasta – but for breakfast?!* He must have been joking on the train. She smiled and devoured her meal. Then she showered and slipped on her favorite silky camisole and began to read in bed. She glanced at Foster fixated beside her, guardian of her Ark necklace while she did her run. It was bejeweled around his neck once again. She removed it from him and placed it around her own. It felt very comforting, as if Bradlee had just placed it on her. She started to review some of the day's studies and couldn't concentrate. Thoughts of Bradlee kept popping into her mind. She held the Ark shell and rubbed it between her fingers and dialed.

"Hello?" Bradlee was partially awake by the fourth ring. He pressed the illuminator button on his wrist watch.

"Bradlee, it's Lyra."

"Yes, I know. You are the only one that I know who would call me at 2:30 in the morning."

"I'll take that as a complement." She giggled.

"It's good to hear your voice again, Lyra. I didn't know if..."

"I'm sorry, Bradlee. I was rude to you last night."

"Apology accepted. Lyra, are you OK? I just had a bad feeling last night, that's all."

"You are very perceptive, Bradlee. Even if you are more than three thousand miles away."

The magnetism had returned. Lyra could sense it. She hoped Bradlee could as well.

"Bradlee, I'm going to be alright. I promise you... Sometimes wives and husbands squabble, right?" She laughed at the reference to the Lady Slipper Inn where Bradlee signed their names in the registry as a married couple.

"Hey Bradlee, guess what I'm wearing just now."

Bradlee thought for a moment. There was the image of Lyra in her milky white satin camisole that she wore to bed that night at the inn. He turned towards her hummingbird needlepoint that he had framed and placed on his nightstand. Her hands were right beside him if he closed his eyes and imagined.

"Uh... a thong below and nothing else?!" He couldn't believe the words from his mouth.

Lyra laughed wildly.

"Really? Is that what you think about when we speak together?"

She was teasing him and again, he didn't mind. He sensed that she was in a very playful mood. He missed that.

"Occasionally, I will admit... OK, more than occasionally. Lots?"

Lyra blushed inside her covers and glanced at Foster.

"Well, I was going to say that your Ark shell necklace is dangling from my neck."

Her voice lowered to a whisper. "Shh... Be careful what you say, Bradlee. Foster is sleeping beside me. You wouldn't want to wake him up. He's big and furry and has sharp teeth."

Bradlee was wide awake now and he jumped out of bed and walked over to the window that overlooked the ocean. The clouds were as wispy thin as he had remembered Lyra's camisole.

"Lyra, you're teasing me now. Who is Foster? You mentioned his name to me before. Is he the one you went out on a date with last night? Because I don't appreciate this kind of humor calling me up when you are sleeping beside another man." His jealousy was gurgling within as his pulse quickened.

"Bradlee, settle down. Foster's my stuffed animal friend. He keeps me warm at night. And he's also the lighthouse keeper of your shell necklace, the one you gave me on the train."

Bradlee relaxed his pace and stared at the ocean again. The shining waves were strikingly beautiful in the moonlight. "Lyra, you looked incredibly beautiful that night in the bedroom at the inn. That's what I picture you wearing."

"Good. Because that's what I have on right now."

Bradlee sighed into the phone. "Lyra, I miss you. I miss seeing you ever since I returned to P.E.I. I really wish we can see each other again…"

"Me too. Very much, Bradlee."

"Can I visit you in Seattle? I can come before or after I'm in Medora over Thanksgiving for the photography exhibit."

"Bradlee, that's why I called back tonight. I wanted to share with you some great news. I'll be in North Dakota at the same time as you, I think. My advisor, Dr. Bonheim and I will be there to begin work on the pipeline project that I mentioned to you."

"Really?! That is amazing news! That's fantastic!!!"

"Bradlee, I really miss you too." Lyra gently placed her right hand over her belly button and let her fingers slide down between her thighs.

"Lyra, I've been thinking…"

"I know Bradlee. Me too… I'll let you go back to sleep now. I wish you pleasant dreams. I had eggplant tonight so I know I'll be having some wild dreams. It always happens to me for some reason." She caressed her labia gently and stroked with her fingers. She did all she could to resist moaning at that moment.

"Save a piece for me next time I see you, Lyra. Can I call you tomorrow night...? And the next day... And the day after that. And...?"

Lyra laughed. "Bradlee, easy now. But I won't mind. We'll make plans for North Dakota tomorrow."

"OK." A long pause. Bradlee glanced at the enlarged photograph frame of the solo wild horse. The stallion's eyes didn't look as forlorn in the moonlight.

"Goodnight, Bradlee."

"Goodnight stars," he replied.

"Goodnight cushy warm socks," Lyra added.

"And goodnight clocks."

"Goodnight room."

"And goodnight cow jumping over the moon."

They laughed one more time together until only their breath lingered.

"Lyra, I think I'm..."

"Shh. Bradlee, don't say another word. But I know the feeling. We'll chat more tomorrow."

She hung up and turned off the nightstand light and focused intently, unashamedly on her hand between her legs.

LESS THAN THREE WEEKS UNTIL THANKSGIVING. Bradlee worked on the finishing touches of his exhibit. The stones he brought back from Newfoundland and tumbled for days were ready for their next assignment. Bradlee assembled two thick oversized custom ash wood frames and inserted a nearly life-size photograph into each. They were the two best photos he had taken of the Badlands wild horses; one was of the entire herd in repose beside the river, the wind in their faces, tolerating the world steadfastly. The other was of the stallion, Bradlee's solo sojourner with those perceptive eyes glaring from the photograph whether viewed from any angle in the room. He carefully gouged the wood frames with his woodcarving tools and created decorative motifs of the Badlands. Cottonwood trees. Meadow sedge and Indiangrasses. Juniper trees. Sunflowers. Asters and Rabbitbrush. Prairie dogs and bison, elk, pronghorns, cottontails. Cedar waxwings and Townsend's solitaires. The memories flooded his mind with creative ideas to add to the wood carvings. He glued the stones along a wood carved streambed. The frames were finally done. He stood back from his work table. They were a labor of love and he was proud of his handiwork. He applied a stain and set the frames to dry overnight. He bundled twenty other enlarged wild horse photographs, the ones he had selected from the thousands of images, and arranged them for shipment to Medora.

He turned to one more enlarged photo. Bradlee had snookered a photo of Jim Clayburn on their horseback ride. They were watering their horses beside a streambed. Jim was standing beside his black stallion and brushing its coat in the dimming light of the afternoon sun. The horse turned its head towards Jim and Bradlee pressed the shutter as man and horse were looking into each other's eyes. Jim's custom saddle, with its metal buckles, was gleaming. Bradlee rolled the poster-size photo and carefully placed it inside a cardboard tube. It was to be a gift for Jim as a thank you for hosting Bradlee at his ranch for Thanksgiving.

Bradlee found his phone and dialed.

"The Lady Slipper Inn. Nancy here. How can I help you?" Bradlee listened carefully. It was good to hear Nancy's voice. Her articulation had improved significantly since her stroke more than three months earlier.

"Nancy, this is Bradlee Lee. We met briefly when I was a guest at your inn at the end of August. I'm not sure if you remember…"

"Bradlee Lee. Yes, of course. Why, you're the hummingbird whisperer!" Nancy chuckled.

"That's right." Bradlee's mind flashbacked to breakfast that morning at the inn when the hummingbird had landed in his palm.

"And your friend. Lyra – that was her name, right? Such a pretty young lady and gentle soul. You have excellent taste, Mr. Lee. I do hope you two are well… I can tell when a woman has love in her eyes. You might want to consider a ring for her delicate finger someday soon, you know."

"Thank you, Nancy." *'Love in her eyes… a ring…'* Bradlee held onto the image.

"I hope you and Thomas are both doing well."

"Well, we're about set to freeze up here in Minot for the winter season but we still get an occasional straggler to the inn who needs a warm and cozy bed. Slow season now but we don't mind the peace and quiet…"

"Glad to hear. Nancy, I wanted to see about —" Bradlee started but was interrupted.

"Oh, and Thomas is plugging along. He thinks he needs to look after me every minute of the day but I'm doing just fine. My talking and walking and writing are improving by the day. And Dr. Cohen has been real pleased with my progress. Says I should be back to ballroom dancing by New Year's Eve… What was that Bradlee?"

"Well, I'll dance with you if Thomas passes!" They shared a good laugh.

"Nancy, I wanted to inquire about a stayover at the inn. I'll be in Medora for some business over Thanksgiving but was hoping to stay a night at the inn before I return to Prince Edward Island where my home is."

"Yes, I remember seeing P.E.I. on the welcome registry. Did Thomas tell you we had our honeymoon on P.E.I.?

That was many moons ago but I was once quite a bicyclist, you know. Thomas could barely catch me back then even if he was at full throttle." Nancy laughed heartily as Bradlee heard Thomas' voice approaching in the background.

"Now hand me that phone, Nancy." Thomas was laughing as well. He picked up.

"All lies, Bradlee, all lies. Nancy enjoyed me chasing her all around that island, I will grant her that."

Bradlee could sense the magnetism between them.

"Thomas Johansen, it's good to hear your voice again. How are you?"

"Oh, just fine Bradlee. Real pleased with Nancy's progress. Dr. Cohen is as well."

"Yes, Nancy told me. She sounds wonderful and very happy. Very glad for you both. May I ask how long you and Nancy have been together?"

"It will be our fiftieth anniversary this spring." *Fifty years of marriage*, Bradlee contemplated the thought but couldn't quite imagine the full breadth of a shared life.

"Thomas, would you do it all again if you had the choice? You know... your life with Nancy."

"Well, let me move into the parlor room out of peeping range. Hold on a second..." Bradlee could recognize Thomas' footfalls. He thought, it was uncanny how each person had a unique sound while walking. A door closed.

"Bradlee, that's a question I used to think about many years ago. Nancy and I, we had some rough patches when the kids were little and I had taken to the booze more than I should have. I suppose most couples do. But to answer your question – yes, wholeheartedly *yes*. I've had a very fulfilling life with Nancy. They say that love is all about romance. Yes, that's true in a way. You've got to have that spark and keep it lit all along the way. But it's a lot more than that as we age, Bradlee. Love means you are willing to do your turn with the dishes, and run out for ice cream on an icy winter's night because the Mrs. has a craving, or take care of each other when the flu strikes, or even worse, a stroke in our case of course, and when a loved one in the family passes and there's nothing but sorrow for many days. You see the passage of time before your eyes. Grandkids. Great grandkids, God willing… It all ends one day, Bradlee. Too quickly, I'm afraid. We all realize that as we age onward. Time accelerating. But my Nancy means everything to me because she's been by my side and when I look into her eyes I see the same thing that she does. *Love*, Bradlee. Just simple God given love. Life's not more complicated than that. I truly believe God didn't intend for the world to be more complicated than that."

"Thanks, Thomas. I really enjoy listening to your thoughts."

"Well, don't thank me entirely. That rabbi who stayed with us years ago – the one who worked on the carvings at the church in town – he shared about all the same ideas as I just mentioned. You might say he had quite the positive influence on me when I needed it most. I sure did adopt a lot of his teachings and I don't regret it. Never have."

"I have a feeling the rabbi knew what he was preaching about," Bradlee added. "Anyway, your words are always very soothing and meaningful… Say, one more thing, Thomas. I have a kind request of Oji if it's possible to speak with her."

"Oh, Oji returned to the reservation last week. She works limited hours here during the winter off-season. Is there anything I can help you with?"

"I was hoping Oji could send me a pair of moccasins. An unfinished pair. Well, finished when it comes to the shaping and stitching but without anything else. Naked, I suppose you can call them."

"Naked moccasins you shall have. I like that phrase." Thomas chuckled. "I'll stop by and find a pair in Oji's living room. I'll ship them to you tomorrow. They are real comfortable. Any particular size you're looking for?"

Bradlee hadn't thought of that detail. "Actually, I'm not sure exactly. Is there a medium-ish size?"

"I'll rummage through and see what I can find."

"Thanks Thomas. You can add the moccasin pair to my tab when I see you soon. I'll be at the inn to stay on Saturday night, two days after Thanksgiving," Bradlee added. Thomas made a mental note of the date.

"How's James doing, by the way? When I'm in town I was hoping you could put me in touch with him. Maybe stop by his place or meet him at Ruby's for a quick visit."

Thomas sighed. "Bradlee, I've got tough news to share with you. James' wife, Caroline – well, she passed away just a few weeks ago. They had just celebrated their own fiftieth anniversary. It was quite the bash. Their grandkids just made a beautiful celebration for them and I think the whole town was there to help James and Caroline celebrate. But then just a few days later Caroline suffered a heart attack and passed suddenly at home. There was nothing the ambulance folks could do by the time they arrived."

Sweet Caroline, Bradlee thought back to the taxi ride with James. The pies he garnered from Ruby's. His vivaciousness. He closed his eyes in sadness. Bradlee wished he could have met Caroline, the love of James' life.

"Thomas, that's awful news. That was his Sweet Caroline... he would *constantly* call her that."

"Yes, I know. Still does. That doesn't have to end after she passed on. We've been friends, James and I, for almost seventy years. All the way back to grade school, Bradlee. I've been visiting James every day at his home since Caroline passed. He's coming around gradually. It will take time, Bradlee. I had my scare with Nancy, as you know. Somehow we must move on after we lose the ones we love. But the loving never ends."

Bradlee's eyes welled up. "Yes, I understand. I'd really like to visit James when I pass through Minot. Maybe I can cheer him up a bit." Thomas gave Bradlee James' contact information.

"Thomas, I really look forward to seeing you and Nancy again as well."

"You take care now, Bradlee. Keep those talented hands of yours safe from harms way. And safe travels here. God be with you."

Thomas and Bradlee said their goodbyes and hung up.

Bradlee stared out the window to the ocean for a long while and thought back to James. He has a kind and gentle heart. That gleam in his eye. '*My Sweet Caroline. She was as gorgeous as I could ever imagine a girl to be... The mind forgets what it's supposed to, you know... It's the good times that really matter...*'

James must be really hurting about now. Bradlee knew that pain. He glanced at Ruthy's framed watercolor beside the window and lost himself deeper in thought.

'*Oh sugar!*' Thomas said to himself after he had hung up the phone. '*I forgot to ask Bradlee if his wife, Lyra, would be joining as well. Surely she would be.*' He notated the booking date in his calendar and held the Hummingbird Room under Mr. and Mrs. Bradlee and Lyra Lee.

LYRA AND BRADLEE SPOKE EVERY NIGHT over the next few weeks up until their scheduled flights to North Dakota. Bradlee spent his time finishing up any remaining tasks on the Heritage Center project. He really needed this project for his career. He had received a new offer for a photojournalism piece about the Nile River and the great pyramids that would have started after the New Year but, once again, Bradlee felt the meager pay just didn't add up for the effort that would be required. Perhaps something else would come along or he'd find work to get by taking wedding photos or children's portraits until the next break came his way.

He received the moccasins in the mail a few days after speaking with Thomas. He set them on his work table and sketched and played with various ideas before setting to work on them. Besides chores around the Marshpillow, strolls along the beach, and bicycle rides to the lighthouse and back, the moccasin project would be his next artistic outlet and an enjoyable use of his creative energy and passion. He was beginning to hope the day would come when the moccasins would be the most special gift he could ever offer.

Every day Bradlee looked forward to his late night pillow conversations with Lyra. The four hour time difference between Seattle and P.E.I. meant that Bradlee needed to wake and sleep by an odd schedule. He awoke very early, usually at 4 a.m. each day, and worked on various projects or exercised and enjoyed nature during its most quiet dawn hours. Early winter sunrises were stunning. He napped briefly in the late morning and arose for lunch. Then he continued with various activities until he forced himself to an early bedtime hour just after sunset. Lyra's usual late night call came between two and three o'clock and they spoke at length. Sometimes a half-hour was the most that Lyra could offer away from her studies, other times far longer when he could entice her to linger into his early morning. Then he returned to sleep briefly if he could quiet his thoughts and fantasies about Lyra. The cycle repeated nightly.

They spoke about their daily routines, recipes, Lyra's studies, strange happenings, and odd coincidences in life. Lyra let Bradlee know about the close friendship she was developing with Angel and her progress running in preparation for the competitive half-marathon race in the spring. Bradlee informed Lyra about Leo and Rachel and Ruthy in Newfoundland and his enjoyment finding a fellow woodcarver to share mutual interests and ideas. He mentioned about Ruthy's watercolor painting and that he had framed it when he returned home and hung it beside the window that overlooked the ocean. He told her about Ezra, his best friend from childhood who was wild and crazy and loved babies and kids and was a pediatrician in Connecticut, but that he needed to reach Ezra again since it had been a number of years since they were last in touch. Lyra commented, teasingly, that "opposite personalities *do* sometimes attract, after all." They had a good laugh. Lyra told Bradlee about the times she used to visit P.E.I. in the summers as a child with her family and with her best friend, Ansley, who now wasn't far away from Lyra since Ansley attended law school at Berkeley. Lyra did *not* tell Bradlee about the assault and attempted rape on Halloween. She felt that subject was done in her mind or at least it could wait for a different moment when she was beside Bradlee someday in the future.

    Bradlee invited Lyra to visit him on P.E.I. the first chance she could get. Lyra said she had tentative plans to visit Ansley and her family in Connecticut for the winter holiday just before she needed to return to North Dakota for the month of January for the pipeline project. She would stop at Ansley's place for a day or two and then fly to P.E.I. to join Bradlee if he could retrieve her from the airport. They could spend the New Year holiday together. But first, they were looking forward to seeing each other in North Dakota. Lyra wasn't informed yet of the exact location where she and Dr. Bonheim would be staying but they would be in touch upon arriving to North Dakota. Bradlee was planning to rent a car anyway so he would map Lyra's location and work out the rendezvous time once they were nearer to each other. And as their reunion approached, the excitement and energy that they shared together continued to blossom.

Part Six

D R. BONHEIM AND LYRA arrived to Billings, Montana in the late morning and then transferred planes to a Cessna single engine propeller plane with enough occupancy for one pilot and three passengers. The Institute had made arrangements to lease the Cessna for their use for the duration of the holiday weekend. Stan met Dr. Bonheim and Lyra at the runway in Billings. After proper introductions, Stan collected their luggage and they walked over to his flight company's Cessna that was parked on the tarmac. He deposited the luggage, carefully balancing each bag's weight, into the small rear cargo bay.

"Lyra, you ever been on a plane as small as this one?" Dr. Bonheim asked as they boarded above the wing.

"Never!" Lyra was quite nervous and excited. The Montana sky was endless and cloudless. It was near freezing outside but the sun warmed Lyra's bare cheeks between her scarf and her wool hat.

"Well then," Dr. Bonheim continued, "you're in for a real treat. These beauties can fly over 250mph at an altitude over 13,000 feet but I don't think we'll be that fast, or that high, today cruising into the reservation."

Lyra settled into the rear seat behind Stan and buckled. Dr. Bonheim fished out her camera from her travel bag and buckled next to the pilot at the front.

"Stan, hope you don't mind if I shoot a few photos along the way. I can't resist my aerials for my photo collection."

"No problem, Dr. Bonheim." Stan checked some of the flight panel instrument gauges and strapped his microphone unit onto his head. Then he flipped a few switches and called to the Billings air traffic controllers and waited for their response. "Ladies, our flight plan will be taking us over some quiet countryside through southeast Montana and then we'll veer northeast, pass near Teddy Roosevelt National Park and then finish up at the airstrip northeast of Medicine Hole on the Fort Berthold Reservation."

He listened to the voice from the tower.

"Roger that, will taxi to runway two. Looks like we're cleared for takeoff. Make sure your seat buckles are securely fastened. Things can get a little bumpy until we reach a usually smoother cruising altitude just above eight thousand feet."

The propeller sputtered and then whirred into ever faster revolutions as Stan turned the wings into proper position at the base of the runway, radioed the tower one more time for clearance, and then accelerated down the runway. Lyra was thrown back against her seat as she grasped onto the door handle beside her, closed her eyes, and began to chant a childhood prayer. Out of the corner of her right eye she could see Dr. Bonheim smiling and readying her camera towards her side door window as the Cessna elevated sharply and reached skyward. Dr. Bonheim quickly glanced behind and witnessed Lyra pulling a paper bag from the seat compartment and holding it over her face. Dr. Bonheim gave a few guffaws.

"Lyra, try to relax. You'll love this in a few more minutes once your stomach settles back down to where it belongs… A mint perhaps?" Dr. Bonheim pulled out a tin with mint candies from her pocket and offered it to Lyra but she refused. She was not amused by the gesture at that moment.

After a few more minutes the plane approached its cruising altitude and flattened its nose to a more tolerable horizontal trajectory. Lyra was able to breathe comfortably again. Her nausea had passed. Dr. Bonheim continued with her aerial photos as Lyra was enamored by the view as she peered out the window and gazed at the earth. Off to the north she could make out some distant snow covered mountains. There were bobbing oil rigs dotted here and there within the geometric farm fields. Massive fields of wheat and alfalfa. They approached near Teddy Roosevelt National Park and Stan pointed out some of the geologic features to them. Lyra spotted a herd of bison and then they passed near a river bed inside a canyon and Lyra surged with childlike excitement when she saw them – a band of wild horses were gathered and slurping from the river. Stan located them as well and did an extra loop while Dr. Bonheim proceeded to photograph the horses. Then they must have been spooked by the plane's propeller noise as the wild horses turned quickly and galloped in a frenzy into the hills and beyond until they were out of visual sight from the plane's window.

"Did you see them galloping in unison?! Just beautiful! That's what Bradlee came out here for, Dr. Bonheim. He was photographing the wild horses for his exhibit debut in Medora the day after Thanksgiving."

"Really?! Well, we'll have to see if we can fit a short excursion to Medora into our tight calendar this weekend. It's not too far a drive from the reservation. I love a nice photography exhibit!" Lyra fidgeted with the Ark necklace and Dr. Bonheim gave Lyra a knowing smile. They relaxed for the remainder of the flight and landed smoothly onto the reservation's airstrip.

"That was fun, Stan! As I get older, I just think I need to have more *plain* fun in life, after all! – no pun intended about the '*plane*,'" Dr. Bonheim laughed giddily. Thanks for the safe flight!" Dr. Bonheim shook Stan's hand generously as she and Lyra dismounted from the wing with Stan's assistance. They collected their luggage.

"My pleasure, Dr. Bonheim. You and Lyra have your accommodations right over there in Trailer #6 adjacent to the washrooms. I'll be across the way in Trailer #1 if you need me at any time during your stay." He pointed to a corral of trailers located just off the airstrip. There was a small platform building located behind the trailers that housed a few bathrooms and showers. Everything looked clean and new. Adjacent to the trailers stood an enormous teepee structure at the center of the trailer corral. Its canvas walls were painted with prints of decorative horses and bison and eagle and hawk feathers. Adjacent to the teepee was a large stone fire pit with a handful of Adirondack chairs. The chairs were all decorated beautifully with Native American designs.

"The reservation folks just placed these structures here over this past summer," Stan explained. "They were hoping to add some revenue by having tourists come and visit the reservation, see what life is like for genuine American Indians, and stay a few nights here before heading home. My flight company has been helping to make that happen. Kind of like fancier glamping instead of camping but with Native American touches. They have plans after the winter thaws to build a stable nearby and really give the tourists a chance to enjoy this more remote section of the reservation. There's some beautiful rugged land out by these parts. Nothing developed yet except for the oil pipeline that'll run somewhere through here if it the plans go through. This area's got some picture perfect sections on horseback and between the glamping and the horseback riding, I'd say they're on to a great idea but it'll need some time to get the word out... Anyway, dinner will be served in one hour at five o'clock sharp. You ladies will get to experience some of that glamping atmosphere. Hope you enjoy it."

"Very cute idea. Well, if they get this glamping project running smoothly maybe they wouldn't have to worry about pumping all that oil through these parts!" Dr. Bonheim remarked sarcastically. The ladies headed for the bathrooms and then unpacked and rested in their trailer.

When five o'clock arrived Lyra heard soothing Native American flute music and men's voices chanting outside their trailer. She opened the door and realized it was being piped in through the speakers hung from the wood carved posts that surrounded the perimeter of the corral. It was near freezing outside. Lyra and Dr. Bonheim bundled up in their winter jackets and wool hats and headed over to the teepee.

A group in traditional Native American dress were gathered inside beside a table and chairs. There were a few pick-up trucks parked behind the corral. Lyra presumed they had driven to the trailer site from the main area of the reservation. Dr. Bonheim and Lyra were joined by Stan. Heat lamps adorned each end of the table and radiated their warmth throughout the teepee. A young boy and girl, dressed in traditional clothing, were at the ready as servers. There were three women preparing and cooking the fresh meal in a small curtained area inside the teepee. First, the children poured warm water over each guest's hands and collected it into a basin and then dried the hands of the guests with a colorfully imprinted towel. It appeared to represent a ceremonial cleansing. Then the meal started with piping hot Knoephla - a creamy potato soup with dumplings. Stan explained that this was not a Native American dish but a North Dakota settler's traditional soup to warm the belly on cold winter nights. This was followed by braised elk shank served with corn and squash and wild rice. There was also a salad of mixed greens tossed with a variety of seeds and nuts and served with a delicious herbal dressing. Lyra passed on the elk but devoured the tasty vegetarian helpings.

The oldest woman who was cooking behind the curtain walked over to the table with a kind smile. "Welcome to our homeland. I am Wichahpi." The woman gently bowed her head towards the guests. "My husband and I were born here and we have lived our whole lives on the reservation.

Someday, we will die here and join our ancestors in the clouds above us. In the times of our grandmothers and grandfathers our people ate very healthy from what was provided by Grandmother Earth. "To the west," she held out her hand, "the mountains brought us pure water to nourish our thirst. To the east," she turned, "the sun brought the arrival of spring, new beginnings, and new gatherings. To the south, the warm summer winds cultivated our plants for trade. And to the north, our forests and plains provided us with the hunt, our elk and deer and buffalo, for eating and warm dress. On behalf of our people we hope you enjoy your meal tonight as we gather in peace."

It was a lovely meal topped off with an Indian pudding dessert made from milk, cornmeal, molasses, cinnamon, sugar and spices. It was served with a heaping scoop of vanilla ice cream with maple syrup drizzled on top and each guest was given a uniquely carved wooden dessert spoon with its handle crafted in the shape of an Indian arrow. Lanyard was used to connect the spoon to the shaft and the handle was adorned with bird feathers. Lyra couldn't help herself. The maple syrup, and all the rest of it was too delicious and so she begged for a second helping before the others had even finished.

The older woman returned with Lyra's second bowl. She explained that this was a traditional Sioux pudding to honor her brothers and sisters from the fellow Dakota tribes. But the recipe was modernized to suit today's tastes, of course. "Many Lakota and other smaller tribes have intermarried over the years. We are one big family in the Dakotas. On behalf of all of us on the reservation, we hope you will enjoy the rest of your stay here."

Lyra and Dr. Bonheim thanked their hosts profusely and then strolled out of the teepee while holding onto their wooden arrow spoons and exited into the frigid air.

Stan wished them a good night. "Weather forecast says

we're headed for a cold blast these next few days, ladies. Make sure you bundle up overnight."

"Thanks for the good news, Stan" Dr. Bonheim replied facetiously and gave Lyra another mock shiver.

"Wow! What a delicious meal! Lyra exclaimed.

"Agreed. These work assignments, Lyra, do have their magical moments sometimes. You will need to have a good sense of adventure if you wish to follow in my footsteps at the Institute someday soon."

Dr. Bonheim paused and raised her eyebrows beneath her eyeglasses. Lyra didn't know how to respond. They turned towards each other.

"Lyra. I've had my eye on you since you arrived to Seattle. Your resume, your college transcript, and your faculty recommendations were impeccable. And I've followed your work ethic and the quality of your research and your writing skills over this past semester. You are a very bright young woman, Lyra. And I need someone who can replace me someday at the Institute. A faculty position as well at the university if you are inclined to continue towards a Ph.D., which I highly recommend you do." Lyra was stunned listening.

"Look, I am not getting any younger. I'm not that far from retirement now... Lyra, I see so much of myself in you when I was your age. We are created from the same cloth. Lovers of the natural world. A desire to preserve the environment at any possible cost. A will to change policy for the better so that humanity can not only survive this planet but also prosper among our fellow inhabitants. These are very challenging times. Your generation *must* replace us. And of those that have come through the master's program these past many years it is *you* that has that passion. That spark, drive, spunk - whatever we wish to call it. Whether you love a fellow human being or your work, or hopefully both, it comes from the same source within here." Dr. Bonheim pointed to her chest. "Think about it,

Lyra. After you finish your master's I would like you to stay on at the university and earn your Ph.D. It will take another five years, at least, but during that time you will be earning income from your work at the Institute. I would like to hire you after graduation this spring. Part-time work at the Institute for starters while you sink your teeth into the Ph.D. program. Hopefully, someday you will serve on the board of the Institute and eventually rise to be its director, just as I am now."

Lyra's mind raced from her childhood skipping along sandy beaches with Ansley to running in the mountains while in college and to her pounding heart while flying over galloping wild horses. She tried to settle her mind but she was just too excited.

"Dr. Bonheim, I..."

"Lyra, enough of Dr. Bonheim this and Dr. Bonheim that... Soon enough we will be colleagues and you'll have your own students calling you Dr. Flurey all the time that you may forget your name was once Lyra... Please, from now on you will call me Carol, my mother's given name for me. I do like it, by the way." She chuckled.

Lyra regained a bit of her composure but couldn't stop smiling. Tears of joy in her eyes.

"OK. Carol it is... Thank you. Thank you for mentoring me. I won't ever let you down. It would be an honor to continue towards my Ph.D. and work at the Institute. I don't think I could ask for a better opportunity."

Lyra gave Dr. Bonheim a long hug. They returned to their trailer and then diligently reviewed work plans for the morning.

BRADLEE'S FLIGHT ARRIVED to Minot in the afternoon. He collected his suitcase and picked up a car at the rental center. Using the car's GPS, he entered the coordinates that

Jim Clayburn had texted him the day prior and headed for the reservation. The trip was relaxing and uneventful as the land quieted just outside of Minot. He meandered south along Route 83 and crossed the Missouri River at Lake Audubon. He pulled over at the wildlife refuge and was able to catch a few glimpses of some late migrating birds in the wetlands. He photographed a shivering pair of tree swallows in their nesting box. Within a few weeks, he figured, the ice would begin to form and transform this lake into an ice fishing paradise. He continued just past Coleharbor and then turned west onto Route 200 through Pick City and onward to Twin Buttes where he made his way to Jim's ranch on the reservation. He exited the car and opened the gate hinge and then stood and stared at the sky. It was endless. Blue shades rising above clumps of tissue thin clouds being pulled and teased apart in the cool winds. They were lit like pink cotton candy as they hovered delicately above the setting orange sun globe ready to plunge below the horizon. *What a place to sit outside on a deck and admire this show every night?!* Bradlee thought.

He pulled out his phone and dialed Lyra. Lyra and Dr. Bonheim were washing up and applying their warmest pajamas and wool socks. Lyra grabbed her phone from inside her jeans which she had placed on the changing table. She rushed to answer the rings.

"Bradlee! Welcome back to North Dakota!"

"You too, Lyra. I hope your flight went well earlier today."

"It was fantastic! Well, except for the first few minutes when I thought my stomach was trying to escape from my mouth." They laughed together.

"I'm really looking forward to seeing you again," Bradlee said.

"Me too. Just had a really delicious meal on the reservation here. Traditional food. Loved it all, especially the maple syrup on top of the Indian pudding!"

"Maple syrup?! You sure they have sugar maple trees in North Dakota, Lyra?"

"They do actually. I learned tonight from our Native American hosts that the '*Acer saccharum*,' or sugar maple tree that provides us with the yummy syrup, grows at the eastern edge of North Dakota along the Canadian border."

"You do know your sweet and hardy tree species!" Bradlee teased.

"Better than you know your shells, Mr. Bradlee Seashell!" A round of laughter between them.

Bradlee checked his suitcase. Leo's maple-stained bowl was packed away safely and unharmed from the flight.

"Bradlee, I've got some great news to share with you when I see you!"

"Really?! I like surprises! Are you and Foster getting married?"

"Not funny, Bradlee." She giggled anyway. "Dr. Bonheim here... sorry... Carol." Lyra exchanged a glance with Dr. Bonheim. "Carol mentioned that we're going to try to make some time the day after Thanksgiving to head to Medora for your exhibit. I think you mentioned the festivities begin at one o'clock at the Heritage Center, right?

"Yes, that would be so awesome to see you there and meet your professor!"

"Well, we're shivering here in our long johns so I need to go find some warm blankets in our trailer and head to bed. We'll be up at sunrise tomorrow. Full day of work ahead despite the holiday."

"OK, I understand. I'm at Jim's ranch. Just pulled up now. You have a great evening and hope you sleep like a full-bellied bear in her lair."

"Goodnight Bradlee."

"Goodnight Lyra." They hung up. He wanted to say '*Goodnight my love*' but he held back. He shouldn't have. He shook his head as if to ring out the shyness that remained between his ears.

Bradlee was greeted warmly by Jim at the entrance to the ranch home. Jim then introduced Bradlee to his wife, Wichahpi. He explained that his wife's name means *'the stars'* in the Lakota language. He winked at his wife as he turned to Bradlee and said that Wichahpi has always been his *'guiding light.'* Then Jim introduced as many family members as he could find sprinkled around the house. His grandkids were all playing or helping Wichahpi in the kitchen in preparation for tomorrow's feast. Jim explained that most of their children and grandchildren were staying for the Thanksgiving holiday either in the main house or in a few other cottages dispersed on the ranch. He proceeded to give Bradlee a tour of the ranch home. Plentiful tribal artworks and paintings and photographs lined the walls and tabletops and bookshelves. Older photos from years past cluttered one wall in Jim's study. Bradlee thought he recognized one of the family members but didn't interrupt Jim's tour. Bradlee was a latecomer tonight. The family had already eaten their dinner meal but he was served a generous portion by Wichahpi - the *'warm-up meal'* - as Jim described the lighter vegetarian fare for the night before the family's annual Thanksgiving feast.

Bradlee awoke early the next morning and went for a stroll on the ranch. The air had significantly cooled overnight to below freezing. His breathing hovered in clouds in front of him and the mist reminded him of Ruthy's watercolor painting. Jim was up early as well preparing his pick-up truck. He informed Bradlee that he needed to head over near Mandaree to meet with some officials regarding the proposed pipeline project but he'd be back by early afternoon in plenty of time for the dinner feast. He invited Bradlee to join him but Bradlee preferred to stay on the ranch for the day and prepare his formal remarks for the photography exhibit tomorrow. The photographs that Bradlee had shipped were already hung on the gallery walls and the Heritage Center had printed his essay about the wild horses into a brochure that also promoted the Heritage Center's purpose and efforts on behalf of the North Dakota community. Fliers were distributed along with newspaper and online advertising for the opening reception.

Jim approached Mandaree and turned onto a dirt road that lead to the airstrip. Wichahpi was just here the night before, he knew, as part of her efforts in helping to establish the trailer glamping business for the reservation. She had returned last night exhausted but carrying a leftover tray of Indian pudding that was as outstanding as he had ever tasted. His wife was always thinking about him and their growing family, many grandkids thriving and a few more on their way into the world. He was blessed all these years and he knew it.

As he approached the entrance to the teepee, Jim noticed that were two women pouring over geology maps of the reservation, and particularly the area around Mandaree where the pipeline was to cross through and then turn inland between Mandaree and the Missouri River. A vehicle was parked beside the teepee. It was left behind last night for the women to use if needed. Jim introduced himself to Dr. Bonheim and Lyra. They were expecting a representative from the tribal council to brief them on any recent updates regarding the pipeline project from the council's perspective. Jim had been serving as Chief of the tribal council for the past thirty years, having replaced his own father in that role one generation earlier. Jim offered to guide them through the reservation's dirt roads and any potential off-roading as might be needed in his more durable pick-up truck. They reviewed the geology maps with him. He grabbed a pencil and drew a more precise updated line on the map to show the latest proposed trajectory for the pipeline from the most recent discussions at the tribal council's last meeting. Dr. Bonheim and Lyra assembled their day packs and piled into Jim's truck as they began to tour the area.

Jim briefed Dr. Bonheim and Lyra about the conflicts on the tribal council and went into further depth about the history of some of the council members' backgrounds and why their positions on the pipeline project would not likely change, whether for or against the proposal. Many had their principles hardened by one life situation or another in their past when it came to dealing with the Federal government and oil corporations. They toured the region extensively. Dr. Bonheim and Lyra collected topsoil and cored underground soil samples and carefully labeled them with links to their exact GPS coordinates and assigned numbers written onto the topographic maps. They would return with these samples to Seattle for the Institute's scientists to study them further. Jim brought them to the locations of the aquifers, reservoirs, and dry bed streams and Dr. Bonheim updated the maps with detailed blue pen markings to represent known water sources.

By noon, Jim mentioned that he needed to be heading home to join his family for the Thanksgiving holiday. He invited the two scientists to join him and his large family for a more traditional Native American Thanksgiving dinner and Dr. Bonheim and Lyra gratefully accepted the kind invitation. They were otherwise facing an evening meal of rehydrated camp food back at the trailer corral. After last night's glamping dinner they weren't going to pass up another prime opportunity. Lyra was going to have her Thanksgiving feast on the reservation after all! Jim returned them to the trailers and they washed up and changed quickly while Jim contacted his wife, Wichahpi, to let her know that they'll be needing two more plates for their family dinner table. Wichahpi didn't mind. She knew Jim's heart better than anyone ever had and he was always looking out for others in need. And Wichahpi always cooked extra helpings for unexpected last minute guests, as was often the case over the years serving as a devoted wife to an Indian reservation Chief. Her hospitality was just one of Wichahpi's many expressions of her love for Jim and they were very blessed with wealth, good health in their aging years, and much love and happiness together.

The truck arrived to the ranch. Wichahpi remained busy in the kitchen along with numerous other family helpers making final meal preparations. Bradlee was assigned to stable duties to help bed-down the horses before dinner. Dressed in blue jeans with a cream colored turtleneck, he donned his cowboy hat and joined some of the grandkids for the job at hand. There was Jim's black stallion, proudly standing in his stall next to a series of other beautiful and fit stallions and mares. The oldest grandson was strictly responsible for Jim's stallion and no one else. They hosed and groomed the horses and then the grandkids gave Bradlee a lesson in using a hoof pick to remove any debris as they inspected each hoof and shoe and then used a stiff-bristle brush to gently scrub any remaining collected mud deposits. They finished by examining each horse's leg anatomy for any further wear and tear that may need to be addressed by Jim's granddaughter, who also served as the reservation's veterinarian.

After introductions inside the home, Lyra left Dr. Bonheim's side as she heard neighing from the backyard area and decided to exit out the porch door towards the stable. From the distance she noticed a handsomely rugged man, clean shaven and dressed crisply. He was wearing a light brown suede cowboy hat and he was at work spreading straw in the stalls. She noticed how gentle he was being with the horses, petting them on the bridge of their noses and whispering in their ears. *A horse whisperer have we here?* she muttered to herself. She thought of Bradlee holding the hummingbird in his palm. They were men of such similar nature.

Bradlee's nose noticed her approaching first. *Jasmine, I know that smell. That's Lyra's aroma!* Lyra was leaning against a post at the entrance to the stable and further quietly studying this man in the cowboy hat off in the far stall. His curls below the hat line looked remarkably familiar to her. He was sitting on an upside down metal bucket and gently grooming one of the mares. He turned his head towards the source of the inebriating sweet jasmine aroma and their eyes met.

"Lyra?!"

"Bradlee!"

He rose from the bucket and ran towards her, lifted her into his arms, and twirled her about.

"Now this is a surprise!" Bradlee screamed out. The younger grandkids were giggling now and then they scurried back to the house, most of their chores completed.

"Bradlee Seashell, if I had known you were a handsome cowboy I wouldn't have dumped you in Minot!" Lyra laughed uncontrollably in his arms and held onto the brim of Bradlee's cowboy hat. She rested her neck against his shoulder and nuzzled him. He noticed Lyra was wearing the Ark necklace. He wasn't going to pass on the opportunity this time. He kissed her neck and inhaled her jasmine perfume.

"Bradlee, I really missed you. I guess you know a man named Jim?" Bradlee laughed from the coincidence of their meeting at Jim's ranch.

"Yes, Jim's the man who escorted me on horseback through the Badlands. If it wasn't for him I wouldn't be having the gallery exhibit tomorrow."

"Another coincidence we've shared!"

"Seems like there have been plenty of those going around since we first met," Bradlee said.

"Jim gave Carol and me a tour of the western edge of the reservation this morning, then invited us to dinner here."

They leaned closer, their eyes fastened to each other. Bradlee noted a small bruise to Lyra's left eyelid above her coloboma but that was all that remained of Lyra's facial trauma. Her nose and cheeks and lips had healed fully. Bradlee set Lyra's feet to the ground and they stood facing each other. Bradlee had his arms wrapped around Lyra's waist. They caressed and their lips met for what felt like an eternity. Their tongues swirled and tasted each other and were as warm and delicious to Lyra as maple syrup on Indian pudding.

The black stallion started to whinny. This triggered the other horses to neigh in their stalls. Bradlee and Lyra started laughing. They were communicating something. Was it a chorus of approval or rejection of their affection for each other? They approached the black stallion together. He had a white striped blaze extending from his lower forehead and down the bridge of his nose. Now studying him at very close range, Bradlee noticed the shape of the stallion's separate small white patch at the top of his forehead. It was an irregular shape, beginning with a wider clump and then extending and narrowing downward a few inches with white hairs emanating as if in a corkscrew pattern. Bradlee looked at Lyra.

"He's got a star marking on his forehead that looks juts like a channeled whelk shell!" Bradlee proclaimed as he gently traced the imprint with his fingers.

"I see it. It's beautiful!" Lyra agreed that it was remarkably similar in shape and pattern to the whelk that Bradlee had shown Lyra on the train.

They kissed passionately once again.

"Another coincidence?" Lyra whispered.

The younger grandkids returned giggling as they stormed out of the house and into the stable. Lyra and Bradlee had their legs wrapped in a pretzel around each other as they were leaning against one of the stall doors.

"Dinner is ready!" the grandkids all screamed and then blew mock kisses. Then they ran back inside giggling all the way.

"To be continued," Bradlee said as he locked onto Lyra's eyes and she smiled coyly. They held hands and walked towards the patio doorway.

"I gather you two know each other?" Jim was leaning against the door frame with a wide grin on his face.

"Jim, this is the woman I mentioned to you on our horseback ride through the Badlands."

Lyra blushed as Bradlee placed his hand around her hips and ever carefully stroked the rise of Lyra's buttocks out of view of Jim. Lyra looked fantastic in her wine-colored blouse and blue jeans.

"And what exactly did Bradlee say about me?" Lyra added teasingly.

"Oh, just that he's seen some real sunshine enter his life and it felt real good, ma'am." Bradlee smiled at Jim's reference to Teddy Roosevelt's love story that Jim had shared along the ride. "Well, come on in folks. The Mrs. has quite the feast brewing."

Lyra introduced Bradlee to Dr. Bonheim and the two quickly discovered their mutual passion for photography as Dr. Bonheim chatted away, comparing their digital cameras and naturescapes and lighting techniques. She was impressed with Bradlee's in-depth knowledge.

Everyone assembled at the massive wood table that extended the full length of the dining room space. Twenty-four adults and children of all ages. Smiling happy faces all among them, none more than Bradlee and Lyra sitting side by side, their hands entwined under the tablecloth. Bradlee gently laid his hand inside Lyra's thigh. A tingling sensation flowed and she felt the moisture between her legs. Her desire for more chased wildly inside her mind as the first course arrived to the table.

The doorbell chime rang and the youngest grandchild

ran to the door and peered through the glass window.

"Oji is here, Papa!"

Jim and Wichahpi left the table to open the front door. Jim embraced and kissed his daughter-in-law who had arrived with her hands full with a large circular cake coated with chocolate frosting. Wichahpi raised her hands and linked them with her daughter-in-law as they touched foreheads. Following behind were Jim's son, Jeremiah and his grandson, Kin. Bradlee and Lyra stood and walked over to the foyer as Jim lifted his grandson and hugged and tickled him.

"Sorry we're running late, Papa. Jerry needed to check on the cattle with the freeze coming on strong overnight and I was finishing up Kin's cake here. I thought we would celebrate together tonight since his birthday is tomorrow." Oji removed her winter coat and then unzipped Kin's. She turned and startled. There was Lyra standing right in front of her. Lyra approached and they embraced warmly.

"Oji, it's good to see you again. I had no idea Jim is your father-in-law! What a coincidence this is!"

Oji was very pleased to see Lyra again. The two had shared a quiet bond back at the inn in Minot. She had wished she would be able to see Lyra again someday and that day arrived much sooner than she thought.

"Lyra, this is my husband, Jeremiah and our son, Kin. He's turning seven years old tomorrow. A big boy now!" Jeremiah and Kin were each wearing cowboy hats and sporting matching brown leather vests. They were a handsome duo.

"Kin is full of heart like his father and has the same eyes as his grandfather's. He can see things from a long distance before anyone else can. His gift." Oji smiled warmly at Jim, and then at Jeremiah, as she snuggled with Kin beside her.

"Come everyone, let's eat. Dinner is getting cold," Jim announced.

Oji was granted the honor to recite a heartfelt blessing for peace and union for all assembled and then they dined. It was a wonderful meal combining traditional Native American squash and corn and wild rice with a variety of cranberry sauce recipes and marshmallow-coated sweet potatoes. Two turkeys with all the fixings and roasted venison steaks adorned the center of the table. Jeremiah was assigned the carving duties. Bradlee, Lyra, and Dr. Bonheim welcomed learning about life on the reservation and the hard work and challenges of working on a ranch from dawn to dusk. There were uplifting and spirited stories that Jim and Wichahpi and Oji and Jeremiah shared about their own childhood. The younger grandkids listened attentively, all wide-eyed, as Jim went on embellishing a few exciting tales about their ancestors. Bradlee could sense the respect that Jim and Wichahpi garnered from the family. They were the current patriarch and matriarch of the family line and it appeared that Oji and Jeremiah would inherit those mantles and the responsibilities one day.

Before dessert was served, Bradlee clinked his glass with his fork and the table quieted for him. A few of Jim's grandkids hurried to a nearby room and brought back a large thin rectangular wrapped package.

"To Jim and his lovely wife, Wichahpi, the shining star of this fine feast. And to your beautiful family..." Bradlee started as he glanced at Lyra beside him.

"On behalf of Lyra and Dr. Bonheim as well, I sincerely thank you for your generous hospitality this most memorable Thanksgiving. You are a very loving family. To honor Jim, specifically, for his role in having me work more hours than I could have ever imagined..." laugher about the table, "I would like to present a gift to your wise patriarch. May he ride on his black stallion until the very end and then may he continue on his journey high into the sky as he and his stallion join with Pegasus, the winged horse above us, eternally. Thank you, Jim Clayburn."

Jim stood and walked over to the gift and removed the wrapping paper. He stood back as his grandkids lifted the framed photograph and he stared for awhile into the eyes of his beloved stallion, thinking back to that painful day of his fall. Bradlee had captured a very tender moment shared between Jim and his prized stallion. He glanced at Bradlee with a keen squint in his eyes and then he reviewed the others assembled as he pondered the image before him:

You didn't need to apologize for throwing me off your back but I appreciate the way you looked me in the eye. We understand each other, don't we? You're one heck of a handsome stallion, aren't you?! And, by the way, that was my mistake for taking you out that day with the lightning storm brewing. Anyway, just so you know, I have no hard feelings my old friend. My femur bone got fixed up and is just about as good as new so stop those sad eyes from now on, will you?

Jim winked at his stallion's photograph and then at Wichahpi. He looked over to the assembled family and guests as he pointed at the majestic image.

"That's one ugly horse, if I may say so. But who's the handsome young cowboy?"

Everyone broke out in laughter and cheered Jim for his sense of humor. And for Bradlee's beautiful photograph of their patriarch. Jim walked over to Bradlee and gave him a long hug and a pat on his back.

"Fine work, young man. I will cherish it until the end. Thank you."

It was time for Jim to drive the ladies back to the trailer corral as some of the family members reached for their jackets and set on foot for their nearby cabins. Dr. Bonheim lingered to admire and study Bradlee's photograph in detail. Bradlee walked Lyra outside to a quiet clearing that overlooked the valley beneath the ranch. The moon had risen and was glowing like an angel's face.

"Lyra, it's been three wonderful months. I know we've been apart most of that time but it feels like I know so much about you and when we speak together on the phone it's as if I'm right where you are, beside you." He nuzzled her neck and inhaled her jasmine perfume once more.

"Bradlee, you're a sensitive man. And serious. And may I add…? very romantic."

"Is there anything wrong with any of those?"

"No. A girl like me can use some romance in her life. And sensitive. And even serious at times. I do like all of those."

"Lyra, there is no *like* when you *love* someone," Bradlee replied.

Lyra thought back to the train. Their first conversation. Bradlee almost said that exact phrase to her right from the very beginning.

Their breath was lit by the moonlight as their eyes reflected in each other. He kissed her and held her against his chest and then they kissed again, and he lifted Lyra into his arms and twirled her as her hair glistened in the moonlight, and then he kissed her again and again as their lips warmed in the frigid air and then their lips parted ever slightly and they stared at the stars above.

"Look, over there." Bradlee pointed upward to the clear sky. There were millions of stars above them. The Milky Way stretched for miles across the vast twinkling darkness.

"It's the constellation, Canis Major. Do you see the brightest star in the sky? That's the star named Sirius," Bradlee said.

Bradlee held Lyra's hand and traced the constellation for her.

"Constellation spotting is very *serious* business for a *sensitive, romantic* chap like me." He smiled and then they laughed together before quieting as their breaths warmed their faces and he kissed her closely and held her again to his chest, enveloping her in a cocoon of warmth, protecting Lyra from the frigid air.

"Lyra, you are my brightest star. You have been ever since I met you. And you always will be." He lifted her palm and placed it to his chest as she felt his heartbeat. "You are here Lyra, in my heart. I need you to know that. And I'm afraid there's no turning back now."

"Bradlee Seashell, you are inside my heart as well. And there is nothing to fear. Now or ever."

They embraced again and Lyra kissed him as passionately as she could.

"Until tomorrow, then?" Bradlee kissed Lyra's forehead. He moved on to the top of her head as he gathered her into his arms like a soft pillow.

"Yes, Bradlee, tomorrow. One day at a time... until the end." She smiled and gazed into his eyes longingly and then... started into unstoppable laughter. Bradlee was caught off guard in the moment.

"I said it!" Lyra pronounced in between scales of musical laughter.

"Said what?"

"Until the end...! Until the end... Until — The — End!!!" Lyra shouted to the heavens with her arms outstretched. Then she settled her laughter to a simmer and composed herself and held her arms around Bradlee's neck, pulling him towards her lips.

"Oh, never mind, Bradlee. All your romanticizing is beginning to rub off on me now, that's all." She kissed him again, slowly and passionately and deliciously.

They parted and Lyra ran to the front door, hugged Wichahpi and Oji, and then hopped into Jim's idling truck. Jim and Dr. Bonheim were settled in the front seats. Lyra tried to calm her breaths and minimize the appearance of her blushing cheeks and wet lips as she brushed her hair back into place with her hands and adjusted in her seat. She glanced out the window at Bradlee, standing like a genuine cowboy up on the hill. *My handsome cowboy*, she thought.

Jim backed out of the driveway. Dr. Bonheim turned her head to have a look at Lyra and then she and Jim shared a glance between them in the front seats and smiled. "Guess we've both been there before, haven't we, Jim?" He smiled and nodded. "Nothing better than that feeling... nothing," he replied and then accelerated down the dirt road.

MORNING ARRIVED TOO SOON as Dr. Bonheim's alarm clock blared at six o'clock. The frigid air had plastered its frozen dewy breath against the sides of the trailers. Ice crystals from sub-freezing temperatures. The arctic front had arrived overnight to the reservation. Lyra and Dr. Bonheim awoke early, shivering out of bed, and quickly climbed into their warmest layers of clothes they could find in their suitcases. Lyra had brought a small camping stove and tea bags and so she quickly boiled a few cups of water and introduced Dr. Bonheim to the soothing taste of piping hot mint tea.

"I know we're not quite at the top of Mt. Everest, Lyra, but it sure feels like it!" Dr. Bonheim exclaimed while truly enjoying her hot tea beside Lyra. Mentor and student were bonding and Lyra never felt happier about her future career plans. They set to work immediately to continue their initial survey of the proposed pipeline route. They would be meeting a delegation from the tribal council at the corral a few hours later. They borrowed the small truck that remained at the corral and drove across the rugged terrain to explore various locations that were concerning to them on the geology map and collected more samples for their research. They returned to the corral by nine o'clock and met with Stan briefly to review departure plans for the next day. The Cessna flight would backtrack to Billings and then they would take a connecting flight to Seattle to be home by the evening.

Seven tribal council members arrived with bags filled with coffee, tea, milk, biscuits, muffins, and oatmeal packs. They gathered around the table inside the teepee. Jim arrived a few minutes later in his pick-up truck. Bradlee and Kin were with him. They exited and headed to the teepee.

The meeting had already begun. Bradlee quietly approached Lyra and whispered teasingly in her ear, "Good morning, my dear. Such a serious face you have on." Their eyes met but decorum did not allow for an affectionate kiss. "Hope you don't mind me being here. Jim asked me to help him fix one of the trailers – something about a piece of siding that he hoped I could help him fix after the meeting was over. Besides, I can make a heck of a big-brother babysitter for Kin while I watch you at work. These chances don't come around too often." Bradlee left Lyra's side and played quietly with Kin in the far section of the teepee.

When Kin was hungry for breakfast Bradlee sliced a variety of muffins onto a tray and poured a few cups of milk for them to share. They sat at a small table adjacent to the kitchen. Bradlee brought out a satchel of rocks and seashells from his Newfoundland beach collection and he laid them on the table for Kin to play with. Kin set the seashells into an unusual pattern and gulped down his milk. He turned to Bradlee.

"I heard Mama Oji talking to GranMama in the kitchen last night. She said that you had telephoned for a pair of her moccasins. Is it for the lady, Lyra, at dinner last night and here in the teepee this morning? The one you were kissing on the lips?" Bradlee smiled at Kin's directness. He placed his hand onto Kin's head and gently patted it and messed his flowing hair. Kin returned the smile.

"And what do you know about kissing girls?" Bradlee

asked him.

"Mama Oji's kisses tell me she loves me here." Kin patted his chest. "But I see what is in a person's head."

"You mean the mind, what a person is thinking?"

"Yes, Mama Oji says it is my gift. A gift she has given me from the day I came into this world. She says she shares this with me. It is in our same blood."

"And what do you see in my mind, Kin?"

Kin glanced into Bradlee's eyes, looked away, and then back again at Bradlee. Then he held onto Bradlee's hand and closed his eyes.

"I see a very bright star. It is surrounded by many smaller ones that are also glowing. The small stars are all smiling together. You and Lyra are floating in the middle of the small stars." Kin raised his hands together and turned them around each other as if he was rotating an imaginary sphere.

"The very bright star is sharing its light between your heads… right here..." Kin touched Bradlee's forehead with his index finger. "This bright light has shined since long long ago, before the time of my ancestors. And I see the light shining between your heads way, way ahead. After you and Lyra are very old and then long long gone into the sky above where there is no pain or suffering."

Bradlee didn't know how to respond. He felt like he was in the midst of some sort of benevolent shaman. A child Buddha or Dalai Lama, perhaps. And he was unafraid. He was simply at ease.

"I help Mama Oji make the moccasins where she works. Mama Oji has taught me that a pair of moccasins are like two people who love. If the moccasins are made right, made from the heart that gives energy to our hands, then the moccasins will not break. They will last a long long time. Just like two people who share long long love."

Kin returned to eating his muffin and then sipped on his milk. "Your mother is a very wise woman," Bradlee responded. "I will remember what you have told me, Kin."

Bradlee turned and glanced at Lyra. She was standing and chatting with some of the members of the tribal council. Bradlee could feel the warmth radiating from his heart to his forehead. In his mind he tried to send a stream of light across the room to meet Lyra's forehead. At that moment, Lyra glanced back at him. Their eyes briefly met and they shared a knowing smile.

Dr. Bonheim and Lyra reviewed their initial research findings with the tribal council members and displayed their updated geology maps that were hung from the teepee's canvas. Dr. Bonheim went on to discuss some of the preliminary environmental risks for the current proposed pipeline map as she delineated the route drawn, overlaying it onto the updated geology map. Lyra then offered a few preliminary alternative, and potentially safer, routes for the pipeline should the tribal council wish to proceed with the project. Dr. Bonheim explained, in more easily understood terms, some of her concerns related to the geologic formations and water sources in the western segment of the reservation. A more thorough analysis would need to wait until the entire pipeline research team from the Institute had more time to study the core samples they were returning with to Seattle as well as further on-site seismographic data collection from highly sophisticated instruments in January. Lyra checked her watch. 10:45 a.m. Dr. Bonheim commented to the council members that the meeting would need to wrap up soon as she and Lyra had another meeting to attend.

As Dr. Bonheim was making her final remarks, a handful of SUV's and pick-up trucks pulled up onto the airstrip, parked, and flashed their lights as they revved their engines repeatedly and alarmingly to those inside the teepee. They followed this by blaring their horns while raising a loud ruckus from slapping the door panels to their vehicles with their hands in unison. Louder and louder. Then some of them exited from their vehicles and started to shout obscenities towards the tribal council members, calling them 'Teepee Toms' and 'Tonto's' and 'Traitors.' Some of the younger council members, along with Jim, Dr. Bonheim, and Lyra exited the teepee and stood facing the protesters.

They began to shout. "Go home pipeliners! This is our land! No one is going to take it from us! We'll destroy whatever you build! No pipeline! No pipeline! They screamed repeatedly in unison. Some of the younger men in the crowd were brandishing metal pipes and beating them against their fists as a threat. Lyra's heart began to pound. A sudden memory of Matt's fist striking her face. Her heart raced and she ran back into the teepee. Stan followed to check on her but she exited through the far canvas door and out of sight.

Jim slowly approached the angry protesters while holding Kin's hand securely. He held up his other hand as a gesture to request their silence. In time, the protesters quieted.

He spoke softly but firmly. "Most of you here know that I have not personally taken a stand on the pipeline project. I have lived here all my life. These are difficult decisions the council members must make on behalf of all of us on the reservation."

"Time to leave the reservation, old man!" A voice shouted. "No pipeline!" a chorus started up again and then quieted as Jim stood his ground.

"Please let the tribal council do its job properly. We have promised everyone on the reservation that there will be a referendum vote among all our people, for or against the final proposed route."

A fuel canister was lit and thrown from somewhere behind a row of vehicles. It landed close to Jim and his grandson and exploded with a loud bang. The crowd began to chant once again, "No pipeline! No pipeline…!" A few men started to walk towards the Cessna plane parked at the other end of the runway. They were beating their metal poles in their hands.

Stan decided he needed to take action. He turned to Dr. Bonheim and advised her that he needed to get airborne fast before there was any damage to the plane. "That's a $500,000 piece of machinery and it's not well insured for willful damages," Stan said urgently. "Don't bother about your remaining luggage. The company will return that to you later. Just head right now to the plane. We'll circle for awhile and then land, if we can, back here at the airstrip if the crowd disperses. Otherwise, I'll bring you to Billings and will return to fetch your luggage tomorrow."

Jim quickly returned to the teepee and addressed everyone present. "This is a dangerous situation brewing. I can't control this crowd. We need to disperse quickly, I'm afraid. Sure hope they don't destroy this corral."

Bradlee was holding onto Kin's hand. Tribal council members headed quickly to their vehicles. Jim's pick-up truck was parked in direct line with the crowd of protesters. They started to smash his rear lights and then they wielded their metal poles and were beating the door frames. Stan grabbed Dr. Bonheim's hand and they started to run towards the plane.

"Where's Lyra?! Dr. Bonheim called back towards the teepee?"

"We'll find her!" Bradlee shouted back. He quickly glanced and realized Lyra was nowhere in sight.

"Bradlee!" Jim hurried over to him. "Take Kin and make a dash for the plane. I need to know he'll be safe. I'll stay here and search for Lyra. I know most of these protesters personally. I think we'll be alright. Now go. Go!!!" He screamed with a determined glare. Bradlee scooped Kin into his arms and ran as fast as he could towards the plane.

Jim spun in a full circle inside the teepee. No sign of Lyra. He ran to the trailers and opened every door and peered inside and called out Lyra's name. *Where is she?* He ran to the shower room and found Lyra slumped on the floor, frightened, shivering, whimpering terribly. He pulled her to her feet.

"Please Lyra, we must go now! You must trust me, Lyra."

Jim didn't let go as he pulled Lyra forward and they exited the shower room. He held her hand vigorously as they ran to Jim's truck and jumped in. He started the ignition just as the front window was smashed and glass fragments flew everywhere. Lyra screamed and wailed and then ducked to the floor board beneath the front passenger seat as Jim quickly reversed into the crowd, braked hard, and turned and sped away from the airstrip. Jim did a quick check and realized that all the other council members' cars had already departed. He was relieved after a few moments passed. The protesters didn't bother to try to chase down his pick-up as he glanced repeatedly at the rearview mirror.

Stan hoisted Dr. Bonheim onto the plane's wing and she quickly seated and buckled in the front passenger seat. Bradlee caught up quickly and handed Kin to Stan who placed him in the rear seat as Bradlee jumped onto the wing and climbed in next to Kin, helped him buckle, and then secured his own strap. Dr. Bonheim locked her door as Stan strapped in quickly and started the propeller. A handful of protesters started jogging towards the plane while wielding their metal poles threateningly. They closed to one-hundred yards. Stan held for a few more seconds as the engine warmed and the prop blades accelerated to their maximum revolutions for take-off. He checked the wing flaps and taxied away from the crowd, turned and accelerated down the runway directly towards the protesters. They dropped to the ground as he approached and then he quickly raised the nose pitch and headed into the sky. Bradlee turned and spotted Jim's pick-up truck racing down the dirt path towards Mandaree. *God, I hope Jim has Lyra with him,* he prayed. He noticed that Jim's pick-up stopped and then turned south towards Medicine Hole but then the plane arced and he lost view of the pick-up as the Cessna climbed higher and headed westward.

"Lyra, please listen to me. You're OK now. You're safe." Jim stopped his truck at the highway junction. Lyra remained crumpled into a ball under the dashboard with her head tucked below her arms. She was shivering with fright.

"Lyra, it's Jim. Please… take my hand. You must trust me."

Lyra released her arms from above her head and glanced at Jim. His palm was open and laying on the passenger seat.

"Please, Lyra. Sit down here. You are safe now. Safe." He repeated quietly.

Lyra elevated from her crouch and sat down on the seat. She leaned into Jim who kissed her on the top of her head.

"It's OK, Lyra. No one's going to hurt you now."

She was still sniffling and her cheeks were reddened from rubbing her tears. Jim reached for a tissue box in the door pocket. Lyra gradually recovered as Jim turned south on Highway 22 briefly and then pulled off onto a dirt road just north of the Little Missouri River. He hid the truck behind some brush. From his vantage he could observe the Mandaree turnoff and determine if the mob's vehicles were heading away from the airstrip and turning north or south on the highway.

"Lyra, we're going to wait here a bit. Let things clear out back at the airstrip. Everyone's evacuated so these protesters should be heading home soon." He thought to himself… *I just hope they aren't destroying the trailer and teepee corral. That was a major investment from the tribal council to help the reservation's budget. That would be a damn shame.*

"Where's Bradlee? And Dr. Bonheim?" Lyra asked.

"They're OK, Lyra. We tried to find you but couldn't locate you right away. Stan has them airborne somewhere overhead in the Cessna. The pipeline protesters were looking to destroy the plane and Stan couldn't let that happen. My grandson, Kin, is with them. We'll meet up somewhere but right now we just need to sit tight for a short while and observe.

Stan flew the Cessna west for a few minutes and then made a wide turn and leveled. He brought the plane on trajectory back to the airstrip to have a look. As the plane approached, Jim was able to track it. He pointed out the Cessna to Lyra who felt relieved. "They must be making a flyover to determine if it's safe to land back at the airstrip," Jim said.

Stan approached above the airstrip and noticed the crowd had remained. A gunshot was fired at the plane and he quickly banked sharply to the right. Stan noticed the mob was stripping off sections of siding from the trailers and bashing the windows. The teepee was engulfed in flames and the protesters were spreading jugs of gasoline around the base of the trailers as well.

Jim saw the dark smoke billowing over the airstrip and his heart sank. "*Damn them. Damn them,*" he muttered under his breath.

Dr. Bonheim, Bradlee and Kin held fixed in their seats without a word spoken as the plane completed its turn. "I think I can take you all into Medora. Bradlee, don't you have an exhibit to get to this afternoon?"

"Thanks Stan. If it's possible I would like to be there." Bradlee couldn't stop worrying about Lyra. "The Heritage Center is expecting me. Hopefully, Jim and Lyra are headed that way as well. Sure wish that mess back there didn't have to ruin such a nice day... But, on a more uplifting note, I think Kin's granddad won't mind if we give him a chance to enjoy some wild horses on his birthday." Bradlee ruffled Kin's hair.

"This pipeline has roused up some serious tempers on both sides. Not sure how they'll ever resolve it between themselves," Stan replied.

"Bradlee, I can take care of Kin while you give your presentation at the center. I'm sure Jim and Lyra will be close behind," Dr. Bonheim added.

Stan turned the plane in a southeasterly direction to head towards Medora.

Jim noted the change in the Cessna's flight pattern. *Stan must be heading to Medora to deliver Bradlee to his exhibit*, he figured. He exited the brush and turned south onto Highway 22 and sped past Medicine Hole. Jim figured the mood at the Heritage Center would be quite subdued once word reached about the protests and violence at the airstrip on the reservation. There were a number of people living on the reservation who had plans to attend the opening exhibit. And a police report would need to be filed but he knew that Lyra needed to be at Bradlee's exhibit. *Couples need that kind of mutual support*, he reminded himself. Lyra sat silently staring ahead. It was about a hundred miles to Medora from their location. Jim checked his watch. 11:40 a.m. He knew his pick-up could do over 100mph if he needed to. He'd deliver Lyra by one o'clock. In time - even if he had to run people off the road to get there. Jim was seething inside while his soul mourned for the whole tribe.

"Stan, can you park this bird in Medora?" Dr. Bonheim asked.

"Yes, I think so. Let me radio to check."

Stan called his company's switchboard and was relayed the necessary information for the nearest landing strip. He checked the dashboard computer. The message lit on the screen.

"Dickinson Theodore Roosevelt Regional Airport," Stan announced. The GPS identified the coordinates and he plugged it into the flight computer. The plane veered east as it adjusted for the new heading. Stan radioed the airport tower and the officials provided the appropriate runway clearance. The visibility was limited due to some gathering storm clouds off to the east but the wind gusts were not an impediment to landing.

"That's the closest we can get," Stan continued. "It'll be about a forty-five minute drive from there to Medora. I'll arrange for a taxi to meet you at the gate for the ground transport."

"Stan," Bradlee asked from the rear. "Can you call down to a ground cell phone while up here in the air?"

"Sure can. He opened a communication line with the onboard computer and patched it directly into Bradlee's cell phone contact list. Bradlee dialed Lyra's phone number.

Lyra heard the phone ringing in her pocket and checked the caller id. She quickly answered.

"Bradlee!"

"Lyra, are you and Jim OK?"

"Yes, we're heading to Medora now. I'm sorry I couldn't make the flight with you. I, uh… I panicked back there at the teepee."

"That's alright. As long as you're safe. Stan is willing to drop us off near Medora so that I can make the exhibit in reasonable time. Can't say I'm quite dressed appropriately for the grand occasion but it'll have to do. At least I've got my cowboy hat with me." Bradlee tried to lighten the subdued mood a bit. Lyra laughed at his last comment.

"Lyra, life can be quite exciting hanging out with you, you know."

"Glad you think so, Bradlee."

"We're heading to Dickinson Regional Airport. Stan says our ETA is..." Bradlee waited for Stan to reply. Stan shouted, "GPS system says... 12:36 arrival time!"

Lyra turned to Jim. "They'll be landing at Dickinson Airport in about forty minutes. ETA 12:36." Jim ran the math in his head. The airport was directly due south on Highway 22 from Killdeer. He had only about forty more miles to cover in the pick-up along a quiet stretch of highway. He could make it there by 12:30, maybe 12:40 at the latest. They'd all be a little late for the exhibit anyway but under the circumstances, Jim realized the Heritage Center would obviously understand.

Jim turned towards Lyra. "Tell them to take good care of my grandson."

"Lyra, please put Jim on the line," Bradlee said. He handed the phone to Kin. Lyra put her phone on speaker.

"It's your grandfather!" Bradlee loudly announced to Kin over the engine noise. Kin put the phone to his ear.

"Papa, I'm feeling like a soaring hawk up here!" Jim gave a long belly laugh.

"That's my grandson! Now you know why we gave you that tribal name when you were just three years old. *Soaring Hawk!* Fits you perfectly now with those eyes of yours up near the clouds. Hope you're enjoying your very first flight! Quite the unexpected present for your seventh birthday today! Now use those hawk eyes and help Stan drop that plane down just right at the airport. Love you, Kin."

"Love you too, Papa." Kin handed the phone back to Bradlee.

Lyra took her phone off speaker mode.

"Lyra," Jim added, "Tell Bradlee to hold Kin tight. He could get a little nervous on the landing. And let Stan know that this chariot will be waiting for them on the runway. This pick-up is going to dust that Cessna... you know, I love an exciting road trip as long as I can be right next to a fine looking broad!"

Lyra laughed at Jim's last comment. He was trying to cheer her up and it was working.

She relayed Jim's message. "Bradlee, Jim says to hold Kin tight for the landing. And take care of Dr. Bonheim as well. She and I will be working together for a long time ahead. I never got around to telling you about the great news I wanted to share with you last night."

"Lyra, we'll talk more on the ride to Medora. Look forward to hearing about it. See you soon. Over and out, 'Sirius Sweetheart.'"

Bradlee disconnected. *Serious sweetheart? Wait, maybe he meant 'Sirius' as in the brightest star.* Lyra contemplated Bradlee's phrase as the warm feelings that stirred inside her were reignited. She closed her eyes and let the memory flood her mind. Bradlee was holding and kissing her in his arms. They were sharing that they were in love with each other. The image was as fresh as last night under the stars.

Jim pressed harder on the gas pedal and watched the speedometer line angle towards 100mph.

Stan had a visual of the Dickinson Airport runway as the Cessna flew over Gorham heading southeast. There were gathering gray clouds off to the east. He checked the onboard flight system and radioed the tower to inform the controller of the plane's current position before addressing his passengers.

"Folks, just another ten minutes and we'll be on the ground and heading to Medora. Looks like our ETA will be a few minutes earlier than originally scheduled with this tailwind giving us a nice push forward." He focused out the windshield as he listened in the head receiver.

"Roger that, main runway for landing," Stan confirmed with the tower. He was bringing the plane down in a very smooth and gradual descent as he crossed over Interstate-94 and spotted Patterson Lake along the approach to the airport.

Kin's eyes focused outside his small window at the right side of the plane. He traced the borders of the lake with his index finger held against the window and observed the marshland along the water's edge. There was a large flock of Sandhill cranes feeding in the marsh. Their long necks were outstretched and searching for an afternoon meal between the reeds. They had beautiful gray feathers, lighter than the darkening clouds off to the east. Their white cheeks were accentuated by bright red patches to their foreheads. A pair of cranes were flapping their wings and jumping into the air. Then they were clasping sticks with their beaks and tossing them. Kin had seen these kinds of behaviors this past spring at some of the reservation's ponds and along the edges of Lake Sakakawea. Back then, many thousands of these same birds were heading northward on their annual migration route. He thought… this flock must be a bit late on their journey returning south for the winter.

As the Cessna glided downward a small group of cranes separated from the flock as they scattered into the air and circled the lake. Stan pointed out the Sandhill cranes to Dr. Bonheim. Their outstretched wings glistened in the sun's rays as their dark long legs gracefully trailed behind them. Dr. Bonheim quickly elevated her camera and began to photograph the spectacle from her vantage. "Just magnificent!" she called out. The cranes turned and began to head in a flight pattern northwest. Stan lost a visual on them as they were camouflaged by the clouds ahead.

"Touchdown in just two minutes folks. Check that your seatbelts are securely fastened," Stan announced. "That tailwind is pushing us so we'll be landing a bit faster on the runway than I usually like but we'll be safe, no worries. Done it a thousand times before," Stan added for reassurance.

Bradlee reached over to Kin and cinched his belt. Then he clasped Kin's left hand into his right palm.

"Kin, landing these small planes can be fun, but also tricky sometimes," Bradlee said calmly to the boy. "Expect a little movement side to side, that's all, with the winds as fast as they are today." Kin nodded as he turned and peered through the front windshield and spotted some of the flock just ahead. They were heading towards the plane.

"Cranes straight ahead!" Kin cried out.

"Where?" Stan quickly surveyed his windshield and then turned his head to peer out to the right and left side of the aircraft. "I don't see any..."

There was a sudden smash and then cracking sounds as the flock barreled into the front windshield, shattering a hole and sending glass chips flying into the airplane front seats. Dr. Bonheim was splattered with blood and feathers as Bradlee saw gray feathers being tossed about the plane with the wind gusting through the open windshield. The plane jolted and veered to the right at a sharp pitch.

Bradlee pulled Kin into his right hip and grasped his right hand around Kin's waist to secure him to his side as he clenched his left hand around a grasp bar attached above his window.

"Kin, hold on to me!" Bradlee shouted.

The propeller blade started sputtering from the impact. The blades were chipped and bent from the flock's impacts. Bradlee leaned forward in his seat. Stan had his hand grasped around the yoke as he tried to stabilize the plane back to the horizon line. He pushed forward on the throttle and the plane accelerated downward. He pulled back and pressed a flat handled switch to adjust the wing flap positions.

"I don't think I can hold her. I've lost control of the wing tail and we're losing thrust speed. The plane was vibrating and being tossed side to side by the winds as Stan pressed a few buttons on the transponder. The plane was dropping in altitude precipitously.

"Mayday! Mayday! This is Cessna 932 heading for emergency landing on main runway! Requesting emergency support!"

A few seconds passed with radio static.

"This is Dickinson tower. Hold your angle, 932. We have a visual. Runway is clear for your approach. Emergency crew is on its way. Get your nose up. You're coming in too hard and low," the controller responded.

"I know that, damn it! We've got troubles here. Bird strike right into the windshield. Damaged prop blades. Rear wing tail is out. Will try to hold as best as I can!" Stan was nervous.

In his twenty-two years of flying all kinds of light aircraft he had never had to deal with a crash landing. A perfect flight record.

"I smell fuel, Stan." Dr. Bonheim added. She was gripping the door panel in panic. Bradlee noticed she had blood dripping from a large cut near her left temple as it ran down her neck. Her camera was shattered into various pieces inside the cabin. Bradlee smelled the fuel leak as well as he glanced out the window. "Altitude, one hundred thirty seven feet and descending fast," Stan said into his headset.

The controller responded. "Copy that. Hold it now. Keep that nose up... steady."

Stan was fighting the winds as the propellers sputtered. He tried to add thrust but the plane wouldn't respond.

"One hundred feet... come on, hold steady. I want to see my 'Darlin' Amanda' tonight!"

A gust of cold air swept through the open windshield. The plane lurched downward and arced to the left. The tip of the left wing struck the runway and burst into flames.

"Come on!" Stan cried out as he pushed the yoke to the right side and pressed the top edge of the rudder pedals.

The left wing rose and then the plane lurched to the right and the right wing scraped the tarmac. More flames arose, this time from the right wing. Stan pushed the throttle forward gently to attempt to elevate the plane ever slightly. One of the propeller blades struck the runway and the nose rapidly pitched forward. The plane toppled over and slid upside down with a harsh scraping noise before crashing into thickets of wild brush on the edge of the runway. The brush ignited where the wing tips were on fire. The acrid smell of burning gas fumes hung in the air surrounding the plane.

Bradlee pushed on the doorframe and kicked the side door open. His head had taken a hard whack against the door panel when the plane flipped. He felt nauseated with waves of dizziness as he moved his head from side to side. He tried to rotate his position by pushing on Stan's seat with his left arm but he felt a shooting pain in his shoulder. He heard Kin screaming. Bradlee grasped Kin with his right arm and pushed him out the door and onto the runway.

"Run Kin! Run fast!!!" Bradlee screamed.

The pick-up truck was passing south of Interstate-94 when Jim and Lyra spotted dark smoke in the sky as they turned into Dickinson airport. They heard sirens blaring and then a fire truck and ambulance passed them as they slowed to make way for the emergency vehicles. Jim glanced at Lyra with fear in his eyes.

"Hold on, Lyra. I know a side road inside the airport on the other side of the terminal building. We've got to get to that runway and see what's happening."

Jim exited the passenger pick-up area and found the dirt road.

"Hold on tight!" he called out as Lyra grasped the door and console. Jim accelerated and struck a locked chain link fence and blasted through it and came to a stop. The runway was straight ahead and Jim noticed the smoke to his left. A young child was running along the tarmac towards them.

"It's Kin!" he shouted to Lyra. He lurched the truck and accelerated towards Kin and came to a stop about a thousand yards from the fiery plane. Jim quickly opened his front door and stood as Kin ran into his arms. "You OK?"

"Yes, Papa."

Kin's face had dried blood on his cheeks and hair. Jim turned and glanced back at the truck.

"Lyra, please take Kin with..."

She was gone. Jim spun around and saw Lyra running as fast as she could towards the Cessna.

"Lyra, hold on!" he screamed at her. That plane's on fire! It can blow any second!"

She was long gone. Her eyes transfixed. There was no sound. As if she was running inside a vacuum tunnel. No air. No vibration. Not even the sound of her breath.

Bradlee righted himself inside the plane. His dizziness undulated inside his head with every rapid movement from side to side. *Blurry vision. Double vision... Damn it*, as he immediately diagnosed that he was concussed. He fell on his knees and then grasped the front center console with his right arm and pulled his body forward to quickly survey. Dr. Bonheim was moaning and waning in and out of consciousness as he tugged on her collar. He could see a contusion forming to the left side of her scalp and her breathing was shallow. He turned his head to the left. Stan's face was smashed against the instrument panel and his nose and mouth were grotesquely deformed by the impact. His body was limp and his left forearm and wrist were also deformed by the impact against the compressed door frame. Blood was seeping rapidly from a lower right thigh laceration. Stan's leg was laying at an obtuse angle below the plane's instrument panel. Bradlee checked Stan's neck for any pulsations. They were weak and thready. Bradlee ripped off his winter jacket and cried out in pain as he felt a bone shift inside his left shoulder. He flexed his left arm and realized it had regained its strength despite the gnawing pain. Then he pulled off his thin shirt, gripped the base, and tore the front section in half. He worked quickly as he wrapped Stan's thigh above the bleeding gash and tightened it with two knots. The oozing blood from Stan's thigh slowed to a trickle and then stopped. He reached over and placed his hand under Stan's shirt and could feel his chest rising and falling. He was breathing steadily but he was unconscious. Stan was alive. Bradlee turned to Dr. Bonheim. Her groaning had ceased. Her head was slumped flaccidly to the right.

"Come on, come on. Think! I'm not going to lose either of you today," he muttered to himself as he focused on what he remembered from his medical school training. *What would dad do right now?* He clenched his fists and tried to focus his mind.

"Dr. Bonheim, wake up!" he screamed at her but there was only a faint groan. He quickly lifted her left eyelid and noticed that her pupil was dilated widely. He felt her breath against his face. Then she awoke briefly as she screamed in pain and twisted slightly in her seat. She grasped the left side of her chest. Bradlee palpated and could feel the crepitations from a rib fracture. She began to gasp for air and then writhed in pain again. He pushed his ear to her chest and listened. There were no breath sounds from the left side. Cracked rib, punctured lung – *that had to be it!* He quickly glanced at her neck. Her jugular veins were distended. *Air leak. Or was it blood filling her pleural space? She's going to die if I don't try to save her now. Bloody hell!* He pulled out his pocket multitool and found the reamer. Then he quickly located the second rib space in the midline below Dr. Bonheim's collarbone and punctured through the skin with the reamer. Dr. Bonheim screamed and tried to bat him away. He jammed the tool further inside her chest until it passed through her rib muscles. Blood seeped from the chest wound. He inserted his middle finger to stretch the wound space open, then he placed two fingers inside her chest and pushed the rib muscles apart until he felt the soft pleural membrane beneath the muscles. He inserted the reamer again, guiding it with his other hand and punctured the membrane. Immediately, a whoosh of air escaped from her chest. *Come on. I need tubing...* He rummaged through the strewn materials throughout the upside down cabin and located a face mask and oxygen bag that had dropped from its compartment during the crash. *Multitool. Cut.* He opened the pocket knife blade on his tool and cut the mask away. Then he quickly spliced a strip of the plastic tubing. He held it between two fingers and guided the plastic tubing through the chest opening and into the pleural space. Bradlee removed his fingers from the chest wound while holding onto the plastic tubing that now emanated from her chest. *That will do for now.* Dr. Bonheim's neck veins were no longer distended and she appeared to be breathing with greater ease despite relapsing into unconsciousness. He checked her neck pulse. It was rapid but strong.

He heard sirens blaring. *Secure in place. Come on.* Bradlee quickly glanced through the debris and spotted a rubber-coated wire cord that was dangling from the mangled speaker box. He clipped a long piece of cord and fastened it around the plastic tube at Dr. Bonheim's chest wall and then tied the cord around her chest and knotted it securely. *That should secure the tube in place for now*, he said to himself. A*irway and neck. Needs to be secured properly*. He grasped his jacket and carefully laid it behind Dr. Bonheim's neck and bunched its sides as he gently adjusted her neck to a centrally aligned position while carefully minimizing any movement of her cervical spine. He rechecked Dr. Bonheim's breathing. It remained slow but the air sounds were equal as he dropped his ear to each side of her chest and then observed her breathing for a few seconds. Then he stared at her neck and placed his hand against her carotid. Her pulsations were steady and strong.

"Bradlee!!!" Lyra screamed as she approached the plane.

"Lyra, I'm alright!!! But we've got to evacuate fast. There's a gas leak! This plane can blow any second from the fire."

Lyra spotted a fire extinguisher tucked under Stan's seat and removed it, pulled the plug and started to blast foam onto the flames along the left wing. She glanced at Stan slumped in the cockpit. Blood had pooled below his legs. She ran to the right side and sprayed the other wing with the fire extinguisher. She turned and saw Dr. Bonheim unconscious, her face and blouse all bloodied, with a tube sticking out from her chest.

The fire engine arrived and six men jumped out. One ran to Lyra, grabbed her, and brought her behind the fire truck and away from the plane. The others hurriedly unwound a wide hose. A mass of white foam blasted from the hose and saturated the wings and engine compartment. The flames subsided. The firemen grabbed smaller extinguishers and sprayed the wild brush fires surrounding the plane. Smoke billowed skyward from the cooling engine and wings. An ambulance pulled up next and two medics pulled the stretcher from the rear compartment and rolled it quickly towards the plane.

"Over here first!!!" Bradlee shouted at them. They carefully extracted Dr. Bonheim and placed her on the stretcher and noticed the oxygen tubing.

"Tension pneumothorax and probable TBI," Bradlee said loudly over the commotion. Traumatic Brain Injury. It was an acronym he had learned and used from his medical school days when he also volunteered on ambulance crews working long weekend shifts for more experience. He wanted his hands in the action. The satisfaction from helping to save lives. That's what he had signed up for when he dreamed about becoming a doctor ever since he was a young boy.

The medics raced with Dr. Bonheim's stretcher to the waiting ambulance and placed an oxygen mask over her nose and mouth. They applied EKG leads to her chest to monitor her heart rate and rhythm and wrapped a pulse oximeter to her finger. Then one medic secured an intravenous line into a vein in Dr. Bonheim's hand and wrapped it carefully.

Bradlee's head was spinning. He lurched to his side and vomited inside the plane cabin.

A second ambulance arrived as Bradlee was pulling himself from the plane. Bradlee hurried over to Stan as he waved at the next ambulance to approach beside where he stood. The medics brought another stretcher and wheeled it towards Bradlee.

There was a deafening noise from the engine of a small jet plane parked at the far end of the runway. A military jet. It taxied down the runway towards the crash site.

Bradlee screamed out to the medics over the jet noise: "I think he's got a compound right femur fracture with an arterial bleed! I've placed a tourniquet but he's lost a lot of blood! And his airway may be compromised with his facial wounds! Also, I suspect life threatening TBI for Stan as well…! They both need to be airlifted out of here to the nearest trauma center immediately! They don't have much time!!!"

The medics quickly surveyed Stan's injuries, secured a tight collar splint around his neck, and gently extracted him onto the stretcher. They inserted a nasal airway and applied an oxygen mask over Stan's mouth and hooked him up to the monitoring devices. One of the medics was on her phone. The jet's engine noise intensified as it wheeled closer. Bradlee cupped his ears as waves of nausea returned. It was a U.S. Air Force jet that had been conducting paratrooper tactical training near the Badlands for a Navy SEAL team. The area was known for its uncanny resemblance to the lower hills and valleys of Afghanistan. The crew was readying for their flight to return them to the Minot Air Force base just north of the city when they watched the Cessna crashing into the runway.

The jet door popped open and one of the SEAL's quickly spoke with an ambulance medic. The jet's rear cargo door opened and a ramp descended electronically to the airstrip. Four Seal members jumped out from the rear cargo bay and quickly took charge of the stretchers from the ambulance medics as they loaded and secured them to the cargo bay floor.

"Lyra, please go with them!" Bradlee shouted at her across the tarmac. His head was pounding from the jet's powerful engine noise. He slumped to the ground and covered his arms over his head. Two firemen started to lift him from under his shoulders and escort him toward the plane's cargo bay ramp. As they lifted, Bradlee screamed in pain. His left shoulder joint dislocated once again.

"They will need someone there for support when they wake up, Lyra. I'll meet you later!" Bradlee's dizziness intensified.

"Lyra, I..." and then Bradlee's knees buckled under his weight and he lost consciousness. The firemen lifted his frame and transferred Bradlee onto a third stretcher. Two Seals ran to meet the stretcher and hoisted Bradlee into the cargo bay with Lyra beside him. One Seal member pressed a large flashing red button and the cargo bay door closed quickly as the plane began to accelerate down the runway.

The Seal members quickly worked to fasten Lyra into a jumpseat before securing themselves to their own seats in the cargo bay. They were airborne just a few seconds later as the jet powered down the runway.

"Where are we headed?!" Lyra screamed out to one of the Seals.

"We'll be at the air base in Minot in just a few minutes, ma'am. The air force will have emergency crews at the ready to transport these civilians to Trinity Hospital in town. They've got a Level II trauma center there. Those folks will take great care of them."

Jim watched the scene unfold. The last he could see was Bradlee collapsing on the tarmac and being brought into the jet alongside Lyra.

'*Tikun Olam*,' Jim was reminded of the words just then. *Bradlee told me about his Jewish faith on the horseback ride through the Badlands. 'Repair and improve the world.'* Jim wondered if this cameraman's hands were truly like a surgeon's out there on that runway. Bradlee probably saved lives, starting with his grandson.

"God, please look after all of them," Jim prayed out loud. He was holding Kin in his arms.

Kin whispered into his Papa's ear. "It was the cranes, Papa. The Sandhill cranes flew into the plane window."

Jim was astounded. "Really?"

"Yes, Papa. I tried to warn them but it was too late." Kin was sniffling.

Jim hugged him even tighter.

"Oh, come now, my little Soaring Hawk. You did well in trying. Your eyes are young and strong. Papa is *very* proud of you... You are safe in my arms now and those people are in good hands. We will pray for our ancestors to bestow their blessings upon them."

"Yes, Papa."

"Come, Kin... we need to clean you up. We have some important errands to do before we can visit our hurting friends later tonight."

Jim stood for a few minutes longer and stared at the jet

until it pierced through the darkening clouds and was no longer in sight.

They exited the runway in Jim's pick-up and stopped at a gas station to use the bathroom sink as Jim cleaned Kin's face and hair from the blood stains and purchased a clean shirt for him to wear. Then they continued into Medora. It was close to two o'clock when they arrived at the Heritage Center. Jim had called ahead to alert Tom and Frank of the plane crash. There were about a hundred assembled visitors at the center awaiting Bradlee's arrival. Some were there from the reservation and Jim particularly welcomed them warmly. All were admiring the details and lighting in Bradlee's photographs as they made their way around the gallery space. They paused to focus the longest on the two massive wood carved framed photographs mounted towards each end of the gallery. One was a photo of the herd gathered into the wind and the other was of the lone stallion. A replica of the lone stallion adorned the cover of the show's brochure and the back page was of the herd. Inside the brochure was Bradlee's beautifully composed essay about the history of the wild horses in the Badlands. All admired how Bradlee had exquisitely captured the true wildness of the Badlands horses through their glares and poses in the backdrop of nothing but raw nature.

Jim made the rounds for a few minutes chatting briefly with many of the guests. Kin studied the photos with his keen eyes and placed his hands gently at the base of one of Bradlee's massive carved frames. He felt the texture of Bradlee's craftsmanship as if he was reading Braille and absorbing energy from the carvings. When finished, Kin returned to Jim's side.

Word had already spread that Bradlee would not be in attendance as he was also transported to Minot for lifesaving care. The expected celebration was transformed into a makeshift prayer service as Jim stood on a chair and raised his hand. The guests quieted. Jim updated everyone on the events of the day beginning with the rampage on the reservation's corral and ending in the tragic crash at the Dickinson runway. A bible was handed to Jim and he leafed through it to find an appropriate passage in Bradlee's honor. *A Jewish man who was a hero today deserves a proper verse from the Old Testament liturgy*, Jim thought to himself. He located the Psalms of David, King of the Israelites, and scanned them until one caught his eye and quieted his unsettled spirit. He read the entire Psalm to himself before speaking.

"Let us pray for Bradlee, a young man with a passionate and loving heart, as we can see from the images that surround us here today. A man who has saved three lives today if our prayers will be answered in the heavens above. And let us pray for his friends who have been traumatically injured today… And I also ask all of you assembled to pray for my people on the reservation for we are a divided nation and we are suffering too as we carry angry and heavy hearts. And now… the burden that we must carry for our part in this unfortunate accident. May we come together in peace and union as is our united heritage. Amen." The gathering responded 'Amen' in unison.

Jim continued: "A passage from the Book of Psalms. Psalm 34, verses 15 through 22." Jim removed his cowboy hat and others in the crowd followed his lead. "Please bow your heads and pray with me."

> The eyes of the Lord are on the righteous, and his ears are attentive to their cry; but the face of the Lord is against those who do evil, to blot out their name from the earth.
>
> The righteous cry out, and the Lord hears them; he delivers them from all their troubles.
>
> The Lord is close to the brokenhearted and saves those who are crushed in spirit.

The righteous person may have many troubles, but the LORD delivers him from them all; he protects all his bones, not one of them will be broken.

Evil will slay the wicked; the foes of the righteous will be condemned.

The LORD will rescue his servants; no one who takes refuge in him will be condemned.

Jim closed the Bible slowly and stood with his head bowed for a long moment of silence among the assembled guests.

The somber mood was in desperate need for something to raise the spirits of all in attendance. Kin climbed onto the adjacent chair as Jim glanced over to his grandson with curiosity. Kin began to speak:

"My Papa's words are true. Please pray for Bradlee, Dr. Bonheim, and Stan. Bradlee is a blessing to all of us. He saved my life today! In Bradlee's honor, please consider a donation to the Heritage Center to help their mission."

Kim raised his arms above his head and formed the shape of a large V as he angled them in the form of outstretched wings. Then he raised his voice louder for all to hear clearly. "And my name is Soaring Hawk!"

The guests suddenly opened into uproarious laughter. Jim glared at Kin but then softened his eyes and caressed Kin's cheeks inside his large hands. He spoke softly and directly. "Your day as the leader of our people will come, Kin, my Soaring Hawk. I am very proud of your heart today." And then he kissed his grandson on the top of his head.

The disposition among the guests turned into a more uplifting atmosphere and the gallery returned to chatty conversation as the hors d'oeuvres were served.

"Kin, let me show you something," Jim said. He brought

Kin to one of the large framed images of the herd. The horses were corralled around a young stallion, perhaps half the size of the adults, and shielding the young horse as their manes were fanned by the cold winds. Kin stared at the image.

"What do you see, Kin?" Jim asked.

"I see many hearts beating with love, Papa. I can feel it inside of me."

Yes, just as these wild horses know instinctively how to love their kind – so must we as one people. One nation. We cannot survive and prosper if we fight amongst ourselves. Our people need the wisdom of our ancestors and traditions. My grandson, Soaring Hawk – you will become a great leader if you are guided by your heart. Not just your eyes. Your strength and respect as a leader will come from living a righteous life for all to witness."

"Yes, Papa. I understand."

"Come now – we have work to do."

Jim thanked some of the fellow Heritage Center board members and catering servers for their work towards making the gallery exhibit a success. Tom and Frank were present and expressed their admiration for Bradlee's work. They asked Jim to keep them abreast of Bradlee's medical condition, as well as the others brought to the hospital, and Jim promised he would. He departed the center with Kin by his side.

Bursts of lightning and thunder punctuated their drive north as the storm clouds rolled across the reservation and discarded their contents in a wrathful vengeance. The pick-up truck returned to the trailer corral as the rains subsided. It was abandoned. Smoke smoldered from the burnt teepee, its fabric laying in crisp tattered shreds inside an ash-filled landscape. All that remained of the trailers were their metal frames and twisted blackened plastic moldings strewn about the area. Jim searched through the rubble with Kin's help in hope of finding any remnants of personal items that belonged to Lyra, Dr. Bonheim, and Stan. He located a few suitcases but their contents were emptied and strewn about the area. Clothing and personal items were burned and melted into unrecognizable forms.

Kin had recovered a necklace from inside a charred zippered compartment of a suitcase and brought it to Jim to inspect. It was a long strand of seashells, all identical in shape. Most of the shells were tinged on their surface into a golden brown hue while others retained their soft white markings, but they were all intact, unharmed otherwise by the fire. It remained an exquisitely beautiful piece of jewelry and Jim surmised that it likely belonged to Lyra since he had seen her wearing a necklace at the ranch that contained a single seashell. Jim placed the necklace in his jacket pocket. Then Kin found Stan's plane logbook. Stan had not had time to retrieve it from his trailer before running to prepare the plane. It was relatively intact in its hard plastic case. Jim located Dr. Bonheim's camera bag but there were only burnt and melted remains of its former contents.

Jim returned to the central teepee area. He searched once again amidst the rubble for anything that could be saved and retrieved a long plastic cylindrical tube below the remains of the charred solid wood table. He opened the top and discovered that it contained the intact geology and topography maps that Dr. Bonheim and Lyra had been using for their pipeline research. At least some of their work over the holiday weekend was salvaged from the fire although the various smaller tubes of collected and labeled soil samples were destroyed.

Kin assisted his Papa with covering any remaining simmering embers with dirt. Jim looked back at the site as he and Kin arrived to the pick-up.

"We will rebuild, Kin. Better. Stronger. Your GranMama's work, and your mother Oji's, will not be in vein. The voices of our ancestors will return here to share their wisdom with all who choose to join us in peace. Your birthday, Kin, someday will be a day for great celebration and joy among our people. A great Chief must become from these ashes... Do not forget what you see before us here, Soaring Hawk. But also, you must learn to forgive and to ask for wisdom as you follow your heart if you wish to lead our nation when I have gone to the stars." He hugged Kin affectionately with tears in his eyes.

They exited and quietly returned to Jim's ranch as Kin napped from exhaustion. They arrived in the early evening. Wichahpi opened the front door and greeted them with saddened eyes. Oji lifted Kin into her arms and held him lovingly as she kissed his forehead and rocked him in her arms. Jim updated the family on the events at the corral and the airstrip. Oji brought bread and butter and tea to the table. "I've made some hot barley soup with garlic and vegetables to strengthen our spirits," Wichahpi said, as she served it to the table. They sat together and ate quietly, each in their thoughts.

After dinner, Jim placed a call to an old friend in Minot. Then he kissed Wichahpi goodbye and Oji accompanied Jim in the pick-up. Jim would not sleep without knowing the condition of his gravely injured friends. He placed Bradlee's bag in the pick-up and they started towards Trinity Hospital in Minot.

They arrived at eight-thirty at the hospital and took the elevator to the intensive care unit. There was a sign informing them that the hospital guest visiting hours were until nine o'clock. Jim and Oji started towards the nurse's station and a voice called out to them.

"Jim, it's good to see you." The two men embraced.

"Ben Cohen, it's been a long time. Thanks for taking my call earlier this evening. I believe you met my daughter-in-law, Oji, when I was hospitalized here last year. Oji's worked many years at the Lady Slipper Inn. Thomas and Nancy's place in town."

"Yes, of course. It's good to see you again, Oji."

"Thank you, Dr. Cohen. I am glad you are in good health and vigor," Oji said respectfully. Ben smiled cheerfully.

"Jim, how's that grandson of yours doing?"

"Kin is Oji's son. It's a miracle that he barely had a scratch on him."

"Did you sustain any injuries from that ruckus at the corral? I'm sorry those folks burned everything. I was worried about that leg of yours."

"Thanks Ben. I was fortunate. Leg is fine, holding as steady as a horse staring into the wind."

Ben chuckled. Jim always had a way with words.

Jim turned to Oji. "Oji, Lyra is here in the hospital somewhere. This might be a good time to see her while we have just a little remaining visitor time. Perhaps we need to invite her to the ranch to stay with us tonight."

"Lyra – is she the young lady who's here helping to care for Bradlee?" Ben asked.

"Yes, that's right," Jim replied.

"She's upstairs with him now." Ben gave Oji the instructions to Bradlee's hospital room and she started towards the elevators.

"Oh, Oji," Jim called out. "And please give Lyra the bag I handed to you earlier. It has something that Kin found back at the corral. It is very likely that it belongs to Lyra."

"I will, Papa." Oji entered the elevator.

"Jim, I think they're all going to live," Ben started. "I know you must have had a long drive here worrying about that. I came as soon as I heard from some of the medical staff that there were incoming trauma patients from a flight out of the reservation airstrip. I was briefed about the troubles that went on there and one of the nurses, who commutes from the reservation to work here, told me that you knew these three patients personally. My teaching position at the hospital allows me access to medical records for resident report on morning rounds. I prefer to keep abreast of details myself from the medical charts so I've been here tonight reviewing their care needs. See if I can contribute some medical wisdom if any is needed. Bradlee has the least concerns. The other two are stable in critical care. I've got the best team working on them now.

"That's very good news!" Jim replied.

"Jim – Stan and the lady, Dr. Carol Bonheim, sustained some serious injuries. Stan was brought immediately to the operating room to fix his compound femur fracture. It was far worse than you suffered yourself last year. He's got pins and rods inside and some bars outside of his leg to stabilize the fracture. Needed some delicate microvascular surgery to stitch his femoral artery laceration. He's already received six pints of blood and his trauma labs are looking stable post-op. But his face is a mess and will need a series of plastic and oral surgeries in the next few months ahead but he's real fortunate to be alive and his brain scan didn't show any serious trauma inside his skull... His wife, Amanda, arrived just a short while ago from Billings and she's with him now in the critical care unit. It was a darn coincidence that Air Force jet was on the runway to get them here as fast as they did. There's no way a helicopter transport would have gotten here in time to save his life with the amount of blood loss he sustained. According to eyewitnesses at the airport, Stan did an amazing job trying to land that Cessna without crashing it into a million pieces. You and I are both men of faith, Jim. I have my suspicions that there was a hand of God involved here. And Jim... the other real hero here is Bradlee. His quick thinking to properly apply that tourniquet saved Stan from bleeding out. It gave Stan a fighting chance to get to us here in time. And that's before I even tell you what Bradlee did for Dr. Bonheim."

Jim listened carefully. He glanced down the hallway and noticed a familiar face walking towards the nursing station. It was the senior intensive care nurse who had cared for him last year after his fall from his stallion when he was riding in the Badlands and the lightning storm came through. She had taken outstanding care of him while he was admitted in the ICU for over a week after his emergent surgery for his own femur fracture and subdural hematoma. The nurse approached Jim and she gave him a gentle hug.

"Sandy, it's great to see you again, although I was hoping to not set foot back here for a long long time."

"I can understand that. You look great, Chief Clayburn. I'm glad to see you well. Very sorry to hear about the troubles at the reservation earlier today."

"Thanks, Sandy. I will need all my energy to help sort through the challenges we're facing over the pipeline plans... It's caused a lot of pain and anger among our people. But enough of that. I came to check on my friends who were brought here from the Dickinson plane crash. You have the overnight shift tonight?"

"Yes." Sandy glanced at Dr. Cohen and he nodded his approval to discuss the condition of her patient further with Jim.

"I'm taking care of a Dr. Carol Bonheim from Seattle. Ph.D. scientist. Sixty-two years old. Professor and prominent environmental researcher and policy advisor. She's on life support now. Heavily sedated. Stable but in guarded condition. The impact at the plane crash caused severe blunt trauma to her chest wall. She sustained multiple rib fractures on the left side and a traumatic pneumothorax from one of the ribs that punctured her lung. She also has fractures in the facets of her cervical vertebra in her neck, C-5 and C-6 to be exact, but fortunately, those fractures didn't penetrate through to her spinal cord or she would have been most likely permanently paralyzed. She also sustained a subdural hematoma just as you had, Jim, from your fall off your stallion."

"I didn't fall, Sandy. My stallion threw me off." Jim kept a serious face but then offered Sandy a gentle smile. Jim knew the truth was a little of both during the lightning storm but he kept his personal concerns to himself. His stallion was spooked alright, as it reared back on its his hind legs when they were on a bluff and a lightning bolt landed nearby. Jim made a quick decision then. If he didn't rapidly slip his boots out of the stirrups and jump immediately from the saddle onto the bluff, then his stallion would have fallen off the cliff edge from the force of Jim's weight on his stallion's back. Both would have perished together off that cliff.

"Please continue Sandy…" Jim kindly requested.

"There was a passenger on board who immediately fixed Stan's arterial bleed. Then he performed a thoracostomy on Dr. Bonheim right inside the plane with his pocket multitool and some oxygen tubing that he found inside the plane. He evacuated a tension pneumothorax that Dr. Bonheim would have otherwise died from within a few minutes. We brought her to the operating room and cleaned up her chest wound. The trauma surgeons fixed her ribcage with wires and she's stable on her ventilator under a lot of sedation and pain medication. We'll need to watch her closely for any signs of infection but so far she's following the post-op protocol quite well…" Sandy felt that was sufficient personal medical information to have shared about Dr. Bonheim's condition before continuing.

"Chief, this kid is something else. He's the talk of all the critical care residents and medical students. Darn hero! Handsome as Superman too, from what I hear from the nurses and residents working the overnight shift." Sandy blushed from her own remark. "But I also hear he's got a cute girl at his bedside guarding him like a leech in a swamp… From what I hear his injuries aren't life threatening. Don't know much else about him other than that he's upstairs on the internal medicine ward and his name is....."

Hold on, let me login to the computer station here to check." She clicked on a chart entry and found a scanned copy of his official driver license. "He goes by a Mr. Bradlee Lee on admission to the hospital but his driver license says 'Baruch Avraham Levitsky.' Kid is from Prince Edward Island. No idea why he'd be in North Dakota for Thanksgiving but I guess he can tell you his story if Dr. Cohen here allows you a visit at this late hour."

"Thanks Sandy. I'll take it from here. Appreciate your efforts as always," Ben replied as Sandy wished Jim well and continued with her tasks.

Jim glanced at Ben. *"Baruch Avraham Levitsky?* Hmm. That's a mouthful of Jewish history right there in one name... Ben, what does the name, *Baruch*, mean?"

"It means '*Blessing* or *One Who is Blessed*,' in the Hebrew language."

"Well, I'll be darned. Makes perfect sense now, doesn't it!" The men laughed together.

"But I might stick with Bradlee for now, as Lyra likes to call him," Jim added.

"There's more to his story, I assure you, Jim. I don't know much more than you about the young man but I've been best friends with Bradlee's uncle, a Rabbi Eliezer Levitsky, for just about my whole life. And Rabbi Levitsky is the brother of Bradlee's father, who is a renowned surgeon and professor in Toronto."

"Small world, Ben. Small world. Amazing how we are all connected somehow to each other... Is it too late to visit my new friends tonight?"

It's best that we steer clear of Stan and Dr. Bonheim. They are in critical care and on ventilators anyway. No use gawking at them through a window with all the pipes and drains and machines they're hooked up to right now. I'll ask Amanda, Stan's wife, if she has a moment to speak with you. We've tried to reach Dr. Bonheim's husband, who's also a university professor. But according to the university he's out of the country in Indonesia working on some remote island on a research project there. It may take some more days until he can be located by the authorities and receive word of his wife's condition."

"How about Bradlee?" Any chance I can spend a few minutes with him? I really wanted to thank him for saving my grandson's life. He deserves that... You know Ben, I've got my eye on Kin. I think he will make a fine Chief to replace me on the reservation one day. The boy has insight and wisdom beyond his years... I won't stay long visiting Bradlee. Chief's promise." Jim smiled as he raised his right hand.

"Of course, Jim. Don't worry about the visiting hours. I'll talk to the nurses on the ward. They won't chase you away anytime soon."

"Thanks Ben. You've been a good friend all these years since we met on the reservation when we were young and reckless. You were a great doctor then and even more so today. You should be very proud of what you've done for our people all these years in the Dakotas. You are one of us. Always have been. Always will be."

"Very kind of you, Jim. Please give my love to Wichahpi."

"And to Hannah as well, from me. Wichahpi and I need to have you over at the ranch again soon. I know you're not much of a horseman, Ben, but I've got a fine old mare for you to ride in the Badlands. She'll be real easy on your behind. You can ask Bradlee about that when you see him again."

The men shared a good laugh together. Ben escorted Jim to the ICU entrance. Amanda met Jim in the hallway and Jim gave her a warm embrace followed by kind words in prayer for Stan's recovery. He handed Amanda Stan's flight logbook that was found at the corral site. The two men then proceeded upstairs to the internal medicine ward. Ben pointed Jim down the hallway to Bradlee's hospital room. They embraced and then Ben returned to the ICU.

Oji answered Jim's knock on Bradlee's door. Lyra approached and embraced Jim. Bradlee was lightly sedated, laying elevated in his bed with a nurse beside him. She was getting to know her patients for the overnight shift as she made her rounds and checked vital signs. He had a heavy sling wrapped around his left arm and shoulder and some bandages on various skin wounds on his chest, arms, and legs. The lights were dimmed.

"It's good to see you, Lyra. Sorry for one heck of an eventful day," Jim started. "How's our hero doing?"

"Let's ask him, shall we." Lyra escorted Jim over to Bradlee's side and pulled up a chair for him to sit beside Bradlee's bed.

"Howdy riding partner, you managing alright? Where I come from, when a man falls off a horse he learns to get back up as soon as he can before the vultures clean up the mess. Unless his bum is too sore to take it." Bradlee laughed at the reminder of his day horseback riding with Jim in the Badlands. He also remembered back to plenty of occasions along his cross country bicycle journey when he had to summon the will to hop back on his bicycle saddle with a sore bum and finish up yet another long day's hundred-mile ride.

"Jim, it's good to see you. Thanks for stopping by tonight."

"Well, I came here with Oji to thank you personally. You saved my grandson's life, Mr. Baruch Avraham Levitsky. I think that kind of blessing deserves a blessing in return from an old Indian Chief for your speedy recovery back to excellent health and good fortune."

Lyra glanced at Bradlee in puzzlement. Jim had called him by a very different name than she knew him to be.

Bradlee met her eyes and then glanced towards the window. Lyra recalled how Bradlee would look out the window of the train when he was in deep thought. Same kind of impulse now, she thought. *Why?*

"So, what does your doc have to say about your condition?"

"I'm being observed overnight tonight. Should be able to be released tomorrow."

"That's it?! You survive a plane crash today and you're already ready to climb back up on Ms. Culpepper? Because she's been asking for you, you know." Jim chuckled.

"Well, not quite so fast but I will take a raincheck for the invitation. My head is still pounding. The doctor says I sustained a good concussion and need a lot of rest over the week ahead. My brain scan was clear so nothing too serious happened between my ears. I also dislocated my left shoulder but the Ortho doc in the ER injected the area with some Novocain to numb it, and then fixed the dislocation with traction on the joint. I'll need to wear this sling for at least a week and start rehab soon to strengthen the joint capsule. Otherwise, I'm real lucky to be alive, I guess."

"I'll second that! Bradlee, my longtime friend, Dr. Ben Cohen, told me you saved Stan's and Dr. Bonheim's lives in that plane crash." Bradlee was surprised by the mention of Dr. Cohen's name.

"You know Dr. Cohen, Jim?"

Jim chuckled. "Just about everyone in North Dakota knows Dr. Benjamin Cohen. He started out in his medical career working on my reservation when we were both just young whippersnappers. Ben and I have been friends for forty years…! Son, you should be proud of your abilities. Your hands took quick action out there. And you must have had the intelligence to know how to do what you did in that short a reaction time. Not sure how – but you did! That's another gift you have. Maybe you should consider becoming a doctor. Have you thought about that?"

Lyra chuckled. "Bradlee told me he attended medical school some years ago. But he didn't finish the program."

"Oh really?! Well, you might want to jump back in, Bradlee. Although I can tell you the gallery exhibit was a great success at the Heritage Center earlier today. Very sorry you had to miss your own show."

"Thanks Jim. If I hadn't passed out I think I could have made it."

Jim laughed at the idea and then feigned a fainting spell in his chair as he pretended to hold a camera in his hands and take a photo of Bradlee in his hospital bed. Everyone laughed as the mood continue to lighten.

But Bradlee ran the idea through his head. He didn't know if he really would seriously consider returning to medical school even if he was offered the opportunity. He admitted to himself that the thought did, occasionally, cross his mind. He was only a few months from graduating and moving on to residency training when he decided to end it all. He was first in his medical school class academically. All honors. His mind flashed to the plane crash. Evacuating a child first – Kin, to safety. Rapid surveillance and triage. Applying the makeshift tourniquet to Stan's leg. Puncturing, evacuating the pneumothorax, and inserting the tubing into Dr. Bonheim's chest. The actions all seemed to come naturally, almost instinctively to him. Not much thinking. Just doing. His reflexes just kicked into gear. A kind of detachment from the emotions of the moment to focus on what was needed to save lives. But he knew those maneuvers from observing his father over the years through college and medical school and his work on the ambulance crew had also helped. His father was a tough teacher. Exacting in his disciplined approach to minimize any chance of medical error. Bradlee scrubbed into the operating room on plenty of occasions that his father invited him to assist. His hands were already seeped in the blood and guts of many patients. He held the retractors and peered inside bleeding chests and abdomens as his father pointed out vital structures and anatomic variants of importance to recognize - the adrenaline pumping through Bradlee's own arteries as his father and the nursing staff rushed to save lives. Trauma surgeon. About the highest stress the medical profession could entertain and his dad was one of the best in Canada. Probably the finest reputation in all of Toronto. Bradlee realized he was exposed to more surgeries and learned more medical techniques than any other medical student could have ever dreamed in their early training years.

"Well, I'll let you get some more rest now. You've been a blessing to us all, young man," Jim said as he winked at Bradlee and laid his hand onto Bradlee's healthy shoulder. He held Bradlee's hand and then stooped to whisper something into Bradlee's ear that only Bradlee could hear. It was as if Jim was the loving father that Bradlee wished he had.

Jim turned and exited the room with Lyra and Oji in tow. In the hallway, Jim told Lyra that she was welcome to stay at the ranch with the family but Lyra preferred to stay. She wanted to remain close to Bradlee and also check on Dr. Bonheim's progress. Dr. Cohen had made an exception to hospital policy. He made arrangements to allow Lyra to use a vacant on-call room, usually reserved for the staff's use, to allow her to rest periodically overnight adjacent to the intensive care unit. Dr. Cohen even waived most patient confidentiality restrictions once Lyra explained her connection to Dr. Bonheim as her esteemed mentor. Besides, as Ben realized, Dr. Bonheim could use the emotional support from Lyra's presence once she became stronger and able to tolerate less sedation. And Dr. Bonheim had no one else to be there for her. "Sometimes you have to bend the rules in the name of giving the best chance for a human being to live," Dr. Cohen said to the ICU staff and they agreed. Jim and Oji said their goodbyes, exited, and started on their return trip to the ranch.

Lyra returned to Bradlee's bedside and touched her forehead to his. They held together for a long time. Then she released and kissed his forehead gently. His arm sling was shifted slightly and so she adjusted it to its proper position as the nurse had instructed her to do. Bradlee winced from the maneuver. "Sorry about that," she whispered and then kissed his lips. She sat beside him on the edge of the bedsheet.

"Anything you'd like to tell me about... Baruch Avraham Levitsky?"

Lyra waited for a response but Bradlee looked away at the pale peach hospital wall in front of him. There was a simple framed oil painting hanging on the wall of a white horse with a mocha-colored mane eating grass in a meadow. The artist hadn't bothered to add any emotion to the horse's eyes or face. Nothing too exciting but it was mellowing to stare at while lying in his hospital bed. A simple piece of artwork that adorned an otherwise dreary sterile hospital room. Bradlee thought about his photographs now hanging at the Heritage Center. His exhibit that he missed attending. They would certainly enliven this place a whole lot more, he thought to himself. Perhaps, he thought, he should donate a few to the hospital in kindness for the care he had received.

"Bradlee, I'm over here... Lyra waived her hand in front of his face and then gently maneuvered his jaw until his eyes met hers and she kissed his lips softly. "You were daydreaming again... Bradlee, I'd like to know who you really are. Isn't that fair?"

Tears began to well in her eyes.

"I'm sorry, Lyra. I had been meaning to tell you but I just didn't ever find the right moment over the phone. That's all. It's not important, really. It's just part of my story, that's all... Look... I sort of changed my name to

Bradlee Lee when I dropped out of medical school for personal reasons. It's not my official name. Never got around to following through on that... I'm not running from the law, if that's what you're worried about... I wasn't completely truthful to you on the train and I'm sorry about that. I didn't want to involve you in my family's problems as I got to know you better. And besides, you hadn't shared anything with me about your own family. I figured we both felt that was for the best for the time being."

Bradlee's nurse returned to the room. Visiting hours had long passed and she asked Lyra to let Bradlee have some rest now. "Just a few more minutes," she informed Lyra before departing again.

"Bradlee... Baruch... whoever you are inside here..." Lyra rested her hand on his chest and then held his right arm to her cheek. She kissed his palm. "We'll talk more tomorrow. I understand how you feel. But someday you'll need to let me inside. To know you for who you are. Imperfections and painful scars and all. We all have them, you know. I want you to trust me Bradlee... and I, you."

Lyra traced a heart inside Bradlee's palm and playfully found his tickle spot at its very center. Then she opened his palm again and studied his creases like a fortune teller.

"Let's have a good look here," she started. "Your love line is very long, Bradlee. And there is a crease here" – as she showed him the spot – "that ends abruptly while the other continues all the way until it nearly wraps beyond the margin of your hand and then stops. I wonder what it means..."

Bradlee smiled at her and knew exactly what it meant. He pulled her gently towards him and kissed her and held his lips to hers as they closed their eyes. He could feel the warmth from her forehead against his, as if there was a bright light emanating between them just as Kin had said. Bradlee felt as if their souls were bonding together and their kisses were serving as the eternal adhesive. It had been a day they would never forget.

The nurse entered the room once again and offered a mock throat clearing gesture.

Lyra turned again to meet Bradlee's eyes.

"Before I go, though... Bradlee, your birth name, 'Baruch'... It means 'Blessed,' doesn't it?"

"Yes, it does. But how do you know that, Lyra?"

Lyra smiled at him and reached over as she laid her head against his chest. "Thank God you are alive, Baruch. Amen to that."

Their lips met again as Lyra was reluctant to leave Bradlee's side.

"Until tomorrow, then?" Lyra whispered. "Yes... until the end," Bradlee replied with a gleam in his eyes as they smiled and then laughed at his phrase once again.

"You are *such* a romantic fool, Baruch Seashell."

"Takes one to know one, Lyra," Bradlee responded." And then Bradlee realized he still didn't remember Lyra's last name and was too embarrassed to ask her at that moment.

THE MORNING ARRIVED. Lyra was exhausted from intermittent sleep as she remained most of the night by Dr. Bonheim's bedside and received updates on her medical condition from the intensive care nurses. Bradlee awoke and dressed, ate the hospital provided breakfast, and then strolled down the hallway. The pounding in his head had subsided to a mild persistent dull ache but he was no longer experiencing waves of nausea or double vision. The left side of his head was very tender at the site of the impact against the plane door, and the scalp area remained swollen, but as long as he didn't touch it or lay his head on that side against a pillow, he found it manageable. The nursing staff were all pleased to see his quick progress and the examining physician was agreeable to discharge him from the hospital on condition that he receives lots of rest over the week ahead. The staff orthopedist checked his left shoulder and adjusted his sling and told Bradlee that physical therapy will start immediately. Bradlee was brought to the center inside the hospital and the therapist demonstrated a variety of shoulder exercises for Bradlee to continue after discharge. Lyra met him at the physical therapy department and escorted him back to his hospital room. Bradlee informed Lyra that he had made a reservation to stay the night at the Lady Slipper Inn when he spoke with Thomas and Nancy some weeks prior and notified them of his plans to return to North Dakota for the exhibit. Bradlee confided with Lyra that he was hoping that perhaps Lyra would have been able to join him at the inn for that night if it were possible with her work schedule on the pipeline project. He admitted he was hoping she would be interested in a quiet romantic evening together. But a lot had happened between then and now. Lyra mentioned to Bradlee that she had the same hope – to be able to stay in Minot together with Bradlee for at least one glorious night together – but Dr. Bonheim's condition remained life-threatening in the intensive care unit. Her professor had spiked a high fever in the middle of the night and Lyra was going to need to remain at the hospital by Dr. Bonheim's bedside. They kissed passionately and agreed to determine when to meet again soon.

    Bradlee remembered the gift in his travel bag. He unzipped his duffel and handed the package to Lyra. She unwrapped it. It was the maple syrup stained ash wood bowl that he had purchased from Leo in Newfoundland. Bradlee reminded Lyra of her craving for maple syrup when they were on the train together and thought she would really enjoy the beautiful handcrafted piece. Lyra admired it and kissed Bradlee again and whispered in his ear that someday she hoped to serve him pancakes with maple syrup in this very bowl, in bed – for dinner! They laughed together and he hugged and caressed her curved frame one last time with his one good arm.

By noon, Bradlee was heading towards the hospital's front doors when his phone rang.

"Uncle Eddie!" Bradlee answered.

"Baruch, good to hear your voice. My friend, Ben Cohen, called me this morning. You remember the doctor in Minot that I introduced you to inside the Scandinavian church…?"

"Yes, of course."

"Baruch, Ben relayed that you were in a small plane crash. He had received a call from Chief Clayburn notifying him. Are you going to be OK?"

"Thanks, Uncle Eddie. I think so. I'm just heading out of the hospital now. Some minor injuries, but I'll be alright."

"Thank God… Thank God… Baruch, Ben also told me that you saved three lives. One of them was a young child too, the Chief's grandson."

"I did the best I could under the circumstances, that's all."

"Well, I'm very proud of you, Baruch. Your ability to think quickly and take action – well, these are traits you share with my dear brother, Baruch. Both of you seem to have the know how and the knack to save lives. Your father would be very proud of you for what you've done. I know I am."

"Thank you, Uncle Eddie."

"Baruch, we still need to get together again when you are in Toronto. Please look me up when you are passing through."

"I will, Uncle Eddie. Thanks for calling to check on me."

"My dear nephew - I love you. I only wish the best for

you, as always. Take care of yourself."

Bradlee exited with his duffel bag over his healthy right shoulder and his cowboy hat safely stowed back on his head. He was beginning to feel like a real cowboy now that he was in North Dakota once again. His third tour of duty through the region in his lifetime. *What is it about this place that I find so attractive?*, he wondered. *All I need now is a handsome pair of cowboy boots, like Jim always wears, and I'll be set! Maybe the locals will call me, 'Superhero Seashell' around these parts.* Bradlee was riding high on happiness. He was the talk of the town and he had a beautiful girl doting on him. And he was in love with her. What more could he ask for from life? He was alive, for starters. And he'd be good as new soon enough.

It was a crisp sunny day in Minot. Snow had dusted the area the night before and the smell of winter freshness pervaded the air. A taxi was waiting for Bradlee at the curbside patient pick-up zone. The driver was reading the local newspaper as he stood against his vehicle holding a sign that read, 'Mr. S U P E R H E R O' and then he recognized Bradlee approaching.

"Well, look who we have here? A genuine Canadian superhero according to this here front page! Look at you all bandaged up with your cowboy hat on and all the rest! You need to work on your superhero swagger, young man." James started strutting around the taxi like a rooster with his head held high as Bradlee broke into laughter.

They greeted each other affectionately as James planted a careful bear hug against Bradlee's right shoulder and patted him on the back.

"You fixin' for some of Ruby's pie and ice cream 'cause I'm sure that hospital food wasn't worth a whole rainforest of vanilla beans?!"

"James, that sounds awesome. Thanks for agreeing to pick me up. And I'm glad you were willing to get out of your house for a bit. I've been wanting to visit you ever since I heard from Thomas about..." Bradlee choked up thinking about the pain James must still be feeling. "James, I'm really sorry about your Sweet Caroline. I know you loved her dearly after spending nearly your whole lives together. I just really wish I could have met her."

"It's OK, son. Thank you for that. Caroline's in a good spot, I believe. She's more than earned her rest in heaven. I miss her every minute, I do. But I'm here and she's there..." he pointed towards the clouds above them... "and we had a glorious fifty years together. I know for sure that she's looking down here and hoping I don't just mess things up. Really, I think she's hoping she taught me enough that I could handle the rest of my life's journey on my own if I needed to. But we've got our kids who have been great, coming by to check on me often, and our grandkids just keep on growing and changing. Life never stands still for very long... One of our sweet little granddaughters, Lois – she's just three years old now, even looks about as darned near a reincarnation of my Sweet Caroline as the angels could have crafted. It's sure helped to be around her and see her blossoming in my arms."

James loaded Bradlee's luggage into the taxi and they set off for Ruby's on the River. They entered and were seated for a late lunch. The place was quiet before the evening rush was to begin in a few hours. Ruby was alerted by the staff and she quickly came hustling over to their table.

"I can swear I've seen you two handsome boys around here before?" she said with a sarcastic grin and a bat of her eyelashes.

Bradlee bounced to his feet and winced as his left shoulder reminded him to be more careful next time with any sudden movements.

"Ruby, life has been a little crazy lately."

She pulled out the newspaper that was folded beneath her arm and showed the front page to Bradlee.

"You sure like North Dakota, Bradlee Lee, 'cause it seems you just keep showing back up here unannounced." Her face was smiling from ear to ear.

"Ruby, I had intended to call you and come by for a visit but a little plane crash got in the way of that. Next time I'll promise to dial you to order takeout just before the crash." They laughed and Bradlee embraced Ruby with his right arm as she planted a juicy red lipstick kiss on his cheek.

"Go ahead and order whatever it is you like, boys. This meal's on the house today for a superhero…!" She glanced at the front page again and left the newspaper on the table for Bradlee to keep.

"And for you too, James. I've got a fresh pie readying to serve from the oven. Either of you ever tasted huckleberries before? You know – the Tom Sawyer and Huck Finn kind munching on these sweet things while rafting barefooted down the Mississippi? Anyway, have a dear friend of mine who drove all the way from Mississippi to visit with me and she brought these fresh berries with her just yesterday." Neither Jim nor Bradlee could recall if they had ever tasted huckleberries.

"Boys, down South they have a saying that huckleberries will get your ticker up-and-ready if you finish it all. So, I'll promise you that." Ruby winked at James and then scurried towards the kitchen. She was all gussied up, as usual, in one of her floral full-fitted dresses and many decorative accessories.

Bradlee sat down again and glanced over at James. James was trying everything he could to avoid making eye contact.

"James, did Ruby just make a little pass at you?" James put down his menu. He was blushing like a young school boy.

"Ruby and I have known each other for a long time, Bradlee. I admit that we've shared a quiet affection for each other over the years. Nothing like you may be thinking. She and Caroline were close friends and I never had anything going on with Ruby on the side. But Ruby's been alone her whole adult life. No husband. No kids. This whole town is her extended family, her love story... Bradlee, it hasn't been two months past yet since I buried my Sweet Caroline. I know Ruby is interested in a relationship with me. Something more physical than what we've always shared. And I do find her attractive in a lot of ways. She's a wonderful woman. Very loving as you know, Bradlee. Will go out of her way to help any soul in need. Reminds me a lot of Caroline in that regard... I guess I just need some more time. My Sweet Caroline and I, our love story, well... it's still simmering even without her presence beside me now. But I can't deny that I'm lonely most days by myself in that house. Winters are darn cold here without someone to cuddle up to next to a fire and share the simple things that make our lives enjoyable. I don't think I was intended to be alone for long, Bradlee. I can tell you that, for sure. Just isn't in my nature." James sniffled and pulled out a handkerchief from his pocket to wipe his nose and then he dabbed his eyes.

Bradlee didn't say a word. He understood. That's what mattered. He reached out and held James' hand. It was worn from all his years of hard work. Leathery, rough, and veiny. But it also had plenty of warmth to it. And strength, as James gripped Bradlee's hand in return.

"Thanks for understanding, Bradlee." James gave him a quick smile and then went back to reviewing the menu as if he'd never been to Ruby's establishment before today.

They ordered the usual delicious burgers and sweet potato fries. There was no use changing things up when both of them knew from experience what was *already* the best meal in the establishment. After finishing off their meal, Ruby then brought out two heaping plates stacked with warm huckleberry pie. On one plate she dabbed a scoop of chocolate ice cream, the other had vanilla.

"Which one you prefer, superhero?" James asked.

"I think I'll go for the chocolate today. Lyra really prefers chocolate so I'll enjoy it in her honor," Bradlee replied. The men laughed together but Bradlee relayed with all seriousness that Lyra was tending to her professor back at the hospital who was in critical condition.

"You tell Lyra yet, Bradlee?" James asked.

"Tell her what?"

"You know. That she's your 'Sunshine girl' and always will be."

"Sunshine girl?! You been hanging around a man called Jim Clayburn at all, James?"

"Chief Clayburn!" James chuckled. "That guy's been telling that same old story about Teddy Roosevelt since he was in diapers on the reservation. Everyone in North Dakota knows Chief Clayburn and his story telling."

"Jim's an Indian Chief?! I didn't know that! Well how about that?! All that time I was riding with him in the Badlands and didn't know it!" Bradlee chewed on his pie and thought back to the details of that day. *Of course – Jim's unique custom saddle. Certainly befitting for a Chief.* And he thought about his time at Jim's ranch over Thanksgiving.

"But it all makes sense now. He's wise all right. Family patriarch, successful rancher, and he has a certain demeanor that he carries with him. A kind of burden that comes with leadership. Responsibility, I guess."

Bradlee conjured an image of Jim wearing a traditional Indian Chief's feathered headdress and deerskin outfit. *He'd sure make a regal looking Chief*, Bradlee realized.

"Why didn't he tell me he was the Chief of the reservation?"

"Jim's a good man, Bradlee. Humble as humble pie, that's for sure. And he's learned not to get too caught up in his head from the title. He's highly respected in the Dakotas and by his people. The reservation has had its challenges over the years but his leadership has been critical. I know Jim' father was the Chief before him and probably his grandfather as well and he can probably trace his roots back quite a ways before TR ever set foot in the Dakotas... I'd imagine he's got his hands full now with the pipeline protests that I read about in the paper."

"Yeah, he sure does. Saw that first hand myself yesterday morning before the plane crash. Well, speaking of Sunshine girl – It's *true* James. When I went back home, I checked Jim's facts about TR. TR did indeed call his wife, 'Sunshine.'"

"Well, at least TR married her first!" James replied. "Maybe that's what you should consider, Bradlee, and settle down. Look at you, pushing thirty years old already, probably older, if I were to wager on it... Have you told Lyra that you love her?"

Bradlee squirmed a bit in his seat as he spooned another bite of pie with his chocolate ice cream.

"I think she knows, James. We've been cozying up real close, especially these past few days."

"Now, how's that girl supposed to know you love her unless you tell it to her straight up?!" James said in astonishment. "I think you're afraid of love, Bradlee. Something about you just makes me wonder why you don't want to commit even when everything adds up... Look, Lyra loves you, Bradlee. She told me that she loves you from her own lips three months ago when she boarded that train from the platform and headed to Seattle. I realize that was all puppy spring love back then between you two, not the full blown kind where you realize that love has eternal responsibilities to care for someone in times of health and sickness, and all that... But I've learned over these many years that a woman's instincts are rarely wrong. Rarely!"

Bradlee thought back to the moment he gave Lyra the Ark necklace on the train. It just felt like the beginning of something very special. Like she was his chance to do it over again and make things right but he had difficulty letting go of his past then. But not anymore. Ruthy and Rachel had fixed that for him in Newfoundland on the summit of Lookout Mountain.

"I do love Lyra, James. I really do. And you're right. I need to tell her straight up how I really feel. That I want to love her forever because that is how I feel inside… James, she's always on my mind now. I can't even eat chocolate ice cream and pie without thinking about Lyra constantly. Because I want to share this with her. To taste what I'm tasting. To share every little thing that makes up a life together between two people who have discovered love for each other. The moments that bring pleasure and hopefully, rare moments with pain… Maybe that's what love is. Nothing more complicated than the simple desire to share all the little moments until the end."

"Bradlee, you remember back when I was dropping you two off at the inn? I had given you some words of wisdom to take home with you." Bradlee had a curious look as he tried to remember the details.

"I'll repeat it for you now so it will really sink in but I can write it down on this napkin if you need me to." James laughed and then looked at Bradlee with the seriousness of a man as if he was on his death bed.

"The mind forgets what it's supposed to. It's the good times that really matter, that you hold onto, and keep repeating inside your head as you age so they're there permanently and you can recall them whenever you want them to be." James snapped his fingers. "Voilà! And they pop into your head again and you smile and feel the love sprouting another root deep inside your heart and soul…" James took a few breaths and examined his pie. His vanilla ice cream was tasty but he realized he preferred chocolate after all these years, just like Sweet Caroline and Lyra. *Another thing women were right about*, he chuckled to himself.

"But I also gave you another pearl of wisdom, Bradlee. I'd hoped you would have acted on it by now, seeing how you and Lyra were getting along that evening... Bradlee, a woman needs reassurance by telling her often that she is loved. That she's wonderful and special and that you want to make her happy. A man needs that too but I still feel that it's more in the other direction and I'd always been OK with that over our fifty years together. It's just how I feel we were created by God. Maybe if Adam told Eve that he loved her more when they were in the Garden she wouldn't have gotten all tangled up by a snake. And the rest is history." James laughed at the association but Bradlee now remembered his advice from their last ride through Minot.

"I got it now, James. Won't forget your advice, either. Ever. Well said..." Bradlee lifted his water glass and James followed. "Cheers, James" and they clinked their glasses together. Bradlee sat back after consuming the remains of his ice cream and pie. A thought crossed his mind as he stared at James, aged yet full of vigor.

"So, *if* I were to ask Lyra to marry me sometime in the future, and *if* she happens to say yes and not knowing any better..." Bradlee smiled. "That's two big IF's by the way... where do you think we should hold the ceremony?"

"Hmm. You know, usually these events happen around where family lives nearby, with plenty of family and friends present."

Bradlee thought about the obviousness of James' comment. But he preferred a more intimate gathering, perhaps.

"I was thinking maybe a destination spot. A smaller ceremony. Not too far away. I don't know, maybe..."

"Why not in Minot?!" James shouted. "You've got plenty of sappy folks here who would love to attend a nice romantic gathering. I sure as heck could use one of those!"

Why not in Minot?! Bradlee laughed at the catchy rhyme but James was right. He and Lyra were developing meaningful friends here these past few months. Friends that could really be considered extended family.

"James, you think Thomas and Nancy could host a wedding at the Lady Slipper Inn?"

"Bradlee, you've forgotten again. My Sweet Caroline and I were married at the inn fifty years ago. It worked for us and it'd be just great for you and Lyra. But you may want to let Lyra know how much you love her first. And that you want to spend the rest of your life with her... you know, all that mushy proposing stuff down on your knees..." James smiled as he stood up and walked over to Bradlee and put a knee to the ground and faced Bradlee with his hands clutched together. They both started into wild laughter by the mock scene and Bradlee felt reassured that the place was empty of other guests to witness James' hilarious gesture. "Sounds to me like you're getting ahead of yourself just a bit now," James added as he arose.

It was time for James to return home. Ruby gave her usual warm farewells with a few more hugs. "You two boys are my most favorite in the whole darn world!" she said as she wished Bradlee a speedy recovery and whispered to James asking him to come around again soon. He promised he would.

James drove Bradlee to the Lady Slipper Inn. They parked and walked up the path to the porch and were greeted warmly by Thomas and Nancy. The pair were bundled up on the porch swing beside each other sharing a heavy wool blanket over their laps and taking in some late afternoon sunshine despite the chilly weather.

They discussed the events of yesterday and Nancy handed Bradlee a gift wrapped newspaper. It was the day's edition of the Minot Daily News, with the front page photo of the plane crash and Bradlee's heroics. It was for Bradlee to keep as a memento. Thomas wondered if Lyra would be joining them later in the evening but Bradlee said he didn't think it was likely. Lyra was occupied at the hospital tending to her professor's more urgent medical needs. Nancy mentioned that she'd leave some snacks in the dining room in case Bradlee was hungry later. Bradlee doffed his cowboy hat to say goodbye to James. Then he lifted his suitcase with his right arm and climbed the flight of stairs. His left shoulder was aching again and his headache was returning. He knew he needed some welcome rest, especially to help digest the huge slice of Ruby's huckleberry pie and chocolate ice cream that were laying comfortably at the top of a full stomach. He opened the door to the Hummingbird Room, removed his cowboy hat and shoes, swallowed a few ibuprofen tablets, removed any remaining huckleberry from between his teeth with a minty brushing, and crashed onto the plush bed. He quickly fell into a deep sleep.

DR. BONHEIM'S FEVER HAD SUBSIDED with more rounds of intravenous antibiotics. The nursing staff fastidiously checked and changed her intravenous lines and bladder catheter to minimize risk of any further infection and the respiratory therapists carefully adjusted her ventilator settings as her condition improved. Her chest wounds were healing gradually and the thoracic surgeons were pleased with her progress over the afternoon and evening hours. Lyra was exhausted. She called Ruby's restaurant and ordered an assortment of Ruby's pies to be delivered to the intensive care unit staff to enjoy. Then she ate some dinner in the hospital cafeteria, checked one more time on Dr. Bonheim's condition, and then she lay down for a nap in her room adjacent to the intensive care unit.

Lyra awoke after midnight in the midst of a fitful nightmare. Matt was attacking her once again and she was covering her face and lashing back at him. Then she was trying to run away but he held her down again and she screamed. Lyra awoke from her nightmare, drenched in perspiration. She walked to the bathroom and washed her face with cold water. The hospital corridors were eerily silent and the only audible noise was a periodic bleep from a cardiac monitor in the intensive care unit. She said good night to the overnight staff. Then she showered and bundled in some new clothes – a heavy sweater and jeans – that Oji had brought to the hospital. Lyra packed an overnight bag, donned her winter coat, and headed downstairs to the taxi station. She decided she didn't want to be alone the remainder of the night.

    The taxi brought her to the Lady Slipper Inn and dropped her off. There was a porch light on but the entrance door was locked. Lyra didn't want to alert Thomas or Nancy by the late hour. She walked through the garden to the side door adjacent to Oji's home. The door was locked but there was a large flower pot on the stoop. She rotated its base and found a key hiding beneath it and opened the door. She removed her shoes to avoid any footfalls and delicately walked up the stairs with her overnight bag and down the hallway to the Hummingbird Room.

    She entered quietly. Bradlee was fast asleep in the king size bed. His cowboy hat resting on the nightstand. She noticed that there was only one bed in the room this time compared to their first visit when the king was separated into two smaller beds with a nightstand between them. Lyra placed her bag on the dresser and removed her winter coat. The room was a bit chilly but then she removed her sweater and slipped off her jeans and silky underwear. She brought her night bag into the bathroom and shut the door quietly. Lyra freshened up and added a light spray of her jasmine perfume to her neck. Then she removed her shirt top and stared into the mirror. Her chest bruises were mostly healed but a few remained to remind her of that terrible night in Seattle. But she set the pain aside, once again reminding herself of her resiliency as she smiled at herself naked in the mirror. She gently inserted her diaphragm deep inside her vulva. Then she slipped on her white satin camisole and returned to the bedroom.

Bradlee had turned to his side with his right shoulder down towards the mattress and his head gently on the pillow. His left arm sling remained attached. He was asleep, breathing quietly. Lyra lifted the down comforter and sheet and rotated her torso so that she was laying sideways and nestled to his back. His muscles were strong and fit as she wrapped her left arm around his waist and nuzzled his neck. He started to stir and then he reached for her left hand and held it in his. "Sami, hold me" he said in his sleep. Lyra held in place, quietly listening to his breathing and gentle mutterings. *Bradlee was in the midst of a dream, perhaps a very good dream.* He quieted again. She kissed him on his neck and gently rubbed her fingers through his thick curly hair. Bradlee stirred again and his eyelids fluttered as he smelled Lyra's jasmine perfume. He turned and they looked into each other's eyes. He reached for her lips and kissed them and let the kiss linger before separating. Then he kissed her cheeks and her forehead before moving on to her neck.

"Lyra, you're here."

"Yes, Bradlee, it's me. I couldn't sleep very well at the hospital and wanted to be here with you. I wanted to…"

Bradlee kissed her again and again. Then he gently traced her lips and cheeks with his fingers and she kissed him back. He sat up and she helped him remove his arm sling. Then she gently removed his shirt to reveal his muscular chest and she kissed each shoulder delicately. She held her hand to his heart and embraced his torso and then she traced his muscles downward to his abdomen and pelvis and unbuttoned his jeans. She moved her hand over his groin and massaged and stroked his long and hard firmness beneath his jeans. She unzipped his fly and grasped his hardness inside her soft palms as he moaned her name. Bradlee ripped off the remains of his clothing with his right arm and they plunged beneath the bedsheets. He caressed her body through her silky camisole and worked his way to her firm breasts and delicately massaged her erect nipples as she lunged her head back. He devoured each breast with succulent kisses.

Bradlee laid her on her back and rested Lyra's head against the soft pillow. He kissed her repeatedly again and again and caressed her thighs. His hand moved upwards and gently played with her moist softness until she was moaning repeatedly. He elevated his torso above hers and she wrapped her legs around his pelvis as they faced each other intensely.

The moon was shining an arc of light through the window curtain. Lyra was lit by its glow against her white camisole and she possessed the intoxicating aroma of a goddess. Their eyes linked and he touched his forehead to hers and felt her warmth spreading everywhere inside of him.

"Lyra, I..." Bradlee started.

"Love," Lyra whispered softly.

"You," he finished.

"I love you, Lyra. I have loved you since the day I laid my eyes on you, but I was a fool then to not allow myself to recognize it and embrace that love. But now I know I will always love you. Today. Tomorrow. Until the end, Lyra. Until the end."

"I love you too, Bradlee. With all my heart. God, I wanted to tell you that so many times these past few months but I wanted to wait until we were together again. Until the right moment. And it's finally arrived."

They kissed deeply and he turned Lyra over until she fully straddled him. She felt herself falling into waves that ebbed into an ocean of stars. The purity of light emanating from above. Lyra felt his love and then Bradlee entered her.

"Gentle Bradlee. Slowly," she whispered to him as he laid his back onto the bed and she stroked her breasts against his chest and fondled his hair and kissed his neck.

They undulated together, enjoying giving and receiving pleasure as he penetrated deeply inside of her. Minutes passed like centuries, and then millennia. Bradlee raised his tempo and Lyra leaned backwards and he kissed her breasts and held her buttocks firmly as the crescendo became fortissimo and the waves were crashing inside of her.

"Bradlee... Yes, that's it. Yes! Oh God! The waves, they won't stop crashing!" she cried out.

She arched and her moans rose ever higher, repeatedly, as she grasped her hands against his chest and was absorbed in rapture. Bradlee slowed his tempo and she paced with him inside of her as her breathing settled. Lyra leaned her body over Bradlee once again, this time with a ferocity of love in her eyes as she kissed him on his lips and nibbled at his ears.

"Cum inside of me, Bradlee. I want you to love me forever."

He maneuvered Lyra to her back and held his torso above her as she wrapped her arms around his neck and her tongue explored his lips. He held her arms above her head and stroked them and kissed them. He worked his tongue down her soft neck and then to her breasts once again. His pace quickened against her pelvis as he caressed her curves from her chest and down to her buttocks and gently lifted her legs to enter her even deeper as Lyra's breathing quickened into gasps.

"Yes, Bradlee, again. Oh, I feel it. The waves are crashing again... Oh God! You are an amazing lover, Bradlee Seashell!"

The pitch of Lyra's voice rose as she met Bradlee's lunges and convulsed her pelvis below him in a release of the eternal energy that is shared between lovers. Bradlee couldn't hold back his milky flow anymore as his voice rose and he released his love inside of her and she felt his pulsations and it felt right and good and everlasting. They collapsed into each other's arms, entwining their legs, and held still as he stroked her hair and they locked their eyes until their breathing calmed.

They held together for a long time. Caressing. Stroking their hands over each other's warmth. Exploring every inch of their youthful bodies. Every perfection and imperfection. Embracing hands. Discovering the newness that is the connection between lovers. They spoke softly of their love for each other and rested quietly between the rise and fall of their breaths and then there was the quiet solitude of the moonlight in their embrace.

Lyra held Bradlee close. She was lying on top of him with her ear to his heart.

"Bradlee?"

"Yes, Lyra."

"You spoke again in your dreams tonight when I came to you in bed. You mentioned the name 'Sammy' just as you had when you had your nightmare that night in this room."

"Yes, I remember it, of course. I'm sorry I woke you then."

"Well, I asked you in the hospital earlier today if you will let me inside. Inside your mind and your heart."

"You have my love, Lyra."

"Bradlee, I want you to trust me, to let out any pain you may have inside, OK?"

"I know, Lyra. I do. And I do trust you with all my heart."

Bradlee held Lyra in his arms. He looked into her eyes and glanced at the ceiling and then his eyes searched the room and he thought about how far his emotions had traveled since he was last here with Lyra by his side. He had grown. Forgiven. Finally able to release so much pain from his loss. He had received the affection and wisdom of others, many he had not yet met back then but now were an important part of his life. *But why? Because of this woman beside him, that's why.* He knew it deep within his heart and soul. His Daphne was alive and real beside him. An animated drawing of a goddess. Yes, she was human and had imperfections and the whole gamut of emotions but he loved her for who she was and wanted to know so much more. *Was Lyra – Sami in reincarnation?* A second chance offered to him to love and be loved until the end. He smirked as he glanced at the magnificent peacefulness of the moonlight. Then he chuckled. *Until the end.* The phrase was becoming *their* phrase - his and Lyra's. Their secret message to each other of their deepening love.

Bradlee inhaled a long breath as the rise of his chest met Lyra's soft breasts. He returned to her eyes and kissed her lids softly and then her nose and their lips met again and held there. Bradlee laid his head back on his pillow and began.

"Sami was going to be my wife," he started. His emotions quickly channeled upwards from a deep source within his heart and he held his words until they simmered and settled and then rested quietly again within. *This is not the time and place for more tears with Lyra in my arms.* Tears that he thought were finished shedding after returning from the top of Lookout Mountain. Lyra didn't need those tears from him now, only the truth.

"We met on our first day of medical school in Toronto. It was freshman orientation and she was in line in front of me as we collected our id badges and course schedules from the registrar. All I noticed was this long thick mane of jet black hair and a pleasant voice. When she turned, our eyes met. Her eyes were shaped like perfect almonds with emerald greens that sparkled in any light. We just stared at each other for a long moment and just knew right then that our attraction was like a powerful magnet pulling us together from that first day onward. Sami — "Bradlee paused. "Sami is what I called her but her full name was *Samia*, which means elevated or exalted in the Arabic language. She was from an Indian Muslim family. Her family had emigrated from India to Alberta, Canada when she was a young child and she was exceptionally bright and stunningly beautiful. She was truly an exalted one."

Bradlee stopped. "Am I upsetting you, Lyra?"

"No, Bradlee. I want to hear your story. I do… honestly… because I want to understand who you are. Please go on." She kissed him on his lips. "Go on, trust Bradlee, trust…"

"At first, we studied all the time together. Medical school had the usual workload of endless cycles of studying and examinations. We were engrossed in Anatomy, Physiology, Pathology, Histology… Lots of '*ology's,*' as you can imagine. Our relationship progressed as we entered our second year and we shared an apartment together. We shared everything, especially our love. I loved her dearly and we were planning our future together, gradually discovering our interests in various fields of medicine. Figuring out which specialty to choose for our career after graduation. I was leaning towards surgery, my father's calling, and she wanted to deliver babies. To be an obstetrician and gynecologist. To help mothers bring new life into this world and women with their needs over their life stages. Her family was receptive to me. They didn't mind that she had selected a nice Jewish boy from Toronto as her life partner. But my father… he saw things differently. He was an observant Jew. Trauma surgeon. I come from a long line of doctors and rabbis on my father's side that he had traced back for many generations into the early 1800's in Europe. Two hundred years of legacy! My father's father came to Canada when my father was just a young boy in grade school as they fled from the Nazis. And, in my youth, Judaism was instilled within me at school and at home and in our community life that revolved around our frequent visits to our temple for worshipping and holidays and community celebrations. I studied the Old Testament – the 'Torah' as the Jewish people call it – and loved and excelled in my studies. I enjoyed worshipping beside my father and my parents were prominent members of the Jewish community. That their son would possibly marry a Muslim girl was intolerable to my father and so he and I had our challenges communicating as I continued my relationship with Sami into our third year. We flew to Florence, Italy during fall break that year in school and immersed ourselves in the romance of the city as we walked through the narrow picturesque cobblestone streets and engorged on heaping scoops of gelato at any time of the day or night and visited the museums where I spent hours sketching the finest sculptures and studying the mythology of their stories. We rented a car and traveled through the Tuscany hills and olive orchards and wine vineyards and were madly in love."

"We returned to Toronto and the remainder of our third year went by quickly as we focused on our studies in the various medical departments at the hospitals and clinics. And then on to our fourth and final year of medical school. By spring break, we were only two months shy of graduation. Sami loved to hike and tent camp under the stars, as did I, and so I planned a beautiful long weekend together for us in the mountains. Winter was dissipating quickly and the scenery along the trail was breathtaking as the spring snowmelts were punctuated by all the signs of new forest growth – new sprigs of tree limbs and soft grassy undergrowth and wildflowers blooming everywhere we turned. The sun's rays lighting the glistening snowflakes dropping from the heavy branches. Long icicle stalactites, dripping cool refreshing pure raincloud water from pine tree branches directly into our mouths as we rested on pine needles and made love together each night inside our tent beneath the stars."

"On the last evening, Sami and I enjoyed a majestic view of a grand pristine valley. Hawks flying above us. Perfect quiet but for the occasional wind. The clouds were gathering off in the distance and the sunset was incredibly beautiful as its rays splayed across the horizon and the clouds were lit pink and then oranges and reds before the indigos of dusk. I kneeled beside her and asked Samia to marry me and presented her with a small diamond ring. It wasn't much but it was all I could afford from my own pocket from savings collected through various odd jobs over the previous summer breaks. She agreed to marry me. And then I held her in my arms and we imagined our future together… no, we envisioned it all right there on the top of that mountain. Our careers, our home, our children, our grandchildren – everything good in life from a loving partnership."

Bradlee paused. This time he couldn't hold back his tears. Lyra wrapped him in her arms and comforted him. She stroked his hair until he dried his eyes and settled again.

"I'm sorry. I thought I had shed my last tears back in Newfoundland."

"Newfoundland?" Lyra said.

"Yes, when I visited there in the fall and called you from my tent under the stars."

"Yes, I remember. That was when I first discovered Foster Point on my jogging route."

"I'll leave the rest of the Newfoundland story for another time," Bradlee replied before continuing.

"It was getting chilly as the sun settled below the horizon. Sami and I set up our tent about a hundred yards from a shelter site off the trail. There were a few other hikers staying inside the wood and metal shelter but we had our tent and sleeping bags and pads with us for the journey and preferred our privacy, especially on that night when we had committed our love to each other. Making love inside a tent in the woods is magical, Lyra. It really is."

Lyra turned to look into his eyes and smiled.

"I'd like to try that with you sometime, Bradlee," she said and tickled his side playfully.

"Sami and I enjoyed a very special evening inside our tent, that's all I'll say about that." Bradlee smiled. "We nodded off to sleep but, some hours later, were awakened by a sudden rush of wind as a storm blew in quickly. It was pitch black outside except for the moonlight. As we quickly shuffled through our belongings I had difficulty locating my headlamp and we were both naked inside our sleeping bags and I needed to slip on my hiking pants as the rains started. Then it quickly moved to thunder and crashes of lightning as the storm was blowing directly over our tent site near the ridgetop. More high winds that tugged at the tent and then it started to pour heavily. The tent rainfly was off. We were enjoying the stars through the thin mesh of the tent. I had slipped the rainfly into an inside tent flap at the beginning of the night and had not expected that we would need it. But I made a terrible mistake. The rain poured down even harder and I found my headlamp and set it on my forehead and unzipped the tent flap and jumped outside with the rainfly in my hands and started to remove the rainfly from its bag when I heard a jarring crack followed by a loud thud as a massive tree trunk came tumbling down beside me and crushed our tent. Sami was in there waiting for me to return. Trying her best to keep our sleeping bags dry from the rain."

"I dropped the rainfly and tried to find Sami under the pine tree. I was entangled by the branches and scraping against pine cones and bark as I drew nearer to the tent. One branch punctured and tore at the skin on my chest and I pulled it away and felt a searing pain as my hand was wet with blood. I continued to pull away anything I could get a hold of until I heard Sami breathing and crying. Her body was crushed by the trunk laying across her chest and abdomen. I screamed out to her as I held her head in my arms, "*Sami – Don't leave me. Hold on, Sami. I'm going to get help.*' I screamed out into the night but no one came."

"I tried to comfort her. She was bleeding from a deep wound in her side and shivering and dying in front of me. She turned to me and quieted her breathing. She held my hands in hers and then she pressed her palm into my chest and felt my beating heart. The last thing she said to me was '*I love you Baruch. I am here inside your heart. I will always be here. Allah is with you.*' And then she gave me one last beautiful smile. I kissed her lips gently......... She closed her eyes and then died in my arms."

Lyra was sniffling as her tears flowed from her cheeks and onto Bradlee's chest as she held him closely and stared out the window into the glow of the moonlight.

"I'm sorry, Lyra. I didn't mean to upset you." Bradlee comforted her with his arms. He reached for the tissue box on the nightstand. Both of them needed to wipe their eyes and noses from their sobs and flowing tears. He covered his face with his cowboy hat and pretended to nod off. Lyra removed it from his head and kissed him.

"It's OK, Bradlee. Your love for Sami will never end. And I'm OK with that too. Sami was in your heart and she was taken away, suddenly, for no good reason that we can possibly understand. Life can be cruel, Bradlee. I know it can."

She settled her head against his chest once again and listened to the sound of his heartbeat for a long time. It was very soothing. Consistent. Stable. She wanted that in her life.

"Lyra, I'm glad I could tell you all of that. Your woman's intuition was right. I needed to trust you with my past. But I told you all of it because Sami is still inside of me. She resides in a compartment inside my heart that I occasionally open, when the time is right or a memory flashes. I hope you're OK with that when it does happen although I will try to keep those times mostly to myself... I loved Sami with everything I could offer her in life. But that was a long time ago and I know I can't change the past. A lot has happened in my life since then. We can talk about that another time. What is important now, and tomorrow, and until the end..." Bradlee smiled at Lyra as their eyes met... "is that I love you. You are real and here and we are each other's futures. I want that to be true." He kissed her gently.

"Me too, Bradlee. Me too... I love you Bradlee Seashell," Lyra replied.

The moon had shifted its trajectory. Its light now a soft sheen in Lyra's eyes. She jumped up to adjust the curtains and was returning towards their bed. Bradlee admired her beauty as if she was truly Bernini's Daphne that had come to life before him. But he noted that there were some bruises under Lyra's breasts and she still had the light bruise to her left upper eyelid above her coloboma. She climbed back into bed and quickly threw the comforter over the top of them as she nuzzled into Bradlee's warmth. They were bonded again and she wanted to remain fixed there until the sunrise.

"Lyra. There are some bruises on your torso." He traced the outline of them as he turned her to her side. "I'm so sorry. I think I've hurt you while we were making love."

She gently nudged Bradlee to his back and settled in the same position she preferred. Resting her torso and head against his. She realized it was her turn to share some truths.

"Bradlee, I have something to tell you and I know it will upset you," she offered.

Bradlee quieted as Lyra had done for him. He stroked her hair. "You can trust me, Lyra. Regardless of what you have to say, I know that I love you. That is enough truth to be able to handle whatever it is you wish to share with me."

Lyra decided to be direct and let it out in one rush. "Bradlee, about a month ago a man abused me terribly in his fraternity room. He hit me with his fists and I fought him and he hit me harder until I couldn't escape. He was raping me. Tearing off my clothes and holding me down and almost suffocating me to death." Lyra started to sob as Bradlee's eyes widened and his pulse quickened with adrenaline.

"I made a terrible mistake, Bradlee. I was lonely and mentally exhausted from my studies and I had doubts if you and I really had any future together being so far away... I thought it would be fun to make some new friends at a Halloween party at this rower's frat house. Instead, he attacked me inside his bedroom. I shouldn't have gone with him up the stairs but I just wasn't thinking right and he had far too much to drink. Beers and vodka punch and who knows what else. It all happened very fast. But another man entered the room and pulled him off from me and told me to run – which I did."

"I called Ansley in San Francisco and she flew late that night to help me through it. A doctor checked me the next morning and, other than lots of bruises and swellings all over my body – especially to my face and left eye – I was going to be OK, physically. There was a woman, a nurse who was walking home from the hospital after I escaped. She found me on the street that night and brought me home and stayed for a long time and took care of me. We've become good friends now. But there's more to my story. This woman – she was someone I had met when I was a small girl in Costa Rica. Her name is Angel – of all names!" Lyra exclaimed. "I still find it amazing that after all these years Angel and I met on a street in Seattle. What are the odds of that, Bradlee?" He nodded and smiled tenderly as he caressed her back.

"It took some time to heal. Physically and mentally. I'm making progress, truly, otherwise I wouldn't have been able to make love with you tonight. And I need you to be gentle with me, Bradlee, as gentle as you were tonight so that I know I am safe and loved in all the right ways."

Bradlee made a fist with his right hand as he imagined punching the rapist until his face was unrecognizable and his arms torn from their sockets. Lyra could sense Bradlee's anger as his breathing paced faster with his heartbeat as she rested against his chest.

"Bradlee, it's alright. He got his due. The man who saved my life ended up pummeling this other guy. I saw the man who hurt me while on my first jog some days later, swollen face and all, and he looked broken. His face unrecognizable, cuts and stitches everywhere, and lost teeth, and broken bones and all. He apologized to me for what he had done but I stared at him without much remorse. I was going to pound him with a heavy stick in my hand but I couldn't do it. Justice was served to him, Bradlee, and I do feel safe at home now although I won't go walking or jogging without mace in my pocket. My friend Ansley saw to that accessory."

"Lyra, Sami once said to me that a man tried to rape her when she was in college but she got away without injury. And plenty of alcohol was involved then as well. Lyra, a woman can be vulnerable to this sort of reptilian instinct that some men can't contain. Add alcohol to the mix and they can explode. I've seen the consequences when I was in medical school working ER shifts. Women coming in, all cut and bandaged and faces bashed – my heart bled when I had to go into their exam rooms and take their history and try my best to help... I will do my best to protect you Lyra – always."

"Bradlee, you're in P.E.I. and I'm in Seattle. Are you going to install video cameras on every street corner and observe my every move?"

"Well, maybe temporarily but I was hoping someday we could change that."

"Oh, really!" Lyra cried out in exasperation. She lowered her voice in mock seriousness.

"The plot thickens. They mount their golden stallion and race off into the hills, young Bradlee and sidekick Lyra, together on a journey to the stars… Ta da!"

Lyra started to giggle furiously and Bradlee had no choice but to tickle her everywhere until she begged for mercy.

He held her side by side and kissed her sweetly.

"Lyra, your bruises are healing well. In a few more weeks they will all be gone. And some weeks after that, I hope I won't be. Somehow we will work out seeing each other more often until…"

He waited as he looked into her eyes.

"Until the end?" Lyra burst into laughter again. Bradlee joined her.

"No silly, until you marry me."

Bradlee held her still in his arms. He searched her eyes.

"Bradlee Seashell. Baruch Avraham Levitsky!" Lyra held his face in her hands and kissed his lips. Then she stared into his eyes.

"Bradlee, will you marry me?" she asked him.

He smiled and then hesitantly laughed.

"I thought *I* was supposed to ask *you* that question?"

And then he held and kissed her again pulling her nakedness closer to him as they sat entwined.

"Bradlee, one thing you will need to learn… no, accept… is that your Lyra is a very modern woman and what Lyra wants Lyra usually gets. Usually well-earned from hard work but when it comes to love, I know what I love when I see it."

She made Bradlee smile as she playfully pushed him down to the mattress and mounted him and kissed his lips like a dominant lioness seeking her prey. He didn't lay helpless for long. He came up for air to rescue himself.

"But I'm a helpless defenseless wounded superhero,

Lyra. How can you take advantage of me?!"

Their play roughened and she let him turn her over on her backside and he held his stance above her and kissed her and then entered her again until she was overcome with more undulating waves as she raised her voice with passion sweeping through her and he melted inside of her again.

The sun was peeking through the curtains. They had fallen asleep in each other's arms but began to stir from the light of a new day.

"Good morning, Sunshine girl." Bradlee could finally say those words to Lyra and he smiled.

"Bradlee," she whispered. "You haven't answered my question yet."

"I wanted to dream on it a bit first," he replied. She leaned into him and hugged his waist.

"Yes, Lyra, the answer is a *trillion* times, YES!!! More yes's than there are stars in the universe or seashells in the vast oceans."

They kissed once more to seal their fate and held still and enjoyed the sunlight as it entered the magical room and lit up all the hummingbird motifs and wallpaper and furnishings until everything sparkled as if in a wondrous dream.

"Oh. I almost forgot. I have a gift for you too, Bradlee, that I had brought with me to North Dakota. Oji handed it to me at the hospital. She said that Kin had found it in the burnt remains of the corral fire inside my suitcase. Our little friend, Soaring Hawk. His tribal name fits him perfectly. As does yours, Bradlee... *Baruch – You are my blessing!*"

She slipped out of bed and rummaged through her bag and returned holding the maple syrup stained ash bowl that Bradlee had gifted to her. She also had a small satin purse in her hand. She found her position, straddling him again, and looked into Bradlee's eyes.

"Bradlee, I will never be Samia. I will always be Lyra and our love will be built from the ashes that will always simmer in your heart for Samia. But I love you and I will promise to protect our love for as long as I live."

Lyra opened the satin bag and pulled out the shell necklace that the street magician had gifted her in Seattle while walking home from Angel's. Lyra placed the necklace in the bowl and served the necklace to Bradlee.

"Any chance you might recognize what these shells are, Mr. Bradlee Seashell?" She gleamed with joy as she elevated the necklace and placed it around Bradlee's neck.

He lifted one of the shells and turned it in his fingers and studied its texture and feel. It was ever slightly tinged a light brown color. Others were as perfectly opalescent as the lone one he had discovered along the beach in Newfoundland.

"I present to you today, *Oenopata harpularius* – *the Harp Lora shell*," he announced in a mocking accent, as if he was an esteemed English professor of malacology with a fascinated audience of pubescent pupils. Lyra broke out in laughter.

"Lyra, the harp... It is *your* shell, Lyra. Your namesake."

"It is not just *my* shell, Bradlee. It will always be *our* shell from this day forward. And it, too, was burned by the fire that now simmers within us. Our eternal love."

He kissed her gently.

"But how, Lyra? And an entire strand! How is this possible?"

"Just another coincidence, Bradlee... Just another coincidence in a series of coincidences that brought us together to this place and to this moment. Perhaps our meeting was written in the stars. Inside the Lyra constellation."

She laughed as he gathered her in his arms and held her tight.

They rested for a short while longer, embraced as if their bodies had always been inseparable. But the new day was upon them and they didn't want their embrace to ever end.

———————————————

Part Seven

BREAKFAST WAS ANOTHER FINE FEAST at the Lady Slipper Inn. Thomas and Nancy were surprised but very pleased to see Lyra joining Bradlee at the dining table. They wondered what time she had arrived so quietly overnight. There were only a few other couples staying at the inn for the holiday weekend. All enjoyed pleasant conversation. As the meal was winding down Bradlee took Thomas aside as they strolled to the gazebo adjacent to the gardens. The gardens were covered with morning dew and only open plots of fertile soil and woodchips remained of Oji's majestic gardens as the ground rested peacefully over the winter season.

Bradlee opened his heart to Thomas as he spoke of his love for Lyra. Their mutual love. He apologized for his indiscretion – that he had misled Thomas into presuming that he and Lyra were husband and wife while registering for their stay at the inn. Thomas understood the false pretense but also revealed to Bradlee that Nancy knew all along but didn't tell Thomas until last night... '*a woman's intuition*, she said to me... *trust me, Thomas.*'

The two men talked business. There was the matter of a wedding that would need to be planned sometime in the near future, hopefully. Bradlee asked if the Lady Slipper Inn could be made available for Lyra's and his wedding celebration and Thomas agreed wholeheartedly to serve as the host with Nancy at the inn. Bradlee mentioned to Thomas that Lyra already informed him that the Lady Slipper Inn would be the most perfect location for their wedding – so long as she and Bradlee could enjoy their wedding night in their 'honeymoon suite' – the

Hummingbird Room. It would always be a magical place for them. Thomas promised to reserve the room for them.

"It's not like we haven't ever done anything like this before," Thomas said. "But every wedding is special and unique with a new cast of characters that bring meaning and memories to the occasion. Bradlee, I believe God will bless your occasion because you two have wonderful souls and Nancy and I can tell that you love each other beyond words, like two halves of a seashell, I'd say." Bradlee laughed at Thomas' eerily familiar remark, the same remark Jim had made on their horseback ride in the Badlands.

"It will be Nancy's and my job to make your occasion as beautiful as you can ever imagine. I know your bride will have her hands into all the decision making, as expected. I'm sure Oji would love to work with Lyra on all the details. And I'll make you a decent price for it all as well, Bradlee... Listen. Nancy and I are comfortable financially after all these years running the inn. We'll be heading into retirement soon enough. In fact, it's about time we start considering selling the Lady Slipper Inn to a young couple looking for a stable business who enjoy meeting all kinds of people as much as we have. With Caroline passing on suddenly and Nancy's stroke, we just feel that our time may be better spent doing some more traveling, seeing the world out there... maybe visit the relatives in Norway... before the end arrives for us."

Bradlee thanked Thomas for everything he and Nancy had done for him and Lyra and for their love and kindness. He would be leaving to return to P.E.I. that evening and would likely not see him or Nancy until the wedding day. "God protect you and Nancy and keep you healthy and safe from harm," Bradlee said. It felt good to say a blessing, a prayer after all these years, Bradlee thought. He was discovering that his roots had not been completely torn from their source within his spirit. The two men parted and

Bradlee rejoined Lyra in the dining room.

With their energy levels replenished from the morning feast after an eventful night together wrestling under the sheets, Bradlee and Lyra helped clear and wash and set the dishes in the cabinetry in the inn's kitchen. They were planning to spend the day together before Lyra returned to the hospital to check on Dr. Bonheim in the evening. She was keeping abreast of her mentor's progress over the phone and the ICU staff were generous in calling her with any important updates. Bradlee asked Nancy if he could put together a little take-out lunch for him and Lyra. She agreed.

He opened the pantry doors and pulled out some items. Peanut butter and wildflower honey. He found some Swiss cheese slices and the tube of mustard in the fridge and then a bag of harvest whole wheat bread on the counter. Bradlee laid out the ingredients on the kitchen island as Lyra observed. He placed a heaping spoonful of peanut butter onto each of two pieces of bread and spread the peanut butter nice and thin. Then he drizzled honey on top of the peanut butter pair. He placed a few slices of Swiss cheese onto a third piece of bread and topped the cheese with a squish of mustard from the tube. Then he created a triple-decker stack by inserting the slice with the cheese and mustard on top, in between the two slices with the peanut butter and honey. He admired his sandwich as Lyra looked on with a smirk on her face.

"What is *that* creation, she asked in between spurts of laughter?"

"This here... well, you're gonna love it, Lyra. Gives you energy to last a hundred more miles on a bike seat. It'll fuel us up just the same when we need it along our hike this morning..."

"What's it called?" Lyra asked as she fingered some of the honey that was drizzling down its side.

"I call it a 'Pe-Ho-Chee-Moo-T'," Bradlee added with a smile. "It's delicious and nutritious!"

"The name sounds very Native American," Lyra replied.

"I agree! I thought it was kind of catchy myself when I came up with it while bicycling through some reservation lands in the Dakotas. It's an acronym for my creation – peanut butter, honey, cheese, and mustard on a 'T' – a triple-decker sandwich! We ate these things like hotcakes on my cross country bicycle trip that I had mentioned to you. Peter, our older and wiser support man, and all around great friend with a contagious joie de vivre... he drove the vehicle and looked after us along the journey... he would make these for us from the back of the van on our brief stops along the way to refuel our energy tanks. They were delicious then and I'm sure this one will be as well. Already starting to make my mouth water just thinking about biting into it...!"

Bradlee thought of something mischievous... "So, when we were near exhaustion but still had many more miles to go in the saddle, Peter would say to us riders: '*It'll get your ticker up-and-ready if you finish it all.*'" Bradlee laughed at his own joke, pirating Ruby's comment about her Huckleberry pie. He figured if it worked for Ruby's pie, as it surely had while loving Lyra last night, then this sandwich might just do the trick as well.

"You mean *your* ticker," as Lyra walked over to Bradlee and planted a ravenous kiss on his lips and gently squeezed his buttocks.

"Bradlee, thank you for last night... and this morning. I feel wonderful inside and out."

They kissed and Bradlee licked the remaining honey off the spoon and kissed Lyra again, this time even sweeter. He sliced the sandwich into two halves... just like two halves of a seashell he thought... and wrapped it for them to enjoy on their hike.

Jim, Wichahpi, and Oji arrived with Kin to the Lady

Slipper Inn. They had driven to Minot from the ranch. Wichahpi was delivering Bradlee's car rental that had remained at the ranch and Jim was dropping off Oji and Kin as they were planning to stay at her home at the inn to prepare for the work week ahead. Kin had grown to enjoy helping his mother make the handmade moccasins and his skill was improving quickly under Oji's guidance. Bradlee proudly took hold of Lyra's waist and informed the assembled group of his and Lyra's engagement to be married, right here at the inn someday soon, God willing. Everyone celebrated together with a send-off toast from Thomas and Nancy.

Bradlee and Lyra departed in the rental and drove south. They stopped briefly at the Paul Broste Rock Museum as Bradlee wanted to see the extraordinary rock and mineral collection from throughout the world. Lyra found some of the items quite fascinating but she knew Bradlee was passionate about rocks and minerals and seashells… and so she enjoyed observing his child-like awe as he made little discoveries that he wanted to share with her.

They continued and stopped at the Crow Flies High State Park and enjoyed the view overlooking Lake Sakakawea, Spanish Bay, and the Four Bears Bridge as they hiked along the bluff and then rested and enjoyed Bradlee's 'Pe-Ho-Chee-Moo-T' creation. Lyra admitted that it wasn't bad at all, quite tasty, and that she could get used to devouring them if Bradlee agreed to future hikes together followed by tent camping under the stars. *Maybe I can devour something else tasty afterwards for dessert*, she teased him. He kissed her and held her close and their lips tasted of spicy mustard and honey and peanut butter all wrapped into a cheesy grin as he felt his groin stir and awaken to attention. *It really works… how about that!* He thought to himself.

After their picnic they traveled to Medora. The Heritage

Center was closed on Sundays but Jim took care of that detail. They were met at the center by Tom and Frank who were profusely thankful for Bradlee's well-being after yesterday's plane crash. Bradlee introduced Lyra to them as the two men doffed their cowboy hats out of respect for the young lady and escorted them to the gallery exhibit room. Lyra was speechless as she walked from one photo to the next and admired Bradlee's work. She caressed her fingers along the intricate hand-carved frames that adorned the larger works at each end.

"Bradlee, these are the wild horses you told me about on the train! They are majestic, regal – like unicorns!" she said with elation. "And their eyes, Bradlee! How did you capture such emotion and passion in their eyes?!" She held him close as she stopped in front of the massive photo of the lone stallion.

"Does he remind you of yourself, Bradlee – all pensive and burdened and serious?"

"He did once. But no more. I think he represents all living things who feel alone in this world, searching. Searching for their soulmate, someone who understands them and will love them for who they are and long to be one equal half of a loving pair. I can sense it in his eyes."

She kissed him and told him how proud she was of his hard work and his gifts. She held his hands in hers.

"Your hands, Bradlee, these are your gifts, your blessing, among many others. You will need to use them wisely in whatever plans may be in store for your future. Our future together."

Tom and Frank asked for a moment alone with Bradlee to manage some business with him but Bradlee insisted that Lyra be able to join them. The men agreed and Bradlee and Lyra followed Tom and Frank as they exited the gallery to the boardroom office and sat down.

Tom started. "Brad, Frank and I want to sincerely thank you for what you've done here for the center. Your work is beyond what we could have imagined. And we are thrilled that you are alive and well after that plane crash the other day and that, from the looks of you today, you're going to be alright. That's a real blessing for us all here in North Dakota. We all prayed for you and for your colleagues on that flight and are glad our prayers are being answered. We missed you here at the gala. Everyone did. It was a solemn occasion but the mood eventually lightened in your honor."

It was Frank's turn. "Brad, I wear the treasurer's hat on the board. The exhibit raised nearly fifty thousand dollars in pledged donations from the attendees here yesterday. That kind of money was not nearly expected but that's not the whole story. An anonymous donor called and guaranteed a matching contribution to the Heritage Center of an additional fifty-thousand dollars. He said it was in your honor, Brad. On the phone he muttered something about 'Tikun Olam' and that he was a friend of your family but Tom and I didn't quite know what that phrase meant... Don't matter to us. The fact is, we've got a hundred thousand dollars coming in and those kinds of funds will keep our center's bottom line healthy for a number of years ahead."

Frank pulled out a checkbook from the desk drawer and started writing Bradlee's name and the date. "As a sincere thank you Brad, the Heritage Center board has agreed to pay you ten thousand dollars for your work as we had originally agreed to in our contract. We're very pleased this all worked out in the end for you and for us."

Bradlee listened carefully and thought about Frank's comment about the anonymous donor's 'Tikun Olam' statement. Bradlee surmised who the donor very likely was. He also realized he had a wedding ring and a wedding celebration to help pay for soon. He kissed Lyra as she smiled at him but he knew it was time for him to speak up.

"Frank... Tom... I'm thrilled the exhibit was a success. I hope the center will enjoy the photos for many years ahead.

Your center does fine work for the community and Chief Clayburn is a good man. In his honor and for the needs of the reservation after the destruction at the corral protest, I'd like to kindly ask you to split my earnings into two checks. One five-thousand dollar check for me and Lyra… and you can write the other five-thousand dollar check to the reservation tribal government council for the explicit purpose of rebuilding the corral glamping area. My hope is that they'll make it bigger and better than it ever was. Hopefully, others will chip in donations to the same cause and we can repair and improve the world together. Gentlemen, that's what "Tikun Olam' means in my Jewish heritage and tradition. Bradlee smiled and Tom and Frank were surprised by Bradlee's knowledge of the phrase. They obliged Bradlee's financial proposal wholeheartedly and then got out their own personal checkbooks and wrote checks themselves to the reservation.

    Bradlee knew what he was doing. He was adding a 'mitzvah' on top of a 'mitzvah,' multiplying one good deed with another, as his tradition was instilled in him from early childhood. He hadn't forgotten that. It was just hiding in the shadows and he knew it was time to open a window to his past and let some sunshine in. That Tom and Frank continued the string of good deeds themselves right before him and Lyra, only validated the essence and purity of this tradition.

    Bradlee and Lyra returned to Minot by the late afternoon. It was time to say goodbye for now. His flight was scheduled to depart that evening for the return trip to Prince Edward Island. Lyra would stay in Minot and help care for Dr. Bonheim until she was recovered enough to return to Seattle.

    They arrived to the entrance of Trinity Hospital. Bradlee opened the door for Lyra and hugged her and kissed her until she was a mess of sniffles and tears. He wasn't far behind in expressing his emotions but Lyra promised she would visit Bradlee on P.E.I. when she headed east for the December holiday week and New Year. She waved and blew him kisses as she entered the hospital. He continued to admire her beauty until there was nothing left of her to see but an empty sliding glass door closing behind her.

BRADLEE'S FLIGHT WAS UNEVENTFUL. He admitted to feeling nervous on the takeoff, and even more so with each runway landing, but he shrugged off his fears from the plane crash as best he could. *No use worrying about things you can't control.* His flight from Minot took him to Minneapolis, then he took a connecting flight to Toronto for a short layover before continuing to Charlottetown Airport on P.E.I.

He called Uncle Eddie from the departure gate in Toronto and shared the good news about his engagement to Lyra and his hope that his uncle could meet her one day soon. Bradlee informed his uncle about the success of his photography exhibit in Minot and his open plans for the time being when he returned to P.E.I. later that night. No specific photography project awaited Bradlee back home but the income from the Heritage Center project would be sufficient for Bradlee until the next job came along. He asked his uncle for a favor – to help Bradlee design and fashion a one-of-a-kind wedding ring for Lyra. One that she would cherish until the end. Bradlee had worked through some preliminary design ideas while on the plane, daydreaming, as he admired the cloud formations from his window seat. He rolled his fingers through the Lyra shell necklace in the same way his father would play with the fringes of his tallit prayer shawl that he wore on the Sabbath or Jewish holidays. He sketched some basic ring drawings with pencil and pad but his uncle's woodcarving expertise would come in handy for the final design and build. His uncle agreed to help. He asked Bradlee if Lyra was Jewish but Bradlee responded that he didn't know, didn't think so, and didn't care either way. Bradlee had been down that road before with Samia and did not want religion to interfere with his love for Lyra, now or ever. Uncle Eddie asked Bradlee if he had informed his parents yet of his engagement. Bradlee said he would let his mother know soon and that she could relay the information to his father. His uncle sighed as he expressed his heartfelt desire that Bradlee and his father could make amends someday and share good things in life together again, starting with the engagement of his brother's only child. Bradlee said he had some remorse about his distance from his father but that life had moved on and he was in no rush to reopen any old sores that he thought had already well-healed with time – at least in his mind.

Bradlee finished the final leg of his flight journey and landed on P.E.I. after midnight. He picked up his car that he had parked at the Charlottetown airport lot and drove the northern, more scenic route through Goose River and Campbells Cove. The moon was shining and he caught glimpses of the ocean to the north. Bradlee did the calculations as his car sped past Glory Lane and then veered south at the East Lake curve.

He had been away from his home at the Marshpillow for only five days but his life had been transformed. *His life...* his life had nearly ended were it not for Stan's smart tactical maneuvering and pure good fortune. *Coincidence that he's alive?* That he and Lyra were now becoming one. *Or was it all destiny?* His head was spinning from thinking about all the '*what- ifs*' in his life. It didn't matter. He was very happy now. And in love. And Lyra would be visiting him very soon. He slowed and turned into the Marshpillow driveway. '*Home sweet home, Bradlee,*' he whispered to himself. But it was very quiet. He missed the solitude but this home was empty of light and love, the kind he remembered so vividly as a child and longed for again. He was a grown man now. Rounding the curve soon of thirty years. Someday he would have a beautiful wife named Lyra who would be ready to greet him at the door with a passionate kiss, or he would do the same for her. He parked in front of the garage. The solitude of the gentle waves reminded him of Lyra's moans when she was climaxing. *The waves are crashing again...!* She was calling out to him. God he loved her. He loved making love to her.

LYRA RETURNED TO DR. BONHEIM'S BEDSIDE. Her mentor remained heavily sedated as the ventilator continued to breathe life into her, every five seconds of every minute, as her chest would rise and fall in a steady metronome. The evening hours passed uneventfully. Dr. Bonheim's tissues continued to slowly heal from her trauma. Her brain's cognitive faculties remained as yet, unknown, as she had not yet been allowed to awaken from her deep state of medically induced sedation. It would take many more days before her sedatives would be allowed to wear off so that she could be removed from the ventilator and be asked to breathe on her own terms.

Lyra returned that night to her small room beside the intensive care unit and settled in for the next many days ahead. Her only job now was to see that Dr. Bonheim would improve. To regain her strength and vigor and intellect. Lyra was there to remind her mentor the same thing Dr. Bonheim had told her. To be strong in the face of challenges. To be resilient and delve quickly into the work at hand. No time for dwelling on what happened in the past. Lyra understood and it was working for her. She felt that resiliency, ever more so now that she was engaged to be married to a wonderful soulful man who loved her dearly.

A man she suspected from the very beginning would be the one from the moment he asked her... what was it he said on the train? *'Do you like Love Stories?'* Yes, that was it. *What man asks a woman that kind of question on first meeting – unless he knew the right meaning of love?* She was tingling as she imagined Bradlee holding her in his arms at the inn. She rested her head on the pillow inside her stark hospital room and replayed the image in the Hummingbird Room, making love with Bradlee, again and again, as she caressed herself into waves of rapture.

A week had passed by and Dr. Bonheim's condition finally began to rapidly improve. Her chest tube drain - placed by the thoracic surgeons who emergently fixed her trauma ten days earlier - was removed and her fevers had long subsided from consistent intravenous antibiotics and proper nutritional support via her central catheter line. Her sedatives were discontinued. Lyra waited by her bedside as Dr. Bonheim's mind awakened. Her eyes fluttered and she began to cough through the ventilator tube and was extubated by the nurse and she was breathing on her own again. Lyra held Dr. Bonheim's hand tightly and calmed her and whispered to her, "Carol, everything's going to be alright now." Dr. Bonheim was back to the wakeful living world, gone from the state of dreamy deep slumber. Her voice was hoarse and dry and her neck was encased in a hard brace to protect her fractured cervical vertebrae. Lyra was soon given permission to offer her some ice chips, then a few sips of water and juice followed. Dr. Bonheim's cheeks flushed with color and Lyra washed her face with a cool cloth and dabbed her lips with Vaseline and gently applied some light makeup and then she showed Dr. Bonheim's face to herself in the hand-held mirror and her mentor was pleased. Lyra mothered her until Dr. Bonheim was smiling and repeatedly thanking Lyra and the entire hospital staff for her care. Her husband was finally reached in Indonesia and he was en route to North Dakota from overseas. Lyra was thrilled to have her back again as she tested Dr. Bonheim's memory of events. Her memory could not recall anything just prior to the plane crash, unburdened by the trauma that she suffered in those final moments on the airstrip. Lyra was thrilled for that and she gave a cursory review of those events to satisfy Dr. Bonheim's endless curiosity and mentioned what Bradlee had done to help save her life and that of Stan and Kin. Next, she told her dear mentor about how much Bradlee meant to her and that in the days that followed they were engaged to be married. Dr. Bonheim glanced at Lyra's hand but was surprised that she was not wearing a ring. "It's OK," Lyra said to her, "Bradlee and I have our trust, our bond, and a ring is not needed until our wedding day."

At that moment, Lyra remembered Bradlee's generosity in offering half of his wages to the reservation instead and she smiled and knew inside her being that there was no precious stone to adorn her finger that could ever provide her with as strong a reminder as her heart felt every minute now of her wakeful hours.

Over the next three days Dr. Bonheim was out of bed multiple times each day, taking painful steps down the hallway locked in Lyra's arm on one side and a rehabilitation specialist's on the other. She was required to wear the neck brace for at least another six weeks to allow for proper healing but the fractures had not affected her use of her arms and legs. She just needed to regain her strength and mobility after the long period of sedation and bedrest. She refused most pain medications despite her broken ribs that would take many more weeks to fully heal. She began to eat real food, advancing from apple sauce and puddings to whole meals. Lyra again ordered delivery from Ruby's and she was rewarded, not just with meals for Dr. Bonheim and herself to enjoy, but the delivery van arrived packed with enough meals and pies for the entire intensive care staff and – *at no cost*. That was Ruby's generosity and all of Minot had experienced it at one time or another over the years. It was just Lyra's and Dr. Bonheim's turn now.

Dr. Bonheim's husband, Robert, a renowned marine biologist and ocean conservationist, finally received word, offshore on a research vessel somewhere in the Indonesian archipelago, of his wife's critical condition and he hurried to Minot by a series of ships, trains, and planes from across the other side of the world. The professorial couple embraced each other and went right to work discussing and critiquing each other's research work in utmost detail as if they had merely skipped a few beats in time together, traumatic accident and all. Lyra was consistently reassured that Dr. Bonheim's mind was as sharp as her wit as she observed the couple's tender quips and barbs like two fencers in a duel that tender kisses and hand-holding resolved moments later. Two great minds in service to make the world a better place. Lyra hoped that she and Bradlee would share even a smidgen of similar fates.

Stan's condition had also gradually improved as he regained his strength and vigor. Amanda was there all along beside him. He surely appreciated receiving his flight logbook as he realized that the crash was to be his final flight. All of those wonderful and successful flights were stored in that book and he realized he would look back fondly on his career as an aviator as time moved on. Retirement was a necessity now. He was in need of multiple complex reconstructive surgeries to his battered facial and jaw bones, muscles, ligaments, and tendons. His flight company arranged for his transfer to the University of Utah Hospital in Salt Lake City where he and Amanda were met by a team of expert facial plastic and oral surgeons to continue his extensive medical care.

By the fourteenth day, Dr. Bonheim was released from critical intensive care and transferred to the rehabilitation unit. She resided there for five more days, continuing to make progress with her strength and her gait with the continued guidance and exercises provided by the attentive rehab staff. She advanced quickly from needing a walker to a cane. And then it was time for her discharge from the hospital. A medical transport plane was arranged by Dr. Bonheim's Institute to return Dr. Bonheim and her husband safely to Seattle where she would continue to rest and rehabilitate at her home with the aid of visiting nurses.

The esteemed professors were escorted by Lyra and Oji to the airport in Minot where heartfelt goodbyes were offered. Lyra exited the terminal building. She was mentally and physically exhausted. She hadn't taken very good care of herself while she remained in the hospital for hours and days on end. She hadn't jogged in many weeks and her fitness and energy level were considerably diminished. Oji brought her back to the grounds of the Lady Slipper Inn and welcomed Lyra to her home as she prepared a comfortable place in the guest bedroom. She cooked healthy meals for Lyra and demanded her to run twice a day despite the cool air and winter snows that had begun to blanket the region. Lyra shopped for warm running clothes and settled back into a healthy pace. Each morning and evening she spoke with Bradlee as they discussed the events as they unfolded and plans for the upcoming winter break that was rapidly approaching. Her excitement for her journey to P.E.I. engaging her as forcefully as her desire to make love with Bradlee again with all her heart.

THE PLANE LANDED INTO T.F. GREEN AIRPORT just south of Providence, Rhode Island. Lyra felt like a squished 'Pe-Ho-Chee-Moo-T' sandwiched between two passengers who either breathed too heavily or squirmed too often in their tightly spaced seats on the fully-loaded jet. The sandwich image that she conjured in her mind, at least, lightened her otherwise anxious concern for flying. Lyra had completed her first semester exams online from Oji's home in mid-December. Dr. Bonheim and the Landscape Architecture department had agreed to that plan as a gesture of courtesy towards Lyra's caretaker role in Minot.

The December holidays were just a few days away. Ansley and Charles met Lyra at the Providence airport and together, they barrel-hugged Lyra to the ground as they congratulated her on her engagement to Bradlee. Lyra's bruises had fully healed and the twelve-day reprieve at Oji's home did wonders to regain her own strength and fit muscle tone. Lyra admitted she wanted to look her best for Bradlee. They chatted over the entire ninety-minute drive south along Interstate 95 and arrived at Ansley's family home in Stony Creek, Connecticut beside the small dairy farm. Lyra used to live next door up until they entered college. Childhood memories flooded Lyra's mind like an array of puzzle pieces when the box is first opened and dumped onto the sorting table. The car turned up the driveway and parked beside a wooded field. Lyra noted the new plantings of birch and maple and pine trees in the field and was pleased that someone had been busy restoring the beauty of the land that once separated their bedroom windows by a mere fifty yards.

Lyra was greeted affectionately by Ansley's parents and welcomed to their warm home by a crackling fire and lit pumpkin scented candles and festive dressings along the tables and stairway. Ansley's parents worked and saved and lived a comfortable life and, being that Ansley was their only child, provided well for Lyra's best friend over the years. Ansley was not want for love or toys or a high school car or leisure travel to various global destinations. Occasionally, Lyra used to join Ansley's family on various adventurous vacations and the same for Ansley, especially for Lyra's annual family summer beach trip to Prince

Edward Island.

Stony Creek was a quaint village by the Long Island Sound. A small market and seasonal restaurant, along with a bait and tackle shop, were the only evidence of a town besides the old fire truck ensconced inside an old building and a single blinking traffic light at the entrance to town. But its tucked-away existence allowed for many days of solitude, rock skipping and boat rides around the picturesque Thimble Islands on Ansley's dad's boat that he had parked at the marina.

The area's small schoolhouse elementary school merged with nearby students into a larger middle school, and then an even more numerous high school census where Lyra and Ansley continued together until graduation. Best of friends for all those years. To this day – despite the arrival of Charles into Ansley's life and the expected retreat by Lyra to give her best friends' relationship with Charles the breath it needed to expand into more mature love.

Over the next few days, Lyra and Ansley took many walks together down to the marina. Ansley was pleased with Lyra's emotional progress after her terrible physical abuse and the two shared stories about the little things that only they knew and hid from their parents, and from the world, as best friends do. They spoke of only the fun and good things and avoided the bad or darker memories. They recalled their secret hideaways. And scary neighbors that had now gone elsewhere, it seemed. They ran over behind the bait and tackle shop where they had once buried a plastic jewelry box – a time capsule when they were just ten years old – and dug it up with a heavy wooden shovel to discover that the rains and worms had managed to get to it first. Time never standing still, digesting memories until they were merely overgrown by a new generation of hungry weed-picking children who passed them by and smirked at their soil-stained, shovel-blistered adult hands.

They said their goodbyes the day after Christmas Day

passed and loving presents were exchanged. They awoke early that morning and Ansley drove Lyra to Boston's Logan Airport for her flight to Charlottetown, P.E.I. They agreed to meet again, the next time in San Francisco along Fisherman's Wharf when Lyra would visit Ansley, dreaming of sharing a delicious bowl of hot soup served inside a giant sourdough bowl before engorging on Ghirardelli chocolates. After chocolates, Ansley told Lyra, they would ride the trolley to the viewpoint on Russian Hill and let the winds tangle their hair. They hugged and shared their special knock against the car door. The knock had become their way to comfort each other, especially for Lyra over her college years - a way to return to happier memories when the only thing that really mattered then was that secret knock at each other's windows from the short distance between their childhood homes. Lyra promised Ansley that she would try to escape to San Francisco for a long weekend in the early spring, if not sooner.

BRADLEE SHOWERED AND GROOMED DILIGENTLY. In his bathrobe, he pranced nervously around his apartment above the garage. Tidying up was not exactly his strong suit but he collected a few loads of laundry, tended to the dishes that were splayed about, dusted, vacuumed the floors and changed the bedsheets. He tried to clean up some of the mess that was his work table, strewn with a sundry of woodcarving tools, frame pieces, and digital prints. He glanced at Oji's raw pair of moccasins, the 'naked' ones as he liked to describe them, and set them in a hiding spot. *No reason for Lyra to see those just now. That would spoil the fun now, wouldn't it?!*

He dressed and felt his hands. They were as if he was a sweaty-palmed high school boy readying for a first date. *Bradlee, now calm your nerves.* But he was too excited to see Lyra. Their distance apart seemed impossibly cruel now. He knew Lyra's plan after her stay in P.E.I. was to return to Seattle for a brief period and then return to North Dakota with Dr. Bonheim to complete the Institute's consulting work on the pipeline project. Bradlee worried about Lyra and the reservation's hostilities. But Lyra tried to reassure him that additional security measures were being implemented by the tribal council after the incidents at the corral and ensuing plane crash.

Despite all that happened over Thanksgiving and into early December, as Lyra helped Dr. Bonheim recover, Lyra received near perfect scores on her semester finals before heading to Connecticut to visit Ansley. Bradlee figured Lyra was probably mentally exhausted. Perhaps physically as well. And so he wanted to provide her with as peaceful and relaxing a visit as possible. *The marsh and the ocean would rejuvenate her, that's for sure*, Bradlee thought. Both waters had always worked for him and he was sure they would for Lyra after a few days of solitude in each other's arms between his clean and crisp bedsheets.

Bradlee arrived to Charlottetown Airport and waited. Lyra arrived towing her rollaway suitcase in one hand and some packages in the other. She looked stunningly beautiful, as always – this time in a low-cut blouse and mid-knee dress that accentuated her curves like a Formula One racetrack as Bradlee's pulse quickened. His mind racing through fantasies of what lay underneath it all. They hugged and she planted a long moist kiss on his lips. Their foreheads touched and held together. It was becoming a habit and new custom for them now, a way to greet each other and let each know that they were inside the other's mind and heart, the light of the stars shining bright, as Kin had told Bradlee. And their airport greeting, to Bradlee, was a grand sign that their upcoming days together would be all that he had been dreaming about each night under his wintry warm covers.

Their first night together at the Marshpillow was absorbed in each other's passions. Lyra desired his love and Bradlee offered it again and again to her until they were exhausted and rested and fed each other sweet treats in bed and then made love again. By morning, they rested as the sunlight streamed and alighted Ruthy's watercolor. Lyra noticed the painting the night before when she first arrived and set about perusing Bradlee's bachelor pad, studying his little nooks and collections and artistic preferences that adorned the walls.

"This painting, Bradlee..." She pointed towards Ruthy's work. "It's absolutely brilliant. I am transfixed every time I glance at it. Was this done by a famous artist?"

Bradlee chuckled. "I shall think it is quite possible," he muttered in his English professorial accent once again. "Perhaps the young seven year old damsel who laid her soft brushes to this canvas will most certainly be – one day indeed!"

He smiled at Lyra and played with her hair. Lyra's cleavage was peeking from beneath the covers into the sunlight as she sat against the headboard of Bradlee's bed staring at Ruthy's watercolor of the Tablelands and sun kissed clouds. Bradlee's mind was on fire once again with passion. Her breasts were like two of the soft clouds in the painting. *Cotton candy. Gourmet marshmallows. No, they were marshpillows. That's it!* He looked away with laughter and Lyra caught him peeking at her nakedness and gently slapped him across his cheek and then climbed on top of him and play-wrestled and kissed him again until he begged for mercy, this time in a thick Irish brogue. "*Please*," he pleaded with her, "*I'm going to die from jasmine intoxication, me lovely Lyra! Help! Call the authorities!*"

And their laughter only heightened their passionate love to ever higher levels beyond the clouds as the bedcovers were swept away once again. They returned to napping, spooned beside each other in blissful repose.

Bradlee's phone rang as he held Lyra, He turned for it and noticed it was his mother by the phone's caller id. *Should I answer it?* He let it ring through to voicemail. She called again. This time he picked up.

"Baruch, good morning son. I hope everything is alright. Are you at home at the Pillow?" His mother liked to condense the name of the family's summer home from Marshpillow to more simply, the 'Pillow.'

"Yes, mom. I'm fine. Everything's fine with the house. I'm just lying here next to my fiancée, that's all. Here, let me put you on speaker phone so you can say hello to her. Her name is Lyra." Bradlee pressed the speaker button on his phone and his mother's voice amplified as Lyra stirred and sat beside him.

"Baruch Avraham Levitsky, why didn't you tell me about this young lady before?"

"Sorry mom. Just needed my privacy, you know. I didn't want to jinx myself until I asked Lyra to marry me a few days ago."

Lyra poked him gently in the ribs and whispered, "*I asked you* lover boy, don't ever forget that," as she smiled and kissed his ear.

"Well, I'm very very happy for you, Baruch. Your dad is here next to me, driving. I'll tell him the good news." Bradlee bristled at hearing his mother's comment and wondered if his dad would ever be happy with any woman his son chose to be his wife.

"Baruch, your father and I will be at the Pillow later this afternoon. We flew into Charlottetown this morning from Toronto. He has a grand rounds lecture to give at the hospital in less than an hour. Tight schedule as usual, as you know, Bradlee. The hospital here is having a trauma surgery symposium all week and he's the featured grand rounds speaker. Something about new techniques in abdominal vascular surgery which, as you know, he's an expert. Anyway, I think we'll be at the Pillow by about five o'clock in time for dinner. Can I make you your favorite homemade pasta with paprika sauce tonight? And please ask your fiancée if she can join us, of course. It will be so exciting to meet Lyra. Very pretty name, by the way."

Lyra was giggling at his mother's suggestion. Bradlee told her about his favorite meal when they were on the train.

"Sounds delicious mom," Bradlee replied. Lyra nodded affirmative for the pasta. "But I'm not interested in dining with my father. Perhaps another time. Can I ask you for takeout from the main house instead?"

"Baruch, I wish it wouldn't have to stay like this forever between you and your father."

"Well, that's the way it is. It's better this way, mom. It just is. See you later."

He hung up. Lyra stared quietly at him and turned to her side with disappointment in her eyes.

They arose and showered and dressed warmly. Then they climbed into Bradlee's car and visited the local market and returned and felt like it was their first morning as a domesticated couple. They walked the grounds of the Marshpillow. Bradlee showed Lyra his woodcarving shed and his lathe for woodturning. He told her about his Uncle Eddie, who was a rabbi and his father's brother, and that his uncle used to spend many hours at the house teaching Bradlee how to make beauty from raw wood from the time Bradlee was barely able to hold a sharp instrument in his hands. Then, he opened the side door to the main house and turned on the lights as they entered. It was still and cold and lifeless but Lyra wandered with curiosity. She found Bradlee's childhood bedroom. Tins overflowing with his old rock and seashell collections and childhood photos from the time he was in diapers. The timeline of his life in photographs.

"Who's this, Bradlee, in the photo with you? You look like you're in preschool here but I can see how your handsome face hasn't really changed after all these years…"

"Oh, that's a girl I had a crush on. We were four years old at the time. Best friends back then. Never forgot her even though we lost touch. Something about seeing her in that photo just makes me feel happy inside. My first friend in life. I suppose we never do forget those… Sometimes, I wonder how her life turned out but I've never contacted her to know. Life just goes on."

"Maybe you should someday, Bradlee. I mean – contact her. True friendships never end, at least that's how I feel with Ansley all these years."

Lyra returned to the living room and examined more photographs. There was a man carrying a very young Bradlee on his shoulders along a beach path. "That's my Uncle Eddie that I told you about earlier. The woodcarver. That's his nickname, actually. His name is really, '*Rabbi Eliezer Levitsky.*' She set the frame down and reached for another. It was a beautiful, elegant woman in a long white beach robe and she was wearing an oversized straw hat. She was posing like a model for the camera. Bradlee noticed Lyra staring at the photo. "That's my mother, Lyra. Jenny is her name," he said.

Lyra retrieved another frame and stared at the photo closely. It was of a middle aged man wearing a colorful Jewish woven kippah on his head. The resemblance to Bradlee was uncanny. She turned towards Bradlee who was observing her quietly.

"Your father, I presume?"

"Yes Lyra. My father."

"His name?"

"Dr. Nathaniel Yitzhak Levitsky. Chief of Trauma Surgery, Mount Sinai Hospital in Toronto and Senior

Professor and Director of the Department of Surgery at the University of Toronto School of Medicine."

"So, he's a great doctor, Bradlee. Is that what you are trying to tell me?"

Lyra found Bradlee's voice condescending and irritating as he described his father's work.

"I guess people think he is. I haven't spoken with my father in more than five years, Lyra. We don't quite see eye to eye on matters. Sorry to bring that up just now."

"Do you want to tell me more?" she asked.

"Not really."

"You are upset, Bradlee. I can feel it."

"Lyra, stop it. My relationship with my father has nothing to do with you and, if I had my way, it never will. Is that clear?" Bradlee had never raised the tone of his voice to her before. He was standing with his arms across his chest and he possessed a stern look to his face that Lyra had never seen before.

"Well, I'd like to know more about your father and mother. Is that too much to ask of you, Bradlee?"

"My father turned his back on me when I asked for his blessing to marry Samia. Why should I give a fucking hell about him now?! He put me through hell after Samia died. Wouldn't even talk to me, console me. What kind of father does that to his only child?! For what? For religion. Because Samia wasn't a Jew?!" Bradlee was visibly angry. "Samia loved her faith. Yes, she was a practicing Muslim and I learned a lot from her about her faith. Her beliefs were hers, not mine, but I loved her anyway, with all my heart… God can damn my father for what he did!" He tensed his hands into a fist and Lyra became alarmed.

"Is that why you dropped out of medical school just before you graduated? Because of your father, to try to punish him for his beliefs and wishes? Bradlee, maybe your father was just looking out for what he thought was best for you."

"My father is a hypocrite, Lyra. Praying to his God and telling me that another human being isn't fit to be my wife as if she is an inferior creature. He was a hard ass on me since I was in primary school. My test scores were never good enough for him. Even with straight A's! I stood beside him in the operating room when I was studying in my surgical rotation, when I was there to learn from my father, the great trauma surgeon – no, only complaints from his mouth the whole damn time. Embarrassing me in front of my peers if I didn't know the answer to a question. Not holding the retractors far enough from a patient's open abdominal cavity. Not doing this or that. Never any praise. Only criticism. Lyra, I was first in my medical school class – no, not enough for him. Never enough, Lyra…! I don't care if he were to live or die tomorrow, Lyra. I wouldn't show up to his own funeral, that's for sure. Damn him!!!"

He was seething with an internal rage. Lyra grew increasingly upset as she raised her voice to match his. Her instincts told her to run fast, get away from Bradlee, the same as she felt with Matt when she was trapped in his room. Her fear mounted as her heart raced and her lips started to tremble.

"You are a fool Bradlee Lee, Baruch Avraham Levitsky! Just look at this photo of your father! Have you picked it up in the past five years even once?!" She was screaming at him. "You look just like him Bradlee, and he does you. Can't you at least try to make up with him? Do it for me if not for yourself, Bradlee."

There was a brief pause between them as Bradlee's eyes darkened and he grit his teeth and seethed. Then he sprang and ripped the frame out of Lyra's hand.

"This is for you and for me! Like Moses destroying the Ten Commandments!" as he smashed the glass frame with all his strength to the hardwood floor between them. Glass shards sprayed everywhere. Lyra shivered in fright, fearing for the blow that would come next from Bradlee's fist.

"You have no right," Lyra said. "Doesn't the Bible say to *honor* your father and mother? At least I learned that in Hebrew School! And at least you still have a father and mother who love you!"

Tears streamed from her eyes as she sobbed uncontrollably and ran as fast as she could out the side door and slammed it shut. She ran to the shed and searched for something. Anything to hold onto and destroy. A rusty bicycle was laying against the wall. She grasped the handlebars and ran outside onto the driveway and jumped onto the seat and started pedaling as fast as she could. She needed to run. To escape as fast as possible.

Bradlee ran from the house and located Lyra as she accelerated down the driveway and away from him.

"I certainly have every right, Lyra!" He started running after her and almost reached her with his outstretched arm but she screamed in fear and swerved and accelerated faster and then she was out of reach.

"Lyra, don't leave me!" he screamed. "Please come back here right now!"

Lyra pedaled faster. A gray haired couple were holding hands and standing by the Marshpillow's mailbox. The woman had her hand to her face and was distraught from hearing their piercing argument. Lyra glared at the older woman. "Please call the police if he chases after me!" Lyra cried out to them as she turned onto the main road and headed south.

Bradlee stopped at the edge of the driveway. "What are you looking at?!" as he turned to the retired couple who lived in the adjacent property. "In all your years haven't you two ever had an argument before?!"

He turned and ran back to the garage shed and searched desperately for another bike. There was a newer model hanging from a hook. He pulled it down and brought it quickly outside to the driveway. The seat swiveled when he jumped on it and he couldn't hold his position steady.

Damn it! He ran back into the shed and retrieved a bike tool and tightened the seat to the post. He got back on and started pedaling, turning at the driveway edge past the old couple and onto the main road. Lyra was nowhere in sight.

Lyra pedaled harder and then banked left onto Lighthouse Road. It was mainly flat and fast as she accelerated as fast as she could away from another madman, she thought. Her hands trembling while trying desperately to hold onto the handlebars. The cold wind burned her cheeks as her tears flowed and dripped onto the slick snow-packed pavement. But she kept pedaling. She looked back and saw no one following. Only wind and sun and snow-covered pine trees and tracks of fallow farmland were ahead of her.

Bradlee pedaled in pursuit. Her words echoing in his mind. *What did she say before she ran off? To honor your father and mother. That she learned that in Hebrew School. At least you still have a father and mother who love you. What did that mean? And what about her parents, her family? She never said a word to me yet about them... God, I don't know. I don't understand. How could I have lashed out at her like that?* Bradlee hated himself and punched at his thighs. *Why so much rage now after all these years?*

Waves of remorse swept over Bradlee as he shifted into the highest gear on his bicycle's cassette and stood from his saddle in search of Lyra ahead. He had spotted her off in the distance when she had made the turn onto Lighthouse Road. It was only just over a mile until the end of that road. He knew it well having spent countless hours training on this very road, cycling to the lighthouse and back, loop after loop, honing his skills, testing his bike speed against an imaginary clock that motivated him to work harder, to build his leg strength and endurance, in preparation for his cross country bicycle trip the summer after Sami died.

He spotted Lyra in the distance again. He was closing the gap. Lyra glanced behind, fearing Bradlee, and pushed forward, forward. She saw the ocean. *Closer, come on Lyra, pedal harder.* And then the lighthouse came into view to her right. The road dipped downward and her speed accelerated even more.

"Lyra, wait for me! Please Lyra! I'm sorry!" Bradlee was calling from behind.

She saw the yellow sign ahead just above the metal guardrail. She squeezed her handlebar brakes. Nothing happened. More acceleration. She squeezed again and then quickly glanced at her brake pads beside the front and rear tires. The rubber pads were worn thin and decayed and couldn't grip the tire. Her bike began to shake and swerve on the remaining gravel and icy path as she lifted her shoes off the pedals and pressed them against the gravel to attempt to slow down her progress. It was too late. She closed hard and fast to the metal guardrail.

Bradlee was only fifty yards behind her. *Why isn't she braking, he wondered?*

"*Lyra! Hold on!!!*" He screamed as loud as he could. Her front tire struck the metal guard rail with a crushing thud and she was thrown into the air and over the guardrail onto the rocky cliff embankment. She was rolling. Her head struck the precipice. Then she was falling downward. She tried to reach and grab onto something. Anything, as she slid further, faster. Her face scraping against the red sandstone. Her small wallet fell from her pocket and descended into the ocean below. Her foot locked against a cropping and she was twisted and contorted and then only silence. She was unconscious. She landed on a rocky ledge that was fifty feet from the summit. Another hundred feet to the ocean waves crashing below her.

Bradlee braked hard and leapt off his bike when he arrived at the guardrail and ran to the edge. No sight of Lyra. He screamed for help. A woman came running from the small wooden building adjacent to the lighthouse.

"*Call emergency rescue! Fast! She's fallen off the*

cliff!!!" he yelled at her. The woman ran inside the building and didn't return.

Bradlee peered over the jagged edge. *"Damn!"*

There was no sign of Lyra. He approached the very edge of the cliff and peered below to what he could see of the ocean and still no sign of movement near the jutting rocks. Only fierce crashing waves.

He set his left foot over the edge and tested the sandstone. A few shards tumbled down the cliff but he could grasp onto the edge and keep his balance. He winced as he tried to use his left arm to grasp the rocky ledge and descend downward. He had to be careful or he knew his shoulder would very likely dislocate again and he would surely fall to his death. No time for pain. *Come on, think Bradlee.* He pulled himself back up to the top of the ledge and ran and searched the parking lot area for something. Metal fencing continued past the guardrail. He peered at the lighthouse and his eyes descended and found what he thought could possibly work. There was rope cord that was strung through wood pilings along the edge of the parking lot. They were simple markers for parking spaces. He ran to the pilings and pulled out his multitool and started slashing at the rope with his knife. He cut through one piece and then ran to the next piling and pulled the cord through the hole. *I need yards of it.* He ran again and pulled the rope through the next piling. He had accumulated enough. *It had to be.* Perhaps about fifty yards of rope. He ran back to the cliff edge. He tied the rope to the guardrail and began to rappel down the jagged slope. His left shoulder screamed out in pain as he shifted his body weight in the wind to compensate. *Come on, Bradlee. Push down with your feet.* The rope cord ripped at the skin of his palms as his flesh bled and he descended further.

There she is! Lyra was slumped onto a rocky ledge. The Ark necklace had gotten caught on the jagged edge of rock jutting from the ledge. Bradlee could see that it had braced her from plunging to the ocean below. *"Lyra! I'm coming!"* he yelled out. *"Hold on, Lyra. Hold on!!!"* He continued down the face of the sandstone cliff and reached the ledge. There was barely enough room to maneuver himself without falling off the edge into a certain death below. He could see the cliff plunging into the ocean. The crashes of the waves were striking huge boulders that had torn off the façade and fallen to their watery grave at the cliff base. Certain death if he or Lyra were to make the same fall.

"Hold on, Lyra." He crouched and carefully detached the Ark necklace from its rocky hook and rolled Lyra on her back while gently gripping and stabilizing the back of her neck. She was unconscious. The Ark necklace remained dangling from her neck, unbroken. He called her name but no response. He pinched her forearm forcibly to check if she could feel pain. Anything. But there was no movement or grimace. He ripped off his light jacket and set it carefully under her head. *Breathing.* He crouched again and felt some warmth from her mouth. She was breathing. *Beating.* He pressed his fingers gently against the side of her neck. There were steady pulsations. Her face was scraped in multiple places and her right forearm was bent awkwardly. He set her arm carefully as straight as he could beside her and adjusted her legs. He waited. He screamed for help. *"Down here! Hurry! We need help, fast...! Help!!!"* he cried out again.

Minutes past. Crucial minutes. He kept rechecking her breathing and her pulse. He lifted her eyelids. Her pupils were dilated and her left coloboma was even more prominent, but her pupils contracted in the sunlight. Her hands were bleeding near her fingertips and he wrapped them inside his shirt to keep them warm. The winds were brutal as they lashed at the red sandstone cliff and through his shirt. He was shivering now. Waiting. *Will anyone come?* Should he leave her and climb back up and call for help. *God, please. Please do not take Lyra from me.* He was screaming and crying and begging as he leaned over her torso to keep her warm and desperately looked below the edge hoping for a fishing boat - anything that could send out a call to rescue her.

There was a rush of red pebbles raining down and he crouched over Lyra even more to protect her from the falling debris. Then an intense downdraft. Helicopter rotor blades whirring above now, observing him. Hovering a hundred yards from the ledge.

"*Don't move!*" A loud booming voice from a speaker.

Stay calm, Bradlee. It was a bright red helicopter with an EKG wave symbol painted on its side. An emergency rescue helicopter. "Our rescue is here, Lyra, *Hold on! Hold on!*" he screamed to her over the blade noise.

A hook attached to a thick metal cable was lowered from above as the helicopter maneuvered high above the ledge. A booming voice again. "Grasp the saddle around your waist and secure it to the metal clip! We need to get you up first! *You! – crouched over the victim!*"

Bradlee put his thumb into the air acknowledging that he understood the voice command. The saddle lowered and struck into the mountain and he reached and grabbed hold of it. He stepped into it and fastened the metal clip to his leather belt and gave the thumbs up sign again. Bradlee was flying off the ledge. Faster. Away from Lyra. His jacket flapping under her head in the wind. He reached the edge of the helicopter and was quickly reeled in by the hoist. He was unclipped by the medic and then quickly pulled and buckled into a small jumpseat and told not to move. He listened. He was thrown a heavy wool blanket and he wrapped himself. His palms bleeding from the raw flesh wounds inflicted by the rope burns. The medic attached a basket stretcher to a larger hook. Another medic attached his thick belt to a separate heavy metal clip and he was lowered with the stretcher. He arrived to the cliff edge where Lyra was lying. He stood and quickly hammered a metal climbing clip into the cliff rock and clipped himself in place with a rope tied to his waist that was attached to a thick metal carabiner. Then he grabbed the stretcher as the helicopter descended and the cable slacked. Bradlee watched it all. The man gently rolled Lyra onto the stretcher while supporting her neck. He cinched three thick padded belts across her forehead and torso and legs and then unclipped his carabiner from the cliff edge. He gave the thumbs up sign and they were hoisted into the air. The other medic onboard positioned the stretcher as it reached the helicopter entry door and he clasped onto the metal hook and unclipped the stretcher and pulled it into position beside Bradlee. The pilot glanced back as the medic quickly entered the helicopter. Ten seconds elapsed as he hovered. The stretcher was secured in place. The pilot throttled up and forward and the winds gusted through the open doors and they were accelerating away from the cliff. One medic tore at Lyra's sleeve and wrapped tubing tightly around her upper left arm. He found a vein and poked it with an intravenous needle and taped it to her forearm and then he connected it to a clear solution as it began to drip. He connected her finger to a pulse oximeter and checked the recording. She had a good pulse. 120 beats per minute. Oxygen saturation – 97%. The medic stabilized her neck with a brace and covered her with a heavy wool blanket. Bradlee was laying perfectly still. Then he tried to reach over and touch Lyra. His left shoulder was throbbing and he realized he couldn't easily move his left arm once again without shooting pains.

THE INTERCOM SYSTEM AT QUEEN ELIZABETH HOSPITAL in Charlottetown blasted a piercing call signal followed by a recorded overhead voice.

"*Code Blue. Incoming Trauma. Lifeflight. Ten minutes out.*"

The message repeated four more times.

The amphitheater was full with hospital administrators, attending physicians, fellows, residents, medical students, and intensive care nurses when the overhead message came through. Everyone present knew exactly what that code meant – that the hospital trauma team was needed to assemble immediately to the emergency room code bay and trauma surgeons from each subspecialty to be scrubbed and ready, if needed, in the operating room theaters. Helicopter arrival was imminent.

Dr. Nathaniel Levitsky was standing at the lectern in the midst of his detailed slideshow presentation of "Novel techniques for rapid surgical approaches to life-threatening abdominal injuries in trauma patients." Everyone paused for a quick moment in time as the code blue message blared followed immediately by a flurry of action. Some of the doctors and nurses quickly stood, left their lunches behind, and ran towards the amphitheater exits. A tall neurosurgical fellow who had studied trauma surgery under Dr. Levitsky in Toronto quickly approached the lectern.

"Nathaniel, come scrub in with us in the operating room. It would be an honor for us here at the hospital." Dr. Levitsky nodded and the two ran off down the hallway towards the OR theater.

The helicopter arrived to its landing circle adjacent to the emergency entrance and was met by four members of the trauma staff. Lyra was quickly wheeled into the ER trauma bay where a critical response team was assembled. They followed the emergency code sequence. Bradlee was brought in by stretcher and was parked in the adjacent bay. He was quickly examined by two emergency room physicians and deemed stable. They called for the orthopedist who reviewed Bradlee's medical history, examined his shoulder, applied sterile solution, injected the joint space with Novocain as a nerve block, and fixed Bradlee's dislocated left shoulder with traction and manipulation. The nurse brought him pain medication to swallow and inserted an intravenous line into his forearm. Then she administered a gradual drip of clear fluids. Bradlee leaned back against the stretcher and observed the concentrated activity in the next bay.

There was a carefully choreographed sequence of events happening before his eyes as physicians, nurses, emergency medical personnel, and supply runners took immediate action around the victim's stretcher. The room was equipped with all manner of emergent supplies. Lyra had a second intravenous line rapidly inserted into her leg and her left arm line was taped more securely. Her obviously fractured right forearm was quickly splinted to an arm board and taped in place. Her lungs and heart were auscultated and chest leads applied and hooked up to a cardiac monitor. She was tachycardic but her EKG showed a steady rhythm. Pule ox, 99% as oxygen was administered via tubing attached to an inflated bag and a mask covering her nose and mouth. There was no need for urgent intubation and ventilation at present. A blood pressure cuff was inserted around her unharmed left arm. It was initially normal, then became erratic, before reaching consistent unacceptably high levels. She was unconscious. She had a boggy swollen area to the occipital region of her skull. She was rapidly wheeled into the CT scanner and images returned within seconds. An occipital skull fracture was evident and she had an ongoing collecting subdural hematoma with a midline shift of her brain tissue. A hurried second series of CT images was taken of her chest, abdomen and pelvis revealing internal bleeding into her abdominal and pelvic cavities. She had a splenic laceration and blood was also pooling in her lower pelvic ring beneath her ovaries and uterus. The CT machine veered and quickly scanned her right forearm and revealed a significant rotational fracture of her radius and ulna bones. The waiting trauma, neurosurgery, and orthopedic surgical teams were updated of the findings and she was wheeled immediately into the adjacent operating room where she underwent rapid sequence induction anesthesia followed by airway intubation. Her scalp hair was quickly shaved and her skull wound site was sterilized. Then her abdominal cavity was draped and quickly sterilized and readied for incision.

Dr. Ibrahim Salim, the neurosurgical fellow, rapidly drilled two holes into Lyra's subdural space to decompress the bleeding site. A drain was placed inside her brain cavity. Dr. Levitsky incised Lyra's lower abdomen with a common lateral approach at the same location as a cesarean section. His scalpel continued through to the peritoneal cavity and retractors were inserted as he peered into Lyra's lower abdominal space. "Suction." The assistant suctioned the pool of blood beneath her uterus. He noticed the source of the bleed. The uterine artery, emanating from the anterior division of the internal iliac artery, was bleeding, spraying fountainous pulsations from a lacerated section above where the artery would bifurcate into its various branches that supplied the ovaries, fallopian tubes, and the uterus itself. The uterus and ovaries looked stale and gray – lifeless – as their vital oxygenated blood supply was compromised. The bleeding pulsations sprayed out of Lyra's abdomen and struck Dr. Levitsky's surgical mask and face shield. The OR nurse quickly cleaned his shield with saline and gauze. "Clamps," he called out and was handed two clamps in succession by the nurse as he carefully clamped each side of the pulsating vessel. "Sutures." He was handed a fine needle attached to suture material that was latched to another clamp. He worked quickly to sew the arterial vessel at its bleeding source. When finished, he waited and observed and then removed the clamps and observed further. No further bleeding from the artery. More saline rinsing and suctioning from the pelvic cavity. The sutures were holding well and the ovaries and uterus flushed with pink tissues once again. He explored further in the abdominal cavity and was satisfied that there were no further bleeding sources as he ran his fingers and examined the small and large intestine. The young victim was nulliparous. He could tell from the appearance of her uterine wall that she had never birthed a child yet. The victim would be able to have children someday, if she so chose. An emergent hysterectomy would not be necessary. He turned to the OR nurse and then to Dr. Salim and nodded approvingly.

"Excellent work, Dr. Levitsky," Dr. Salim said. "This woman will surely thank you someday in the future."

"And you too, my colleague and dear friend," Dr. Levitsky responded.

The two surgeons each completed their separate tasks. An intracranial pressure monitor was inserted into Lyra's brain and her abdominal cavity was carefully closed with care to future cosmetic appearance. Dr. Salim and Dr. Levitsky exited the operating room and removed their surgical garments and washed. The orthopedic team entered and quickly reduced Lyra's right forearm fracture with traction and rotation followed by a series of X-ray images to confirm the appropriate bony alignments. Her forearm was casted. Her facial abrasions were cleaned and she was wheeled to the recovery area for further post-operative care.

"Did we get a name yet for this patient?" Dr. Levitsky inquired as he was escorted from the OR by Dr. Salim. "Not yet, sir. She's currently listed as '*Jane Seashell*' in the system. The hospital already has a '*Jane Doe*' admitted – an elderly woman with dementia who may have wandered from a nearby nursing home without any id. Our mutual trauma patient – she was rescued by the chopper medics from a rocky bluff over along the northeast side of P.E.I. They noticed a seashell dangling from her necklace, hence the pseudonym they selected for her in transit here. I will go have a word with the ER staff and check if they have an update for us on her true identity. Then I need to make some brief rounds on a few other patients in the ICU before I return home. My wife and daughter and I have a red eye flight to catch out of Halifax later tonight. We are headed to Paris for a few days and then we return to India for a long overdue extended vacation visiting our families. The grandparents will be meeting their vivacious granddaughter, *Samia*, for the first time." Ibrahim's eyes lit up with joy. He and his wife, Sofia, had decided to honor his love for his deceased sister by naming their first child after her.

"May my goddaughter's name be exalted in heaven," Nathaniel said.

When Samia was first born, Ibrahim had approached Nathaniel and Jenny and asked them if they could take the responsibility of being Samia's godparents, in case of any unexpected tragedy that might befall Ibrahim and Sofia. Nathaniel and Jenny had agreed, further establishing an even stronger fatherly bond between mentor and pupil.

"I'll meet you in the lounge just after my rounds are completed soon. I will stop by to see you off as well, Nathaniel." Dr. Salim departed.

Dr. Levitsky headed to the physician's lounge. A delayed lunch was being served as he filled his plate with kosher vegetarian items and took a quiet seat at a small table. He closed his eyes and recited a Hebrew blessing for his meal and then he stated the trauma victim's name, 'Jane Seashell.' *God knows who this woman truly is and let Him now do his work of healing.* And then he quietly mumbled a prayer for the trauma victim. This had been his routine since he had first begun as a surgeon in training. He had no doubt that prayer could help patients recover from their trauma. And then he opened his eyes and enjoyed his meal in solitude.

Bradlee was interviewed by the police while in the emergency room. He gave his full birth name and age and a detailed report to an officer of the events that occurred at the lighthouse cliff.

"And the victim's full name who was with you?" the officer asked.

Bradlee hesitated in thought. "Her name is Lyra, officer. Lyra Sasha... Bradlee could not remember Lyra's last name once again. He searched his mind for a visual clue. The train ride. *She mentioned her name to me when we first met on the train. God, tell me now, what was it?* The policeman was surprised that Bradlee could not recall his girlfriend's last name.

"You said she's your fiancée. Is that right?" the officer asked.

"Yes," Bradlee responded. The officer looked puzzled. He informed Bradlee that he needed to go check a few things in his squad car and return.

Bradlee was exhausted. A second traumatic experience in less than a week and he had had enough of near life-ending events for a lifetime. He felt waves of guilt over Lyra's trauma. He had made a terrible series of mistakes after having such a beautiful night and morning together with Lyra. He was angry at himself for deflecting his anger at his father towards Lyra. She didn't deserve to be the recipient nor serve as an intermediary between him and his father.

Ten minutes went by. The police officer returned and stood at the base of Bradlee's stretcher.

"Mr. Levitsky, I've run a report of your name in our database," the officer said directly. "It appears your name is linked to the death of a woman named '*Samia Salim*' five years ago. Is that right, sir?"

"Yes," Bradlee replied. "She was killed by a fallen tree when we were camping in the mountains."

"Yes, I can see that description given from the database report. I'm going to need to file a report on this matter today. The police investigative unit will be contacting you shortly. We tend to look suspiciously as a department when there are two potential deaths of young females linked to the same individual. Mr. Levitsky, you are now under investigation for potentially two homicides, if this current victim doesn't pull through."

Bradlee stared at the officer as if he was just struck by a metal bat across his gut.

Was Lyra truly in jeopardy of dying in the operating room?

"Officer, I didn't do anything to hurt Samia. She was my fiancée. Or Lyra. Lyra and I had just gotten engaged a few weeks ago. I had nothing to do with her bike striking that guardrail and Lyra falling off the cliff."

The officer was astonished by Bradlee's report that he was recently engaged to two separate female victims just before each of their traumatic accidents occurred. He wondered if this man in this hospital stretcher was truly a serial murderer. He wanted to arrest Bradlee and bring him back to the police station at that moment but, as he called and relayed his findings to police headquarters, his superior officer informed him to let Bradlee be discharged from the hospital without arrest for the time being. Bradlee was instructed that he would need to return to his home on P.E.I within twenty-four hours after his hospital discharge or an arrest warrant would be issued. He would be required to remain there until further questioning by the detective investigative unit.

Bradlee continued to stare in shock from the officer's accusation. The officer left his card and informed Bradlee to call him if he needed to add anything further over the next few days. He suggested to Bradlee that he might want to seek an attorney to assist him through the legal process ahead. Then the officer informed the ER clerk that the victim's name who was wheeled in beside Bradlee was presumably, '*Lyra Sasha.*' No id was found on the victim to say otherwise. The ER clerk entered the name in the computer and kept the surname, '*Seashell,*' in place in the medical record.

Dr. Salim entered the intensive care unit to review his new trauma patient's post-operative care. The occipital surgical site was covered by a dressing and it had not accumulated any significant or unusual fluid leak. Intracranial pressure and peripheral blood pressure readings remained stable on appropriate intravenous medications. Then, Lyra's arms and legs began to convulse in awkward pulsations. She was having a seizure. Dr. Salim quickly informed the nurse to administer a bolus of an anticonvulsant into Lyra's intravenous port and her seizure quickly subsided. He remained by her bedside for a while longer before returning to the ER to check on whether any further neurosurgical consultations were needed. There were none. The ER was quiet again in the late afternoon. He glanced at a patient in an arm sling who was in the distance at the ER trauma bay but couldn't make out his face in detail. He thought he may have looked familiar to him. The man in the sling was being questioned by a police officer. Dr. Salim was then distracted by a resident asking him for a curbside consult on an ER patient.

Then he logged into the computer and checked the admission screen. *Lyra Sasha Seashell. We finally have a real name for our trauma victim.* He was aware of the report that the patient was rescued by helicopter from a cliff's edge. *Cliff jumper, perhaps? Suicidal?* He wondered what her story truly was. But he was curious about her name as he peered at the screen. '*Seashell*' remained as her last name in the computer system. That was odd, he thought. He departed and located Dr. Levitsky in the physician's lounge.

"Come and join me, Ibrahim. You're just in time for dessert." Dr. Levitsky stood and greeted one of his finest surgical pupils that he had ever mentored.

"Thank you, sir. Any baklava available today, Nathaniel? Dr. Levitsky chuckled as he thought of Ibrahim's love for the sweet flaky dough traditional Middle Eastern dessert treats.

"I'm afraid not today. Not even babka or rugelach either! Perhaps tomorrow. There's always hope for us fellow sons of Abraham. At least we share our love for delicious sweets," Dr. Levitsky responded teasingly and affectionately.

The two men, mentor and student, had grown fond of each other over the past many years. Ibrahim had met his mentor through his sister, Samia, who was Bradlee's girlfriend at the time. Ibrahim was one year behind his sister in his educational track at the university medical school in Toronto. When Samia died, Dr. Levitsky had remorse over his falling out with his son, although he maintained his strong opinion that Bradlee and Samia should not have married due to their religious divide. Ibrahim, highly intelligent and possessing gifted hands just like Bradlee, became a surrogate son to Nathaniel despite his personal devout Muslim beliefs and practices that Nathaniel learned to tolerate, and then appreciate and accept, of Islam's many spiritual and cultural similarities to Judaism. His relationship with Ibrahim became a way for him to try to maintain some kind of link to Bradlee despite the weeks and months and years that rolled by without any direct communication between them. Ibrahim served as the bridge for a period of time, a courier for messages between father and son, but eventually that role subsided as Bradlee distanced himself further when he dropped out of medical school and disappeared from his usual circle of academic friends. Eventually, despite their affection for each other as future brothers-in-law, Bradlee chose to discontinue contact with Ibrahim as well. For Bradlee, the memory of Samia's death was too painful for him to experience it repeatedly through her brother's eyes.

Ibrahim sat down beside Nathaniel and spoke. "Our patient is stable and her post-operative labs are encouraging. She is being transfused now with two pints of blood in the intensive care unit. Her blood pressure has stabilized and her intracranial pressures are acceptable to me. Her splenic laceration is stable as well on follow-up imaging. The staff is most appreciative of your willingness to step into the OR and perform as you always have, Nathaniel. To save a life is the highest good one can do in this world. But to also leave intact the ability of a young woman to reproduce, to bring new life into this world, is an even greater mitzvah."

Nathanial and Ibrahim chuckled at Ibrahim's use of the word, 'mitzvah.' Both understood the connections that linked their cultures all the way back to Abraham and Sarah, the original patriarch and matriarch in the Old Testament. Nathaniel recalled the verses in the Torah: *'Two nations are in your womb; two people will come from you and be separated.'* It was the fundamental origin of their shared brotherly connection. Both had been well schooled in the teachings of their faith and traditions.

"Her name has been updated in the system, Nathaniel. You can find her listed now as – *Lyra Sasha Seashell* – in the medical record when you make rounds after you finish your lunch."

"Thank you for checking on her, Ibrahim. And for your kind words, as always... *Seashell*? Now that is a very curious last name. An alias perhaps, Ibrahim. I will leave that for you to decipher the mystery. I will be departing soon with Jenny to return to our home on the east end. You are always welcome to join us there with your family or take the house for your own family vacation as desired when you have some time off to enjoy the island."

"Thank you, Nathaniel. Very kind of you to offer."

The two men caught up on events in their lives. Nathaniel informing Ibrahim of his desire to retire soon and travel more with his wife. Ibrahim, updating Nathaniel on his lovely wife and their nine-month old daughter, all wide-eyed with energy, crawling, and chattering away in her own excited jibber-jabber of primitive first words.

They departed the physician's lounge and embraced goodbye. Nathaniel went to check on his patient, Lyra Seashell, in the unit as Ibrahim exited the hospital and found a halal food truck parked outside and ordered a falafel pita sandwich. He returned inside carrying his late afternoon lunch and found a quiet seat inside the cafeteria.

Dr. Levitsky arrived to the ICU to finish his post-operative care. He reviewed the patient's vital signs and lab results and checked her abdominal incision. All appeared stable. He was readying to leave after chatting with the patient's nurse but then Dr. Levitsky returned to her bedside and held Ms. Seashell's hand in his and recited another quiet prayer for her. He would likely never see her again, he presumed. He signed off to the staff trauma surgeon who assumed responsibility for Lyra's remaining care. He departed, met Jenny in the physician's lounge, and they returned to collect Nathaniel's laptop computer from the amphitheater lectern and exited to the parking lot to begin the drive to their Marshpillow home.

BRADLEE WAS DISCHARGED FROM THE ER and went to check on Lyra's condition. He had hoped to receive an update from the intensive care staff. Her very survival overwhelmed his mind with grief and remorse. He approached the intensive care unit security clerk and asked permission for entry to visit Lyra. He desperately wanted to be by her side again. To touch her and hold her and beg for her forgiveness. The security clerk requested Bradlee's full name, the patient he was requesting to visit in the unit, and the nature of their relationship.

"Her name, sir?" the clerk asked.

"Her name is Lyra Sasha..." Bradlee hesitated.

"Her last name, sir...?" And Bradlee froze in place. He didn't know Lyra's last name. There was no wallet or personal items found in the ER. Only a simple single-shelled necklace on a lanyard was found on her neck and the clerk showed it to Bradlee and asked if he recognized it.

"Yes, *of course*, I do. I gave that as a gift to Lyra."

"And her last name, sir," she asked Bradlee again.

Again, Bradlee pondered and could not recall it from the train ride just as he couldn't report it to the police officer in the ER.

The clerk searched the computer under the name, 'Lyra Sasha,' and noticed the full name was actually 'Lyra Sasha Seashell.' Probably an alias, the clerk presumed.

"Are you her boyfriend?" she asked Bradlee.

"Yes... No... I am her fiancé," Bradlee responded.

"There was no ring, sir, on her finger, that we found. Can you prove that you are engaged to each other?"

Again, Bradlee thought. There was nobody he could think of calling who could provide any specific evidence. He had given Lyra his trust and his promise and she the same for him. But no ring was exchanged for want of money and interest in such matters.

The clerk paused and sat back in her chair. "I am sorry, sir, but under the conditions I cannot allow you entry or visitation. The hospital has very strict confidentiality protocols and you do not qualify for medically supportive family access. We cannot allow entry to any visitor unless he or she is the spouse or immediate family member – wife, husband, parent or child. All others are allowed entry only with prior written consent of the patient. The clerk checked in the computer and noted that the patient did not have any listed allowances. Bradlee's name did not fit any acceptable category.

"Here is our standard hospital visitor badge and discount food coupons. You are welcome to remain here in the unit's visitor lounge or in the cafeteria," the clerk added.

Medically supportive family access, Bradlee muttered to himself. *What a euphemism for 'loving care!' Medical jargon, be damned!*

"I understand," was all he could reply. He had run out of options to see Lyra or receive any updates on her medical condition.

Bradlee lingered in the intensive care visitor lounge, hoping to see someone check-in on Lyra's behalf. Perhaps a family member of Lyra's was already informed and on their way to the hospital. He could hardly think straight. Waves of sleepy exhaustion mixed with gnawing shoulder pain as the lidocaine block was wearing off from his procedure in the ER. As time passed in quiet observation, no one arrived seeking entry to visit Lyra. Bradlee exited the lounge and returned to the elevator. He needed some nutrition. The hospital cafeteria was downstairs.

IBRAHIM HAD FINISHED HIS LUNCH and was standing in the hospital lobby, waiting for one of the bank of elevators to bring him upstairs to the intensive care unit.

Bradlee was descending inside an elevator from the ICU lounge to the ground floor. The door opened and Bradlee exited. A tall man with a jet black closely groomed beard, and wearing a long white physician's coat, was standing in front of Bradlee.

"Ibrahim, is that you?" Bradlee called out. The two men

greeted each other warmly. It had been a number of years since they had seen or spoken with each other. Bradlee was careful to maintain his left arm in its proper position in his new sling to avoid further pain.

"Hello, my brother," said Ibrahim. "It's good to see you again."

"And you as well, Ibrahim."

"Baruch! Baruch Avraham Levitsky! It's been a long time, my brother." Ibrahim looked over Bradlee who was disheveled and unshaven with red clay and dried blood stains to his shirt. His hands were wrapped in gauze across his palms.

"What happened to you? You look like you've been in a street brawl," Ibrahim asked with concern. He pointed to Bradlee's sling and facial abrasions and hands.

"I'll be alright. Just had a rough day today trying to save lives," Bradlee replied thinking back to the times he shared with Ibrahim when they were medical students, wet behind the ears with only basic medical knowledge and dreaming of their future surgical careers that lay ahead for them.

"Where are you headed, Baruch?"

"I was hoping to visit someone very important to me upstairs in the intensive care unit. And to receive an update on her care. Her name is Lyra. She had a terrible accident earlier today. I, uh… I did everything I could to try to save her life." Bradlee looked down with pain in his eyes.

"I operated on this patient just a few hours ago, Baruch. She needs to rest now." Ibrahim paused as he looked at Bradlee's exhausted face.

"Baruch, I am headed to the unit now to check on her. Come and join me, old friend."

They rode the elevator together and exited to the unit. Bradlee explained to Ibrahim why he was denied access to the unit over the past number of hours.

"Wait here in the visitor lounge… Let me see what I can do." Ibrahim returned a few minutes later. "Baruch, I can't override access to the unit for you. This security clerk follows hospital policies strictly by the book. You and I both know that if I allowed you entry, under the circumstances, that would be a serious breach of hospital confidentiality policies and my position here would be in jeopardy."

"Ibrahim, listen – you were a class below me and Samia in medical school. And now, look at you – a Neurosurgery fellow doing trauma and critical care rounds here on P.E.I. I'm very proud of you, Ibrahim. You've done well. Your family must be proud."

"Thank you, Baruch. You were the top student in your year. I'm sorry you were not able to finish and move on to your chosen specialty training."

"Ibrahim, we were almost brothers-in-law. I loved Samia with all my heart. And I wish I could take back that night she died in my arms."

"Baruch, I have no anger towards you. I mourned my sister's death for many months, just as you, but she is with Allah now and I am here. We are here until our last day has come as well. Look Baruch, I mean you no harm... Tell me... who is *Lyra Sasha Seashell* to you and tell me about this cliff fall at the lighthouse?"

Bradlee glanced at the ground and then into Ibrahim's patient eyes.

"She is everything to me, Ibrahim. Lyra and I are engaged to be married sometime this spring. And I know this sounds crazy but, for the life of me, I can't recall her last name. It is not '*Seashell*,' that much I can tell you. The hospital must have selected that name for her because she was wearing a beautiful shell necklace when we were rescued off the cliff. A necklace I gave Lyra some months ago when we first met. Lyra and I met on a train four months ago heading west across the country. And then we spoke over the phone and had a few wonderful visits that we shared together and I just never secured her last name in my mind and, eventually, was just too embarrassed to ask her what it was. I figured it would come up, eventually... We were rescued along the cliff edge beside the lighthouse at East Point near my home earlier today. Her bicycle brakes failed and she was catapulted over the railing and down the Cliffside and landed on a ledge... I did everything I could to stabilize her until help arrived in the form of a rescue helicopter that brought us here... Ibrahim, I haven't seen any visitors coming or going to the unit while I was sitting in this ICU lounge. Can you at least tell me if the hospital knows her real last name by now? Any other visitors – any family, friends?"

"There have been none, Baruch. And no, I do not have her last name either to share with you. We have not been informed yet of who she really is. It is my understanding that the police authorities are investigating."

"And her condition, Ibrahim? Please, I love Lyra with all my heart just as I had loved Samia. Please share something with me to give me hope."

Ibrahim looked at his wristwatch and walked over to the clerk to discuss a few matters. Then he returned to Bradlee.

"Come, let us walk together."

He took Baruch into an empty hospital room and they sat in two visitor chairs. Ibrahim leaned over with his elbows on his thighs and placed his hands in a prayerful position.

"Baruch, we will speak as if we are truly physician to physician. I know your knowledge is keen and likely remains very sharp despite these many years away from your studies and your father... Your fiancée has suffered a serious bleed to her subdural space in her brain's occipital region. I evacuated the bleed in the OR and placed a drain tube which remains in place. Her blood pressure has been only mildly unstable post-operatively and she is being maintained on several medications. She has an intracranial monitor in place which has been tracking reassuring pressure readings. She had a brief seizure when I was at her bedside but she stabilized quickly with a sedative bolus. Her brainstem reflexes are intact and she is moderately sedated but her condition remains guarded. She is in a state of coma, most likely from her traumatic fall off the cliff and onto the rocky ledge where you found her but I can't deny that her neurologic state is also partly iatrogenically induced at this moment by her sedative medications… By the way, the CT scans also revealed a nearly complete detachment of her left retina from her posterior globe. The ophthalmologist requested more detailed orbital scans and this specialist is of the opinion that this detachment was not something new but rather from an older traumatic injury that Lyra may have sustained. It is difficult to date when this retinal injury may have occurred. Perhaps if Lyra is able to inform us someday whether this condition was known to her it would help the ophthalmologist in determining if any surgical or laser intervention may be potentially beneficial in reversing her condition. Baruch, Lyra is nearly completely blind in her left eye but her right eye is intact and appears to be in excellent condition. It will remain to be seen whether any parenchymal damage to her occipital lobe may impair her cortical vision. In other words, her right eye may be perfectly normal structurally but her brain, if permanently damaged, may not be able to interpret her visual input properly…"

Bradlee understood the consequences. Lyra could be permanently blind in both eyes.

"Oh – and Lyra also has fractures sustained to her right forearm – radius and ulna – these needed to be aligned in the OR by the orthopedics team. She is casted, of course, but that injury is quite minor in comparison to her brain… And Baruch, I'm not sure if I should tell you this but I will. Your father was visiting here and offering the staff a state-of-the-art grand rounds lecture when the Code Blue was sounded overhead. I asked him to scrub in for Lyra's surgery. Lyra had a life-threatening uterine artery bleed that needed an emergent laparotomy but your father fixed it quickly in his own fastidious way. He's a perfectionist, as you well know, and I've always admired his exceptional skills in the OR... Baruch, Lyra's brain needed urgent intervention in the OR but she would have bled to death on the table before I could finish my work were it not for your father's attention to detail and proper intervention."

Bradlee placed his hand to his forehead and rubbed his tired eyes. *My father? How could that be?* The bitter words he exchanged with Lyra resounded inside his head. *My father turned his back on me. He is a hypocrite...* And yet, did Ibrahim just say that his father had saved Lyra's life? *My Lyra?!* The image conflicted with everything he held against his father for the past five years since Samia had died and he was struck again by a renewed awareness of the coincidences that have occurred over the course of the past four months of his life.

"Does my father know I am here, Ibrahim?"

"No, not unless you had run across each other in the hallways."

"No, we haven't. Is he still here at the hospital now?"

"No. He left a short time ago with your mother to return to your home at East Point. Baruch, he is not aware that the patient he operated on has any connection to you. She is simply a stranger to him. *Lyra Seashell*, that's all. Not that it matters to him. He utilizes his intense intellect and abilities just the same for any human being in the operating room, his personal prayer included afterwards, as you know, at no extra cost. Only his faith that God will listen and help repair those in need. Lyra Seashell is simply an unknown patient from a vast collection of patients he has saved from entering their graves prematurely."

Bradlee digested Ibrahim's information with another wave of astonishment and mixed emotions. "Ibrahim, will Lyra live?"

"Yes, I have faith that she will but it is in Allah's hands. She is young and appears to be in excellent shape, physically. Her prognosis for survival is greater than ninety percent."

"And will she be normal, neurologically speaking?"

"That I don't know yet, Baruch. Only time and excellent care and monitoring will reveal the answer to that. We will see if..." he paused... "After she awakens from her coma. We will have far greater prognostic indicators at that time."

"Can I see her? Just for a moment... Ibrahim, I know my father prays for his patients but that is no longer in my nature to recite words of prayers. But I do believe that we each have a healing energy that can be transferred by touch, by our minds, from one to another. You and I have both seen this with our own eyes. Can you let me into the unit to see her just for a few minutes?"

Ibrahim sighed and held his hands together.

"I think we can arrange that. Go and wash up a bit, get a bite to eat for dinner, and meet me in one hour at the unit's entrance desk. The clerks are on a shift change just now. I will have a word with the new clerk and try to make the arrangements."

"Thank you, Ibrahim." Ibrahim winked at Bradlee and they exited the room.

BRADLEE TOOK THE ELEVATOR TO THE ENTRANCE FLOOR and entered the gift shop. He purchased a travel-size razor, shaving cream, toothbrush and toothpaste, and a hair brush. He added a new shirt and sweater, paid at the register and found the nearest bathroom. He washed his face and shaved and brushed his hair and changed into his new outfit. *'Just in case I'm lucky and Lyra wakes up before my eyes. Perhaps she'll forgive me if at least my appearance is more presentable.'* He knew he wasn't in denial of her condition but he was pleading in his mind for her survival and recovery. Then his mind felt a sense of detachment. As if Lyra was a patient and he was the doctor trying to analyze and discern, calculate and adjust. A professional approach that had survived the test of time. The doctor-patient relationship. Why did it survive in this detached fashion? he wondered. Because it works. Because a doctor's emotions cannot interfere with the cold truths of the body as a machine, an unstable often dysfunctional collection of parts that fails us with sickness or the depravity of aging. The cruelty of nature and the fragility of our own life form. Our bodies vulnerable to the slightest of insufficiencies or diseases or genetic programming errors. Bradlee knew an intensive care patient on a ventilator was largely the modern story of humans vs. machines; rarely was there a patient who could talk and walk who belonged in an ICU bed. No, they were discarded when able to breathe on their own accord and then quickly transferred to the walking sick units until they were well enough to return home or perish.

But he and Lyra shared a bond that transcended bells and whistles from machines. He needed to touch her again and exert whatever force of will that he could provide. To reenergize her spirit like a movie superhero. Or just hold her again in his arms, if only he could, and whisper that he loved her more than ever. That he would take care of her regardless of her condition. Neurologically intact or not. Able to speak or hear or see, or not. It didn't matter.

Love transcends all of these. Love is the acceptance that life has its way of smacking one human being in the head and then leaving the other - the loving partner who is the luckier one – to deal with the consequences and accept nature's lot, he thought. *And provide for the one who is the less fortunate. Until when, Bradlee? Until when does the providing stop? Yes – until the end. That's right. Until the end comes. James knew that with his Sweet Caroline.*

Thomas had his scare with Nancy's stroke and now I know that. It's my turn now with Lyra. God help us.

And then Bradlee walked outside to the sun-setting evening and he sat on a bench and he cried. And cried more. For all the good and the evil and the bad shit that happens for no God damn good reason. For his father's rejection of Bradlee's first love and his mother's complicity. For Samia's no damn good reason to die in his arms. For Lyra's punishing abuse in Seattle when he could do nothing to stop it from happening. And then his mind went silent. He stared at the clouds and thought of Ruthy. Such purity in childhood. Laughter. Goodness. He had that too as a young child. When love was the simple gestures offered by a dear mother or father or uncle. He had no siblings. No one he could share his childhood with. But he had friends then. And he has new ones now. But they are far away in North Dakota. Lyra was his friend and lover and his everything. She needed him to be strong for her now. And he would do just that.

Bradlee wiped his eyes. He was hungry. He walked over to the food trucks. Pasta did not sound appetizing. Nor did a burrito or Pad Thai or Indian curry. There was a Chinese food cart. He would order vegetarian in Lyra's honor. Maybe it was time he changed his ways and did his part to leave the animals alone. *Did they not have souls just like his?* He ordered an assortment of vegetables with fried rice. He devoured it. It was light fare yet filling. The sun was performing its magical light show as the clouds were lit from beneath in pink and rosy hues. He finished his dish and glanced at the takeout bag. He pulled out a fortune cookie. *Why not open it?* Maybe something will make sense out of this week of near-life and near-death experiences. He cracked it open and ate the sweet sugary cookie. He held the message in his hand and prayed in Hebrew. The prayer his father taught him when he was a young child. Then he repeated it in Arabic as Samia had taught him. A prayer for God to heal the sick. He said it again and again. And when he had exhausted his mind from prayer and looked quietly at the sky and the clouds he opened the paper and read his fortune:

Nothing is Impossible to a Willing Heart.

Bradlee pocketed the message and walked inside the hospital. He took the elevator to the intensive care unit. He met Ibrahim at the clerk's desk and he was escorted by Ibrahim to Lyra's bedside, no questions asked further of him. They stood there together as Bradlee cupped Lyra's left hand into his and felt her warmth. The ventilator was steady and undeniably monotonous but Bradlee sat beside Lyra and stared at her. Her chest rising and falling just the same as the hummingbird who flew into his outstretched palm that morning at the Lady Slipper Inn and settled quietly, trustingly in his hand. Slow breaths. Calming. Lyra was eternally beautiful. His Daphne reincarnated. That would never change regardless of whether she could never see herself again in the mirror. He began to cry.

Be strong, Bradlee. You must be strong for her.

He looked at Lyra for a long time as the nurse departed and gave them privacy. Ibrahim stood in the curtain's shadow. Bradlee leaned over and held his forehead to Lyra's. He wanted to transfer that eternal energy. That bright star that Kin spoke of.

Love. It is what we human beings call it. But what is love but the eternal and infinite understanding of all living things in the entire universe. And that awareness always resides deep within us if we focus on it and accept it.

But there was more. Bradlee knew…

Love of two souls. And all souls. Where there is no past, present, or future. Time disappearing into meaninglessness.

Love. The positive force in the universe that serves as the interconnection of all things. Yes. Yes! – That is love. And love is the only thing that has ever mattered or ever will.

He concentrated. A tender warmth rose from his heart and expanded and encompassed all of his mind and then it began to seep from him and out the surface of his forehead and he sent it inside of Lyra, forehead to forehead. He transferred that message to her willing heart.

Lyra, nothing is impossible to a willing heart. Nothing is impossible to a willing heart. Nothing. Everything is possible…….

"Baruch, it is time," Ibrahim said softly.

Bradlee lingered against Lyra's forehead and then he kissed her above each eye.

"Yes, I know… Thank you, Ibrahim. She's going to be alright… Before I go, Ibrahim, I wanted to show you something." Ibrahim approached.

"May I borrow your pen light?" Bradlee asked.

Ibrahim handed it to Bradlee from his white coat pocket. Bradlee turned out the overhead lights in Lyra's cubicle. He opened Lyra's right eyelid and shined the light for Ibrahim to see. Her pupil was perfectly round and constricted normally by the light and then dilated as he moved the pen light away. He moved to her left eye.

"Look, Ibrahim, your trauma team may have overlooked this. Bradlee shined the light into Lyra's left eye and the coloboma was evident to see. The pupil constricted and dilated just the same but the iris coloboma was there.

"Ibrahim. I've been aware of Lyra's coloboma jutting inferomedially since the moment I laid my eyes on her. Did you or your neurosurgical colleagues or the ophthalmologist detect it on physical examination of your patient?"

"No, Baruch. I didn't notice it, myself. The ophthalmologist only looked at Lyra's CT scan images. The ones that showed Lyra's left retinal detachment. They were going to examine her when she was more stable post-operatively."

"Well, I wonder now if she's always had her retinal detachment. Since birth, perhaps. We will know when she awakens, God willing. And I have faith that she will, now that you have given me the chance to be with her again. And her coloboma, to me, is probably her one and only defect. What humanizes her to me. That makes me realize she is vulnerable and needs my love. I feel something when I touch her forehead. As if she too has lived with deep pain from loss. But her coloboma, to me, is the window to her soul and we have only begun on our journey together. Please take good care of her... And Ibrahim, I will always be sorry for losing Samia. I shouldn't lose you as a friend as well. No - we were meant to be brothers. I'd very much like to have a brother in my life again."

Ibrahim put his arm around Bradlee's neck and embraced him.

"Baruch, the word 'like' does not describe what two brothers should always share – and that is love. Brotherly love. You and I both have the same willing heart, Baruch. And so it shall be as you wish for us again. I have wished for it too these many years learning from your father. You and I are as two brothers from the same father."

They exited the unit together. Ibrahim informed Bradlee that he would be departing to India with his wife and daughter, Samia, in a few hours. He explained to Bradlee that Samia was named after Bradlee's fiancée and Ibrahim's dear sister who perished. Bradlee hugged Ibrahim and held him close. Ibrahim handed his key to the physicians' on-call overnight quarters at the hospital. He wouldn't be needing it for the next three weeks anyway while in India. With this access, Bradlee would be able to sleep and shower in the hospital as he wished and remain close to Lyra even if he couldn't visit her at her bedside.

"Oh, and Baruch, I spoke with your father just before you arrived to the unit tonight to visit Lyra. I mentioned to him that I had run into you at the hospital and that you had a patient admitted here who you cared for deeply and wished to visit but were denied access. I did not mention the patient's name. And then I handed my phone to the clerk parked outside the unit and your father made the arrangements to grant you access to whichever patient you needed. Your father has that kind of respect here at this hospital and across the medical community in Toronto, and across P.E.I… Baruch, give your father a chance. He seeks your forgiveness after these many years apart. He has changed in ways you don't realize. Good ways. Decent. More accepting. More compassionate. And I suspect you two truly wish to find a way to make peace together."

THE PHONE RANG AT THE MARSHPILLOW MAIN RESIDENCE. Jenny and Nathaniel were relaxing, quietly chatting in the living room and reading the newspaper. The shattered picture frame had unsettled them on arrival earlier in the evening but Jenny cleaned up the mess and restored order as she was used to doing over the past many years. The thought of Bradlee smashing the frame troubled her and she wondered whether that was how the mess really happened.

Bradlee's engagement announcement weighed on Jenny's mind as she prepared the cup of wine and Friday evening Sabbath candles for lighting. The two men in her life that she most dearly loved – her husband and only son – were as divided as the Red Sea. Try as she had over the past five years, she was exasperated in her attempts to bring them together and make peace. It just wasn't right and she wondered what the loss of shared time would mean when the day arrived and she and Nathaniel would become grandparents. She dreamed of being a loving and dutiful grandmother when Bradlee was ready to settle down and start a family. She wished he would find new happiness to lighten his often somber moods whenever he was near her for brief visits if his father wasn't also present. The division was an ever-present burden to carry for all involved. Hearts that were shackled by family strife and the simple undeniable stubbornness that stood defiantly between their stoic defenses or the alternative – a hope for a détente that could bring happiness, joviality, the sharing of time, and God willing, a return to love.

Jenny answered the call. "Shabbat Shalom, Jenny." It was Uncle Eddie. He was calling just before the Sabbath was to begin.

"Eliezer Levitsky, what a nice surprise! How is everything by you?" Jenny asked.

"Baruch Hashem, thank God, all is well. I have some good news to share with you and my brother. I spoke with Baruch yesterday when he called me from his airport layover in Toronto. He mentioned to me that he was recently engaged."

"Yes, Eliezer. Baruch informed me this morning when we spoke by phone but we haven't yet had the chance to meet Lyra."

Nathaniel's ears perked up from the paper. *Lyra?* It was the same name as the trauma patient that he performed lifesaving surgery on earlier in the day. And restored her fertility. It was an unusual name. Quite beautiful, as he thought about its origins from mythology. *Lyra, the harp. Majestic enough that a constellation was named, Lyra. Perhaps a mere coincidence*, he presumed.

"Jenny, may I speak to my brother?" Uncle Eddie kindly asked.

"Yes, of course. He's right beside me."

"It's your brother, the concerned Rabbi," Jenny whispered to Nathaniel with a wink. Nathaniel accepted the phone.

"Rabbi Eliezer, how *is* my younger and only brother? Good Shabbos to you as well," Nathaniel said with joviality.

"All is well, thank God. Nathaniel... Listen – I tried to reach you earlier today but was unsuccessful. I haven't got much time now before the Sabbath begins. I spoke with Baruch from the airport in Toronto. He is engaged to be married, Nathaniel, as I'm sure Jenny has informed you by now. He sounded well to me and in fine spirits. I'm not sure if you were informed about his recent small plane crash on the runway in North Dakota?"

"No? Is he OK?" Nathaniel focused.

"He told me he had some minor injuries, that's all. Nathaniel, do you remember my childhood friend, Ben Cohen, the doctor in North Dakota who I mentioned to you at times before?"

"Yes, of course."

"Ben relayed to me the story of what happened as he heard it from his friend, Jim Clayburn. Jim's the Chief of the Indian tribal council on the reservation near Minot where Ben started his career years ago... Nathaniel – from what Ben told me, your son saved the lives of three people in that plane crash. One of those lives was a young boy, the Chief's grandson. You should be very proud of Baruch."

Nathaniel listened. "I am, Eliezer. I always knew my son had a good soul."

"*Has* a good soul, Nathaniel. Thank God, Baruch is alive and well... Your son was in North Dakota for a gallery exhibit of his photography work. Apparently, it was very successful. I am very proud of his artistry, Nathaniel. You know my nephew holds a dear place in my heart for all these years since I was the Sandek for his Bris. I welcomed him then in my arms, as a newborn being circumcised into the traditions of our Jewish faith."

"Yes, I remember the day well, like it was yesterday, Eliezer," Nathaniel said.

"Our tradition states that as we welcome a Jewish boy to the faith of our ancestors, we offer three blessings, Nathaniel: for this boy to grow to manhood fulfilled by the teachings of the Torah; for him to find eternal love as he reaches his wedding day; and that his heart and soul commits to a worthy life filled with the performance of good deeds."

"Yes, Eliezer, these are beautiful blessings in our tradition."

"And did you not name your own son, Baruch, because of your faith that God had finally blessed you and Jenny with an only child in your later years – just as God did the same for our patriarch and matriarch, Avraham Avinu and Sarah?"

Nathaniel was wondering what the purpose of his brother's sermon was for the approaching eve of Shabbat. But they *were* beautiful words. Pure.

"Nathaniel, Baruch expressed his remorse to me on the phone about your lack of connection. His heart still hurts as I know yours does too. He had tears in his eyes when I saw him in North Dakota some months ago and he and I spoke quietly. Even with the passage of time, you cannot deny your bonds as father and son. Baruch needs your understanding. Your compassion, Nathaniel. He has found a new love and he deserves peace and happiness after his tragic loss of Samia... Nathaniel, I know in my heart that Baruch wants to forgive you and you must forgive and accept him for who he is and desires for his own sake. His life journey is his own now as a young man. He is responsible for what he chooses to believe or not from our shared faith. Baruch is not you, although he favors your intellect and gifted hands. He has his mother's heart, though. A loving woman, Jenny has always been. Nathaniel

– listen to me. Find a way to reach out to your son. Not just to hear him but to really listen. To know your son as you have not before. It is time for forgiveness. For both of you to forgive. So that we can forget the troubled past and replace those memories with many loving ones ahead. I ask this of you as your only brother."

Nathaniel had tears rolling from his eyes as his heart winced with the pain that only a father can feel for the loss of his son. And Baruch had gone so far as to even deny his birth name. First and last. Further embarrassment to him and his own mother. Nathaniel knew enough from others that Baruch had taken an alias – '*Bradlee Lee*,' over the past five years, even if he still cashed birthday checks from his parents as Baruch A. Levitsky. He hadn't yet changed his legal name with the authorities – that much his father knew. But Baruch was still his son and he was alive and well. His soul in the present, inside his youthful body. His vitality in full bloom if only he could see Baruch with his own eyes. Nathaniel closed his eyes and prayed quietly as Eliezer waited. It was time for new beginnings.

"Eliezer, I do live with pain, every day. You are a wise brother. And I have made mistakes raising my son. I know that now. It is painful. But I will make a promise to you, on our Shabbos candles, that I will go and find him and seek his forgiveness. I can only pray that he still wishes to reconcile with me… May I ask you a favor, Eliezer? Please talk to Baruch and let him know that I wish to meet if I don't see him first."

"I will, Nathaniel. Good Shabbos. My love to you and Jenny."

They hung up. Nathaniel departed from the room after hugging his wife. He walked down the hallway and stood at the entrance of Baruch's old bedroom. Then, he stared at the memories covering his son's walls.

BRADLEE NEEDED SOME FRESH AIR. His energy level seemed depleted after his conscious gift of love and healing that he offered as his forehead touched Lyra's. He took the elevator to the ground floor, exited the hospital, and walked down the entrance road. He crossed over Murchison Lane and noticed a walking path along the water's edge. The inlet was calm and the air crisp with the scent of expectant snowfall. He strolled along the path and then found a bench to sit and observe the water in solitude. Away from ventilators and bleeping monitors. Memories of his father came to him. Good memories from childhood. Innocence. His father tossing him into the ocean and teaching him how to balance on his first two-wheeled bicycle. Bradlee had played the role of a doctor in a primary school play and his father's face was there in the audience, beaming with pride. He recalled his Bar-Mitzvah. Bradlee had studied well and his father placed his tallit over his head and blessed Bradlee and kissed his head with so much pride. *What had gone wrong since then?* - From the moment his childhood quickly melted into young adulthood and his father became stricter; a disciplinarian requiring perfection from his son. An unswerving urgency for Bradlee to dedicate his years ahead towards one goal – to become a physician, just as his father had chosen and so many others had chosen in the Levitsky line.

Bradlee's mind returned to Lyra. He still hadn't been able to recall her real last name. The investigator would be contacting him soon and he needed more information. Knowing Lyra's name certainly wouldn't hurt his cause. *What man doesn't know his fiancée's last name, for goodness sake?!* He admitted his story would be implausible to believe. He worried. The 'what ifs' returned and were sharply poking at his gut as if they were like needles entering his flesh.

'*Needles*' – wait... '*Needles*,' he repeated to himself. Lyra's needlepoint. "That's it!" he cried out. Lyra's farewell gift to him when they first stayed at the Lady Slipper Inn. "She sewed her initials into the needlepoint!" he shouted to himself. The needlepoint remained framed by his bedside at the Marshpillow. *What was her last initial? Think, Bradlee. Think.*

L, S, …… but his memory failed him once again. He dialed his mother's cell phone and she answered. "Mom, I need you to go to my bedroom…" He gave her instructions for what she needed to locate. She found Lyra's needlepoint.

"Baruch, it's very beautiful. Lyra is very talented!"

"Mom, please. It's important. Just tell me the letters at the bottom right-hand corner. What are they?"

She read them. "She sewed three letters, Baruch: L, S, and F, with a heart at each end."

"Thanks mom! Love you. We'll chat again soon."

Bradlee quickly focused his memory to the train. *The letter 'F.' What was her last name? I know she told me.* He pressed his arms to the sides of his head and tried to squeeze out the memory. *Lyra – Sasha – F…. Gosh, nothing.* He punched his chest in frustration. *Where did she say she grew up?* He closed his eyes and focused again on the scene in the train. He replayed as much as he could in his mind as they sat diagonally across from each other. *She said she summered on the beach on P.E.I. with her family… from where? Think.* Connecticut popped in his mind. *She told me that Dr. Bonheim once taught at Yale University close to where she had lived in her childhood. The 'shoreline,'* she said. She must have lived somewhere along the shoreline outside of New Haven. He entered 'Lyra Sasha F, Shoreline Connecticut' into his phone's search bar but nothing linked of any value to solve the mystery.

Bradlee next ran through names. Anyone he might know who lived in Connecticut. There was Ezra, his once closest childhood friend from primary school. They had grown up together and entered as medical school classmates in the same class in Toronto, sharing the same dream of becoming physicians. Bradlee had fallen out of touch with Ezra when he chose to drop out of medical school. His friendship with Ezra another casualty of Bradlee's desire to leave his past behind after Samia's death. He remembered that Ezra had accepted a residency in pediatrics at Yale-New Haven Hospital. Perhaps he took a job in the region after he finished his three years of general pediatrics residency? Or he may have stayed on at Yale to specialize further. Ezra loved children. A natural fit to be a pediatrician if ever there was one. To Bradlee, Ezra seemed to permanently have one foot seemingly stuck in the quicksand of childhood innocence and he knew Ezra had no interest in ever removing it. Bradlee dialed Ezra's number that he still had saved in his phone's contact list.

"Yo bro! What's up, Baruch?" Ezra answered the call as if he had seen Bradlee just a few minutes ago. Immediately, Bradlee knew he missed Ezra's childish humor and manners of speech.

"Ezra. Great to hear your voice!"

"Well – I'm getting ready to shit, shower, and shave. Have a hot date tonight, Baruch. Hope *your* love life has improved lately, bro." Ezra was referring to Bradlee's depression and detachment after Samia's death and Bradlee knew it.

"I'm very happy for you, Ezra." Bradlee raised his voice to a falsetto pitch: '*Don't forget to brush your teeth, Ezra!*'" Bradlee teased him as if he was Ezra's loving, but sometimes nagging, Jewish mother.

"Good comeback, bro," Ezra said in a deep but playful voice. "You been cycling lately, Baruch?"

"From time to time. Hoping to head over to Europe someday for the next leg around the world. You interested in joining me?"

"That would be cool, bro – we'll see if I can get a block

of time off. Tougher as we get older. Damn adult responsibilities. Better to be kids. This growing up thing really sucks, bro."

"Agreed," Bradlee added.

"Ezra – I was hoping I could ask you a favor. I need help locating a certain name – someone's last name."

"Why, you in trouble? Or are you a detective now after dropping out of med school?"

"Neither. There's a certain friend I was hoping you could help me locate. I need her last name, actually. No dark motives. Only good. She grew up somewhere along the Connecticut shoreline near New Haven. I was hoping you could, maybe, visit some of the local high schools and see if you can find a match from yearbook graduation photos. Searching online is getting me nowhere."

"Sounds like you sure are a detective, Baruch, but also sounds like fun. I think I can swing it. What's this girl's first name and what year do you think she graduated from high school?"

"Her name is Lyra. Lyra Sasha… something. I just need her last name. All I know is her last name starts with the letter F. Look Ezra, I'll be straight up with you. Lyra's sick and in the hospital and nobody's come to visit yet from her family and I'm trying to reach anyone I can. But I need her last name to try to locate any family members." Bradlee and Ezra tried to guess Lyra's likely age and high school graduation year and agreed to a realistic range of dates to search.

"Got it, bro. The shoreline covers a handful of towns east of New Haven. You're lucky I've got a few more days off for the New Year holiday break from work. I've got some time tomorrow morning. I'll see what I can find and give you a call back… Hey Baruch, this Lyra chick. I can tell from your voice. Is she as sweet as a lollipop treat?"

"She sure is, Ezra. You can add a huge scoop of vanilla ice cream with maple syrup. No… better than that, a generous slice of your mom's chocolate chip sour cream cake…! Hey – thanks old friend! Sure hope the kids in your pediatric office are loving you."

"I love 'em back, bro. I'm always goin' to be a glass half-full kind of kid at heart! You know that better than anyone. Later dude." They hung up.

Bradlee peered at the inlet. The water was still and the moon reflected a long silvery line across the surface. It was as if Lyra's tapestry needle was pointing him in the right direction all along. He just needed to open his eyes and see how the threads connected. He strolled back along the same path as snow flurries began to fall. He tasted a few as he stuck out his tongue and then remembered that sensation from when he was a young child – the first snowflakes of winter when he would run outside to experience that exciting tingling sensation on the tip of his tongue. He reached out his hand and a single snowflake landed in his palm. He watched its metamorphosis - from a solid weightless fragile thing of intense and unique beauty, into a formless shapeless droplet of clear liquid. Bradlee reflected. He had also been transformed over the course of the past four months. He had opened his heart again to love another woman. *Maybe it was also time to revisit my relationship with my father.* He sipped the droplet of water and then reached out his hand to collect some more melted snowflakes to quench his thirst. He returned to the hospital, reinvigorated by the possibility of change despite his physical exhaustion. He found Ibrahim's overnight on-call room and fell into a deep sleep.

"HEY, WAKE UP, BRO!" Bradlee had answered his buzzing phone and checked his watch. It was already eleven a.m. He had slept more than twelve hours straight.

"Ezra – how's the search going?"

"I found her, man! That's why I'm calling you now! I've been running around the shoreline area like a kid flying a kite on the beach. Crazy! But, I drove up to Old Saybrook High School and then started working my way back towards New Haven. Nothing at Old Saybrook. Then Westbrook, Clinton, and Madison. Nothing in those spots either. I was getting discouraged when I walked into Guilford High School. At first, the librarian wouldn't let me take a look at the stacks since I wasn't an alumnus of the school but I revved up the charm index, man, and handed this chick a seashell that I found along the beach in Madison where I stopped for a late breakfast – figured if seashells always worked for you to charm the ladies then I might as well try it myself – and, what d'ya know!, she got all smiley and melty chocolatey smushy, then loosey goosey with me and led me over to the stacks herself. I was in, dude! She helped me locate a mishmash of yearbooks. Actually, she thought this whole detective chase thing was kind of cool. Romantic, really. Anyway, this librarian chick was real cute, about my age, so I got her phone number and we're going to go out later tonight to…."

"Ezra, did you find her. Did you find Lyra's picture?"

"Oh sorry, bro. Back to business – Yup, sure did! So this librarian chick and I – we flipped through pages and pages together of the high school senior classes. And there it was, her picture staring right at me on top of her name! **Lyra Sasha Flurey**. I took a picture of her photo with my phone. I'm sending it to you right now…" Bradlee waited for a few intense seconds.

"Got it!" Bradlee opened the text. It was Lyra alright. Her last name was '*Flurey*.' *Of course!* It all came rushing back to him now from the train. Flurey – like snow flurries on the tip of his tongue from last night! He laughed at the coincidence in his mind and promised to never forget her last name – ever again. Lyra Sasha Flurey was like his

Snow White, asleep but not in her own princessly bed. She was in a hospital in critical condition. If only he could place one snow flurry to her lips and then kiss them gently – perhaps Lyra would awaken from her deep slumber as he aroused her to life again. The waves of guilt returned and crashed against his chest. His foolishness arguing with Lyra over anger with his father that preceded her desire to run from him. And then, her fall off the cliff. Bradlee stared at Lyra's photo. She was incredibly beautiful then in high school but even more so now that she had matured even further. She was just a slightly younger version of her current self. An innocence about her. She was smiling through her shiny braces. Bradlee looked closely at her eyes. There it was. The coloboma in her left iris.

"Ezra, I can't thank you enough for what you've done for me!"

"Hey man, that's not all I found. So this librarian and I were curious and we checked through the rest of the yearbook. Turns out, this Lyra chick was her class Valedictorian. Numero uno, man! She's a foxy lady alright, but she's also got to be as smart as a whip!"

"She sure is both, Ezra... OK, I must tell you. Lyra's my fiancée. I'm in love with her."

Ezra thought it was odd that Baruch didn't know her last name but he didn't press further.

"Couldn't have figured that out, dude. Man, I remember like it was yesterday when we were little and couldn't stand girls!" Ezra laughed, sarcastically. "Well, I'm really happy for you, Baruch. I know you deserve Lyra after everything you've gone through."

"Thanks again, Ezra."

"Anytime, bro... Hey... Baruch, personal question between old friends... How do you know when you find the right one? It hasn't really clicked for me yet, you know."

"Hmm... I think it's when you realize that everything

happens for a reason. I don't think coincidences happen for no reason at all. When you meet the right one, you'll know Ezra. Just trust your heart and take the leap when it feels right."

"Will do. Thanks man. Hope to see you again soon, Baruch. Maybe at your wedding?" Ezra laughed.

"Sounds great. Sure hope so. You'll get the first invitation mailed out!"

"I'd like that, old friend."

Bradlee ended the call. He stared again at Lyra's yearbook photo. He showered and shaved quickly, dressed, and then sat down at the computer workstation in the on-call room and started searching on the internet. He entered in the search bar: 'Lyra Sasha Flurey, Guilford, Connecticut, Valedictorian' and his chest tightened.

THE POLICE DETECTIVE STOOD IN THE EAST POINT LIGHTHOUSE parking lot and studied the crime scene. He walked over to the guard rail and noted some paint scrapes and a few dents in the metal barrier. He stepped over the barrier and walked to the edge of the cliff. There were fresh markings of disturbed rock and red sandstone dirt as the cliff plunged deeply. He peered over and couldn't see any evidence of where the victim may have landed below but there were a few good shoe prints at the top of the cliff. He asked his deputy to take some photos and measurements of them. They'd return later in the morning to make a casted impression of them and see if they matched either the victim's shoes or the suspected assailant's – a Mr. Baruch Avraham Levitsky. Then they hammered a few stakes into the frozen ground and ran some yellow tape across the crime scene.

The detective, Gordon McCallum, had been with the

Royal Canadian Mounted Police for almost twenty-five years. He had transferred to the police headquarters in Charlottetown, P.E.I. just a few years earlier, after spending nearly his entire career in the hustle of Toronto. He figured P.E.I. would be laid back, a way to ease into retirement. Mostly petty crime and domestic violence cases. But, rarely any severe crimes, let alone homicides, out in these parts. He thought he had seen it all by now over the course of his career. But, as he stared over the cliff top and out to the ocean, he realized this scene was about as dramatic a location as a potential homicide could be. A cliffhanger better suited for a blockbuster Hollywood movie than for this quiet corner of Prince Edward Island in the winter time. The investigation would be a real nuisance, he thought. Probably three or four weeks, at the minimum, trying to drum up all the facts and collect enough evidence to make his case for a prosecution of the suspect. One young lady dead five years earlier, another on life support. The thought of this man walking free irritated him. *That*, he knew in his gut. Enough to do his job the same professional way he was trained and carried it out all these many years.

Detective McCallum and his deputy got back into the police cruiser and slowly, they retraced the bicycle path back to the Marshpillow home. The only evidence they could see were the tire treads from two different bicycles. The deputy took some more tread photos and measurements. Mr. McCallum had already interviewed the elderly couple. The retirees next door to the Marshpillow had called the police with a tip after watching the news about the helicopter rescue along the cliff. They described a young man chasing after a young woman. They identified the suspect as Baruch Levitsky, who they had known, affectionately, since he was a young boy but that he rarely was friendly to them over the past many years of his adulthood. He lived alone most of the time at the Marshpillow home, they said. And they rarely saw any other visitors come and go while he was present. And the young lady – she was crying and pedaling away from him as fast as she could on the morning of her demise. They said to the detective that Baruch was angry and screaming at the young lady with rage in his eyes. And then Mr. Levitsky began to chase after the young lady and he glared back at them, standing beside the mailbox on their mid-morning walkabout, to the point that the older woman was as distraught as she had ever recalled from fear for the safety of this young woman, if not for her husband and herself as well.

The detectives arrived to the Marshpillow driveway, parked at the entrance and surveyed the surroundings for any possible clues. They glanced inside the shed room. There were two other bicycles hanging from rafter hooks The deputy continued with further photos and measurements. Perhaps these bicycles matched the same models as found at the crime scene at the lighthouse.

Detective McCallum rang the doorbell and then knocked on the front door to the main house. Jenny answered.

"Good morning, ma'am."

"Good morning, gentlemen." She noted the police vehicle in the driveway.

"We are detectives from the RCMP looking for a Mr. Baruch Levitsky for questioning. Is this his residence?" Detective McCallum opened his badge for the woman to see.

"Yes, I'm his mother, Jenny. But our son isn't home right now. We expected to see him last night for dinner with his fiancée but he wasn't home when we arrived and we haven't seen him this morning either. I was hoping when you rang that it was Baruch at the entrance just now. But it's nice to meet you, officers. Please come inside from the cold. I will go and fetch my husband, Dr. Nathaniel Levitsky, to have him join us."

They settled in the living room and Jenny brought a fresh pot of hot coffee with an assortment of biscuits for the officers. They appreciated her kindness. Jenny found Nathaniel. He was in the home office reviewing a draft of his latest journal article for submission to be published in the Annals of Trauma Surgery. He decided to write-up the surgical case he had just completed in Charlottetown: "A young woman with blunt trauma presenting with an unusual case of a ruptured uterine artery: Approaches to acute management with attention to intraoperative pelvic anatomy." Jenny interrupted his writing and they returned together and sat down across from the officers.

"Dr. Levitsky, thank you for joining us. I'm Detective Gordon McCallum and my partner here is Will Tatum. We're from the RCMP based in Charlottetown. We're here as part of an investigation involving your son, Baruch Avraham Levitsky."

"What kind of investigation, detective?" Nathaniel said.

"Domestic violence, sir. Possible homicide if the victim doesn't survive her traumatic injuries. Mr. Levitsky had a prior incident some years ago that resulted in the death of a young woman. That case was closed and believed to have been a purely accidental death due to a tree fall at a shelter site in the mountains. But this case involves a young woman as well so we are quite concerned that your son is not what you might think he is in this community."

"Are you saying you are suspecting our son tried to murder either of these women?

"I can't say that for sure. I suspect the evidence we collect will help a judge and jury make those decisions either way."

Nathaniel and Jenny clasped their hands together and squeezed them tightly.

"Officers, my son and I... well, we haven't spoken in a number of years. His mother is in communication with him from time to time. We do love him despite our family's challenges. I have no reason to suspect any foul play on my son's part."

"I understand your concern. But I will need to interview him very soon. He has a right to legal representation, of course, but I do have the right to bring him to the station for further questioning and issue a search warrant to this property and an arrest warrant if we have reason to believe he is evading the law. Do you happen to know where we might find him now?"

"We don't know," Jenny replied as tears began to well in her eyelids. Nathaniel remained silent.

"Ma'am, I know this is all difficult to hear. We are not directly accusing your son of murder or any other crime. He is a suspect needed for further questioning, that's all at this moment. Now, what I can tell you is that he was discharged from the emergency room at Queen Elizabeth Hospital in Charlottetown yesterday afternoon. There was an incident at the cliff over at the East Point Lighthouse. I'm sure you know the spot down the road. His fiancée, a Ms. Lyra Sasha Seashell..." Nathaniel's eyes widened. "...had an apparent bicycle accident and went off the cliff. Your son's story is that he chased after her, climbed down the cliff side, and tried to rescue her. An emergency services helicopter collected them and flew them to Charlottetown. Your son sustained relatively minor injuries but Ms. Lyra Seashell is in intensive care with a number of serious medical concerns."

"Officer, I was at the hospital yesterday afternoon offering a lecture to the medical staff. I'm a trauma surgeon and professor in Toronto. I was asked to operate on an acute trauma case flown in by helicopter and was eventually informed of her presumed identity. That's her name sir. I took care of this patient until I signed out to the hospital staff and we arrived here last night."

Thoughts raced through Nathaniel's mind. Lyra Seashell. Baruch's fiancée, as Jenny had informed him.

Impossible! It couldn't be! But then, the irony of the moment. His strained and fragile relationship with his only child. A chance for good to come from all of this. But Baruch – he couldn't accept that his son was to blame for Lyra's suffering. Or for Samia's, years ago. That was not the child he and Jenny had raised with the kindness of his soul and empathy for others that were always his nature.

"Then let me suggest that you try to contact your son as soon as possible. The RCMP will be patient but we expect Baruch to be available here, at this location within forty-eight hours. Otherwise, we will issue an arrest warrant for him. Is that understood?"

"Yes detective," Jenny said glumly. "We will do our best to reach him and have him join us here. Our son is not who you think he is."

"I understand. These are difficult matters to deal with... Here is my card. You can reach me once you hear from your son. Detective Tatum and I will be in the immediate area for the next few hours before we head back to Charlottetown this evening. Please call me once you locate your son... And ma'am, thank you for the hot coffee and biscuits."

They departed.

Nathaniel and Jenny closed the front door and tried to fit the pieces of the puzzle together in their minds.

AT THE TOP OF THE SEARCHES, Bradlee clicked on the internet link. It was an obituary published in the Guilford Courier newspaper dated three days after Lyra's high school graduation. There was a photo of Lyra beside a teenage boy on one side of the page. On the other, a few photos of older family members. He read the story:

Community Mourns Loss of Stony Creek Family in Tragic House Fire

On the night of June 28th a fire rapidly swept though the Flurey family residence on Leetes Island Road in Stony Creek. Fire trucks from Stony Creek and Guilford stations raced to the scene but the family home was engulfed in flames by the time the firefighters arrived. At present, the fire marshal's investigation suspects that an electrical source is to blame, possibly due to an overloaded circuit in the basement.

Survivors include the family's two children, Lyra Sasha Flurey, who was not at home at the time of the fire, and her brother, Jared Chaim Flurey, who managed to escape from the basement. Ms. Flurey, who had graduated just earlier that afternoon from Guilford High School as class Valedictorian, reported that the family had been in the midst of renovating the upstairs kitchen and bathrooms and that she and her brother had moved downstairs to the basement temporarily.

Family members who perished include the parents of Lyra and Jared - the late Christopher Flurey and his wife, Leah Shem-Tov Flurey; tragically, the grandparents of the surviving children, who were visiting the family in honor of Lyra's graduation, also perished in the fire. The late grandparents include: Rabbi Yehoshua Shem-Tov and Leora ("Lyra") Mazel Shem-Tov of Jerusalem, Israel; and Henry and Emma Flurey of Seattle, WA. Of note, Lyra Mazel Shem-Tov was a Holocaust survivor and descendant of the 18th century Jewish mystic, Rabbi Israel ben Eliezer, known amongst Jewish scholars and Kabbalists as the 'Baal Shem Tov,' who has long been considered the founder of Hasidic Judaism.

In lieu of flowers, the children kindly request that community donations be sent in honor of those who perished to the Marshland Habitat Restoration Society, a non-profit organization in Guilford where Mrs. Leah Shem-Tov Flurey volunteered and served as the director over the last twenty years of her life.

A community service will be held at the Temple Beth Tikvah Synagogue in Madison on Wednesday evening at 7:00 p.m. and a candle lighting vigil will be at the First Congregational Church on Sunday morning followed by scattering of the ashes at the Stony Creek pavilion beside the water.

Bradlee slumped in his chair, bowed his head, and wept. He cried for Lyra and for the family members he would never know. Her line was wiped out in one terrifying moment. *Why didn't she tell me about this tragedy?* But Bradlee understood. Sometimes burying the pain from losing loved ones is best not shared when new love is blooming inside. He was just as guilty of that as Lyra was, not revealing Samia's loss until months later.

We all die eventually. He understood that harsh reality of finality. *Yes, some by fire and others by disease or the cruel frailties of old age. But the vigor of youth denies that life has an end. Only new beginnings await, events and wonders that seem endlessly available from one breath to the next. Eternal love must not die. It simply can't ever be extinguished. The soul must live on and rejoin the greater universe and then it is reborn and we live again and learn something new each time, discover our true soulmate if we are fortunate and that soulmate enriches us even more until we don't need to return anymore. We join the light of the universe. Where the harps are plucked and happiness and only goodness and kindness rein.*

He wept for all that hurt inside. Samia's smile and tender heart. His bitterness towards his father. He thought of the simple yet powerful tale that he read and reread when he was a child and then forgot to heed its wisdom; Antoine de Saint-Exupery's, 'The Little Prince.' *The fox's advice – what was it?* Yes, that to know someone or something beyond the ordinary was to make its connection very special and its relationship unique – that it contains at its source not just something to be *liked* but to be *loved*. "*It is only with the heart that one can see rightly; what is essential is invisible to the eye*," the fox taught the Prince. Yes, anyone who dares to love realizes this painful finality of seeing loved ones pass into the night, into the clouds, and then become the stuff of stardust. Lyra may never see again, he thought, if her brain did not heal, but he would love her all the same and ever more. He would be her eyes if she needed but *could she ever forgive him for his mistakes?*

Bradlee departed from the room and walked the stairs down to the hospital chapel. It was a simple condensed room. Small rows of wooden benches. Quiet solitude. No symbols other than a light with an artificial electric flame above the platform at the front.

He took a seat in the second pew from the front and lowered his head. He was alone in his thoughts. He wanted to pray but no words came. Only memories of his childhood. His parents. Friends he left behind. New ones that arrived along his journeys. And then Samia. Her face – Bradlee would never forget her. He blinked – and then there was Lyra staring at him on the train, her head rotated as her right eye gleamed with her smile. *Lyra was named after her grandmother's nickname. What did they share together? Were they close before the fire?* Then Lyra was in his arms at the inn. They were making love together. Through the night and into the morning light. His own 'Sunshine girl.' *Jim Clayburn was right*. Every man needed his own Sunshine girl to light his way through an otherwise dreary life of quiet desperation. Men were merely disordered messes despite their mothers' best intentions. Perhaps a little more tidy then when they were toy-tossing toddlers but, all the same, all men were merely inherited projects for their lovers. *Until the end...* he smiled. The quiet words spoken between lovers who laugh like children and who know all of life's truths can be summed up in one simple word – *Love*. Two lovers embraced, enjoined like two symmetrically balanced halves. A castanetted seashell, completed. Made whole as the grand designer of nature had intended all along.

Bradlee exited the chapel and searched on his phone for 'Jared Chaim Flurey, Kansas.' Lyra said her brother was in Kansas, living on a ranch. *That fact*, Bradlee remembered. He found a link to a ranch with his name. He was the assistant director for troubled youth – teens who came to the ranch to learn how to ride horses and be absorbed in nature and have someone to talk to who could perhaps show them a better way, away from their difficult pasts, tortured souls from abuse or neglect or trauma. Bradlee called the ranch. The main office located Jared and Bradlee explained who he was and what had happened to Lyra and that she had no family by her side. And Jared said yes, he would be there as soon as he could, and Bradlee hung up and felt that at least Lyra would have one person from her bloodline who could hold her hand inside the unit where the only music was the sound of a digital heart monitor singing to a ventilator pump. Lyra would have one recognizable voice from her family. Someone who loved her and who she loved, he hoped. Her brother would be there soon. Perhaps Bradlee could join him inside the unit beside Lyra and everything would be alright in the end. Bradlee would kiss Lyra and she would awaken from her dream.

Then Bradlee returned inside the chapel because he thought it would be safe. He had nowhere else to go. He was now a crime suspect but surely the authorities would not enter the sanctity of a chapel. He sat down again in the same pew and stared at the eternal flame above the platform. He thought about Kin and Ruthy and then Ruby and James. Lyra unconscious on the ledge. And then his mind went silent. He was tired of thinking all the time. Why couldn't he just turn off the damn thinking switch in his mind and give his life a good rest. The flame's randomness of movement was puzzling. No order. No pattern to it all. Maybe that's what life is about. The unpredictability of it all. No destiny. Only randomness. Unfairness. And so he focused on the flame and tried not to think of anything else. Then he closed his eyes and simply breathed.

The door opened and an older man walked slowly up the aisle. He had visited Lyra upstairs in the unit when he arrived to the hospital with his wife. Lyra was resting comfortably. She remained comatose despite attempts to arouse her by withdrawing her sedatives. He left his wife by Lyra's side and then he came to the chapel to pray for her. To pray for himself and the fate of his family and his misdeeds. He needed to ask God for forgiveness but his misdeeds were really not between him and God. They were between him and his fellow man. His flesh and blood.

He paused along the way and stared at the flame and noticed the same as Bradlee. The unpredictable randomness in its electric movements. The disorder was uncomfortable and then he continued his slow gait and then sat beside the younger man.

He noticed Baruch was in quiet contemplation with his eyes shut. He did the same. In time, he reached out with his right hand and placed it into Baruch's palm. Baruch recognized his father's hand. He responded with a gentle squeeze and they held their hands clasped. They knew. They knew the feel of the other's touch. A boy never forgets his own father's hand, regardless of age or infirmary. And neither does a father, his son's.

"Baruch, I made some mistakes." Nathaniel swallowed and breathed through the pain. "A father shouldn't need to ask for forgiveness from his son. But I do. I judged you too harshly and interfered with your decisions and I shouldn't have. Yes, I wanted what I thought was best for you but it was really what I thought was best for me. And that was selfish. A father has no right to interfere with a son's or daughter's love."

Bradlee took his other hand and rubbed his forehead as he turned his head gently away.

"Your mother and I have loved each other for many many years. I want you to have that love with the woman that you choose. It is only fair and I know now that it is entirely your right to choose. My beliefs may be different from yours, Baruch, but I have widened my faith in humanity and I realize now that it's a far larger and more complicated tent that we all live under. I've changed too, my son, in these past five years. Perhaps more spiritual and less religious although I do find prayer and rituals meaningful and fulfilling to carry out."

"Dad, you don't need to ask me for forgiveness. I need to ask you. I was selfish and angry and turned my back on my faith and even some of your guidance when, at times, it may have made all the difference. Samia would have been alive today if maybe I had called you from that ridge. But I was upset by our strained relationship. I had wanted to share a photo with you and mom of Samia and me standing in front of the most beautiful sunset I had ever seen when I asked her to marry me. Dad, had I sent a text of our location, you would have reminded me, come nightfall, not to camp on top of that mountain ridge. But I didn't call you or text you even though I knew you were an expert hiker for so many years and had hiked the same trail to that very spot. And I never did share that sunset with you. And then Samia died and I was angry at you for not ever accepting her and I felt trapped by my own family and lashed out. I wanted out. Of everything from my past. Medical school. My family home. You. Mom. My friends. Yes, even my name. To run away from it all and find something else that would bring me peace and happiness. I had told myself that my father was a hypocrite. He would never learn to accept and love anyone who I loved. Never good enough for him. Samia was pure and believed in the goodness of people. She wanted to deliver babies into this world, for goodness sake."

Bradlee's father turned towards him in the pew.

"Baruch, listen to me. We must forgive each other. I am opening my heart to you. We must find a way forward from the misfortune that has struck you."

"I have, dad. Her name is Lyra and she is lying in a bed upstairs in a coma. You know that, don't you? You saved her life."

"As did you, Baruch, on that cliff edge. A detective came to our home and asked of your whereabouts and informed us of the events with you and Lyra."

"The police think I may be a serial killer," Bradlee interjected.

"I'm not worried about their investigation. That is frivolous and unnecessary but they must do their job given the circumstances. I did not know who Lyra was, Baruch, when she was lying on the operating table before me and Ibrahim. We worked quickly and Lyra Seashell survived. She was just another name, another human being who needed care. And now we wait for healing and for her awakening."

"Lyra Seashell," Bradlee repeated it a few times and then started to laugh. And he laughed louder.

"What's so funny, son?"

Bradlee settled. "When we first met, Lyra soon started to call me 'Bradlee Seashell.' In time, she would call me by that name whenever she wanted to playfully tease me, when she wanted me to know – at least I *thought* so – that she loved me. Or, that she was *falling* in love with me. I had given her a simple necklace while on a train when we first met. A shell that I had rescued from the gutter in a street in New York City and I recognized it for what it was – a common yet uniformly beautiful Ark shell that needed a rightful home. Someone who could wear it and make it special to them. I cleaned it and placed a lanyard through the shell's hole. The lanyard wasn't long enough for her to easily see the shell around her neck without a mirror. But she could feel its texture and realize, in time, that what was essential *was* invisible to her eyes. That I was the one who had gifted it to her and that it wasn't the shell that really mattered or the shell that she needed to love but it was me – because *I loved her*. I loved her from the moment I laid eyes on her and there was this incredible energy and magnetic attraction when we spoke that I hadn't felt since I was with Samia."

"Bradlee, Bradlee..." Nathaniel repeated it a few more times. "It's an interesting name, Baruch. I don't mind that much that you prefer to use it over your given name, although you will always be our blessing. Your mom and I were very blessed to bring you into this world in her later fertile years. You might say you were a surprise, but very much a desired one. And so we blessed you with the very name itself. When I pray, Bradlee, as you know, we say 'Baruch' at the beginning of nearly every Jewish blessing. And it is impossible for me to not think of you nearly every hour of every day of my life."

"Dad, you saved Lyra's life but I also know that you restored Lyra's gift to have children if she wants to someday. I haven't spoken with her yet about her wishes for children or not. But I know that to have that option, and to have it taken away, can be devastating. My hope is that she desires children and that she wishes to forgive me and that we can bring a child into this world together. I feel it is our destiny. And we will love that child with all our hearts and souls."

"Only *one child*, Bradlee, like your mother and I brought

you into this world?"

Bradlee chuckled. "We'll see. Your patient upstairs will need all of our prayers and blessings first. And to accept my forgiveness for what I have done. Her accident falling off the cliff was a reaction to an argument she and I had over *you*. My anger with who I *thought* you were. Really, over my frustration with our lack of communication – you and me. I got angry and she ran off on a rusty bicycle lying inside the shed and then disaster struck. I hope God will listen and forgive me too. And is there not more power if we unite together in prayer? As it should be. Beside each other. Father with son."

Nathaniel reached out and held Bradlee's hand and squeezed it tight again. Bradlee felt the warmth and vitality from his father's gifted hands. He glanced at his father's right hand cradled in his. He had aged. The tissues were not as supple as when he last held his father's hand years ago. The surface was blanketed by brown freckles and solar lentigines and tortuous veins.

"Dad – I want to repair what has been broken between us."

"Me too, son. Then let us try to forget the pain from what needs to be forgotten and build new memories together."

It was the same advice Bradlee recalled James giving him in his taxi when he and Lyra first arrived to Minot and then again while enjoying ice cream and pie at Ruby's. The wisdom of the years. Of sacrifice and loss and redemption.

"Dad, I found out today that Lyra lost her parents and her grandparents in a terrible fire at her home when she graduated from high school in Connecticut. She and her brother are the only survivors. He's on his way here. He'll be arriving soon from Kansas.

"God works in mysterious ways, Bradlee. Sometimes we will never have an answer for terrible tragedies. I'm sorry, Bradlee. That is terrible news to hear."

"Yes, and her mother's mother was a Holocaust survivor just like your father."

Nathaniel absorbed the meaning of that news. Lyra must have Jewish bloodlines, he surmised.

"Bradlee, I meant what I said earlier. Your love for Lyra is *your* love. Not mine. Not your mother's or mine, for now at least, until your mother and I are welcomed by Lyra as in-laws so that we can also love her. Perhaps now ever more important and meaningful, as surrogate parents for Lyra, given her family's tragedy. And I will not interfere between you and Lyra. I would have accepted Lyra regardless of religion or race or anything else. It's the truth. But I thank you for shedding light in the midst of darkness."

"I don't know if she practices any specific faith, dad. We haven't discussed it at all."

"You will work through those issues in time, Bradlee. In time." The two men quieted and stared at the flame together in thought.

"Dad, I've also been thinking we could learn something new together like we did when I was a child fascinated by seashells and rocks and minerals. You would go searching for books that we poured over until I had all their names and details mastered."

"Yes, I remember those times very fondly, Bradlee."

"I've been reading about Kabbalah and the Baal Shem Tov while sitting here in this chapel over the past few hours. I want to try to better understand the reason behind the many coincidences that have shaped my life. Something tells me his teachings will have greater meaning to me over the rest of my life."

"Very interesting. *Kabbalah* study, Bradlee?"

"Yes, dad. You know it. The spiritual mysticism that the Torah can teach us if we open our minds to it. Some of the deeper answers to the 'Why' questions that I have always wondered about. That maybe life isn't really *just* a series of coincidences."

"I've thought the same thing these past few years, Bradlee. I thought it might bring solace to an old man's broken heart. But now, I feel it mending and I feel the teachings would make me stronger." Nathaniel placed his arm around Bradlee and rubbed the back of his son's head affectionately.

"I think it's a wonderful idea, son, and I happen to know a rabbi who is a real Kabbalah expert."

"You do?"

"Yes, you may know him as well, Bradlee."

"Who?"

"His name is Uncle Eddie, I believe."

They both laughed together and then they hugged. Tears of joy, only tempered by Lyra's tenuous condition, for what they had missed these many years. For Samia, and for the future. A very bright future that was ahead of them. Then they sat quietly for the next hour and prayed.

Nathaniel's phone rang. It was Jenny. Bradlee could hear her voice clearly beside his father's ear.

"Nathaniel, come quickly. It's Lyra, she's…"

Bradlee ran out of the chapel as fast as he could and then up the stairs. He reached the lobby to the intensive care unit. Another visitor was exiting. He was gasping for air. The day clerk recognized him from their previous encounter. Bradlee had no time for any bickering. He darted past her and held the door open quickly for the departing visitors.

"Sir, you are not authorized to enter. Sir!" Bradlee didn't acknowledge her. She was not yet made aware of Bradlee's allowed access into the ICU.

Bradlee was fearing for Lyra's life. He entered the unit and quickly approached Lyra's bedside. Bradlee's mother was beside her.

Lyra was coughing. She had awakened and was forcibly

pulling out her breathing tube from her throat. Various medical personnel came running to her bedside. The tube had exited and so her nurse quickly suctioned Lyra's mouth. Lyra was trying to breathe on her own now. The nurse fit an oxygen mask over Lyra's face. Lya caught a glance of Bradlee at the base of her bed. Her left arm tried to extend it towards him and he grabbed it gently and held her hand.

"I'm here, Lyra. I'm here for you. Keep holding me. Now you be strong for me." Lyra coughed again. "Settle down now," Bradlee encouraged Lyra as he stroked her hand gently.

Lyra continued to be combative with the nursing staff. She choked up some more phlegm and then she finally settled. She brought her left hand to her mouth and lifted the oxygen mask off her face.

"*Please*, I'm a runn'r. Take dis off'f me, now!" She was slightly slurring her words. The nurse checked her lungs and observed Lyra's oxygen saturation level that was constantly being monitored from her right index finger pad. 98% on room air. It held steady without any need for supplemental oxygen. Lyra was breathing comfortably. She looked at her right forearm and noticed the cast. She flopped it about but it was too heavy for her to lift from the bed. She reached again with her left hand and placed it on her scalp and felt her baldness. Then she moved it backward until she felt a large bandage over her scalp wound. She winced from the pain as she located the incision sites.

Jenny had brought a hat with her to keep warm. It was a colorful splash of died wool appropriate for the winter on P.E.I. She placed it in Lyra's left hand and then she helped Lyra apply it gently over her scalp.

"Your mutter?" Lyra tried to say. More slurred now. Her eyelids were groggy. "Very bueful."

"Yes Lyra, my mother, Jenny." Lyra smiled at Jenny

and squeezed her hand in hers.

"Tell'r... I Iuvyu, Ba-ru-ee," she was whispering now, sleepily. Lyra had jumbled his names, Baruch with Bradlee, together. And then she fell asleep. The nurse gave Bradlee and Jenny a big smile.

"She's going to be just fine. This girl's a fighter, alright! This kind of grogginess and muscular fatigue is normal but it'll settle over the next few hours and I expect she'll be much more lucid soon."

Dr. Levitsky arrived to the unit. The clerk was incensed by Bradlee's unauthorized access and she had a few stern words to share with the gray-haired surgeon. But he tried to reassure her that Bradlee meant no harm. He asked the clerk to check the computer where it should state Bradlee's allowed access but she refused. The young man had defied her and had not followed the appropriate check-in protocol. She decided to call for security back-up to the unit. Bradlee was informed by his father to hustle out of the back door of the unit and down the flight of stairs. He complied and headed back to the safety of the chapel. Two armed security officers arrived and questioned Dr. Levitsky and the hospital staff extensively. One officer departed to make a phone call while the other officer stood guard at the entrance to the unit for added safety measures. Under no circumstances would Baruch Levitsky be allowed access to the unit without the verbal consent of the patient, Lyra Seashell.

The officer who departed placed a call to the RCMP detective's office and spoke with Detective McCallum. The detective replied that he would be there in less than an hour. Time went by slowly as Bradlee waited for Jared's call. Finally, Lyra's brother had arrived to the Charlottetown airport. Jared took a taxi to the hospital. Bradlee texted his mother who replied that the detective was present and waiting for him in the lounge outside the unit. Detective McCallum was receiving an update on Lyra's condition from the hospital staff.

Bradlee arrived first and Detective McCallum verified his identity from his parents. Jared then arrived as the elevator doors opened to the ICU lounge. He had to duck under the elevator post. Jared was at least a foot taller than anyone present. He towered over the assembly with lanky arms and loose fitting jeans over long thin legs. He was quite thin but possessed a rugged muscular build through the length of his torso. His hands rough from gripping the reins over countless rides through the ranch lands in the Flint Hills of Kansas. His eyes were the same emerald hazel blend as his sister's. Perceptive eyes. He was wearing a cowboy hat and everything about his quiet, observant demeanor suggested that he was born to be one.

"Mom. Dad," Bradlee spoke first. "I'd like you to meet Jared, Lyra's brother."

"Welcome son." Dr. Levitsky introduced himself with a firm handshake and Jared tipped his hat towards Jenny with a brief smile and a nod.

"And this is Detective McCallum," Dr. Levitsky continued. "He's been appointed to review the conditions regarding Lyra's traumatic injuries." Detective McCallum made the usual introductions and then glared into the eyes of Baruch Levitsky. Usually, he could sense from a person's body language whether they were nervously evading the truth. Most of the time those initial instincts were right. But Bradlee didn't have that demeanor of nervous fidgeting or shaking. No straying of the eyes. Either he was a great poker player, the detective surmised, or this suspect may not be as dangerous as the RCMP force was portraying him to be.

"Jared, I'm sure you would like to see your sister now," Dr. Levitsky said. He explained that he was one of the surgeons who operated on Lyra and he reviewed her current care needs with Jared before they entered. "Your sister's head is shaven as well so please do not be alarmed. She needed emergent neurosurgery but her brain is responding well and she has only a large gauze wrap remaining to protect her scalp incision towards the back of her skull. She has been resting over the past few hours. If we are lucky, we may be able to rouse her from sleep to briefly chat with her before more rest is needed overnight."

"I will have some questions, Dr. Levitsky, as part of my official duties," Detective McCallum added.

"That will be fine, if Lyra is able to respond," Dr. Levitsky replied.

They gathered around Lyra's bedside. Detective McCallum's first request was directed to Jared. "I would like to know the legal given name of the victim."

Dr. Levitsky interjected. "Can we please use the term '*patient*' while inside the intensive care unit?"

The detective ignored the physician's statement.

"The victim's last name please…"

Jared stated that it was '*Flurey*,' the same as his. It was from their father, Christopher Flurey. The detective wrote it down. Then Dr. Levitsky spoke quietly with Lyra's nurse. The nurse proceeded to stop the flow of a medication that was dripping steadily into one of Lyra's intravenous lines. They waited. Some minutes later Lyra stirred and her eyes fluttered. She gradually kept them open and tried to focus on something in front of her that looked familiar but her right eye was blurry and her left was uselessly absent of any visual input. Darkness, only darkness, she realized.

"Bradlee, is that you in that cowboy hat? You've sure grown since I last saw you." She smiled her fantastic smile that Bradlee loved so dearly and turned her head towards her left shoulder, just like she did on the train so many times, and then stared at the assembled group, one by one with her right eye facing the crowd of onlookers. She blinked a few times and her right eye began to focus better, gradually – enough to make out more refined facial details.

Jared approached her and held her hand.

"Lyra, it's Jared here. I'm sorry for what you've been through." He hugged her and gently kissed her forehead.

"My baby brother. It's good to see you again. How are all those horses in Kansas?"

Bradlee was very pleased. Lyra was remembering details. Details about her past. Her traumatic injury and coma may have *not* induced the retrograde amnesia that he feared most. That she would have forgotten him entirely. Tabula rasa. To potentially have to start over again after everything they had been through.

Jared chatted briefly with Lyra but remained somewhat detached. Bradlee sensed that something was distant between them. It was not the kind of reception he had expected from two siblings who had lost their parents in a tragic accident and had not likely seen each other in quite some time. Jared stood and deferred to the others to continue.

The detective began.

"Lyra, I'm Detective McCallum with the police force. Do you know where you are at this moment?"

"In a hospital."

"Which city or region, ma'am?"

"Uh… Canada. I love maple syrup with pancakes, by the way... Prince Eddie, I think." Bradlee smirked at Lyra's maple syrup passions but particularly at Lyra's crossed reference to his uncle. He'd have to remember to use that one on his Uncle Eddie one day. '*The Little Prince-Eddie,*' perhaps?!

"And the time of year, Lyra?" The detective continued his inquiry.

"Winter." Lyra began to sing: "*Winter, spring, summer, or fall; all you have to do is call, and I'll be there, yes I will, you've got a friend.*" She was uninhibited, and for the first time Bradlee heard her sing and it was absolutely beautiful. It was the same song he heard Lyra playing into her earbuds while on the train. It must be one of her favorites. The Carole King poetic lyrics roused the nursing staff to join her in harmony. Lyra stopped singing after a few more stanzas and continued: "I can sense the smell of snow on your clothes, Detective McCallum. And I do love my new hat. Thank you, Jenny."

Bradlee was pleased Lyra was already remembering new faces and names. And she was discovering her voice…! Perhaps her head trauma had released some new and exciting features to her personality, or was reinvigorating long buried talents from her early childhood.

Lyra's answers were good enough for Detective McCallum to suggest that she was mentally competent despite her apparent disinhibitions.

The detective continued. "Lyra, besides your brother, there is another young man here beside me. Can you state his name for me, please?"

Lyra peered with her right eye at Dr. Levitsky and then over to Bradlee. Then back to the older gentleman. She remembered his photo from the Marshpillow but that was all she remembered from the incident at the home.

"He's very handsome. These men look very similar. It's as if I have double vision."

Bradlee chuckled and glanced at his dad who returned the gesture with a smile. Lyra's wit was ever present.

"But his beard is not my type. If a man's going to grow a beard then you might as well go all-in and let it go for at least a month, preferably two or three. Let it be as wild as a pack of wild horses. Then we can truly see if it suits him well and enhances his handsomeness."

Dr. Levitsky couldn't contain himself as he began to laugh. Bradlee was stunned by Lyra's craftiness. As shrewd as a fox. His valedictorian was awakening.

Lyra pointed towards Bradlee with her left index finger.

"He's the one you're after, isn't that right, detective?"

"Possibly, Ms. Flurey."

"He did something very bad, did he?" Bradlee's pulse suddenly quickened. What was Lyra trying to say?

Bradlee took a few steps towards Lyra but the detective warned him away with his outstretched arm. The armed security guard, standing in the shadows, kept his hand on his revolver, just in case this got ugly.

"Lyra, tell me what you know about him."

Lyra studied Bradlee from head to toe before carefully focusing on his steady gaze. Bradlee was gripped by fear of the unknown. *Her brain.* Could it be trusted this soon after her surgery? *She could be delirious.* Lyra brought her left hand to her neck and touched the Ark necklace. The nurse had let her wear it again after Lyra had awakened a few hours ago.

"His name is Bradlee Seashell. I don't care what anyone else calls him. That's his name and always will be. She was staring at Bradlee now, intensely. Bradlee softened his stance a bit and breathed deeply.

"Ms. Flurey. You sustained severe injuries from a fall off a cliff. I don't know if you've been told this news yet but the eye specialist discovered that you likely have no vision in your left eye. Your retina is nearly completely detached from the back of your eye socket. I need to know if your left eye blindness is a result of your fall down that cliff the other day. And did this man, this Bradlee Seashell, hurt you? Did he argue with you and then chase you and push you over that cliff?"

Lyra held her thoughts for a moment. Sometimes painful memories need time to mull over before conveying their secrets.

"I've been mostly blind in my left eye since I was born, Detective McCallum. My pediatrician discovered it in elementary school when I had my first reliable vision test. The eye specialists my parents brought me to couldn't offer any correction for my defect. My eye never formed properly in the time before I was born."

The detective turned to Jared and asked for confirmation of this detail and he acknowledged that it was true.

"Sir," Bradlee interjected, "Lyra has a small, almost imperceptible, coloboma of her left iris. I noticed it the moment I met her."

Dr. Levitsky and the detective approached the left side of Lyra's bed. Bradlee's father asked for a pen light and, with Lyra's permission, proceeded to shine the light into her left eye. Then he checked her right. Bradlee was right. It was something he knew he should have checked himself, as thorough as he prided himself for every one of his patients. But he didn't this time.

"Did you say cliff, detective?" Lyra asked.

"Yes —— I did," Ms. Flurey.

"I didn't fall down a cliff. I was abused by a *terrible* monster of a man. He held me down and *punched* me until I couldn't resist… and then he tried to *rape* me."

Detective McCallum was ready to handcuff the suspect at that moment.

Bradlee's mother couldn't stand it anymore. Tears flowing. She grasped onto Jared's arm and pulled at him as they left Lyra's side, escaping from the horrid news that Lyra was relaying. They quickly exited the waiting room. *Her own son! How could he do such a thing to this beautiful and tender woman?* she thought.

Lyra continued: "But I fought and I escaped with the help of another man who came to my rescue. And then there was a woman named Angel and another named Oji. All of them restored my dignity in time. But what remaining sight I had in my left eye was extinguished by that man. He got what he deserved, thankfully." Lyra cleared her throat and reminded herself to remain strong just as she had in the weeks that ensued after that terrorful night. Just as Dr. Bonheim had instructed her from her own experience.

"But there is one person who helped me to fully heal. To trust again. To love him because he loves me for who I am and for what I had been through. To be gentle. And that man is right here beside me. And if that is his horrendous crime then I ask you, detective, to arrest him and take him away from me forever."

Bradlee jumped to Lyra and held her to his arms. He kissed her gently.

She whispered into his ear. "I love you Bradlee Seashell. I will always love you until the end......... but Bradlee... What cliff? I don't remember any cliff? Did we argue or did you just chase me because you've been chasing me for all of these months... haven't you? And I let you catch me because I wanted you to, from the very moment we met." She kissed his earlobe.

"It's OK, Lyra," Bradlee answered. "You're going to be OK. Sometimes the mind chooses to forget the memories that it should but keeps only the good or more important ones for our healing. The most meaningful if not always the least painful."

Bradlee knew Lyra had retrograde amnesia for her most recent traumatic events at the cliff. Short term memory loss – but her brain did not forget everything. She remembered the painful moment in Seattle but more critically, her memory of Bradlee was intact. Not just her memory, but her love for him. Her brain held on to those emotions. Perhaps it was the way the brain heals best. Mother Nature protecting from further harm. Closing most wounds, sometimes healing to perfection, and other times leaving remnants of scars as reminders of where one has been so that the same mistakes never happen. But truly, most hidden or cleansed from view just as only the heart can see what is most important, what is most right, and genuine, and eternally true. What is essential is indeed invisible to the eye.

Dr. Levitsky turned to Detective McCallum.

"Are you done with your questions, sir?"

"I think so. It appears there is nothing further needed here. On behalf of the RCMP force, I apologize for this misunderstanding. I wish you a speedy recovery, Ms. Flurey. Or do you prefer that I address you as Ms. Seashell?"

The detective smiled at Lyra and embraced her hand gently. Then he shook Bradlee's hand as well.

"I wish you both well. You make a fine couple. Please be safe moving forward. And if I may add this thought – it appears to me that your love story has just begun." And then the detective departed the unit with the armed security officer beside him.

Bradlee exited and found his mother, distraught in the lounge. She had noticed that the detective and security guard had exited without Bradlee in handcuffs and they had wished her a pleasant evening. *That is very odd*, she thought. Bradlee approached her cautiously.

"Mom, it's alright. I'm not a murderer or an abuser. I'm sorry you had to even imagine that. Lyra explained things to the detective in her own witty way. Everything's going to be alright now, mom. And mom… I love you and I love Lyra very much. Our journey as a family has just begun – dad included." He hugged and kissed his mother.

"Dad and I had a long talk this evening. We're going to work things out…" Jenny smiled effusively. "You know mom, one thing I learned along the way is that nothing is impossible to a willing heart. Nothing. I think dad and I both learned that lesson." He held her close. He realized how much he missed hugging his own mother.

"Mom, Lyra is an amazing and strong woman. I'd like her to stay with us at the Marshpillow after she is released, at least until her health is restored enough to return to school. She has a life waiting for her in Seattle where she is attending grad school."

His mother agreed to welcome Lyra to their home. But, on one condition. That Lyra help Jenny with her chocolate seashells. Jenny had decided to return to P.E.I. in preparation for the summer season. She had asked her husband of forty years to take a sabbatical from his surgical and teaching duties in Toronto and he agreed to her request. They would return to a long summer together at the Marshpillow. Something they hadn't done in many years as a couple. Their own long and winding love story needed some work after all these years – "*a little battery recharge*" – as his mother confided. And Jenny had plans to restore her old business. She missed bringing so many people happiness. And love. Apparently, the goat's milk chocolate shells had accumulated fans far and wide.

"And Bradlee – a nice lady named Ruby even wrote to me from Minot, North Dakota of all places!" his mom declared with astonishment. "Perhaps Lyra could help me design the next custom line of aphrodisiac goat's milk chocolates? We can name it the 'Lyra Seashell Collection.'"

Bradlee asked his mother and Jared to wait in the lounge while he said goodnight to Lyra. He returned to Lyra's bedside and kissed her. They held their foreheads together. He was continuing to enjoy that new tradition as they met each time. As if always for the first time.

"Bradlee," his father said, "Lyra and I have been getting to know each other a little bit better."

"Well, I hope you don't believe everything my dad tells you, my dear. He tends to exaggerate on the details."

"Your father said you have very gifted hands, Bradlee. And that he was proud of your photography and your woodcarving. But he also said that you were quite the prodigy in medical school as well. Is he exaggerating about all of those things too?" Lyra had a way with words. Bradlee wondered if she should have gone to law school instead. She'd make a fine prosecutor, or perhaps better, a public defender, saving the world from any unjustly accused – whatever she chose she would have succeeded at. And certainly in any career that she desired ahead.

"Maybe a bit. I'll take my father's comments as a kind complement. I've missed those from him these past many years." Bradlee smiled towards his dad.

Lyra began to speak. "Dr. Levitsky ——" but she was abruptly interrupted by Bradlee's father.

"Please Lyra, I think you should get used to calling me, '*Nathaniel.*' The sooner the better. It is the name my mother had chosen for me and I do like it."

"Bradlee thinks the word '*like*' is just a euphemism, most times, for what someone really means to otherwise say from their heart," Lyra remarked. "What they really mean to say is that they '*love!*'"

"My son is a very loving person."

"*That*, I already have discovered." Lyra squeezed Bradlee's hand.

"Nathaniel, I'd like to… no, I'd *love* to be able to thank the doctor who saved my life. Is it possible to arrange a meeting at my bedside while I'm still here in the hospital?"

Nathaniel thought for a moment and looked over to his son.

"The doctor who saved your life isn't here now at the hospital, unfortunately. He left for vacation to India for the next few weeks with his wife and infant daughter. He's from there originally but has lived in Canada for many years and I know him well. He is a very gifted neurosurgeon. I will reach Dr. Ibrahim Salim myself by phone and personally send your thank you and warm wishes. Perhaps someday you will be able to meet him and his family. His daughter, *Samia,* is very special to me and Jenny. You know Lyra, Ibrahim was once going to be Bradlee's brother-in-law?!"

Lyra smiled at Nathaniel. The connection clicked in her

mind. Nathaniel didn't need to explain any further.

And just at that moment, Bradlee knew how much he loved his father. He was humble and pious. He didn't take any ounce of credit for Lyra's survival, let alone her future fertility. His father had given Lyra the chance, perhaps, to have his own grandchild. The irony astonished Bradlee but it was his father's humility that would remain forever in Bradlee's mind from this shared moment at Lyra's bedside. Perhaps, one day, Lyra will hear the whole story. Perhaps not. Either would be fine.

Lyra turned to Bradlee. "Coincidence, huh? Just another simple coincidence in our lives, Bradlee?!"

She began to laugh and then tears of joy came flowing down her cheeks. Bradlee held her and Nathaniel squeezed her left hand. Lyra felt like she was being adopted into a new family at that moment, one where a father and mother and son could love her as her own family had before. The twinges of painful memories now being swept away by a steady flowing current of love by their acceptance that was filling her with happiness.

"Lyra, I think you may need some more rest tonight. You will regain your strength with time and a healthy appetite, and from the excellent care you have been receiving here from this wonderful staff," Nathaniel said as Lyra's nurse nodded approvingly. "The medical staff will update us on your progress or if any concerns arise."

Nathaniel raised Lyra's left hand and kissed it gently. He said goodnight and then joined Jenny in the lounge.

Bradlee lingered. "Lyra, my father and I have agreed to forgive each other. We will make new memories as we move forward. Most of those will involve you, I'm sure. Maybe some little ones running around the Marshpillow one day as well, down the road if you wish someday..."

"Bradlee, are you asking me if I'd like to have a child with you someday?"

"Well, I guess I was hoping you might like to."

"Then the answer is... No." She said it adamantly, almost defiantly.

Bradlee was shocked but then he softened as he allowed himself to accept their future without the possibility of children together.

"Come here," she motioned with her index finger. As Bradlee approached she teasingly pulled on his shirt until they were thoroughly embraced. The nurse winked at Lyra and then departed and closed the curtains to give them a moment of privacy.

"Bradlee Seashell. Don't ever say the word '*like*' to me again when it comes to what is only '*love*.' Only love, Bradlee Seashell. Until the end. Only love." She kissed him sweetly and then their lips separated but lingered as closely as two halves of a complete Ark shell. "And I would *love* to have a child with you someday. Hopefully more, if it is our good fortune."

"You are a clever one, aren't you," Bradlee replied with a smile. "But, thank you, Lyra. I'd like... oops... I'd *love* that very much..." He chuckled from teasing her but knew she seemed to inevitably have the upper hand there. He would forever need to mind his chosen words around her. She glared at him and then softened again. "Until the end, Lyra. Until the end," Bradlee whispered.

They kissed, passionately.

Bradlee informed Lyra that he would be staying at the Marshpillow with his parents. Jared would be there as well. And that Lyra was welcomed by his parents to recover at the Marshpillow until she could return to Seattle. He would return to the hospital tomorrow evening. There was New Year's Eve to celebrate together then.

IN THE MORNING, Bradlee dressed and entered the main house. His mother was in the home office sifting through some old paperwork for her chocolate seashell business. His father was quietly reciting morning prayers in the sunroom facing the ocean just as Bradlee always remembered. Bradlee approached quietly and sat down and observed his father's rituals. Bradlee wondered if he would ever desire to pray again as he had when he was a young child. He was quite similar to his father in many ways but they differed now when it came to religious practices and observances. Nature, to Bradlee, remained his spiritual hideaway. His ability to connect to a higher source, perhaps. From rocks and seashells to flowers and butterflies and hummingbirds, insects and amphibians, and all the rest of nature's diversity. He thought he saw God's hands shaping his when he was immersed within the natural world, imbuing his mind with the creative impulses that allowed the most opportune and enlightened – yes, truly *spiritual* – moments for his own gifts to shine through.

His father finished praying and they made breakfast together. Jared was off on a long walk through the marsh trail and along the shoreline. Bradlee recalled that his father used to castigate him for his disinterest in prayer. But not now. Not today. His father seemed more at peace. There were no words of bitterness or condescension from his lips towards Bradlee. After breakfast, Bradlee prepared two bicycles from the shed. It was a beautiful late morning with only wisps of clouds painting the blue sky. It was the last day of the year and Bradlee asked his father to join him for a short ride to celebrate new beginnings together. Bradlee examined and tested the gears and brakes to be sure they were in good working order. He oiled the chains and adjusted the tire pressures. They pedaled down the driveway, turned south onto East Point Road, and then left onto Lighthouse Road. Bradlee wanted to return to the lighthouse to show his father where Lyra had fallen. To reveal more of the story.

They arrived to the lighthouse bluff. The waves crashing

below, doing their job as Nature had assigned them to do. The waves were there to create awe for any living thing who dared to peer over the cliff's edge. The power of Mother Nature. He showed his father the bicycle treads and the paint scrapes along the railing. And then he showed him the disturbed cliffside rubble and the tumbled path. Bradlee told his father the whole story from the moment he and Lyra argued at the Marshpillow until the end on the cliff's rocky ledge.

Nathaniel turned to his son.

"Bradlee, you saved Lyra's life. You asked for help from a stranger and she listened and called the authorities. You climbed down and kept Lyra safe from further harm, didn't you? Protected her neck and torso as you were taught to prevent spinal injury. You spoke with her and gave her hope even though she was already unconscious but somewhere inside, the brain knows a familiar loving voice. And then you protected her from the winds and covered her. And you held on to her on that ledge, didn't you? So that she wouldn't fall to her demise. All of these – at the risk of your own life…"

Bradlee listened and averted his gaze to the ocean.

"My son, I know I pray to God wishing He or She – whatever entity of God we choose for us to try to understand in physical form – that God will answer my prayers. As if God can directly intervene in our affairs here on earth. Maybe God can but we will never fully understand when the choice is made to intervene or not. We ask ourselves as a Jewish people – why did the Holocaust have to happen? for instance. Or any other heinous or immoral crime or any otherwise terrible misfortune – if there is a God who could intervene like a superhero and save us, save this planet for that matter, from harm. But we will never fully understand the works and decisions of God. What I can accept and make sense of is that every human being is born with something unique, something that is a gift, perhaps many gifts if most fortunate, and you and I share one of those. We both know how to save lives, Bradlee. I heard from Eliezer that you saved three lives on the runway in North Dakota. And now, Lyra as well, here on this cliff. Those are not coincidences. Bradlee, I save lives in the operating room – you know that. You've witnessed it as my assistant many times. So we deeply share something in common. Perhaps that is God's way. To transfer that gift from one generation to the next since our lives are finite and we must replace ourselves with others and then teach them well. Bradlee, I am sorry I was so hard on you in your later years of schooling. Sometimes I pushed too hard because I wanted you to be the best. But it was because I saw in you that same capacity to save lives with what is here…" Nathaniel pointed his finger towards his head, "and with these…" He held his hands in front of him and tensed his outstretched steady fingers, his palms like Atlas elevating the grand celestial sphere.

"Our minds and our hands, Bradlee. You have your mother's heart. But you and I share an intuitive medical mind, problem solvers with gifted hands." Nathaniel lowered his hands to his side and looked out across the ocean as he stood beside Bradlee.

"So why do I say these things to you now?" His father asked rhetorically.

"Because, I have wondered these many years if you have given any thought to finish up medical school someday. To rejoin the profession of your father and your grandfather and many others that came before us in our Levistky line."

"I have, dad. I've given it a lot of thought."

"Well… soon, God willing Bradlee, you will have a wife to care for. Perhaps the financial responsibility that comes with children…"

"I know, dad. I'm thinking about that too."

"Then, if I may give a bit of fatherly advice to my son

after all these years apart – my favorite and only son…" Nathaniel smiled at Bradlee. "Bradlee… Baruch… there is a time for *thinking* in one's life, and then a time for *deciding*, and then most critically, for *doing*. For taking decisive action… You asked Lyra to marry you recently, didn't you, for instance, and she agreed?"

Bradlee chuckled.

"Well, actually dad, Lyra asked me to marry her." Bradlee started to laugh. "Dad, Lyra can be very assertive sometimes. I didn't mind it then and don't think I ever will. One of the things I love about her."

"Well, if you want to be assertive about returning to medical school, young man, then maybe you should speak up for yourself someday soon, that's all. It is quite likely the university will grant you permission to be reinstated in Toronto. After all, you only had a few more months before you were to graduate and then begin your residency training in whatever specialty you would have chosen."

"Thanks, dad. I *will* give it some more serious thought and let you know soon. *I will*."

Bradlee wished he had his camera with him at that moment. There was a pod of very large-headed whales moving steadily with the warm current about two hundred yards from the shore. *Eubalaena glacialis*. Bradlee was sure of it. He had sighted the rarely seen Right whales that visited this region along the Northern Atlantic off the coast of P.E.I. and Cape Breton in the summer. But here they were in the winter, swimming before his eyes. Sometimes nature provides an unexpected surprise if one's eyes are open to see. The observing. But it comes from a deeper source of awareness, *before* the observing by the visual sense takes its prominent role. There is the desire, the thirst for knowledge, for understanding, for exploring. It is in the doing, the act of doing something to further one's understanding, which nurtures one's growth. And that creates the awareness of what is needed to make the world a better place. To repair and improve. The 'Tikun Olam' of life's journey.

Is the decision to return to medicine as right as a Right whale swimming before me in the winter? Bradlee thought. Sometimes things just happen out of the normal temporal sequence of expectations. To complete what he had once started and excelled at. Photography and woodcarving could always be there. Perhaps they should be hobbies, important ones, not to be cast aside as if these gifts are inconsequential. He knew it would be a difficult living to make from them with family to help support and nurture. They could remain as creative outlets to express his emotions. What would arise from the depths of his willing heart and allow him to engage his hands fully with the breadth of his creative inspiration. He had to reconcile his engagement to Lyra with the reality of his gifts. He had a new love blossoming ever more each time he was with Lyra. Her life restored by his simple measures and his father's, and Ibrahim's, knowledgeable and disciplined interventions. The two surgeons were *also* master craftsmen who worked hard to hone their skills for the sake of human life itself. Perhaps Bradlee also deserved a place at that table with his father and with Ibrahim and Ezra and all the rest, including Samia. Bradlee wanted to believe, from her last breath in his arms, that Samia was now delivering angels, if not babies, inside the clouds above as God's helper.

Father and son mounted their bicycles for the journey back to their Marshpillow home. Bradlee returned to his workshop to sculpt some prototype designs for Lyra's wedding ring. He contacted Uncle Eddie to collaborate further. He showered and dressed more formally for the New Year ahead to be celebrated that evening by Lyra's bedside. Jared joined him and they drove to the hospital.

Unfortunately, Lyra had developed a fever in the early afternoon and the doctors restricted Bradlee's and Jared's visiting time to just one hour. To the intensive care unit staff, New Year's Eve was just another regular disciplined shift caring for fragile patients. It was a subdued hour but Bradlee understood. Lyra needed rest and careful attention to her wound sites at the base of her abdomen and her posterior scalp. It wasn't clear where the source of her fever was emanating from but she was placed on a cocktail of antibiotics through her intravenous lines, just as Dr. Bonheim had needed. Lyra rested while the New Year arrived.

Three days later, Bradlee received a call from Lyra's nurse. Lyra's fever had broken and her elevated white blood cells and inflammatory markers were improving. Lyra was mending and her demeanor and energy improving rapidly. She was now walking the hallways regularly, her strength regaining quickly. By the tenth day in the hospital Lyra was ready to be discharged. Bradlee arrived to retrieve her and they returned to the Marshpillow. Jenny had arranged the sunroom as a bedroom for Lyra, better to enjoy the view and the healing morning sunshine. Lyra was fed well as Bradlee's mother cooked contentedly for her growing family. Then Lyra began to more rigorously exercise – first by walking the grounds of the Marshpillow, discovering the old goat tracks and the marsh paths and imagining a future garden that she desperately wanted to landscape for the premise. Designs and planting options dancing through her mind. Then, Bradlee and Lyra gradually began to take long walks along the beach, discovering and sharing new finds that trickled along the shore with the tides.

By the seventh day at the Marshpillow with Jared and the Levitsky family, Lyra started to lightly jog for short distances, marshaling her strength and flexibility. Her desire to heal quickly motivated her to accelerate her workouts. Her resiliency of mind and body, returning. She was finally shaking free of the stagnation and drudgery from days lying in a hospital bed. She asked Jared to join her, this time without Bradlee, for a walk along the beach in the afternoon sun. The siblings had not spoken much since she was discharged from the hospital. Bradlee continued to sense that something wasn't right between Lyra and her brother. And so, when Lyra kissed Bradlee goodbye inside the house and told him she wanted some alone time with her little brother, Bradlee understood that it was his cue to not interfere. To give them the space they needed. Bradlee wrapped Lyra in a warm sweater and jacket, protecting her right arm in her cast and sling. He covered her scalp, now sprouting new strands of flowing thick hair, with the wool cap his mother had given her at the hospital.

Lyra and Jared set out along the beach path as Bradlee watched from the sunroom until they were out of view. The siblings strolled quietly together along the water's edge. Her brother was intensely quiet, reticent to begin conversation. It used to not be that way between them when they were younger. Lyra reached and held her brother's hand.
"Jared, we need to talk. From the heart," Lyra started. He remained silent but nodded towards Lyra in acknowledgment.
"Jared, I feel like you've been beating yourself up ever since the fire marshal's investigation was released. His report stated that the fire was likely started from the outlet plug that was overloaded with plug-ins from an extension cord. You know, all the gaming paraphernalia you were using that night in the basement. Well, I haven't told you this ever before but I'm not so sure that was the reason for

the fire. I have a confession to make to you, Jared." Lyra stopped walking and stood in front of Jared.

"That evening I was dressing and doing my hair with a plug-in curling iron. I went over to Ansley's next door to continue partying after our grandparents went to sleep. And, to this day, I think I left the scalding hot curling iron on the top of a towel in the bathroom. And I don't remember ever turning its switch off. I think I left it on, Jared. And, I have lived with not really knowing which truth was right. I just can't remember. I wanted to tell you in the days and weeks that followed after the fire but you were so upset that summer that all I could do was to find you help. You turned to alcohol and drugs with friends that I didn't know you ever had and you drowned your sorrows and rage and guilt – I am sure, *all* of these emotions. And I just wanted to find the help you needed before I went to college in the fall. Thank God we had friends of the family who took us in and cared as best they could for us. But I know it was difficult for you after I went off to college. In and out of rehab facilities and dropping out of high school."

Jared stopped to rest on a stone ledge. An outcropping of boulders was jutting out to the ocean from the shoreline. Lyra sat beside him.

"Look Jared, neither of us will ever know the exact cause of the fire. But, I don't think that really matters anymore, does it? Neither of us can bring back our parents and grandparents who we loved and they loved us dearly."

Jared still remained silent. Lyra reached over and pulled his chin slowly towards her tearing eyes.

"Jared, we had a beautiful small family. And it was all taken from us in the most hellish way possible. But thank goodness you survived... You're the only family I have left... I need you, Jared. We need each other moving forward. I love you and I carry no anger or bitterness towards you. I hope you won't with me. If we can only do just that. Jared, I suffered through my own guilt from not revealing to you until now about the chance that it was all my fault. I just don't know, because I – can't – remember!" Lyra sobbed and wiped away more salty tears. "But you suffered too. Terribly. From your own feelings of guilt. I know you did. Those last few years in and out of high school and rehab centers were awful and yet I kept my distance as I was off in college trying to make my own sense of the cruelties of this world. And you struggled to finally receive your high school diploma. I was so proud of you for your efforts despite the pain inside your heart. And then you moved on, Jared. Our friends in the community deserve so much more from us for taking us into their homes and comforting and caring for us. And I know I may be repeating myself but this really hurts to talk about with you."

"Lyra, it still hurts," Jared began to speak. "It hurts every damn day I wake up and look at myself in the mirror and see our father's face in mine and I replay that horrid night. The fire took to the stairwell so fast that I couldn't run upstairs to save them. I ran out the back basement door like a coward. And by the time I got to the front door our entire home was an inferno. Yes, every day I think about how foolish I was to have overloaded all those plug-ins together onto that minimal power strip. That I feel the fire marshal should have reported me to the police and thrown me in prison for the murders of my own family!" Jared was crying now. His lower lip trembling as Lyra squeezed his arm to try to console him.

"Jared, we'll never know why. And it doesn't matter now. *It Just – Doesn't – Matter! Do you hear me?* Both of us may have contributed or neither. Maybe it was something entirely different that triggered the fire but was overlooked in the rubble… Things happen and who knows what the real truth is. Like I said, it just doesn't matter now. But Jared, we can let it burn inside here, inside our hearts, until it kills us or we can forgive each other. Forgive me,

Jared as I have forgiven you. I want to have my brother back in my life again. Really present. Not all gloomy. But alive. Smiling again. The Jared that I used to know. You were once my best friend as a child, besides Ansley, of course." Lyra smiled for the first time through her tears. "You and I had goodness and kindness towards each other and we teased each other in the usual ways that siblings do. I want us to really care about each other's lives ahead. To visit. Share some holidays when we can. Our future children. Everything a family needs to do to keep the caring and the loving going on for generations beyond us."

"Lyra, I've grown these past number of years. My work at the ranch with all the troubled high school kids has made me more compassionate. More resilient like you, I think." He smiled affectionately. "I think our relationship just went cold because I wanted it to at the time. I needed my own space to try to make peace with what happened to our family. I'll never be able to forget it. But I've been learning to live a bit more with the pain these past few years. A lot of counseling has helped. The countless horseback rides I've enjoyed on the ranch have helped too. Probably the most. The Kansas Flint Hills are beautiful, Lyra. I wish you had the time to visit. There are wild horses on a stretch of land nearby and I'd love to share them with you someday. I find staring at them, observing their mannerisms, very soothing."

They were beginning to share again. Lyra was sensing it.

"Come here, little brother. You're a darn lanky giant, you know, towering over me like a giraffe, but you'll always be my little brother." She teased him lovingly.

Jared removed his cowboy hat and they gave each other a long embrace.

"Jared, do you remember when we were kids in elementary school together. We shared a bedroom back then and you used to like hearing me recite to you our family's stories so many nights after we turned out the lamps and we were cuddled in our beds. I'd like to remind you of one now, here on this beach, that is very meaningful for me. It's been a long time and we can't forget these memories now. They're all we've got of the past besides each other with everything burned and gone. Even all the photos..." Lyra paused to collect herself. The thought of not even having a single photo frame of her parents and grandparents pained her.

Jared agreed. He wanted to hear a story again.

"Jared, you know that I preferred to go by my middle name, Sasha, during my college years after the fire. I couldn't face waking up every morning and looking in the mirror as well and having my first name, Lyra, remind me of our grandmother who we both loved dearly. Yes, her real name was Leora, but we called her Lyra because that's what she preferred ever since – as she told us time and again – she arrived to New York as a child refugee fleeing from the Holocaust. She was secreted away by the Krawczyk family in Poland who shuttled her into hiding spots and then arranged for her to travel underground to France and then onto a kinder transport ship to the United States for Christian parent adoptions. This was the difficult way Jewish children had to be rescued from the Nazis. But Safta Lyra, as she asked us to call her by her Hebrew title for 'Grandma' – she had told us many times that she remembered watching her parents being lead off from their family home in Poland, away from her own outstretched arms as an eight year old child. Separated to never see them again. As far as she knew, her parents were killed in a concentration camp. Never to be seen or heard from again.

Safta Lyra grew up with her adoptive Christian family in New York and eventually met our grandfather, Yehoshua – our 'Grandpa Yeshi.' They married and moved to Connecticut as their finances improved and they were seeking a quieter life away from the stresses of Brooklyn. They had an only child – our mother, Leah, and they provided her with everything they didn't have in life as children. When our mother was in high school she went on a cross country trip and fell in love with the beauty of the Pacific Northwest. She applied to colleges in that area and was accepted to the university in Seattle, the same one that I now attend as a graduate student. Our grandparents, Safta Lyra and Grandpa Yeshi, understood but missed Leah deeply and visited her periodically in Seattle. But, in time, Grandpa Yeshi became more fascinated with the little Judaism that he knew from his childhood and he desired to immigrate to Israel to live out his years with Safta Lyra. They departed to Jerusalem when you and I were still quite young, where Grandpa Yeshi eventually became a practicing rabbi. And that is where they stayed, with as many trips as they could afford to visit us in Connecticut over the years – until they arrived for my high school graduation ceremony followed that night by the terrible fire."

"Our father, Christopher, met our mother at the university in Seattle. He was not Jewish, raised in a conservative Christian home, but our mother and father were in love and his parents, our Grandma Emma and Grandpa Henry, tolerated their love as did Lyra and Yeshi in Israel. As best they could, they made their own peace with the arrangement. Then our dad's job took him and our mom back east to Connecticut and closer to where she was raised. You and I arrived into this world a few years later, spaced a few grades apart in school. Our parents decided to not emphasize religious instruction for either of us although, as you know, we attended Hebrew School when we were quite young and a bit of Sunday school and Christian Bible camps as kids. The holidays remained enjoyable and festive despite the lack of emphasis on beliefs or prayer rituals. They were smaller occasions with grandparents far away, and you and I gravitated towards our friends nearby to enjoy the various festivities. But

Jared, you know we had our favorite grandparents, as most grandchildren do. You know I favored Safta Lyra just as you favored Grandpa Henry…"

Lyra paused. She and Jared had spotted a pod of whales feeding offshore. They were exhaling through their blowholes and seemed to be playing in the current. Lyra and Jared focused on the scene for a few moments.

"Jared, I'll stop there. I don't want us to forget, that's all. All we have is each other now. But I'm engaged to be married to a wonderful man and into a loving family. Bradlee's family happens to be Jewish and I've given a lot of thought to that and what it means with our legacy. Yes, I'd like to learn more since, as you and I know, neither of us were schooled very much in Jewish prayers and practices. Bradlee doesn't care much for these things like his father does but I know he is quite knowledgeable from his youthful studies. Bradlee had a very rough period away from his family after he lost a woman that he loved some years ago. But he's found me and I feel very fortunate to have found him too. Jared, Bradlee and I love each other and I want to be with him until the end. And I really want you to be an important part of our family ahead. Of this family. The Levitsky's are very welcoming and loving as you have already witnessed from their hospitality, and regardless of your or my views on God and faith."

"Lyra, I'm very happy for you. I have no intention of forgetting our roots. I was able to save *one* family picture when I ran out of the basement that night. I thought you knew but I guess not. Staring at the photo on my nightstand does give me comfort as the years have gone by. I will mail a copy of the photo for you. I promise."

"Thank you, Jared." Lyra reached up on her toes and kissed his cheek.

"One more thing, Jared. Do you remember the story that Safta Lyra told us about her name?" Lyra asked.

Jared smiled and asked Lyra to repeat it again. Each time it was as if the story had taken on more meaningfulness. A twinkle of magic, perhaps.

Lyra disguised her voice as if she was their grandmother and then took on Safta Lyra's persona.

"My dear Einiklach," Lyra spoke using the endearing Yiddish word for 'grandchildren' just as Safta Lyra would say it. "I was born on a full moon. And so my parents decided to name me, '*Leora*,' because it means 'my light.' They told me many times as I was growing up that I was born into this world on a beautiful moonlit and starry night in the summertime in Poland. And there was an exceptionally *bright* star above in the sky that night. My parents went to the rebbe in the village and asked him if it meant anything special. The rabbi said it was the light of God shining upon them and so the rabbi asked my parents to give me a middle name as well, which was '*Mazel*.' It means constellation or destiny in Hebrew as in the expression, "*Mazel Tov!*" that we announce at joyous celebrations. That God may bring us good destiny – good fortune... They asked the rebbe from which constellation the light was shining so brightly. He studied the sky and smiled tenderly. 'It is the Lyra constellation. The ancient harp, just like the one King David of Israel would play so beautifully, perhaps as he composed his Psalms of love and compassion,' the rebbe answered them. And so my parents decided to call me, ever since I was a newborn in their arms, by the nickname, 'Lyra,' instead of Leora. The rebbe also knew that the family name was Shem-Tov, from the line that stretched back to the great Baal Shem Tov and founder of Hasidic Judaism. They used to tell me that the rebbe sat for a long time that night, even after everyone had gone to sleep in the village, staring at the sky in wonderment."

Lyra returned to her natural voice and to herself. Safta

Lyra had passed from within Lyra's spirit. Lyra turned towards her brother.

"So, as we both know Jared, we come from an interesting history. Maybe it's just a story that Safta Lyra made up to soothe her pain from surviving the Holocaust while her parents, our great-grandparents, perished for no good reason. But, maybe there's something to it if we have a willing heart in search of more answers... Perhaps, when the time is right. When the time is right," she repeated and Jared agreed.

"Jared, one more thing before we return. When I was in the hospital, I searched the name, 'Baal Shem Tov,' on my phone. I was curious. Bradlee's father mentioned to me that he and Bradlee were interested in studying Kabbalah, or Jewish mysticism, together and that Bradlee's Uncle Eddie, a rabbi in Toronto, would oversee their learning as their spiritual guide.

"And what did you discover?" Jared was curious himself.

"As I read and tried to make sense of the rabbinic terms, many which I didn't understand – what struck me was the theme the articles all seemed to agree on – that here was a man who lived in the pre-industrial 1700's who knew how to live a life of love and kindness. That's what I understood was the essence of all of his beliefs and teachings to others. Love and kindness, Jared. That God – try as we may to make sense of our own existence and everything around us, of the terrible things that happen in life or the wonderful – that God is just that. A creator and an eternal source of love and kindness... Jared, there was a term that I read online – '*Eyn Sof*' in Hebrew – I think its basic interpretation is that it means, '*There is No End*' – and if we were to even possibly be able to comprehend the concept, it is that God, or 'love and kindness,' *has* no end. Eyn Sof is just another name, or perhaps it *the best* name, we can attribute for 'God.' That we don't just go on and live out our lives until the end of our earthly days, Jared. Something within each of us that is imbued by our Creator - call it our *soul* – remains into the beyond. Into eternity. I am beginning to believe more so that this is the case. That everything is interconnected around us and that love is that unifying force of the universe. The glue that binds everything together into a massive web beyond our comprehension of time and space. Maybe physicists will discover that there is the 'love particle' that is truly the grand unifying force they've been searching for in all their smashing experiments in those particle accelerators. Maybe there will be a mathematical equation they will decipher to try to understand it all. Call it the '*God Equation*,' if you like. But it will likely be an equation without a true beginning, or a middle, or a real end to it all. Only an equation that can explain the transfer of matter and energy from one state to another far better than even Einstein imagined. The Eyn Sof, perhaps. Jared, I know this is heady stuff for our first good talk in a long while but we are adults now and I am being completely honest with you about how I feel inside, just as I hope both of us will be to each other forever..." He nodded in agreement. "So, maybe humans created these ideas about the soul only to soothe ourselves when we each approach our own death, or to soothe those who remain behind from the pain of losing a loved one. A hope for the future. That good mazel... good fortune... lies ahead. I used to lean in that direction before I met Bradlee. But Jared, there have been far too many coincidences these past many months as Bradlee and I began to share our lives together. It is as if our paths were truly destined to meet. I can't explain it better than that. The 'Mazel' is working its magic and I believe it now."

    Lyra quieted. It felt good to have her brother back in her life again. Someone who she felt understood her from their childhood years together. Someone she could truly confide in as her only surviving family member. Jared rose from the stone ledge and held Lyra's hand and then he entwined his fingers gently with his sister's.

"I know how you feel, Lyra, even though I haven't studied these metaphysical issues in such detail. I'll chew on them more when back at the ranch. I promise you that, alright sister?"

"Yes, of course. I just wanted you to know how I feel."

"Thank you for sharing, Lyra. We need to get back to that more often. I'll share more with you about my feelings in time. I promise – again."

"Your promises are piling up, little brother." He started to tickle his big sister in playful jest. He took off running and she chased after Jared down the beach, casted and slinged forearm in tow.

"You know I can still kick your butt in the mile course, don't you?!" Lyra exclaimed while huffing.

"I'm sure you can, big sister! But I can whip yours on any horseback ride, any day!"

Lyra laughed playfully, kicking up sand as if she and Jared and Ansley were back on the beach as children, somewhere here on P.E.I. A different place and time, but all the same. The child sparks were being reignited and it felt really good and right inside her soul.

They returned to the path that would lead them towards the Marshpillow. Lyra changed the topic to her work in North Dakota on the pipeline project. She would be departing soon to return there for a few weeks before she would need to begin her next semester in Seattle at the university. She told Jared about Dr. Bonheim's mentorship and her offer to Lyra to remain in Seattle to continue her studies towards a Ph.D. degree. And that she would be joining Dr. Bonheim's Institute as a research fellow. Jared expressed how proud he was. And also how proud mom and dad would have been.

Lyra corrected him. "How proud they *are*, Jared – they *do exist*, only in the realm of their souls now – but I *believe* they exist – *eternally*." Jared felt comforted by the concept even though he hadn't fully wrapped his mind around it.

Bradlee peeked out the window as he heard their voices and spotted Lyra and Jared in jovial conversation as they approached the entrance. He watched Jared stop and turn towards Lyra with his long arms. He cradled his sister with an endearing hug just as their Safta Lyra and Grandpa Henry used to give both of them as children when love was transferred from one generation to the next by mere touch alone. They entered the Marshpillow home in time for yet another delicious dinner spread, prepared by Jenny, and waiting for everyone to be seated at the table. Lyra gave Bradlee a warm smile followed by a generous hug and Bradlee knew that something wonderful and meaningful had just happened on Lyra's walk together with Jared.

Nathaniel drove Jared to the airport in Charlottetown the next morning. Jared needed to return to his work at the ranch in Kansas. A new group of at-risk troubled high school kids were to arrive shortly for the spring semester of residence and guidance at the ranch. Jared was excelling at his work and his promotions continued with his efforts. The personal challenges he had faced and worked through had provided him with a certain cache of resoluteness in his workings with teens that were carrying tormented fragile egos not dissimilar to his own after the fire. Jared sat back in his airplane seat and studied the clouds as the flight tracked southwest and across the Midwestern skies. Perhaps ego wasn't the right word. Perhaps it was his soul, after all, that was in need of redirection. Healing. Redemption. Lyra was probably right – smart ass as she was, he chuckled in loving recognition. He slept briefly and then awoke refreshed in the awareness that he had a sister again in his life and it felt real good inside. It made him stronger. Yet another hurdle he had overcome and a strength he could harness for more good towards his life's work. '*Tikun Olam,*' he said to himself. He knew what it meant from his grandparents' teachings. That was his motto each morning and, once again, he was ready to tackle the next group of teens with it until they broke. *After all, those troubled teens were just like taming a wild horse!* He laughed, imaging the dangerous work really involved for those kinds of cowboys.

Lyra remained another week at the ranch to fully recover her strength. Her right forearm cast was removed by the orthopedist who replaced it with a soft brace to use for another few weeks. She was healing quickly. Her surgical incision to her posterior scalp had fully healed and her hair had regrown substantially. It was coming in generously now, a full and lush 'mane,' as Bradlee called it – "*like a wild mare's mane in the Badlands,*" he teased her. Lyra's running workouts continued to improve despite the winter blasts of frigid air. She began to ritually clock her times for her runs. The routines comforting her just as she had done in Seattle. There was still that competitive half-marathon race she looked forward to kicking-butt in the spring.

On the last evening at the Marshpillow, Lyra was showering after dinner in Bradlee's apartment above the garage. The bathroom door was slightly ajar and as she exited from the shower, Lyra stood in front of the bathroom mirror and studied her lower abdominal incision. It ran horizontally along her smiling pelvic crease. She realized instinctively that it was where a Cesarean section incision would be made. She was pleased with its appearance. It would be a minimal scar, easily hidden under her bikini bathing suits. Her body was returning to its well-toned shape and she thought it would be nice to wear a bikini this coming summer if she were to return to the Marshpillow after their wedding day. *Wedding day! I'm going to be married soon!* The thought struck her like never before.

Marriage and children and grandchildren raced through her mind. *All because Bradlee asked me if I liked Love Stories.* She ran her fingers gently across the thin fibrous scar tissue of her abdomen. Bradlee teased open the door and approached her from behind as she smiled in the mirror. He caressed her abdomen and held her and kissed her neck and then he interlocked his fingers with Lyra's. Together, they moved their fingers along the length of the scar as he gently kissed her lips.

"Someday Lyra, someday this scar may need to be reopened to bring our child into this world."

"I know, Bradlee, I know, my love. And I'll be just as strong, if not stronger on that day."

He turned Lyra and kissed her lips again and then her neck and caressed her softness and she teased him with her stroking hands. He lifted her in his arms and brought her to bed and he was gentle and passionate and teasingly hungry. They reunited as the waves began to crash inside her. Bradlee entered her gently and held still. She could feel his pulsations, his strength and desire, only to match her own. He remained gentle and then he could feel a rush of infinite energy coming to the surface, uncontrollably. "Lyra, I love you. I will always love you," he moaned in her ear. And she took all of him inside of her. And then they melted once again as the cool breeze meandered from the open window and slowly cooled the volcano that raged beneath their sheets.

"I will miss you terribly, Lyra."

"I know Bradlee. And I, you."

And they were sleepily entangled in each other's arms and legs, entwined like a pretzel once again. Bradlee smiled as he remembered his dark and somber mood in Medora sitting at the bar and glancing at the bartender and his girlfriend in passionate embrace. His turn had finally arrived and it felt wonderful. Magical. Not just the act of making love but the connection, the grand interconnection that he felt he and Lyra shared. It was as if the whole world was full of possibilities for them to explore together and to do something wonderful with their lives. And together, those possibilities seemed endless.

Part Eight

Lyra relaxed on the plane to Minot. Dr. Bonheim had cautioned her that their work would be extensive, and potentially exhausting with long days ahead. Lyra had begun communications again with Dr. Bonheim over the last week of her recovery at the Marshpillow. Dr. Bonheim was mending as well. Her chest wound had fully healed despite twinges of neuropathic pain that seemed to remind her frequently throughout each day that her body was not as resilient as young Lyra's and needed far more time to fully heal. But her brain was just fine and Dr. Bonheim's work at home – and gradually her return to her university office, classroom teaching sessions, and her directorship of the Institute – resumed accordingly.

Jim met Lyra on her arrival to the Minot airport terminal. Lyra informed Jim that she preferred to call him 'Chief' from now on out of respect for his position and for everything he had done for Bradlee and for Dr. Bonheim. He obliged reluctantly. Dr. Bonheim arrived shortly afterwards on her flight from Seattle. This time, she had brought an additional cadre of experts from the Institute. They caravanned together to the pipeline site in an entourage that included Chief Clayburn's pick-up truck and a few van rentals pre-arranged from the airport.

The corral site had been cleaned of its debris from the mob fire and restored with new trailers – this time with more than twice as many as before. There were now two massive teepees that adorned two matching corral areas, eight trailers surrounding each teepee site with two sets of shower and bathroom blocks. A large stable was under construction and could be seen off in the distance at the end of a walking trail from the corrals. Lyra was very pleased and texted Bradlee with the great news and attached some photos.

Chief Clayburn explained that over the past six weeks since the fire destroyed the site, the tribal council had many meetings with the reservation's members to try to reach a consensus on the pipeline project in advance of a vote by all reservation members. When word had spread of Bradlee's generous donation to the tribal council to rebuild the glamping structures, many residents on the reservation opened their wallets in remorse for what had occurred among a rogue group of bandits. But these bandits were still tribal members and Jim knew who they were. He knew where each one worked in the region and lived on the reservation. And he knew their families. And so he went – with Kin beside him at every step – from home to home, business to business, and personally confided with each member in solitude along quiet walks. Anger was in their eyes, as he first approached each one. Until each softened from his consoling and thoughtful words. His measured humility. He was their Chief, as was his father and grandfather, tracing the Dakota tribes to a time and place of harmony among all of his people. He was wise and patient and listened carefully – just as he had done with Bradlee when Bradlee had stormed out of the meeting at the Heritage Center, frustrated by the stark reality of the diminished financial deal. Leadership required a gentle touch with a strong constitution from earned respect over the years of hard decisions and empathy and compassion. And Jim won over each tribal member steadily, one by one, including other longstanding tribal council members, until there was no further opposition to the pipeline. Jim understood the reality: that the pipeline would come to them, regardless, as powerful oil politics is as it is. But if his tribal members could control their own destiny, through more careful planning, then the potentially harmful risks could be dramatically minimized. All that remained were further details – the most optimal position to run the pipeline through the reservation land, the quality and durability of its construction, and the safeguards necessary to protect the watershed, agriculture, and grazing lands. Those were big items but the Chief reassured his people that Dr. Bonheim's consulting group would achieve these goals and the project would be a boon to the reservation's financial health for all its people.

Dr. Bonheim led her troops like a platoon officer across a harsh and difficult landscape. Lyra was instructed to join one of the teams responsible for environmental buffers and protections – water tables and soil samples needed further complex analysis beyond their initial cursory survey over Thanksgiving – to create the exact pipeline pathway that would pose the least risk. Dr. Bonheim led the other team of experts who focused on pipeline design and safety measures. Together, the teams met each evening and into the night after gathering further data throughout the day. The reservation provided the trailers and all the services, including the delicious glamping dinners each evening coordinated by Wichahpi. By the end of the second week, the Institute's staff wrapped up their work. Lyra returned with Dr. Bonheim, and the rest of the staff members, to Seattle. Lyra now truly felt like she was being most useful, enjoined in the real world issues that Dr. Bonheim was tutoring her as her mentor. She was being readied to officially join the Institute in the coming summer.

Lyra poured herself into her academic coursework as the new semester began at the end of January. She returned to her torrid schedule of a full day of lectures and labs and landscape designs in the daytime which then continued into the writing of research papers and further landscape schematics into the night. On top of all of that, Dr. Bonheim assigned Lyra to help compose a draft of the

Institute's final report of their findings and recommendations. The report would serve as Lyra's master's thesis for her degree.

At least, for brief stretches, Lyra's creativity shined as she offered herself one passionate diversion. Lyra had chosen a final landscape design project for her added master's degree. One that was dear to her heart and would allow her to daydream of Bradlee at least for an intense but brief period each day. She had brought back with her to Seattle, detailed measurements of the plot of land in front of the Marshpillow home. Land that had remained wild after the goat pens had long gone. She would design a beautiful garden for the front entrance to the Marshpillow, one uniquely different but just as beautiful as Oji had designed and installed for the Lady Slipper Inn. Lyra hoped that Bradlee and Jenny and Nathaniel might take a liking to her drawings one day ahead. Perhaps after her wedding day. Perhaps it would be her gift to them and heartfelt thanks for welcoming her into the Levitsky family.

Bradlee worked clandestinely in his studio on Lyra's wedding ring, out of view of his parents who were busy restoring their own personal love story. Bradlee's design, in consultation with Uncle Eddie, had been finalized. He called Leo in Newfoundland and ordered a block of wood. *Acer saccharum. Lyra's favorite,* as he smiled. *Pancakes for dinner!* It was a hard maple – the same tree which is tapped in the early spring for its sticky sap. Lyra's ever indulgent sweet maple syrup cravings. The sap then boiled and concentrated and filtered and cooled.

As Bradlee worked, carving out two smaller blocks from the larger chunk, all he could imagine was placing his custom ring on Lyra's finger. To cherish her with this ring as a reminder each day that his love for Lyra will always be sweet and unbroken. *Until the end.* He loved pondering those words... until the end. Three simple words they shared together, forehead to forehead, even if they could only imagine doing so from a distance right now. But as the weeks turned into months they found their ways of sharing moments over the phone. Lyra's jasmine scented love letters were read and reread hundreds of times along with shared pleasant surprises, flowers and chocolates, and handmade tidbits that meant everything would be alright. That the embers of their love were simmering, waiting patiently for their union.

It was a simple yet elegant design that won Bradlee over. From one solid piece of maple he carved an intricate spiral pattern, reminding him of the passion of two lovers entwined in eternal embrace. He left a thick section at the top which he whittled down meticulously until a bed of maple wood rested above the spiral. He finely sanded the raw maple until it was as smooth as a baby's cheeks. Then he polished and stained the maple a dark amber hue. It almost looked edible by the time he had completed his tasks. He removed a single shell from the Lyra necklace that she had gifted him. He chose one of the shells that had an amber tint, slightly tinged, but its strength and durability unharmed, by the corral fire. It would serve as a reminder to them that love should always burn as an eternal flame. A flame that should always guide them with pure hearts through the lifetime of tasks and challenges that await them. Bradlee set the Lyra shell in place and then diligently carved further as the shell was fastened by a durable set of wooden clasps that hugged the shell permanently into place. It was as if the clasps resembled his arms surrounding Lyra, embracing her with his eternal love.

He measured his own ring finger and proceeded to carve a simple but hardy circular ring of maple. He polished and stained it the same dark amber and set it aside. It would be his ring to wear until the end. Then he returned to Lyra's ring. He polished and applied stain fastidiously to any remaining finely detailed areas until he set back in his chair and rested. He had worked the last of the design through the night.

At dawn he rose from his seat and took a long walk along the beach. Thinking. Remembering. Everything seemed right with the world and with Lyra. He was happy and knew their lives were set to begin together. But he returned to thoughts of his career. He stared at his hands. His fingers were sore from their detailed work dedicated to his artful creations. But his hands were birthed into this world for many tasks that could combine the sheer will of his focused mind and heart.

His father was right. Bradlee needed to accept what his calling continued to whisper into his ear each night. That his intelligence and his hands, combined with his heart, would enable him to not only craft beauty from a blank block of wood, or a memorable and emotionally enlightening photograph to impress on a person's conscience, but also that he could be a gifted physician in service to others who needed him. *Who needed him to save their lives.* It would be the greatest good, he thought, to humanity. Every person needed to be loved, and hopefully had someone to love. *If I could save even one person's life then that meant I would have enabled love to prosper.* The universal force would be stronger for it and he would have made his proper and sufficient contribution. He would be making an offering, perhaps many hundreds or thousands in the form of each individual human being who would become his patients – many offerings of 'Tikun Olam' to the universe – and the universe would accept his offerings with open arms.

Bradlee returned from his long morning walk. He cleaned up the scraps and then set the plain 'naked' moccasins on his studio table. His mother was calling him for lunch. She had made him his special meal. Homemade pasta with tomato sauce. All the aromatic spices that he loved were included in the dish, especially paprika. He devoured it all and hugged his mother as if he was a young child in her arms.

He returned to his studio and then searched on his phone for the number. He placed the call.

"Cohen Internal Medicine. How can I help you today?" A friendly curious voice answered.

"Good morning, ma'am. This is Bradlee Levitsky. I was hoping to reach Dr. Cohen, if he is available. It is a personal matter. I'd be happy to leave him a message."

"Not to worry, sir. Dr. Cohen just arrived to his office." Bradlee looked at his watch. It was nine o'clock in Minot, adjusting for the time difference from P.E.I.

"Thank you," he replied. Voices muted but Bradlee heard chatting on the other end.

"Dr. Ben Cohen here. Bradlee, is that you calling?"

"Yes sir. I hope you have been well, Dr. Cohen."

"Thank you. As well as a seventy year old mule can be, I suppose. Takes a little longer each morning than I remember at your age, but I don't mind. It gives me more time to observe which toe is acting up the most with my arthritis." Dr. Cohen chuckled.

"So I here your photography show was a grand success in Medora. I enjoyed it myself when I had the time for a brief visit to the gallery and also swung by to see my old friend, Jim Clayburn."

"Dr. Cohen, your donation to the Heritage Center was very generous. It meant a lot to them."

"How do you know about that, Bradlee? That was supposed to remain confidential."

"Well, I was just following my intuition, sir."

"I see. And *your* donation to the reservation was very kind as well. I heard about that too. It set up quite the frenzy to not only repair that glamping corral that had been destroyed but also to improve it, expand it for the future. I have confidence in Chief Clayburn. The reservation's got a nice set of leaders in place. And his grandson, young Kin –

who you saved Bradlee, from that plane crash – he's being groomed to take over the reins one day for Jim. Even Chiefs don't live forever, Bradlee."

"Yes, I admire young Kin's insightfulness. And thank you again, sir."

"So Bradlee, you're calling me to chat or to ask for another donation?"

"Neither sir. I've given a lot of thought to my future, sir. I've made some decisions recently. I'd like to complete my medical school training..." Bradlee paused a brief moment. "Uh, correction, Dr. Cohen... sir: I'd *love* to complete my training. I am sure of it now, sir. I want to be a physiain with all the dedication and effort required from my mind and heart."

Bradlee paused to let his words sink once again into his own mind. He finally said what he had been thinking about for far longer than a few months. Not a day had truly gone by since he had dropped out of medical school after Samia passed away in his arms that the thought was on his mind to return and finish. He used to think he should return for her sake, in her honor. But that wasn't enough. It had taken him five years to understand that this decision was for him, for his own life, and it felt rightful now. At this time and place in his life.

"Well, quite frankly Bradlee, I've been waiting for this call from you ever since we met at the Scandinavian church in town with your uncle's introductions."

"You have, sir?"

"Yes. Listen Bradlee, I've got over forty years of experience behind me as a physician. That's a long road. One day you'll be in my shoes looking at a young person who has all the gifts and yet needs a little time to sort through other things that interfere and cloud the mind. I look for those types even more when I sit on the admissions committee interviewing the newest crop of medical school candidates here in North Dakota because those are the types who I know *really* want it. They've suffered through some soul searching until the truth burns inside so deeply that they can't deny what nature intended for them. And you're one of those, Bradlee. So, welcome back, son."

Bradlee didn't quite know what to say. Maybe Dr. Cohen knew him, he thought, better than he knew himself.

"Thank you, Dr. Cohen." Bradle's emotions began to well to the surface. But his tears now flowed with goodness. No sadness. No pain. He was being welcomed but with a renewed spirit within his being. A healed heart and soul.

"Bradlee, enough with the 'Dr.' salutations. My name is Benjamin, as my mother – may she forever rest in peace - would call me when she was irate over one thing or another that I had done as a child." He laughed. "I've preferred Ben over my adult life and career. '*Big Ben*,' like the London clock. I figure if Clayburn gets his 'Chief' title then the least I can have is to add 'Big' in front of my name. I have a bit of the stomach size to support it now." He laughed again.

"So, let me know this, Mr. Bradlee Levitsky. It's March 1st today. If you were to hop on a plane tomorrow, would you be interested in finishing up your last few months of medical school training here in Minot? That is, provided you can pass a comprehensive exam on arrival to demonstrate your competence in the basic sciences and clinical medicine that you might be a bit rusty with after the long pause. Bradlee, I serve on the admissions committee and the medical school is based in Grand Forks. But fourth year students are dispersed throughout North Dakota to complete their clinicals and electives. I'm sure we can integrate you quickly into the hospital here in Minot. You can even spend a little time with me at my office if you are at all interested in Internal Medicine as a specialty after graduation."

"That is an incredibly kind offer, Dr. Cohen. I've had

good fortune ever since I first stepped foot in North Dakota. But as to my specialty, I am thinking of Emergency Medicine. I want to be on the front lines to save lives, Ben. I think that is my calling, similar to my dad who is a trauma surgeon. But also, the shift work hours in ER medicine may allow me to squeeze enough free time to continue to enjoy my photography and woodcarving hobbies."

"Got it. Just like your Uncle Eddie and my good friend all these years, with his work as a rabbi and a woodcarver. Bradlee, you come from a very talented and gifted family, no doubt… My offer stands on the table. You accepting it? Going once, going twice, three..."

"Yes, Ben. Yes!!! Thank you. I'm on the first plane to Grand Forks tomorrow morning. Promise! But, *planes* that is. Don't imagine there's a direct flight from P.E.I. to Grand Forks."

"No, there sure ain't! But you'll get here eventually. Try not to crash along the way, will you son?"

Bradlee laughed and Ben joined him. Enough time had passed by then, where humor could replace trauma. After all, humor was truly the best medicine for the mind. Both men knew that.

"I'll alert the university admissions office that you'll be arriving tomorrow. They'll make all the arrangements needed from there. Call me once that's all finalized over the next few days. I'll expect you to report for hospital duty here in Minot the next day after that. Time is of the essence with the medical school graduation ceremony just about three months away."

"Yes, sir."

"Oh, —— and Bradlee. You may want to open up a few medical references while on the flight over. That exam can be a doozy. Hate to see you need to repeat third year again after the rigorous training you received in Toronto. So – study, study, study! Crash study! Ha!" Ben started to laugh again. "See you soon, young man. I have full confidence in you. Like I said to you in Minot, if your uncle thinks you've got the right stuff, then I have no reason to doubt him. He's a wise man."

"Agreed. My Uncle Eddie certainly is. Thanks Ben. From my heart."

"Your welcome. Take care, Bradlee. Safe travels."

They hung up.

Bradlee glanced at the wedding rings. Then over to Ruthy's watercolor. And finally, at Ruby's empty pie tin that he had brought back with him from Minot as a souvenir from his lunch with James. Life's puzzle pieces were falling quite nicely into place. He glanced out the window towards the ocean. God, he missed Lyra. He picked up his phone. Lyra would be in class by now at this early morning hour.

He decided to text her:

Returning to North Dakota tomorrow. Have a craving to save more lives.
It appears Dr. Seashell will soon earn his prefix after all.
Love and Kisses, Your favorite malacologist.

Lyra received the message while in her first class of the day. Dr. Bonheim had returned to lecturing and she was enjoying learning from her mentor once again.

Dr. Seashell? malacologist… a craving to save more lives.' She reread the text message and let it sink in. Bradlee liked casting riddles in texts for her to decipher.

She texted back:

No sheshells by the sheshore in ND. Sorry to disappoint. Save more lives? Suggest stethoscope and white coat for starters.

Leave multitool in pocket.
Willing to volunteer for thorough physical exams from gifted hands.
My B will need lots of practice. Medicine can be exceptionally hard to master.
As hard as a hungry moon snail must work for his seashell.

Bradlee opened the text and started to laugh uncontrollably. Hysterically. "Touché, Lyra!" he uttered happily. She remembered every last detail going back to their first discourse on the train. Their first touch of hands. *She's darn crafty and teasing, alright!* He loved her for those traits too. *And such a flirt!* God only knew how much he wanted to be with her right then to celebrate the good news.

THE MIDDLE OF MAY ARRIVED. Bradlee flew from Minot to Seattle to enjoy Lyra's graduation ceremony. Summa cum laude. Lyra had not only earned both of her master's degrees in just one year but she had excelled with the highest distinction possible from each department's faculty. Dr. Bonheim set Lyra's tassel across her graduation cap as Lyra marched onto the stage to accept her diplomas. Then she hugged Lyra as only a mentor could offer – respectfully and affectionately.

As Lyra walked across the stage she noticed a very tall and muscular African American man who was standing in his cap and gown off in the distance, hugging his sweetheart. He was towering above the assembled crowd. Lyra descended the stage and approached him as he turned.

"Carl…" but that was all Lyra could say before tears came to her eyes. Carl turned and approached Lyra and she reached to give him a hug. Carl wrapped her up and held her close.

"Thank you, Carl. Thank you. You saved my soul and my life. I will never forget that," Lyra said quietly to him as she held on.

"It's OK, Lyra. I'm very proud of you. You look like you're doing great now. Congrats on those diplomas. Two of them, I see, in your hand. Very sweet!" Carl replied. "Hey, great news to share! I've been drafted into the NFL. I'll be a defensive lineman playing for the hometown team, the Seattle Seahawks, come September. I'll send you a pair of tickets to my first game next season." His face was beaming with pride. "Hey, let me introduce you. This here is my fiancée, D'vash. She's told me it means 'honey' in the Hebrew language.

"A pleasure to meet you, D'vash. *Love* your name! Carl here is a great man. He came to *my* defense when I needed him to. I wish you both much love and happiness together and a wonderful career, Carl. Please be safe on the field. I know it's quite dangerous out there."

Lyra and Carl exchanged their contact information in their phones. Lyra hugged them both and said goodbye and then located Bradlee through the crowd.

"I just found him, Bradlee. Carl – the man who saved me that terrible Halloween night. It was good to see him again and thank him, finally. What a coincidence meeting him here in this massive graduation crowd!"

"I'm happy for you, Lyra. I'd love to meet Carl someday – to thank him myself."

"Oh, I think we will. Important people in our lives don't go away forever. They tend to come back around. It's just the way it is," Lyra replied.

Bradlee kissed Lyra, passionately, as she opened the cardboard tubes and unwound her two master's diplomas.

"Very proud of you, Lyra, Very proud! Your family would be too. Very much. You know that in your heart."

She smiled and hugged Bradlee and knew that, someday, she would raise a family of her own with this wonderful man in her arms. Happiness was not enough to describe how elated she was at that very moment. The pieces of the puzzle were all coming together, blissfully.

The next day, Lyra and Bradlee flew to Grand Forks together. It was Bradlee's turn to be awarded his degree – Doctor of Medicine. The medical school based in Grand Forks had accepted all of Bradlee's credits from his previous course of study in Toronto. Dr. Cohen saw to that by virtue of Bradlee's near perfect score on his entrance exam. This was followed by impeccable knowledge, clinical skills, and empathetic bedside manners as demonstrated every day during his last few months of hospital rotations in Minot.

Dr. Cohen had decided to make one more call on Bradlee's behalf. While he would miss not seeing Bradlee remain in North Dakota to further his medical career, he knew that Bradlee needed to join Lyra in Seattle as she continued in her Ph.D. studies and work at the Institute. Perhaps another 'Chief' might be of assistance. Ben acknowledged the benefits that had been derived over his career befriending various chiefs of all kinds. In this case, he picked up the phone and dialed an old medical school friend who was the Chief of the Department of Emergency Medicine and Professor at the University of Washington in Seattle – Dr. Simon Shapiro. A man with hundreds of publications to his name and teaching awards from just about every medical society that could offer him one. Ben liked playing the role of matchmaker. He hadn't brought Bradlee and Lyra together but he was going to do his best to ensure that they would not live apart as they would soon begin their married lives together. And he knew that Bradlee was a gifted student and now, physician. A younger Dr. Levitsky had joined his father, among the generations of esteemed Levitskys that preceded them, as a caring physician. A life saver, God willing.

Simon Shapiro listened to what 'Big Ben' Cohen had to

rave about this young smart whippersnapper of a physician, and then agreed to make an exception to accommodate Bradlee's highest skills and recommendations from his trusted friend. Dr. Shapiro added a residency spot in Emergency Medicine for Bradlee at the main university hospital. He would be due to start three weeks after his medical school graduation.

The next few days were a whirlwind of activity as Lyra and Bradlee quickly rented a car and departed from Grand Forks. Their route westward across North Dakota mostly tracked the same cross country path beside the train tracks as when they first met. They passed Lakota and then stopped along the shores of Devils Lake to admire the pelicans that inhabited the pristine lake and wetlands beside the Spirit Lake Reservation. Then, onward through Rugby as Bradlee pointed out the stone monument that he had stopped at along his bicycle journey to mark the half way point across North America. They continued to track the railroad as it passed adjacent to acres upon acres of quiet solitude of northern prairie. It was truly a romantic day traveling through the breadbasket of the heartland. The springtime was flushed with the young sprouts of wheat dancing in gentle breezes. Bradlee stopped the car and walked over to Lyra's door. He escorted her into the midst of a massive field of wheat as the stalks caressed their legs and tickled their noses.

Such beauty in time slowed to the pace of a wandering wheat stalk in a Midwestern breeze. The passionate thought had remained with him ever since his first encounter with Lyra on their westbound train. How fragile life is but secure in the arms of the one you love.

He turned and embraced Lyra in his arms and then fell onto one knee. There would be no witness today other than the heavens above them. He wanted *his* chance to ask Lyra for her hand in marriage and he had no better a place to imagine doing so than in this expansive prairie in the sunshine of glistening wheat stalks and hay bales. Her jasmine perfume enticing his desires and moving his soul to bond with his destiny. *Equality needed equality in their relationship after all*, he thought as he smiled and recalled Lyra's strength and courage. Lyra was truly *his* blessing. And he wanted her beside him for the remainder of his days. Yes – Until the end...

Bradlee removed his cowboy hat.

"Lyra — will you marry me and make me the happiest man on earth? And in all of the heavens above us?" Lyra blushed in her lilac spring dress. She played with his curls.

"Yes Bradlee, I will and I will forever!" He lifted Lyra in his arms and they kissed passionately. He set her onto a hay bale. Then he pulled a stalk of wheat and wound two strands for rings. He placed one on Lyra's ring finger as they kissed again. And then Lyra did the same for Bradlee's finger. Bradlee reached inside his jacket and pulled out a pair of moccasins. They were made from Oji's amber-stained deerskin softness and covered in the most beautiful array of seashells from his Newfoundland collection. It was Bradlee's simple wedding gift for Lyra yet he knew the moccasins would last their lifetimes together. He slipped them onto Lyra's feet and looked deeply into her eyes.

"Lyra, just as the sea provides a seemingly infinite source of seashells and sand, so shall my love be for you, eternally." He lifted her again and twirled her in the field under the glorious sunshine. And he whispered to Lyra that it was enough for him – to declare their intentions to the heavens above in this field. To Bradlee, their wedding day would be just a formality now for the assembled guests but it shall be a grand occasion to celebrate among loving family and friends.

May 22ⁿᴰ arrived. The Lady Slipper Inn had never looked as beautifully incarnated, with heirloom roses upon roses hanging from every planter and bannister. Oji had clipped hundreds more from the garden and Zach had worked continuously through the previous night delicately fastening the roses onto a trellis constructed inside the gazebo. Oji briefly ran back to her home with Kin to work on some last minute details. Together, mother and son had crafted many pairs of moccasins that would serve as parting gifts for each family member and friend in the wedding party. She was so proud of her son. Kin had honed his skills to the point where he was responsible for the initial cuttings and creations of the moccasins themselves. Oji could now focus exclusively on the creative decorations for each pair.

The guests were assembling now. Angel and Guillermo arrived with Isabel and Gabriel in their finest dress. Then Leo and Rachel appeared with Ruthy in tow, holding her small backpack that contained her watercolors and a small canvas. Ruthy proceeded to sit quietly in a chair and prepared her items for the ceremony to soon follow.

Peter arrived to the occasion with his lovely wife, Elaine. He looked very dapper in his tuxedo with a bicycle-wheel checkered handkerchief stuffed in his breast pocket. He scurried to the inn's kitchen. Then, he fondly meandered about making everyone's acquaintance as he offered bite-sized tastes of his 'Pe-Ho-Chee-Moo-T' creations from a silver serving plate. Everyone who knew better indulged and admired his creativity and poignant sense of humor.

Carol and Robert, the professorial pair, were having a lively conversation with Thomas and Nancy, describing the incredible beauty of the Norwegian fjords. They were encouraging the innkeepers to take that glorious trip they had been only dreaming about for so many years.

Tom and Frank, from the Heritage Center, arrived fittingly dressed like the true cowboys that they actually were. They meandered with their lovely wives about the grounds and mingled with the crowd of well-wishers from the Minot community.

    Ruby was escorted hand in hand by James. They looked wonderfully happy together. Bradlee knew. James had called him a few weeks earlier to tell Bradlee the good news – that he and Ruby were now engaged and planned to tie the knot themselves very soon. James had discovered new love with Ruby, just as Bradlee had with Lyra. And Bradlee could feel their happiness knowing they would enjoy the remainder of their lives together. The two men were growing closer, understanding and respecting each other even more, in their need and desire to find new love. And Ruby had brought a multitude of boxes of her delicious pies. She and James had spent hours together in Ruby's kitchen cooking-up the many bite-sized varieties and garnishing their hors d'oeuvres with sprinkles of rose petals for the occasion. All the better to bring new love together as Ruby believed her magical pies had done for Lyra and Bradlee.

    Kin joined his mother Oji's side along with her husband, Jeremiah. And then Chief Clayburn arrived with Wichahpi and numerous other family members from the reservation. He was dressed in the robes and headdress of his traditional tribal Chief attire and Wichahpi had donned her traditional deerskin outfit as well. Wichahpi had arranged for a handful of spirit drummers and dancers to join from the reservation. It was considered a great honor to have their presence for the occasion as they proceeded to dance and chant prayerfully for the assembling guests. The dancers were performing a ritual ceremony of peace and blessings for the bride and groom as the drummers paced the dancers through the rhythmic beating on their deerskin drums and announced calls to the skies like soaring hawks.

    The drummers paused. One of the dancers hurried to help seat any remaining guests from the community. The great lawn in front of the gazebo was arranged with twenty rows of white chairs. A few hundred guests had arrived, most from the nearby Minot community who were there as witnesses to the disseminated news of a great North Dakota love story.

The dancers surrounded the gazebo. Silence among the assembled guests. Then a single drum beat echoed across the grasses and magnificent gardens. It was their cue to begin. Thomas and Nancy descended from the inn's patio and walked slowly down the aisle. Honored host and hostess for the grand occasion. Nancy setting her cane carefully with each step. The pair radiating kindness and decency from a full life lived amongst the Minot community. The aging loving couple looked regal. Thomas in a fine gray tuxedo and Nancy in a long flowing emerald gown. They took their seats in the front row.

The steady drum beat continued. Ezra, in a colorful collage of whimsical clothes, escorted Ansley down the aisle, arm in arm. Ansley looked sensational in her rose-colored dress, made by the hands of Oji. They entered the gazebo and took their place on each side.

Harry kissed his wife, Susie. He was balling and sniffling in tearful joy. The pair were seated in the front row beside Thomas and Nancy. Harry composed himself and then jiggled up the three gazebo steps in his old fashioned black tuxedo, tails and purple top hat, and stood at the center. To the crowd, indeed he looked as genuinely a wizard could be with his long curly mustache and cherubic cheeks. He was beaming with happiness and pride for bringing Lyra and Bradlee together on *his* train. Bradlee had managed to reach Harry through Amtrak's headquarters and he was thrilled to be offered the chance to officiate for the occasion. Bradlee just knew that Lyra would love to see him and Susie again and so the surprise was in store for her.

Uncle Eddie was next. He quietly and unassumingly

sauntered down the aisle to the drum's steady beat and took his place beside Harry. In his jacket pocket was a simple glass.

The lone drummer paused and raised his arm for silence. Now, two drummers began to beat and they chanted in slow soulful tones. Bradlee exited the inn, hand in hand, with his dear mother. They descended the steps as Jenny escorted her son down the aisle. Bradlee looked smashingly handsome in a dark blue tuxedo and tails and a crisp white shirt. His silver cufflinks were a gift from his father and they bore the markings of the staff of Aesculapius, the ancient mythical God of medicine. On his head was a traditional Jewish kippah but it was magnificently colorful. Lyra had learned from Jenny how to weave its threads and so Lyra decorated Bradlee's wedding kippah with images of hummingbirds and dragonflies. Only Angel and Bradlee knew what these symbols truly meant to Lyra.

Then, out popped Ruthy in a beautiful pink satin dress. Alongside of her stood little Samia in a pure white dress. Samia was gently holding two small handcrafted wooden boxes between her outstretched palms. Ruthy guided Samia as the two stepped forward, slowly down the aisle. Samia was smiling and peaceful despite the crowd. The guests encouraged the little toddler onward as Samia brought the gift boxes that contained the wedding rings and climbed up the gazebo steps. Bradlee knelt in front of Samia. He reached out his hands to collect the boxes. He kissed Samia's forehead. And then, Samia reached out her hand and held her palm over Bradlee's heart for a long moment. She smiled at Bradlee – as if from an eternally knowing place – and then scurried off to join Ibrahim and Sofia. Bradlee knew there was no coincidence to Samia's outstretched hand. He inspected the contents of the carved wooden boxes and then turned and placed them into Rabbi Eliezer's hands. Ruthy returned to her seat and continued to watercolor the gazebo scene unfolding before her.

No one present knew, beside Lyra and Bradlee, that Rabbi Eliezer had asked the engaged couple to set their wedding date for this specific date of May 22nd – for it was the day that the Baal Shem Tov's soul had passed on to heaven so many years ago. Their wedding day was not only to honor their eternal love for each other but to celebrate the Baal Shem Tov's legacy of spiritual union – of love and kindness. A distant relative that Lyra now felt a certain kinship across the ages. And so, the 'Mazel' would only be intensified in commemoration of this day.

Utter silence descended. Now three drummers joined forces together. A steady strong beat alternating with waves of faster and more intense sound. Then lighter, more gentle taps. The cycle repeated. It was like an ebbing and flowing of the energy of the universe. Of the union of two spirits. Solemnity. And the drummers' voices rose and unified their chanting into one clarion voice. They were calling for the bride.

Nathaniel heeded their cue as he opened the door from the inn to the porch. Lyra came forward onto the patio and descended the steps, held carefully by Nathaniel's hand. She was like a breezy hummingbird in flight. Her wedding dress was an assemblage of iridescent colors that illuminated in the afternoon sunlight. Her gown flowed to a long train that swept behind her. The train was covered in peacock feathers. Lyra had sewn her own veil out of ornamental white satin rose patterns as it covered her fully grown thick hair strewn with jasmine vines freshly cut from the inn's garden trellis. She was absolutely incredibly stunning to all, but especially to Bradlee Avraham Levitsky who stood at the gazebo entrance and accepted his bride from his father's arm.

Bradlee and Lyra walked up the steps, arm in arm, and stood in front of Harry and Rabbi Eliezer. On their feet were two sets of moccasins. Bradlee chose a pair without any adornment. Only the purity of plainness. Today was his bride's special day. And Lyra – she was wearing Bradlee's gifted moccasins that he had offered her in the wheat field as a remembrance of his eternal love. Where Lyra walked, Bradlee would follow, and he would care for her until the end.

The drummers held silent.

It was Harry's turn – finally, and he could hardly contain himself any further.

"Now don't y'all look so gussied up like copperheads in the tallgrass?! What a fine lookin' couple, we have here!" The audience burst into laughter as the somber mood lightened. Harry's belly jiggled with laughter as he winked towards Bradlee, blew a kiss towards Susie, and gave Lyra a generous smile.

Lyra whispered to Bradlee as she glanced at Harry's wedding ring. "Harry and Susie are husband and wife?! How could I have missed that? Bradlee, thank you for inviting Harry. We will never forget this day now, won't we, she said amusingly." Lyra nuzzled Bradlee and then they stood straight before Harry, trying to keep their composure.

"Ladies and gents, children of all ages and sizes – I present to you our bride 'n groom!" The audience clapped and whistled as if they were attending a circus performance. Harry continued. "When Susie and I got hitched forty-four years ago she was fixin' for a lickin' of some peach punch before we'd even been kissin'!" Lyra glanced at Bradlee and whispered something to him. Harry caught them.

"Now wha'ch y'all whisperin' to each other?" he said.

Lyra's face grew serious before Harry started to laugh again. It was infectious and Lyra could hardly contain herself.

"Folks, I have a few words to share with the bride and groom if they'll indulge this ol' wizard before the rabbi gets on with the hitchin' show." Harry winked at Lyra and teased at his mustache. Then his demeanor grew serious for a sudden change.

"It goes like this, Lyra and Bradlee... We are born, we live, and we die. But I think there's more to our story than that. When I met Susie I knew she was the one for me. Why? I asked myself the same darn question when I couldn't shake her from my head like a coon dog chasin' an armadillo. Susie was the one 'cause she was my better half. She had what I was lackin.' I needed her confidence, her people lovin', and some of her brain power and plain common sense. And maybe a good ol' kick in the pants from her, at times, to get things done in my life. To let me know when the thinkin' becomes the doin'. In my job and around the house. But without my Susie, I surely wouldn't have become nearly half the man that I am. So, you see folks, two halves *are* needed to make a whole. And when that whole is wrapped up in love, then *anythin's* possible."

Harry stared intently at the young couple.

"Lyra... Bradlee... be good to each other. Love each other from the source – what resides within your hearts and souls. Forgive and forget. Laugh more and cry less. And always remember to toot each other's horns when you most need to. The rest of life will take darn good care of itself... until the end... until the end." Harry winked at the bride and groom.

"So, I ask now of all you good people assembled here today. Is there anyone among us... and I mean anyone!... who objects to the union of this here lovin' couple... then come'on forward now... or forever hold your peace?"

There was a long moment of silence as Harry's eyes darted across the audience. He was a showman on par with the best there ever was. Lyra was loving it all.

"Good now, 'cause if there was... I'd a thrown the darn weasel straight into this here big ol' vat of peaches and cream pie that 'Sweet Ruby' has concocted for us all." The crowd went wild with uproarious laughter.

Harry lifted his purple top hat and waved it to the crowd. More cheers and laughter. He turned towards the rabbi and said: "That good enough for you, Rabbi? I sure warmed 'em up for you, didn't I?" Harry affectionately grasped Lyra's and Bradlee's hands and then stepped aside for Rabbi Eliezer.

The drummers began a slow methodical beat as they waited for the rabbi to take his position in front of Lyra and his nephew. Then silence again. The rabbi started to sing a beautiful melody. Bradlee was taken aback by his uncle's booming melodic voice. Something Bradlee had never known was yet another of Uncle Eddie's many talents. It was Lyra's cue to slowly encircle Bradlee seven times. Ansley held Lyra's flowing train as Lyra completed the task and returned to her place beside Bradlee. The rabbi had chanted the traditional Jewish wedding blessings in Hebrew, and then in English, with each of Lyra's turns. Then, Bradlee turned to Lyra and opened the wooden box. He lifted and placed his crafted ring on Lyra's finger. Lyra stared at Bradlee's carved work of utter beauty – the woven maple wood with a Lyra shell cradled in its magnificent setting. With tears in Lyra's eyes, Ansley handed Lyra the other wooden box and she opened it and placed Bradlee's circular maple wood ring on his finger. Meaningful symbols of their eternal love. Bradlee lifted Lyra's veil for all to see her beauty. They sipped from Rabbi Eliezer's wine cup. And then Bradlee kissed Lyra passionately and they touched their foreheads together and held. They were wedded. Their new journey had begun. Rabbi Eliezer then placed a simple glass that he had wrapped in a napkin onto the gazebo floor. He gently covered the glass with a thin piece of maple wood. Bradlee glanced at the audience and then jumped in the air and smashed the wood with his moccasin foot. The glass shattered. A round of 'Mazel Tov' ensued as all assembled repeated the phrase together.

Bradlee returned to embrace Lyra. Again, they held their foreheads together and felt the warmth of their bonded energy ascend through their hearts and into their minds. And then it ascended above them and into the clouds. Ruthy saw it rise. So did Gabriel and Jim and Oji and Kin. They knew. They were the lucky ones who could see the unity of their souls. The secrets of the universe. Just as Lyra and Bradlee knew it at that very moment.

"Let's get this party started!!!" Peter cried out. The drummers drummed, and the dancers danced, and then a DJ took over the show as Lyra and Bradlee descended from the gazebo and into the arms of well-wishers. Then they started to dance the afternoon away in the soft spring grasses. It was rock 'n' roll and romantic ballads and all the fixings for a grand occasion. Thomas and Nancy had catered a feast for all in attendance. And there was love and kindness everywhere. Ruthy put away her watercolor sketch. She would refine the details later when she returned home to Newfoundland. She spotted a young boy of similar size on the porch and walked over to greet him. Kin was in a fine outfit and she sensed his kind soul. She reached out her hand to Kin and he accepted it and they shared a knowing smile as they glanced at Lyra and Bradlee and then returned to each other's eyes. Then, without a word spoken, Kin pointed a finger towards the sky and the clouds above them as they shared a glance upwards. Something moved inside of them. Ruthy blushed and Kin withdrew his hand into his pocket. But for a brief moment there was a comforting knowing that electrified their two innocent souls.

Rabbi Eliezer spotted a man he recognized standing by the white fence at the far entrance to the inn. He had been observing the wedding from the distance. It was an old man in a black suit and a long grey beard. He had a twinkle in his eye as Rabbi Eliezer approached him with an outstretched arm. They embraced affectionately.

"They found each other, Rav Chaim. You were right all along," Rabbi Eliezer said to the old man. "You always believed that it would happen someday and it has arrived. Would you believe it started on a train ride, Chaim, of all places…?! There were dark trains to Auschwitz. But then there are trains that bring us to a love story. Redemption. You agree, my dear mentor and friend?!"

Rabbi Chaim Shem Tov looked deeply into Rabbi Eliezer's eyes.

"God works in mysterious ways. We've known that our whole lifetimes, Eliezer. But the light that has guided their love started long before they boarded that train. Long before… And it will continue now, into eternity. Eyn Sof, my dear friend. If there is love and kindness, then two willing hearts *will find their destiny*. Their Mazel. As the Baal Shem Tov said, 'From every human being there rises a light.'"

"Rav Chaim, may you go in peace now. You have been a blessing to me. May your light of wisdom and truth and love… shine forever."

Part Nine

THE WINTER SNOWMELT TRICKLED DOWN THE MOUNTAIN and collected into the streambed. It was a beautiful morning in Newfoundland. The air still cool but spring was gaining on its predecessor, ready to overtake the winter chill at any moment.

Lyra and Bradlee ascended along the trail. Ruthy followed them and guided two little ones lingering behind. The stragglers were busy tossing pebbles into the streambed and smelling wildflowers. Towards the apex of Lookout Mountain the stairs confronted them and Ruthy lifted the smaller one into her arms while Bradlee gently grasped the larger against his back. They climbed steadily to the apex. Lyra and Bradlee took their seats in the comfortable wooden chairs and admired the view from the summit. The others played as they tumbled in the grasses under the watchful eye of Ruthy. Ruthy took her responsibility quite seriously as a doting God-niece. She liked her new title that was bestowed upon her four years earlier. Ruthy was now a blooming young lady, a teenager, and her artwork had begun to receive its just notoriety, adding good fortune to Leo's and Rachel's studio.

As the little bear cubs danced and shouted about, Bradlee took Lyra's hand and they climbed further up the hill, even closer to the clouds. There was silence as they peered to the horizon in awe.

Bradlee then spotted something glistening in the morning dew and reached down to collect it into his palm. "Well, look what we have found…" he said.

It was a seashell – a lightning whelk – the kind that Lyra most loved.

"Now look here, Lyra. Give me your hand." She complied as he placed her index finger onto the shell at its natural whirling starting point.

"I've always loved tracing my finger around a shell's grooves. It begins here, from the source, and then it continues round and round…" Bradlee continued to slide Lyra's finger, "… until the end."

Lyra couldn't help but smile coyly.

"Now Bradlee Seashell, you can't expect a girl like me to fall for *those* lines again?!"

"Well, why not, Lyra Seashell?"

"Because you are an incorrigible romantic, that's why."

She smiled and turned her head to glance at Ruthy and the others below with her right eye and then she peered into the clouds.

"Bradlee?"

"Yes, Lyra."

"Do you see them in the clouds, too?"

Bradlee looked skyward and followed Lyra's eyes to the same spot. They stood silently and peered at the clouds together.

"I do, Lyra. They are beautiful souls that have joined us, aren't they?"

Jasmine and Benji darted up the hill towards them. Four years old now. Twins brought into this world from Lyra's fertile womb. They ran, giggling all the way, into their parents' outstretched arms and hugged them for shelter. Ruthy stood and smiled. She knew they were in safe hands. Ruthy then glanced to another area in the sky in wonderment. She waved to her mother and blew her a kiss just as she always did before.

They began to descend from the mountain. The children

were in the midst of euphoric play as they gave chase to dandelion seeds lofted into the winds by Ruthy.

Lyra stopped and held Bradlee's hands as she leaned to touch their foreheads together.

"Bradlee, hold me now." He held Lyra tight to his chest as the winds picked up over the ridge and rushed through the valley.

"Tell me, Bradlee. Am *I* your love story?"

"Yes Lyra. Yes – you are and always will be." She smiled and kissed his lips.

"And am I *yours*, Lyra, until the end?"

"No Bradlee – not until the end. Until beyond the end."

"Until eternity?" Bradlee asked her.

"Yes Bradlee, until eternity."

"And beyond that too, Lyra. Far beyond. Eyn Sof... Eyn Sof..." he whispered quietly into her ear and then to the clouds above.

They kissed passionately. Their love ever finding new ways, each day, to express itself. Then they chased after Jasmine and Benji but their children's energy continued to sweep them down the mountain. They stopped and peered into each other's eyes just the same as the day they were surrounded by wandering wheat stalks in a Midwestern breeze.

"Dr. Baruch Avraham Levitsky, will life *always* be this adventurous with you?" Lyra asked him.

"I'm afraid so, my dear, Dr. Lyra Sasha Flurey."

"I thought so. Then where shall we explore next?"

Bradlee then remembered someone who had great meaning in his life when he was younger. *Perhaps it is time.*

"There is a good friend of mine, Lyra. His name is Yusef. He has lived as a monk for many years in the Abbey of Monte Oliveto Maggiore in Asciano. It is in the beautiful

Tuscany region in the Italian countryside. I thought we might pay him a visit soon together…"

Lyra welcomed the offer.

Bradlee then clasped Lyra's hand and they continued on their journey.

Author's Note

It is an emotionally cathartic undertaking to compose a love story. Like most middle aged men I have lived long enough to understand the significance and complexities, as well as the fragility, of love. I've been hurt by unrequited love and thoroughly repaired by love.

The plot in *Until The End* took various twists and turns as I sat down to write in the time available to me away from my regular duties as a physician. Sometimes, I'd have only brief moments to jot an idea or a paragraph. Later, I'd work at the keyboard for hours at a stretch, even occasionally through the night, to compose a lingering thought into text or draft a tender dialogue between characters, drawing from ideas that sprang forth from certain experiences in my own life or pure imagination. Many ideas arrived during frequent pleasant strolls through the nearby woods with my dogs. Streams of conscious – and perhaps subconscious – nuances forming ideas for plot and connections between characters. And so the characters I developed have ended up meaning something more to me. They are as virtually real in my life as my own family. I think they always will be. Like the characters who guide Dorothy in "The Wizard of Oz," some, but not all, of the characters in this story do represent real people in my life, including myself – yet it still remains a work of complete fiction.

On a family vacation to South Carolina's coast I was enjoying a morning walk along the beach, collecting a few stranded seashells. A momentary idea was born to have a young man entertain a certain avocation as a malacologist. A lure as a conversation starter with Lyra and also a symbol – the Lyra shell – that would subsequently be the inspiration for her chosen name. And Lyra… when my wife and I were visiting our daughter who was studying abroad in Florence, Italy we visited the Uffizi Gallery adjacent to the Piazza della Signoria. I have always loved marble sculptures. And there before me was the four-hundred year old Bernini masterpiece, Apollo and Daphne. Daphne's utter chiseled beauty and expression and poise metamorphosized into Lyra as I began my story. Fiction mirroring life, a harkening to the wisdom of ancient mythology and to the eternal needs and desires for love.

And the settings: Well, they derived from a menagerie of life experiences. I have traveled twice across North America and circumnavigated Nova Scotia – these journeys all while on the seat of a bicycle. Thoughts such as... *"Such beauty in time slowed to the pace of a wandering wheat stalk in a Midwestern breeze."* Birds chirping. Sun baking. The mind has time to think while bicycling a hundred miles day after day from dawn to dusk. To reminisce and imagine and absorb meaningfulness in the surrounds of breezy silences and the aroma of the native soil. These were glorious moments in rapture that begged for a proper setting for romance. I'm not quite sure why my travels through North Dakota particularly struck a nerve, as if I was having déjà vu experiences – but bicycling through the Badlands National Park in Medora, staying at the Dakotah Rose Bed and Breakfast in Minot with generous hosts, and dining at an upbeat restaurant in town – provoked me to imagine The Lady Slipper Inn and Ruby's on the River, and create the various characters who Bradlee and Lyra would befriend in this story. If my readers haven't been to the Dakotas, I encourage you to explore the landscape, the solitude and relaxed pace, and the wonderful hospitality of the people in the region.

My wife and I have also vacationed in Nova Scotia and Newfoundland. While visiting the magnificent Gros Morne

National Park in Newfoundland we hiked from Woody Point along the Lookout Trail that wound to its apex, known as Partridgeberry Hill. There really is a long rise of wooden steps to climb to the apex where two colorful Adirondack chairs indeed are waiting for you to relax one's behind into and rest weary arms and languid legs and enjoy the vast view of the Tablelands, Gros Morne Mountain, Bonne Bay and the tangible cloud formations. The scene in the book between Bradlee and Ruthy, from that exact lookout, was spawned by one of those permanently etched vibrant memories that I shall always savor. And so in the novel I just wanted to share this little secret place with the world.

The wild horses chasing Bradlee in Kansas… yes, it really happened to me and my buddy on one of our bicycling journeys. How could I ever forget the adrenaline rush and the quaking rumble from that serendipitous stampede. The hummingbird landing in Lyra's childhood hand and again in Bradlee's at the breakfast scene at the Lady Slipper Inn – also implanted into the story from a real happening – only it was from my own family trip to Costa Rica many years ago. My young daughter had a hummingbird land gently in her orange-laden palm while she stood perfectly still as I looked on with a loving smile. Ruthy, the child artist with an insight into love beyond her years, is a reincarnation of sorts of my own dear mother who has passed on now. My mother was born an artist and lived her life through her artistic creations. Her joie de vivre. Gifted eyes and beautiful creative hands that I had always admired. Bradlee's conflict with his father, Nathaniel… this evolved from personal challenges with my own father, albeit quite different in nature than the one described in my novel. Yet the source of that pain was real for me just as it was for Bradlee and may strike a cord in some readers who have endured difficulties with their own parents. It is my hope that, just as Bradlee and his father were able to come to terms, my novel can serve in some way as an opportunity for reflection and hope for any reader inspired to open a new chapter with their own parent. Life is finite. Most often the chance one takes to open dialogue and to listen quietly will be rewarded with love and forgiveness for our errors and faults, even if there must be some pain shed in that process of healing.

And the cloud formations: On a simpler plane, they represent the pure innocence and wisdom of a child. Youthful optimism. But more deeply, the clouds represent love itself. A loved soul. The sharing of beloved moments and memories in life and after death. To me, the clouds symbolize the very essence of the entire story – the concept of "Eyn Sof" (that there is no end, only the infinite and eternal) in Kabbalistic theology.

Lastly, a dose of Dalai Lama-esque humor is surely needed when it comes to thoughts and meanings of love. One might say that I believe in ascribing greater meaningfulness to apparent coincidences that have happened throughout my life. Perhaps I do buy into the concept of clues strewn about along one's life path. That there is a guide – call it a Creator (or any other term one prefers for God or Angels among us) – who at least makes attempts to steer us in a proper forward direction if only we have our eyes and souls open to accepting who we are and what gifts we can offer the world. With that said, I do enjoy Chinese fortune cookies. And so I opened one from a take-out restaurant shortly before I began to compose this story during this past year of global Covid-19 trials and tribulations, and there before me on the simple white strip of paper was the following quote: "*Nothing is impossible to a willing heart.*" Voila! Inspiration for a romance novel! I repeated the phrase time and again like a mantra and a story soon began to take form. All I had to do was fill in a few details here and there typing away on the screen before me... and eight weeks later Bradlee and Lyra were born into the world of the imagination. And as the story weaved its way, it was only a matter of time until they inevitably would overcome their challenges and be joined together.

Namasté... *Until the end,*
David

Book Club Guide

Group Discussion Points For Consideration

1. This book is designed to be a dramatic love story. After all, it does have a happy ending for Bradlee and Lyra. When do you think our pair first "fell in love" in the story? And how would you describe this concept of "falling in love?" What do you think is the author's concept of love?

2. Lyra does not discover Bradlee's true identity until many months into their relationship. And even when she did, it initially didn't seem that Bradlee was willingly interested in revealing his past. Is this a significant character flaw in Bradlee? Is it fair that he chose to lie to Lyra and others about his real name? Think about a situation in your own life, a past or present relationship, where you may have also been reticent to share information with a partner or close friend. Would you have changed your approach in hindsight? Why or why not?

3. The novel turns when Bradlee and Lyra separate from each other upon departing in the morning from their initial stay at the Lady Slipper Inn. Bradlee meets Dr. Benjamin Cohen and he must also confront his Uncle Eddie at the Scandinavian church. How did the scene inside the church alter your impression of Bradlee? Did you have a sense that Bradlee might very likely

end up confronting and repairing his relationship with his father as the novel progressed? Did you think Bradlee might end up returning to medical school to complete his studies? How did you think Bradlee and Lyra could possibly get together again once separated?

4. Bradlee's strained relationship with his father, Nathaniel, is unfortunately an all-too-common occurrence between a parent and child in the real world. How did their father-son conflict make you feel about your own relationship with a parent or a sibling. Would father and son have been able to forge a rapprochement even if Nathaniel was *not* a gifted surgeon who helped save Lyra's life? And if so, do you think Lyra's character was strong enough that she could have ultimately brought father and son together again?

5. Chief Jim Clayburn, Dr. Benjamin Cohen and James all have strong influences on Bradlee. These men may all be considered as surrogate fathers for Bradlee. And Dr. Carol Bonheim as a surrogate mother for Lyra. Describe what you think those influences were from these elders. Think about mentors (or a true surrogate parent) you have had in your own life and describe how you feel they influenced you? Would you have become who you are without them in your life? Are you serving as a mentor or surrogate parent to others and in what way? Did the novel influence you to change your approach to mentoring by any measure?

6. The novel adds Native American scenes to emphasize

concepts about the importance of preserving and protecting the natural world and living spiritually amidst nature. Oji quickly develops a kinship with Lyra because she possesses a shaman-like awareness of human nature and hidden emotions. It is as if Oji can truly feel Lyra's pain and love. Have you ever met someone who seemingly has that kind of deeper empathetic awareness? Who understands your emotional state to the degree that you can trust and confide in them?

7. Ansley and Angel serve important roles in the story as meaningful old and new friends who help Lyra begin to heal from abusive trauma. Do Ansley and Angel resemble a close friend in your own life? Did you think of this friend while reading the novel? Do you think Lyra's challenge and ability to overcome her trauma was realistic?

8. Bradlee is portrayed as a hero in the novel. On the runway after the plane crash he reacted quickly to be sure Kin escaped and then instinctively intervened to help save the pilot and Dr. Bonheim. Later, Bradlee must risk his own life once again to protect Lyra from an impending fall from the cliff as he awaits their rescue. In what way might Bradlee be considered a flawed or genuine hero? Do you think he had to be the one to save Lyra's life from a cliff fall in order for them to be together forever? If Lyra had not survived could Bradlee have overcome yet another personal tragedy?

9. The novel is organized as a series of apparent coincidences linking Bradlee and Lyra together.

Describe some of these coincidences and then think of your own life. Did you also have apparent significant coincidences that brought you to a certain place, career, or togetherness with a partner. Do you feel these coincidences were merely random or, on some greater level, deepened your sense of spiritual connection?

10. The author titled the book, *Until The End*. This phrase was used by a number of characters throughout the novel until Bradlee and Lyra adopted it as their own. What do you think about when you say the words yourself? Does it lead you to reminisce? To wonder about the "what ifs" in your life? Does the novel have you question concepts of faith or souls or soulmates and whether life has some greater meaning beyond our full comprehension?

11. At the wedding, Uncle Eddie meets a fellow rabbi who was standing at the inn's gate and observing the event. The rabbi has the same last name (Shem Tov) as Lyra's maternal ancestors traced to the Baal Shem Tov (the founder of Chasidic Judaism and revivalist of Kabbalah – Jewish mysticism). What do you think the author's intentions were to add this encounter at the end of the book? Does it tie up any loose ends in the story? What do you think the encounter between the two rabbis really means?

12. If you were to imagine a sequel to *Until The End*, where do you feel the story is headed next? What themes might be addressed next by the author? Which characters from the novel would have an important role in the sequel as time marches on and why?

Made in the USA
Columbia, SC
10 April 2021